Robert Dunn

Pink Cadillac

Pink

Cadillac

A musical novel by
Robert Dunn

A Coral Press original, ~~June 2001~~

Library of Congress Catalog Card Number:
2001126489
ISBN: 0-9708293-0-2
Manufactured in the United States of America
1 3 5 7 9 10 8 6 4 2
First Edition

Book Design: Anna Manikowska
Author Photograph: Chris Carroll

www.coralpress.com
Coral Press
252 W. 81st Street
New York, New York 10024

For my parents, Mary and Gerry Dunn

Part One
Kismet

THE CAR APPEARS FIRST as a speck in the dust-flurried road, comes closer under the canopy of cypresses and Spanish moss, the constant noonday boiling sun above her, and she halts herself, setting down her cardboard suitcase with the decal that reads PARIS, FRANCE over the picture of an airplane circling the Eiffel Tower (decal she spent candy money on years ago, along with one that read HOLLYWOOD over a bevy of klieg lights and NEW YORK twirled round the Empire State Building) and giving her hip a tiny hitch as she raises her thumb and lets it sway honey-bee slow in the stillborn air.

Car coming closer, and she sees it's an unearthly color—it's *pink*—and long, with fins ... a Cadillac, she's almost sure, just like the pictures with starlets perched on them in the movie magazines. Fins high as waves, not that she's ever seen a real ocean wave. Floating like a pink vision in its own swirling cloud of road dust, yet closing now, about fifty feet away. There's something huge and black strapped to the roof of the car, she has no idea what it is. She's been walking this road from sunup, after sleeping the night in a stolen-into barn, still picking straw out of her berry-blonde hair, and breakfasting on ... come to think of it, she hasn't had anything to eat all day, not that she's unused to going hungry ... yet for a minute she believes she's hallucinating the whole mirage.

But now she can hear it, thrumming engine, louder and louder; it's running smooth, but she picks up a subtle but definite ping, ping, ping in the pistons. The car's ripping right at her, the girl boldly takes a step forward, the pink Cadillac edges left but slows, she can see three men inside, a beefy dark-haired guy in the back, blond string bean riding shotgun, and a beautiful man with a wave of pitch-black hair nearly as high as the car's fins behind the wheel, and they're all looking at her—bump that hip!—and she can tell the driver's thinking of stopping, but the shotgun boy turns toward him and waves his hand toward the backseat, which—now that they're right next to her, she can see is stuffed roof-high with tweed-covered boxes and long guitar-casey things—and like that the Cadillac speeds up and Daisy Holliday eats dust.

And glowers. It isn't that she's more than a slip of a thing anyway, as her aunt Ruth always said, and she's sure she could have fit in some ways, even if the car was rocking full.

She's somewhere between Kentucky and where she's heading, Memphis, hoping she's closer to the river city, but not knowing; the last three days have passed in a wearying blur. She has less than $40, the only money she can expect until she gets to Memphis and finds some kind of job, and has eaten from swiping eggs and vegetables. What she'd give for a hamburger. But Daisy keeps telling herself this is the long walk, the dues you gotta pay, the way when you start singing and the records start selling that you'll know what it all means. Remembering walking the road. The sun. The dust crunching in her teeth. The dream shimmering bright in front of her....

She climbs a hill and, freed from the tree canopy, squints for a second in the full bloom of the golden sun, then looks down the curling road and laughs to herself. There, dust all settled now, is the pink Cadillac, its baby-outfit-colored hood canted up; and the three men, sweat now on *their* brows, poking and prowling round a steaming engine, clearly to no earthly avail.

＊ ＊ ＊ ＊ ＊

THE RUMORS PEAKED at a record show in Sheffield, a long room filled with the usual vendors with the usual milk crates stuffed with worn, cloth-soft cardboard LP covers, the usual classicals from the '50s and '60s sporting buxom Scheherazade models, fans swirled over their privates, and that to-die-for black banner across the top: RCA LIVING STEREO, as well as lots of early rock, *Ricky Sings for You*, Elvis's *For LP Fans Only*, Chuck Berry's *After School Session.* There were the usual denizens in their stretched, too large black T-shirts and black motorcycle boots and the pressed-chino-wearing, public-school-teaching jazz aficionados. Colin Stone hawkeyed his way through the crowd. He'd long ago given up the hope of finding anything he could use at shows like this—in the CD age, almost everything worth hearing had been put out, lots of it through his own label, Blue Moon Records—but there'd been a recurrence of the story of what Colin called the Great Lost 45, and here he wason this drizzly Saturday morning with all the music geeks, ears up.

What had brought him here was a phone call from a friend/source named Spider Kaesburg, who said he'd met a man in Dusseldorf who said he'd actually seen a copy, at a Saturday show in a small Bavarian town, Bad Potlach. Colin quizzed him closely. The label was Bearcat Records, the artist billed as Daisy Holliday. The disc itself was a wide 78, which sounded plausible since 45s were still a novelty in 1956. On the phone, Colin felt his fingers glow hot.

But Spider's contact hadn't bought the record—it had been for sale for a ridiculous 21 DM—which seemed suspicious. How could he not have grabbed up what might be the only copy of this signal moment in rock history? Something seemed funny. Who was the dealer? Dieter said a man named Firth, no one anybody knew well. Englishman. With a modest six boxes of old wax discs. Possibly a hobbyist. From the north.

Englishman named Firth. Colin racked his brain. He knew a bloke named Frith, Edgar B. Frith, who used to handle rockabilly out of Leeds, but a call up there brought only the question, "Colin, you still obsessing 'bout that myth? Only cuts Bearcat ever put out were with Sonesta Clarke and the other black players on that album you already put out. 'Sides, wasn't Bearcat Jackson dead when you have him making your 'missing link' record?"

Colin said no firmly, but only in his head. On the phone he thanked Frith and said he was sorry to bother him.

Firth. A phony name? No, didn't make sense. Twenty-one DM—that was about £6, which was what you priced records simply because they were old. Which meant, if the disc actually existed, this Firth saw it only as a 78 on a label he'd never heard of, which meant he didn't know anything.

Which made Colin more suspicious. Even his self-penned liner notes to his Bearcat collection mentioned the rumors of the Great Lost 45 (or 78 or whatever). The A side—the only side—was supposedly called *Pink Cadillac*, produced by Thomas "Bearcat" Jackson, with Dell Dellaplane (who went on to score films in Hollywood in the '60s) playing sax. He'd talked to people who had heard it over WHBQ—swore they had. That when it was first played it caused a buzz as bright and loud as the first time the same station and DJ played *That's All Right* by that glory-craving mama's boy, Elvis Presley. 'Cept this time it was a *girl* singing. A bluesy voice everyone thought was black—same deal as with Elvis—and rocking with grit and passion like there was no tomorrow. Recording played on WHBQ for a week or two, then mysteriously pulled off the station.

And was it ever pressed up for sale?

Colin had never seen a copy, no one had that he could trust. Just the rocking song, the spine-rippling voice frozen in the memories of now aging housewives and car salesmen in Memphis ... and the story so much like that of Presley's that

Colin sometimes wondered if it was all just a wishful-thinking hallucination, the nascent myth of a Queen of Rock 'n' Roll to go along with the world-changing power of the King.

'Cept one woman had actually sung him a lilting, truly catchy chorus: *I don't care if I ever come back / In my Pink Cadillac, my Pink Cadillac.* Just that kind of lyric, devil-may-care, spit-on-it-all. Colin's pulse had jumped.

And if the record existed? Then there had been a Janis Joplin in the South ten years before the doomed belter, an interracial band working eight years before the Stax house band, a singer who right now might have the glory afforded Elvis. (Colin, in the States on other business, had watched on CNN the 20-year death ceremonies from Memphis and wondered somewhat wryly if he were observing a religion in formation that mimicked nothing so much as that from when the calendar jumped from negative numbers to positive.) If the record existed, almost everything known about rock history would have to be rewritten.

And that was before he saw a picture of Daisy Holliday.

It was a picture of her later, though, when she was singing on that '70s love boat, but she didn't look that much older than she must have been in '56—blonde hair up just so, soigné nose, a vivid, sassy cut to her mouth. It was just a glossy get-work head shot, Daisy Holliday in a wide-collared, low-cut blouse, her hair half-teased, but even with the banal period trappings, the picture spoke to Colin. She wasn't just lovely; there was an intense focus, a beautiful determination that ... well, that he had found once before and against all reason these nine long months later was evidently still hopelessly....

No, don't go there, he told himself, at least not now, and with vivid effort he pulled his thoughts back from that cacophonous London street corner to the record, *the record....*

He knew how much he wanted *Pink Cadillac* to exist.

What he didn't understand was why, if there really was a record, *everyone* didn't know about it. How could it be lost? Why was he standing in this flyblown record show in this grim northern city waiting for . . . what? Would he have to go through every stack of records looking for the Bearcat label? (There weren't that many 78s, but who was to say the disc hadn't ended up in the LP bundles.) Could he just ask? Oh, sure, and then hear the old, "Right, Colin, you still tooting that Lost 45 tune? Yeah, sure I got it. Yeah, yeah. How much Blue Moon Records willing to pay?" And what of this Edgar B. Frith?

He was strolling the back row of the show, elbowing past the wide-shouldered guys burlying up to the record boxes, with their practiced fingers flicking through the stacked records, when he came to a breathless stop. A small table, a black-haired man with a cowl and a pointed chin—positively medieval looking, Colin had to say—with a small name tag that read EDWARD G. FURTH. New man, Colin didn't know him. With a feather duster, scratching it over what was mostly promo CDs. Unlikely, yet—

"You do any old records?" Colin asked, standing before the waist-high table. Nobody else was bothering with Furth's goods.

"LPs? Sure." A high-pitched voice.

"I'm thinking 78s, American."

"You a blues guy? Chess, Aristocrat?"

"Sun?" Sun Records was the label Bearcat Jackson should have been on, except the story was he was too proud to work for anyone but himself.

"Don't have any Sun, sorry."

"Anything else from around that time?"

"Nothing." Shrug from the short man.

Colin said, "Anything lately, might have sold?"

"You must be looking for something special, mate. If you want to put in an order—"

"Rare record, not even sure it exists. Called *Pink Cadillac*." Close look at Furth's eyes, nothing. "On the Bearcat label."

Ah, a flicker.

"Bearcat, you say. Name's familiar."

"He had his own label in the early '50s. Maybe resurrected about '56."

"Sounds like something I should know about. The artists?"

"Sonesta Clarke was the big one. Couple others. Guitar player named Clayton Booker. Played with Ike Turner, cut some sides with Bearcat, had a later career in Chicago with Willie Lee Reed."

"Booker, Booker." The wolflike man closed his eyes. "Clayton, Clayyyy Booker. I can see something with that name." Quick nod. "Might have had that."

Colin took a step forward. "Any idea where it went?"

A shrug. "Records come and go, mate."

Well, that must've been it. *Booker's Boogie*. Ripping instrumental. A raw, barbwire sound to Booker's guitar. The Bearcat himself ostensibly playing harp. Colin owned three black-lacquer copies.

"Should I take your name, mate, for this *Pink Cadillac* thing?"

Quick thought, then Colin shook his head. "No, appreciate your time, though."

"Anytime, friend."

It just didn't exist, did it? It was too good a story to actually be true.

But . . . he had the feeling again. Tingle in his fingertips, quickening of his blood.

It was the only pulse quickening he could muster these days. The *only* strong counter emotion to what he felt every time he started to think about his wife, Robin, which, dammit, was still all the time.

Concentrate on the record. Had anybody ever looked into this? Colin's tingles now told him he would be off on a singular adventure. To the States, eh? He flew into New York a couple times a year but hadn't been to Memphis for the four years since he'd met ... well, since he'd met Robin there. He'd been working on the Bearcat release then, chasing down rare discs, interviewing the usual suspects—Sam Phillips of Sun, Rufus Thomas, the famous DJ Nat D. Williams—and he'd found her his last night in town, in his hotel's lounge, where she'd been singing all week, Colin hustling past the velvet-curtained door chasing the Bearcat's scent.

But that night he was ready to relax. A beer in front of him. The place almost totally empty. And this blonde singer curled over a Martin guitar with a glass slide on her finger, fretting out startling blues.

In the next week, as he extended his visit, courting Robin Longworth assiduously, successfully, flying with her back to England as his slightly stunned but joyful bride, he would in quiet moments ask himself what first caught his eye; and the best answer he had was that it was a simple shape: the evanescent curve her hair would make falling across her left cheek as she leaned over to dig into the guitar. Sure, there was her voice, strong yet gentle, and her eyes, a startling blue; and certainly in practical terms the way Robin was immediately *ready* for someone like Colin—a serious man who could love her and move her out of the stuck place *she* was in—just as he was ready for a wife, even if he couldn't quite admit it to himself. But it was in the moments the curve of her hair met the flawless arc of her face—the flutter of light and shadow; ever-lost seconds of fragile perfection—that remained the most moving vision; and it was the memory that always moved him most now that she was irretrievably lost.

Could he go back to Memphis? Face her hometown again? Maybe feel compelled to call on her parents? Was he ready for that? Or—a thought that was still more academic than real—could he not begin to move beyond his grief until he went back there?

He hated that word *grief*. It seemed so obvious, so afternoon talk show, so insufficient for the gray hovering deadness he swam through nearly every day.

Yet he could just about hear that voice he'd never heard, on a record he had scant evidence even existed, sung by another beautiful blonde who if still alive would be almost 60 years old.

Our hearts jump in the strangest ways.

At least, Colin sighed, they jump.

✳ ✳ ✳ ✳ ✳

THE FIRST THING you see is a dusty parking lot, empty but for a couple broke-down-looking jalopies, a wide-hipped black Ford pickup truck, and next to it a totally out-of-place sea-green MG sportster, little beauty that looks as funny out here in the middle of nowhere as you do. It's a car just like a model you built a couple years back, when you were still into kid stuff, and as you walk past you admire its polished wood dash and gleaming black-leather seats. But you're hardly out here to peep at expensive sports cars.

Indeed, you're not quite sure why you're out here. Sixteen-year-old kid from east Memphis with sandy hair and big ears that seem to pop out of your head like something just spooked you (yet girls, thank God, still call you cute); sophomore in the all-white high school, honors your last semester, idea you might become a doctor; and yet this overweening passion has risen up in the last six months: This negro music you hear at night over radio station WDIA, the way you sneak it into your room on the radio you got for your fourteenth birthday to be able to get the baseball reports, but the record names already nudging baseball heroes like DiMaggio and Kiner out of the pantheon of your imagination. Each syllable is magic, like notes from foreign lands: Chuck Berry, Ivory Joe Hunter, Little Richard, Sugar Pie DeSanto, James Cotton, The Prisonaires, Sonesta Clark, Heddy Days, Howling Wolf, Ike Turner, all these ranters and shouters, crying like the very sky is falling, and churning up this wild beat that makes your feet start tapping and your hips shake when you're up in your bedroom with the radio pressed to your ear doing your trigonometry homework. A smile. Mr. Frederick, I was working really hard last night, and I think I figured out the cosine of *Moanin' at Midnight*. Can I get extra credit?

It's still a secret the way you love this negro music; you know your dad would skin you he heard you listened to it, and Mom would get the long face like she did the time you slapped a baseball through her kitchen window. Most of the kids at school don't quite feel they can admit it though you know you're far from the only well-brought-up kid going gaga over the new sounds. Some of the louder ones, though, the guys with souped-up cars and friends at Humes High in town, wear their love proudly. They call themselves rockers and have outlaw sideburns and piled up pompadours of Brill-Creamed hair and play WDIA loud as they cruise out to Willie King's for burgers and malteds. In your hugely growing secret self you sort of wish you could look a little like that, except that ... your dad would skin you and Mom would get the long face.

But the secret has an unsettling power, just like the stirrings of your desire for, God, how many of the girls in your class—Beverly Domino and Barbara Smith and Nancy Jo Singer with the butterfly in her golden hair—and the need for the music seems amazingly linked to this discovered desire for these girls: Like you just discovered there was this whole part of your body down there with a blooming life of its own.

But the negro music hits you all over and makes you feel loose and slaphappy and just beaming with good feeling. Makes you even think negroes—you're careful to call them by the respectful name—might be different from the way you always heard; might be something there you could learn from, they make a music so jumping great. And more than just the music. It just amazes your white brain that there's this whole world of ... blackness ... and that nobody says word one about it. A world of mystery, fascination, power, and astonishing music that blows anything else you know away, and it's right there all around you, and yet it's as faceless as the field hands you drove past on your way down here.

It took all your courage, and even now you're looking back over your shoulder to catch if anyone might see you, just like that afternoon when you sneaked into town after school and walked up and down Beale Street. That's how you heard about the roadhouse out here. It was from a pawnshop owner with a shock of hairs spraying from his nose. "This is where the nigras say the true music comes from," the white man said. "This is the home of the Bearcat."

The Bearcat. Even the name spooked you, like some huge beast risen up in the forest in your dreams. You had heard his records, of course, especially *Cryin' Shame* by Sonesta Clark, often still played on WDIA, but from the wild sounds, you sort of thought they might be cut on the moon.

"That record, it was made right in this house," the pawnshop man said, pointing to the X he'd drawn on the crude map. "Yessiree. Bearcat hisself bought a record cutter from me back ten years ago. Got to give that boy credit. First nigra to cut his own music. What you think about that?"

What you thought was: I have to see this.

And so you borrowed Dad's Buick, saying you were heading to the lending library to study, turned south down Highway 61, and here you are.

You're surprised it's such a big place. It's got two stories and looks sort of like it was once a hotel, dotted with windows up top like there're lots of bedrooms, but recently walled up below except for two windows up front. It's a funny building, crumbly and worn in a way like nothing you see in east Memphis. Course, it's a negro house, and like your dad says, they ain't got pride.

Except you sort of like the weathered wood siding, the wide porch out front that's bowed like waves, the stacks of crates of empty bottles—it's all kind of comfy and lived-in. Not like the squeaky new suburban house your parents bought after Dad got back from the war. That house has a gleaming new refrigerator full of those new-fangled TV dinners, and bright and shiny plastic covers that Mom keeps on the furniture. Nothing like that at all. As you creep up to the building, you feel like you're creeping up on a haunted house—just that kind of feeling, sneaky, forbidden, heart bumping up and down in your throat—yet the place itself couldn't be more open-seeming and inviting. Look, there's even a sign above the door that reads WELCOME Y'ALL TO BEARCAT'S LARE.

But welcome to you? Not much going on, but you'd bet bottom dollar they don't see many white kids out here. 'Cept why not? If you love the music, and music's for everyone, then why not for you? This race thing you think for the thousandth time, it just don't make sense.

Still, you know you're not supposed to be here, and you don't want to get caught, so you're not going to go walking in the front door, and you're not going to be looking in the front windows, and that's why you're thrilled to find around back a small side window perfect for peeking into.

You find a discarded milk crate that holds your weight, take a deep breath, peek your eyes just up over the sill, and ... is that him? God, it has to be! He's big, bigger man than you've ever seen, and amazing looking, wearing a wide-shouldered flash blue suit, his hair conked back, his nose wide and shmushed, and this brilliant gold tooth firing up his mouth. He's talking to someone, you can't make him out, but there are other people there, lanky negroes, some in equally flash clothes, others wearing overalls.

And then they start playing. You lower your head, place it against the wall ... someone's blowing a sax. And good. Bright, bell tones, but ripping.

You raise your eyes to the window, and what you see's the most astonishing thing yet: There is somebody playing the sax, but he ain't black at all. He's a white boy, pretty much a regular-looking guy even if his reddish-brown hair is grown out longer than the cuts fashionable at your high school; well-muscled, if a bit wiry, with a football letterman jacket on over a tight-necked white T-shirt; good looking and pretty damn confident, you'd say, being out here with the flashy nigra. Then the most amazing thing of all: The white boy's leaning back and blowing for all he's worth into a golden saxophone—and he's sounding good.

Your jaw drops. You keep listening and wondering, wondering and listening, but you don't really understand. It's not just that this other white boy beat you out here, it's that he's actually up on a stage, playing with negroes. You blink, pinch yourself. How could that be?

* * * * *

INSIDE THE ROADHOUSE the young man filled his lungs with the smoky air, kissed the mouthpiece, sucked up all of his doubts—he'd been building to this audition for what seemed years now, dreaming of playing the real music with the real men, mixing in a way he'd never heard of down here before—but he told himself it was all just music, he just had to get that right; then he arched his back, like a teetering question mark, and blew again into the saxophone and felt more than heard his buzz-saw tone lift away from him, then rip through the exposed rafters, down the beer-stained walls, across the dirty linoleum floor, and out the windows open to the steamy

September air. He pulled fuller into himself, felt his lungs swell, the thin braid of music start deep in his stomach, then spin up and out the sax. He was going for a tone so pure and bluesy it would stop time. And he was close, but as he grabbed another breath, he knew not yet close enough.

"Hold it! Stop. 'Nuff. I ... heard ... enough."

Dell Dellaplane took the sax from his mouth and looked down from the bandstand at the huge shadowy man seated at one of the empty club's tables. Saw, even in the crepuscular light, his wide shoulders, massive zoo-beast head, sparkly, sly, nothin'-gets-by-him eyes—then the splintered glint of his gold tooth.

"You got something, 'specially for a white boy. Where you learn to play like that?"

Dell let his sax hang loose on his neck, put his hands together. "Practice, Mr. Jackson."

The large man laughed. When he spoke, his voice was big and round as a circus tent. "Hold it, son, you can just call me ... Mister." A deep belly growl. "Like, Mister Mister."

Dell leaned forward, half off the stage. "Mister Mister?"

A round of laughter from the shadows now, reminding Dell they weren't alone. Rest of the band, plus a clutch of afternoon drinkers, nothing-else-to-do-ers, the regular hangers-on.

"That's a joke, son." The big man stood up, came toward the stage. "Bearcat's fine."

The big man moved slowly, like his bones were far more delicate than his appearance would make you think, but it was a smooth movement, and for the first time Dell realized that he did move like his namesake: half lurching bear, half padding big cat. He was clearly a strong man. His shoulders looked like they could knock down doors, and veins like cords popped out on his neck. And what a suit he was wearing! It was midnight blue, deep, yet made of a fabric that seemed to subtly sparkle and glow with every move, like a phosphorescence floating in the sea. He had some sort of big white stone stud keeping his shirt buttoned below his couple-triple layers of chin. Yeah, the big man was dressed awful sharp, yet what was that strange, greasy leather bag hanging from his belt?

"*Mistah* Bearcat," Dell said, still wanting to be deferential, but planting a barb in the *Mister*, too.

"Yeah, yeah, *Mistah* Bearcat. That's the way a white man should speak it, right boys?" Titters and guffaws from the shadows. "O.K., let's try you with some competition." The Bearcat went up to the bandstand. "Think you can go with *me*?"

Dell ran a hand down the shiny side of his saxophone. "You mean, keep up?"

"I mean hold your own, whiteboy."

"I wouldn't dream—"

"I don't care nothin' 'bout dreams. I'm talking 'bout the here and now. One *musician* to another."

"It's my dream to play with you," Dell said, and he was young enough that he was simply speaking earnest truth.

"Then let's see we make it real. Boys."

The Bearcat's drummer, "Sticks" Miller, his bass player, Earl "Thumper" Johnson, and the guitarist, Clayton Booker, climbed up on the stage. It wasn't in truth much of a stage, just a cobbled-together platform about a foot and a half high, raw plywood set on a frame and butted up against the wall about twenty feet away from and flanked by the makeshift bar. There were twelve wobbly seats before the bar, which was a beautiful piece of burled oak. Beer signs for Falstaff and Connoisseur were stuck akilter behind the bar, the provisions of which consisted of half a dozen bottles of a cheap whiskey called Old Scotchman, a pail filled with 'shine brought out from North Carolina twice a week, a hot plate with a coffee pot, and a four-by-six-foot ice cooler filled with brews, a constant puddle at least half an inch deep all around it. (Salt, the bartender, carefully wore shoes with pieces of wood nailed under the soles.) A couple strings of Christmas lights, lit 24 hours a day, were strung merrily around the beer signs on the wall.

In truth, though, in the afternoon light the roadhouse had a gray, forlorn feel to it, as if this place were outside any flow of life. Funny thing about the blues, Dell often thought. Nothing else but playing them made him as happy—for him blues were pure joy. But this afternoon, this place ... this place was *stone blue*.

The musicians' boot heels clattered on the hollow wood. Sticks rattled his snare, Thumper whooshed his electric Fender bass. Then Bearcat took the stage.

Dell felt him like a natural presence, first his smell, earthy, even spicy, like he was a pot of beans cooking all day, but then just a flow of energy—like he was a huge stone radiating solidity but also animal grace. The big man picked a harmonica out of the side pocket of his loose electric-blue suit jacket, ran his mouth over it.

"Now you understand, you're playing *behind* me," the Bearcat said.

Dell nodded.

The rhythm section fell into a slow, grinding beat, and Clay danced ninth chords behind them; then Bearcat mouthed his harp and pulled a deep bluesy riff out of it. He played through twelve bars, then gave Dell the nod.

Dell reached down inside himself again, spurted out a round of on-the-spot horn patterns, honking, blatting notes that slithered and jumped like quicksilver. He felt Bearcat's eyes on him.

"Son," the big man finally said, "that's different. That's that new rocky-rolly we been hearin' 'bout, ain't it?" He turned to the band. "That's that rocky-rolly, boys. What you think of that?"

Behind Dell he heard grunts, shuffles.

"Don't pay 'em no mind, son," the Bearcat said. "They's

blues players, they got a stick up 'em 'bout the blues, and no problem with that. You know, this new rocky-roly, it's just the blues, 'cept it's—" Bearcat waved a hand, looking for a word.

Dell quickly said, "It's different."

"Hey, hey." Huge cackling joyful laugh. "Tha's it, *but different*. No, you and me, let's keep going, see if we can get a little more of the old blues in your playing, maybe some of that rocky-roly in mine." A turn and a flourish. "Boys."

Silence.

"Come on, a one, a two—"

Silence still.

A spin to face the band, then a low growl: "Hey, I know what you thinking, but let me tell y'all black asses something. Things are changin'. You listen to the radio and hear what Daddy-o Dewey's playing, y'all know something's happening out there. Now I can't keep filling this place up playing blues no more, and you know it. So maybe we get over this li'l thing, or we all just be niggers followin' tractors again." A loud bark: "Now play."

Sticks and Thumper started in again, same twelve bars, but this time, following Dell, there was just a little more of a punch in it. Dell, confidence flying, arpegiatted down the V IV transition, and Bearcat, honking his harp almost saxlike, came out of the IV V, *moving* those notes.

"Hey, hey, hey!" The big man, in his black shoes the size of PT boats, did a light-footed dance over the wooden stage. "I like that. Maybe we gettin' ourselves something here."

There was a loud noise in the back of the room. Three middle-aged black women came through the door. The women were dressed, from pillbox hats to heavy pumps, all in black, though the one in the middle had red piping around her formidable suit. They walked in with a solemn, sniffy air.

"Well, look what the cat finally dragged in," Bearcat called out in a wry tone.

"Yeah, well look what a drag the 'cat is," the woman in

the middle said. This was Sonesta Clarke. She harrumphed, then moved with her two friends, her "sisters," Lil and Lurleen, to the long bar, where Salt poured them all coffee.

"Hey, hey," Bearcat went. Dell heard a different tone in his voice, something slightly forced, not the confident playfulness the big man had had with him but something falser, edgier, even angry. Then: "Where y'all been?"

"I been prayin' for your soul, where you think I been?" Sonesta spun herself around on the stool. She was in her early forties, with sleek black hair in large curls, side bangs spit-pointed down by her ears. She had lively, fun-loving eyes, though they were clouded over now. Her lips were painted with a deep-purple gloss. She wore gold rings on nearly all her fingers. Her two sisters were not nearly so glamorous. But like good backups, they spun too, just a few seconds later.

"And has it been doing any good?"

"What do you think? Here you are, on the Sabbath, and you're—" Sonesta froze, shielded her eyes so she could see better. "What's he doin' here?"

"We're playing music, woman. Something you used to know something about."

"No, I mean *him*." She pointed to the bandstand, to Dell Dellaplane.

"He's sitting in, teaching us ol' fogies some of that rocky-roly."

"But he's—"

"Yeah, he's white. So what?"

"So *what*?"

"He's a musician—plays damn good. That's all *I* need to know."

Dell swelled at the direct praise. He pressed his sax closer to his body, where it fit just right.

"What you *need* to know is what you *do* know. That you got troubles out here, nigger." Sonesta stopped swinging back and forth on the bar seat and faced Bearcat. "And they ain't troubles gonna be helped by bringing no white boy round."

"When you start singing with us again, you can have yourself a *musical* opinion," Bearcat said. He gestured behind him, and Sticks gave him a rim shot. "Till then, you just taking up space."

"That's what you call it? *Taking up space?* After all these years?"

"You're not singin'."

"Yeah, I can think of a few things you ain't doin' like you used to, too."

Bearcat took a large step toward Sonesta. "You gettin' smart with me?" Up went his hand.

Sonesta held her ground, but it was clear to Dell, if not everyone else, that she flinched involuntarily; she pulled her shoulders and chin back, lowered her eyes.

Bearcat kept moving toward her, but his voice shifted to something gentler. "Sonesta, you should listen to it, this boy's got some of that new sound, the rocky-roly you know all the kids are listenin' to. Like that Presley boy used to hang out here had. Remember him?"

Sonesta rolled her eyes.

Bearcat, ignoring this, simply went on entreating. "Now why don't you get on up with my boy here, see if you can catch that new beat—"

Sonesta just pursed her lips.

"Come on, boys, let's lay it down, see if we can get the Church Lady to goddamn sing for us." Bearcat flicked his fat fingers.

The band started playing, halfway between a slow blues and backbeat rock and roll. They didn't quite have it yet, and Sonesta stood looking straight at them, her arms crossed before her chest.

"They's a sorry lot doing this," she finally said. Her two sisters had come up right behind her, nodding along.

"Oh, they just need some help," Bearcat said, thinking fast. "They need some sweet inspiration."

"Sounds to me like what they need's a whole new education."

"Yeah, and who better to show 'em than you?" Bearcat's voice suddenly dripped honey, and Sonesta made an involuntary pinched-up face.

"I don't know nothing 'bout no rock n' roll."

"But you know music." A glint of Bearcat's huge gold tooth. "Honey, you *are* the music."

Sonesta cocked her still pretty head back, gave him a long look.

"Bearcat, stop it. I don't know what I like better with you, this phony sweetness or your usual sour self."

Bearcat stifled a quick glower, kept up his blooming smile.

"It ain't sweetness, darlin', it's music. Just want to get it right. Get us a new start."

"A new start?"

"Yeah."

Sonesta stood there, thinking this over. "Like what?"

"Like we get us a new way of playing. Like we get some new material, do that crossover thing like Chuck. Like we start with this Dell Dellaplane here, playing rippin' sax."

Sonesta started at the name Dellaplane. "Oh, my," she sighed. But Bearcat clearly didn't notice.

"Come on," he went on, all butter. "Let's show 'em. These boys do need some dire help, don't they?"

Sonesta's eyes were going wider, and Dell could see her breathing deepen, her chest rise and fall. He was too young to have ever seen Sonesta Clarke sing, but he knew her songs from the 78's he bought with his allowance when other kids were buying yo-yos and baseball cards. He was looking at her with righteous encouragement.

"Well, they sure do at that," she finally said.

Bearcat, Dell, the band—everyone was smiling. The musicians kept playing, even tightened up some, and Sonesta took two steps toward the bandstand, when her sisters came and stood right next to her.

"That's the *devil's* music," Lil said hissingly to her.

But the singer was looking straight at the microphone atop a spindly pole.

"Come on, let's try it," Bearcat said. "Not like you wasn't up here a few months back and all."

"But this is the *Lord's* Day," Lurleen, the second sister, said. "You just comin' from church."

Sonesta hesitated, then took another step forward.

"But you ain't all the Lord's woman, now are ya." The Bearcat grinned.

Tippety, tippety, Sticks brushing the snare, and it was a seductive rhythm.

"You still got those blues in ya soul. I seen 'em, woman, in ya eyes, in ya lips ... and in ya *hips*."

Tippety, tippety, tippety, and one of the hangers-on, bone-thin guy named Walter, wearing a pair of plaid pants barely held up by rope, got up and started dancing, wiggling his bottom and shaking his shoulders, doing a kind of chicken peck. Dell had never seen anybody move quite that way, all hibblety-jibblety, and he was staring at the man when he saw Sonesta's feet start to move. She was swaying side-to-side, the beat run out like a hook and catching her. Hey, hey! Dell leaned back and let his sax crow bold. Tippety, tippety, then, *whomp*, tippety, *whomp*—the bass drum sounding its dead hollow beat.

And like that the whole room sparked alive. Lil and Lurleen reached out for Sonesta's hands, but she was already away from them.

"Come on, woman, do it."

"Darlin', remember *the Lord*!"

Sonesta got up on the bandstand, her arms still stiff over

her bosom, but her feet moving, shuffling to the strong beat, and her wide hips starting to swing....

When there came a loud rapping at the front door.

"What tha fuck?" Bearcat cried, spinning around.

The door slammed back, and a mid-sized man in a tight-cut gray uniform strode in.

"Well, well, well, this is one interesting picture." This was Sheriff Josey Trump. He was in his late thirties, a thin mustache on his lip, his hat cocked down over his sharp gray eyes. He was looking straight at Dell. "Tell me, whose fancy sports car is that out there?"

"It's mine," Dell said. His sax hung limp from his neck.

"You want to show me a license?"

It was clear the sheriff wasn't going to go any farther into the roadhouse, and equally clear Dell wasn't going to leave the stage.

"I'll go get it," another of the hangers-on, a friendly-faced man named Hosea, said. He scampered toward Dell in his faded overalls before the Bearcat froze him with one look.

Then Bearcat gave his head a nod, from Dell toward the sheriff.

Dell pulled out his wallet and carried the license to the uniformed man.

"Your father know you're out here?"

"You tell me."

"You gettin' smart with me, boy?" The sheriff pulled up his height, puffed out his chest.

Dell was silent, lifting his own chest in pride. They stood there for a minute, silent. But Dell could feel Bearcat's eyes on him, feel what he was telling him: Now's not the time. Finally, Dell answered softly, "Oh, no, sir."

"That's better. Now what's your business out here?"

"We were just playing us some music."

"What kind of music?" Hooded eyebrows.

"Well, sir, I was just teachin' Mr. Jackson here how to play the blues."

Loud escaping guffaws from the band.

"Y'all think that's funny?"

"No, suh, no, no." Mumbles from Sticks and Thumper.

The sheriff rocked a little side to side. "Listen, Jackson, what business this boy got with you?"

The Bearcat, silent heretofore, smiled and said, "Just like the boy said, we wuz playing music."

"Playing with trouble's what I think. Don't you think the last thing you need out here these days is, um, negative attention?"

"Sheriff. . . . "

"Jackson, come here if you're talking to me." Bearcat lowered his thick head into his shoulders and did a well-practiced shuffle over to the white man. The sheriff leaned in to him and whispered, "Now, Jackson, you know people are looking 'specially close at you. *Specially close!*"

"I know, but you the Man, Sheriff." Bearcat reached around to the back of his pants, pulled out a fat scuffed black wallet, fanned it open. "You always be the Man."

"Put that away." A loud hissing whisper. "What you think? You can just fool with 'em downtown? Do what you damn well please? Bring white boys out here—'specially *that* white boy."

"What's so special 'bout him?"

"Why don't you ask him?" The sheriff threw a glare over to Dell.

"Oh, I will, I will."

The sheriff took a step closer to Bearcat, leaned in to his ear. "Listen, Jackson, there's only so much I can do—"

The Bearcat had folded up his wallet, but not before he had palmed a $50 bill.

"Now looky here, Sheriff." The Bearcat stretched to his full height and put an arm around the sheriff's shoulders. "You not the only white man who can help me. I got another great old friend, Mr. Abe Lincoln here." He deftly slipped the folded bill into the sheriff's breast pocket. "And I want you to remember what Mr. Abe said. He said I'm a free, free man—"

The sheriff went to interrupt, but the Bearcat kept going.

"Now I want you to tell all them bigshot speculators, I got me a *deed*. And then you tell 'em I pay my taxes—all my taxes. I don't got 'nuff to feed my boys, feed Sonesta, I *pay those taxes*! You tell 'em that."

The sheriff, quiet with the big man's left arm around him and his right hand tapping his chest, where he could hear the crinkle of the crisp folded bill, now took a step back.

"Your friend Abe's long dead, Mr. Jackson. Just you remember, I might be the last friend you got. And I sure am hoping you're not lookin' for trouble out here."

"Just lookin' to live my own life," Bearcat said. He threw his arms open wide. "Play me some music. That's all I's ever lookin' to do."

The sheriff looked deeply at him, as if to say *You been warned*, then left the roadhouse. Outside he saw a white kid with jug ears in the parking lot, backing away from the roadhouse, and called out, "You, son, you don't belong out these ways. Now you get going back to Memphis, you hear?" The kid hopped in a brand-new Buick and took off.

In the roadhouse, Sonesta, all thought of performing gone, glared down from the lip of the stage, and said, "Ain't that great."

"Shut up."

"You think you some friend of the Man's. You nothin' but a fool playing with fire."

Bearcat raised his huge hand, palm out, cocked it back. "Don't you start with me!" All his earlier sweetness gone, he threw a dark glower at her. "You *know* 'bout messin' with me." Then he turned to the band. "All right, boys, that's enough for today. Y'all git out of here!" He kicked at a chair, sending it tumbling over the beer-soaked floor. Then to no one in particular: "A goddamn woman can drive you to the end of a rope faster than any goddamn man of the law."

The band was slow picking up; the hangers-around were not yet out the door.

"Go on, git!"

Bearcat only had to take a couple long steps and everyone in the roadhouse scooted along. A curious, gray, half-dead silence—a deep emptiness—descended on the place; Dell was feeling it, blue on blue, as he followed the bass player, Thumper Johnson, out the door.

"Hey! Hey, you, stick here."

"Me?" Dell said, glancing to his side. He was the one closest to the door.

"Yeah, you." Bearcat was sitting on a chair by the stage, strumming a well-beaten shaded-top Gibson.

Dell, his saxophone still around his neck, bumping his chest, walked slowly back into the roadhouse. In the gray light, even sitting down, the Bearcat looked huge.

"Maybe this wasn't such a good idea, me coming out here—"

"Well, let's let me decide that." Bearcat started picking flatted fifths on the guitar. "Tell me a little 'bout yourself."

"Like what?" There was an open chair six feet from Bearcat, and Dell lowered himself into it.

"Like how you learned to play like that." Nod at the gleaming saxophone.

"I worked at it."

Bearcat threw his hands up, off the guitar, which nonetheless kept ringing out. "Oh, I'm sure 'bout that. I mean, play the way you play."

"It's what I love."

Bearcat furrowed his wide black brow. "Yeah, but how'd you *hear* it?"

"You mean 'cause I'm—"

"No, I mean 'cuz you're you! You got a feeling for it, can't deny. You understand the blues, and you understand that new rocky-roly, too. But how? I mean, with a car like that in the lot—"

"The car ain't nothing."

Bearcat laughed. "Don't be a fool, boy. Car can be everything to a man. Car can be your wife and your children—your whole life sometimes." He went back to picking the Gibson. "But it means you ain't *born* to the blues, now, right?"

"Well, I never followed a tractor, if that's what you mean."

Bearcat laughed hugely. "And you think I did?"

Dell leaned forward. "You said—"

"Oh, sure, I said. What you think? All us niggers be field hands?" Loud guffaw. "My daddy was edycated. He was a doctor—till he died."

"I'm sorry," Dell said softly.

"Oh, that was decades ago. I was just a kid, fourteen. And I gotta say, came pretty close to the fields after that. But I put me my music before everything."

Dell leaned forward, clearly intrigued.

"My mother, she married this—" Bearcat gave a wide shake of his oiled head. "I don't like be talkin' 'bout it."

Dell thought of his own father, the stormy battles, the way he'd always had to hide what he loved, and said, "That's what I had, when I didn't have anything else. My sax. The way I could go off by myself and play it. My father, he never seemed to—"

"Let me ask you one thing," the Bearcat interrupted. He was leaning back, nodding slowly, but his gaze shot forward, suddenly knife-sharp. "How come the sheriff there knows all 'bout your daddy?"

Dell started, tightened up; held the Bearcat's gaze.

"'Cause he's nothing but a brown-nosin' piss-ass." There was heat in his words.

Bearcat laughed in spite of himself. "The sheriff, or your daddy?"

Dell defiant: "Both."

There was a long second there when it looked like Bearcat was turning something over in his head, but then he said, "But you—you really want to sit in with us?"

"Nothing more." A glance down at his sax, still hanging round his neck, as if for comfort. "You think I'm good enough?"

Bearcat started plucking the guitar again, this time a slow, country blues reminiscent of his old acquaintance Son House—this wild kid Bearcat had known when *he* was a wild kid, too.

"Look, I don't got to tell you things ain't so great out here these days. You got everyone I came up with either dead, moved north like Heddy Days and the Wolf, or full of the—" his gaze swung up the stairs, where Sonesta had gone "—the religion. Things been changing here—there's that new music out there, the rocky-roly—and we ain't gettin' half the business we need.

"But now there's something new." Bearcat fixed Dell with a steady glare. "You hear anything 'bout a highway coming out here? 'Bout something called a *clover leaf*?"

"Nothing much." Dell's hands stroking the barrel of his sax. "Just what anybody hears. Times are good, the town's growing, spreading—" A shrug. "You mean something special about the roadhouse here?"

"Well, what I'm hearin' is a low rumble. But it ain't just talk. It's the sound of a bulldozer getting ready to run this old roadhouse over."

Dell looked visibly startled. "But this is all your place, isn't it? You said you owned it—"

"Owned it like a black man."

"But—" Dell leaned forward. "This place, it's *historical*."

Bearcat lifted an eyebrow at the patent enthusiasm in Dell's voice.

"I'll say. But maybe that's part of the problem. I listen to the radio, I know what's happenin' out there." Bearcat waved his hand through the gray air. "It's all changed. Now it's tutti-fruttis, rock-a-boppin' hillbillies, signifyin' monkeys, and who knows what all! But you know where they got it all from, don't you?"

Bearcat dug into the guitar, hit a few crisp, syncopated ninth chords.

"Yeah," Dell said, "the blues."

"Damn right, my son. It's all the blues."

Bearcat looked emphatically at Dell, then was silent, as if he was waiting for something. There was a silence, then like that Dell was alight with a new idea. It was burning huge and wonderful in his head.

"So make it happen again." Dell's feet were doing a little dance.

"Yeah, sure."

"But that's what you were saying to Sonesta Clarke."

Bearcat rolled his eyes.

"No, no, why not? You got the band, you got the touch. And like you were saying, maybe I could—" Dell's enthusiasm was making him wave his hands now.

"You're forgetting one thing, son."

"What?"

"I need a goddamn woman who will sing!"

"There must be lots of singers out there," Dell said.

"Oh, I'm sure there is. There's that Patti Page, she got the blues, for sure. Connie Francis."

"No, I mean somebody young, somebody new."

"Yeah, where she gonna come from?"

"I don't know, maybe we hold an audition." Dell heard the word *we*, and it left him emboldened.

"Oh, I've held auditions," Bearcat said. "I've gone to town, gone to schools, gone to goddamn church! But nobody had it. *Nobody*! It just don't work that way, auditions. What we're talking 'bout, it just has to happen. It has to be—" Bearcat lifted both his hands, opened them, supplicant to the skies "—just has to walk in the door."

"Yeah, well you could be waiting till hell goes to ice before that happens."

"Oh," Bearcat drawled, "you never know. You just walked in the door this morning, didn't you? Nothing on your mind but playin' music, right?" That tight, questioning glare again. "No trace of no thoughts 'bout no . . . clover leaf?"

"I'm sure we could do something," Dell said, quickly turning the question aside.

But Bearcat was hung on that word. "Yeah, well, only clover leaf I know's got four leaves. You find me one of those, maybe I put it here in my mojo bag." He tapped the worn leather pouch hanging from his thick belt. "You know what this is, huh?"

"I heard some 'bout that sort of thing."

"You did, huh? You sure your name's Dellaplane?"

"Only my name. And that ain't my fault."

"Jes' that I been hearin' something 'bout someone named Dellaplane. Sonesta, she been hearin' it, too."

"I thought we were past all that 'bout my father." Dell stood up. "If you're gonna hold him against me, I'm out of here right this second."

"Whoa, whoa, hold on there. I'm not saying that."

"Don't you put what I was born into against me."

Bearcat smiled, gold tooth with a muted glint. "Guess that's only fair. Ain't like nobody ever held what I was born into against me." A sniff. "And I didn't have to worry 'bout being born rich and white. Lucky me."

"I didn't ask for none of it. And I go my own way." Dell

stretched himself. "And I don't know shit 'bout no goddamn clover leaf."

"O.K., O.K. Down, boy, down. I'm just foolin' with ya." Gave Dell a big moony smile. "What say we get on with bizness."

Dell held fire.

"What say I actually have a true four-leafer in my hand." He held his meaty black hand up, pinched his pink fingers daintily, twirled an imaginary clover leaf. He fixed his gaze on it, and his breathing slowed. Dell felt his breathing fall in with the Bearcat's. Then the big man began to slip into what looked like a trance.

"Clover leaf, spirit root, crow's foot," he started saying, words drawled long and curvy, floating there like balloons. "Plant me a sockful outside ... conjure me up a woman who can sing! ... oh, yeah ... give her some sun, give her some rain ... hell, call her Clover Leaf, or maybe Easter or some other holiday, what you think 'bout that?! ... maybe she drive a tractor ... she play a little guitar, yeah?"

"Yeah," Dell said, swayed by Bearcat's trancespeak, pictures popping magically behind his eyes.

Bearcat smiled, kept on. "And maybe her daddy be a preacher, but maybe with her that religion didn't quite stick!" Raised his head. "Maybe he went bad and she had to find her own way ... maybe she comes like she's hollerin' from pickin' roots ... makes no difference long as she can *sing the blues*. Just let her sing to me, and then shoot me dead...."

Bearcat suddenly hit the guitar with the back of his hand. Dell flinched.

"You listenin' to me, Sonesta?" he shouted up the stairs to the second floor, where the bedrooms were. "GODDAMN YOU, WOMAN, YOU LISTENIN' TO ME?"

There was no answer, and Bearcat let the silence hang in the smoky room. Finally, he turned straight to Dell, bore in with his gaze.

"If we could get us just one new song and have Dewey spin it on the radio, what you think? Huh?"

"Yeah," Dell said. "Yeah!"

"Maybe get us a little more scratch, 'nuff to keep them sheriffs and bulldozers away? 'Nuff to give us a little presence with the big boys in town?"

Dell took the Bearcat's furious gaze, held it, and turned it back.

"Nothing," the boy said, "could give me more delight."

Bearcat hung there for a moment, eyelids heavy, a touch of his trance state still with him, looking like he was thinking, *cogitating*.

"So what was that you were doin' with the sax?"

"When?"

"Before. Went something like this."

Bearcat rested the guitar in his lap, pulled his harp from his jacket pocket, and blew a bright, rocking riff. Dell put his sax to his mouth and copied the Bearcat. Then he went off blowing on his own.

"That's something," Bearcat said. "It's the blues, but it *ain't just the blues*. It's got some of that sound. Come on, let's work with it some more."

And that's how they spent the rest of the afternoon, Bearcat blowing and tonguing his harpoon, Dell picking it up, then leading the big man on his sax. When they finally parted they had a strong melody worked out—a tune that felt like something new to both of them. Both men stood at the same time, the Bearcat opened his arms, and before Dell knew quite what was happening, he was being gathered in to the big man, hugged tight enough to almost snap his bones.

Dell, who couldn't remember the last time anyone had held him like that, broke away gasping.

"You're O.K., boy," Bearcat said. "We'll see you again out here, soon, right?"

Dell was so full of joy he couldn't speak.

Back at the white-pillared two-story house he'd been born in Dell didn't go immediately to his quarters in one of the auxiliary carriage houses but, surprisingly hungry, went into the big house's kitchen, where Carl, one of the servants and, on musical matters, Dell's secret confidant, made him a sandwich.

"A good afternoon, Master Dell?" Carl said as he polished down the stove.

"Oh, Carl, amazing, amazing. Let me tell you all about—"

At that moment Dell's mother, her early-gray hair swept up, her prized cameo broach on her estimable bosom, strode in.

"Carl, there's a problem with the car. Can you—"

She pulled up short.

"Dell, what a surprise. We never see you. What've you been doing?"

He gave his mother a bright, empty smile. "Nothin'," he answered quickly, then gathered up what was left of the turkey sandwich and went out to the carriage house a good quarter mile away.

✳ ✳ ✳ ✳ ✳

SHE LOVED TO PLAY man tricks on men, and they came easy to her. Specially mechanicals. Even before her mother died and everything went to hell there'd been some things her daddy had taught her good, what with Daisy not having a brother, even though there were other things she wished she'd never had to learn. But cars? Cars and trucks and tractors, she knew inside out. Hunting. Trapping. Fishing. Gutting a fish. Gutting a pig....

She could tell the shorter man and the bigger man were put out. They stood round the engine, watched her work her magic, and started making *Oh, that looks easy* noises. *That wan't nothing. We coulda done that.*

But the pretty boy/man with the greasy black hair and the bold sideburns, the splatter of acne and the luscious eyes, just stood back in admiration, asked her name.

"Daisy Holliday. Two *l*'s."

"Elvis Presley," the boy/man said, holding out a delicate white hand. He looked to see if there was recognition, but saw none. "Only one *l*."

"That's a curious name."

"You don't know who he is?" the short man said with a straining upward voice.

"Do you know who *I* am?" Daisy said.

Elvis took a step back, regarded Daisy with direct interest. "So, who are you?"

"I'm a singer."

The small man and the big man started snickering.

"You mean," Elvis said in a drawl, "you're no Formula One auto mechanic, you just do that in your spare time?"

"I'm on my way to Memphis to sing." Dug-in-her-heels determined, Elvis could see that.

"And you're walking?" A lift of his eyebrow. He loved to flirt with girls and was still astonished at how ready they were these days to flirt back.

A smile from this very pretty, if dirty and ragged girl. She wore her miles on her, but they hadn't really worn her down. She kept a fresh-burst energy, like a flower just popped out of the bud.

"Not anymore." She looked from Elvis Presley to the small man, who was Elvis's guitarist, Scotty Moore, and the larger one, who was his bassist, Bill Black, and when Elvis started laughing, she knew she was home free.

* * * * *

THE FIRST THING, Colin thought, was to find out which of them were still alive. From his research on the Bearcat

Jackson CD, he knew Bearcat was dead, well, unless he was working in the same bowling alley as Elvis up in Minnesota, but Dell Dellaplane and Daisy Holliday would have been right around 20 in 1956, which would make them only sixty-something now. He winced for a second, thinking of other old rock 'n' rollers he'd seen at record shows or concerts, especially the one-hit wonders: formerly pompadoured teen idols now with hair combed ear-to-ear over liver-spotted scalps and with little pot-bellies popping over pegged Italian pants, and hot bouffanted girl singers gone to skin tucks, Lycra stretch pants, and harlequin glasses. Still, you couldn't take this away from any of the old stars: that there had once been a moment of such pure vitality and expression that, drop a needle on one of their scratchy singles, and the room would brighten, your feet would jump, and a little bit of heaven explode in your head.

Colin's reverie on the Virgin Air flight from London to New York. It was that leave-in-the morning, get-there-in-the-afternoon, huge jet-lag flight, but he was pretty excited about hitting the States. It had been over a year, and as much as interesting things were going on in Brit Rock, there was nothing like being back in the cradle of it all.

He had already arranged a dinner that evening at the apartment of his old friend Skeeter Rankles. Skeeter had the largest record collection of anyone Colin knew, every wall of his four-room apartment covered with floor-to-ceiling metal shelves, each packed tight with LPs—and that wasn't counting the storage room he rented on Long Island. Colin had called Skeeter a couple days before and told him he had some clues on the Lost 45.

"It doesn't exist," Skeeter said over the bell-clear transatlantic line. "If it did, I'd have it."

"But why have so many people heard it?"

"Why do thousands of people go to Roswell each year?"

"You think *Pink Cadillac*'s a blinking UFO?"

"Colin, my friend, come and see me—we'll talk. You sound like you need a trip anyway." A pause, then Skeeter's voice lowered. "Hey, how have you been, um, holding up?"

Holding up? Colin hadn't even known Skeeter knew he'd gotten married, let alone what had happened nine months back. He was a little surprised that someone as eccentric and troglodytey as Skeeter Rankles could also be intuitive and perceptive. Holding up, indeed.

"I'm fine," Colin said.

"Good. I'll see you in a couple days then."

Skeeter lived in Brooklyn, a section they called Park Slope. It was around four in the afternoon. Skeeter's day job was as a mailman, and he promised he'd be home from his route around then. Colin took a cab from Kennedy and got out on Skeeter's tree-lined street.

"So, the *Pink Cadillac* bug finally nipped you hard," Skeeter said. They were sitting in his non-bedroom room, not simply floor to ceiling with records, but stacked so that moving about the room was like walking through a maze. There looked to be twice as many albums as when Colin was last there, five years before. They were alphabetized by year (Colin loved to note fans' cataloguing modes; putting them by date meant that Skeeter was confident he knew in his head any artist's whole career—an awesome accomplishment). "Why now?"

Colin answered quickly, "Because no one's ever run the whole story down, have they?"

"*Goldmine* did a piece a couple years back."

"But that was just on what's known about Bearcat Records, it was mostly cribbed from me. And they only noted the rumors."

"And something happened in Germany?"

"I got a call from Spider Kaesburg that there was a disc called *Pink Cadillac* with the Bearcat label for sale at a show in someplace called Bad Potlatch. Seller was British, he said.

Name of Firth. I found a guy in Sheffield called Furth who said he'd had a couple Bearcat label discs, but the only one he could remember was by Clay Booker—"

"Which itself would be pretty rare."

"True. But not—"

"Not *Pink Cadillac*." Skeeter leaned forward. He was pole thin and, as Colin remembered, ate only brown rice and steamed vegetables (when they got to dinnertime, Colin was going to insist on taking the collector out). He had long, skeletal fingers—he'd been an acoustic bass player as a kid— and used them exotically to buttress his speech. "So why are you here with me rather than rattling around Deutschland?"

"I need the story," Colin said, leaning forward himself. "I need to know what happened, whether there ever was a record. I need that more than chasing the dubious attention spans of record-show people."

Skeeter nodded. "But me?"

"Who better to know where they might be now?"

"Bearcat's dead—true dead." A thin smile.

"Of course. I found the death certificate. Couldn't quite make out the date though. Looked like fifty-something, six or seven. Cause of death was clear: *Natural causes*, it read." Colin raised his eyebrow. "Who knows what that means."

"Means one dead black man."

"Agreed. But the singer, Daisy Holliday. The saxophonist, Dell Dellaplane. Where are they? Then there's Clay Booker. Is he still alive?"

Scooter leaned back, folded his arachnid fingers before him.

"Dellaplane's in the Hollywood Hills somewhere, still gets a movie job now and then, though no longer the best movies."

Colin leaned forward. "Have you ever talked to him?"

Scooter shook his head. "I've never known anyone, either on the record or off, to get him to talk about his

Memphis days. There's even one school that says he wasn't even there—that at one point it didn't hurt in Hollywood to have a perceived Elvis connection, and that Dellaplane met the King when El first got to Hollywood and, because he fell in with the Memphis Mafia, played up a story taking him back to the South."

"What do you think?"

"I don't think there's a whole lot of deep soul in the soundtrack to *Pedal-pusher Girls* or *Glory on the Mount*."

Colin nodded. Dellaplane wouldn't be his first choice to look up anyway.

"Daisy Holliday?"

"Nobody knows much. If there is no *Pink Cadillac*, then there's nothing on record at all. We know that someone named Daisy Holliday was a bit player in teen flicks in the late '50s, and that someone with that name sang on cruise ships in the early '70s."

"I have a picture," Colin said. "It was in the *Goldmine* article."

"But no record, right? Nothing anyone's ever put on a turntable. So, if this is the same Daisy Holliday, and if she was as good as the stories have it, then why didn't she record anything?"

"Do we know anything past the '70s?"

"I don't. But I don't know if anyone's looked that hard. Remember, I don't think anything like *Pink Cadillac* exists."

"So she could be—"

"Dead ... or married to a gall bladder specialist she met on a Princess cruise. Living in Wisconsin. A grandmother now.... "

"I did a Web search last week from the office. Nothing."

"You look for Clay Booker?"

"Of course."

"Nothing there, either, right?"

"I don't think he's dead," Colin said. "He would've gotten an obit somewhere."

"Probably. You talk to *Living Blues* magazine? They keep tabs on all these guys."

"Good idea."

Skeeter smiled. "So, you want me to cook us up some dinner? I have—"

"No, no, I'm taking us out," Colin said, all flying elbows. He started to stand, but something checked him. It wasn't that Skeeter hadn't been helpful, it was just that something was missing. He pursed his brow. That was it, he wasn't feeling any closer to the record. Sure, he had some leads, but they were about people who might or might not know something. What he needed was to touch the *sound*.

"That's great," Skeeter said. "I know this really good macrobiotic—"

But before his fellow collector got fully out of his chair, Colin sat back down and leaned forward.

"What do you think it sounds like?" he said.

Skeeter heard the sudden serious tone, said, "I never thought of it."

"Never?"

"It's not *my* obsession, buddy." Then, seeing how serious Colin was, he added, "I mean, we know *Cryin' Shame*—"

"But this wouldn't be anything like that. This was four years later, and after Elvis happened. There were whites involved."

"But that's what makes it all sound so crazy. Wouldn't Bearcat know what kind of shitfire that would bring down?"

Colin closed his eyes for a second, remembered the picture of the Bearcat he'd used on his CD. It was of a handsome man, in his twenties then, with coal-black skin and a large, distinguished nose, yet sharp cheekbones and fiery, focused eyes. As he'd written in his liner notes: In the picture it looked like this man could see into the future. Wouldn't he know exactly what was happening around him? His roadhouse wasn't that far out of Memphis, and was on the direct road down to the Delta. He'd have a radio. And he'd be bold. From all Colin had turned up, this Thomas Jackson was always bold—if at times a little crazy, too.

"But think where things were at," Colin said. "For years Thomas Jackson was the Man. You hear of black music in the South, he was there. Touring with a jump band, producing blues artists, hell, starting the first black record label anywhere. But things were changing."

"So?"

"So the old music wouldn't cut it. Bearcat knew that. Business was falling off at his club. Four years before it was the hottest place around Memphis, that's what I was told. People were swinging from the rafters. Bearcat had his own label. He had *Cryin' Shame* charting with Sonesta Clarke. Hell, he was *living* with Sonesta Clarke!

"But by '55 things were dead. That's what I heard when I was doing my research. That for some reason after *Cryin' Shame* Bearcat, who up till then was playing with everybody, cutting all kinds of records, just got quiet—"

"Yeah, exactly," Skeeter said from his chair.

"But you're counting him out," Colin went on. "What I'm saying is that that man had overcome so much—his parents died when he was twelve, and he was shipped off to an aunt whose husband was a tenant farmer and never wanted him to play music, used to beat him silly and drive him out to the fields. We're talking about a man who ran away from home at 16 and made it all the way to New York, where he sat in with the likes of Lonnie Johnson and Bill Broonzy. Man who hung with Son House! Man who had his own band in his 20s. Man who did more than just play, but actually produced. Man who cut record deals with white men back when almost no white man would talk to *any* black.

"This man's just going to quit? No, something happened. He might have been lying low, might have felt discouraged, but around 1955 or '56, right before he died, he saw an opportunity. He saw the goddamn future."

Skeeter was looking at his old friend closely. "But isn't that what I was saying? If there's a *Pink Cadillac* at all, it's another Bearcat record—"

"No, no," Colin said, and he was half out of his chair now. "If it was going to be just another record, then why would Bearcat do it? As far as I know, *Pink Cadillac* broke a four-year recording drought. What I need to know is why that was—what this Dell Dellaplane had to do with it? Where Daisy Holliday came from? What caused this genius musician to make that leap—to jump into a future that wasn't really even ready to happen for another, what, six or eight years."

Skeeter folded his long fingers before him, then nodded lightly, as if he were almost persuaded. "What does it sound like to you?"

"You probably don't really care—"

"Hey, come on, I do." Skeeter fixed him with his Ichabod Crane face. "'Sides, you're buying dinner."

Colin gave him a look, then he sighed and closed his eyes again. "*Pink Cadillac* ... the title's so much like a novelty record, *doo doot doo*, but I don't hear it that way. Sure, it rocks. Sure, it's up-tempo. But I don't think it's just a throwaway. They're not just riffing on pink Cadillacs 'cause Elvis drove one and they were in the teenage mind—no, it's like there was some *real* pink Cadillac, and it meant something special to them. One person quoted me a chorus: '*I don't care if I never look back / In my Pink Cadillac / Pink Cadillac.*' "

"Sounds pretty frothy—"

"Oh, sure, sure," Colin said, "optimistic as hell. *We're cruising ahead, I'm driving this ridiculously beautiful car, blah blah blah.* But this is Bearcat Jackson producing. This is a man who has a damn good idea what they're trying to get away from."

Skeeter focused with new intent. "So it's pop, but it's blues, too."

"And then there's Daisy Holliday."

"The cruise boat singer."

"What I heard, she could cut it like no white girl before her. Like Big Mama Thornton, like Ruth Brown. Like fucking Janis ten years earlier."

"That would be something," Skeeter said softly, but there was disbelief under the awe.

"But why not? That's what makes the story so great—if I knew the goddamn story. You have this woman with this *voice*. No voice like it before. It's got froth and sunny days, sure, but it's also got a blues rip and a soul tug." Colin closed his eyes again, spoke slowly. "What I hear is something deep ... boundless. This woman can pull *anything* out of herself with her voice.

"Now think of it: They're up on a stage—people I talked to years ago in Memphis swear they saw her perform— and there's this blonde woman, thin, wearing a sparkly dress, but solid, big shoulders, a real head on her. She's got this long blonde hair, but she's unschooled enough, it just sort of hangs there, but it's beautiful blonde hair, and if you're in the audience, you just want to touch it, run your fingers—"

Colin's own fingers were spritzing the air.

"And then she starts to sing. There's this huge black man next to her, and she's learned from him, and she's drawing from him, and there's this bright, punky kid behind her, blowing sax, and she's learned from him and is drawing from him, too, but they're all in awe of her because they know what's really getting to 'em is coming straight out of her—"

"Colin. Colin, I—"

"There's never been anything like it, Skeeter. That sound, that voice, that look—"

Skeeter suddenly gave a quick frown.

"I think I got it now." He was nodding fast to himself. There was half respect, half sadness on his face. "*That sound, that voice, that look. . . .* Do you think this *Pink Cadillac* record you're obsessing about, that probably doesn't even exist, Colin—*that probably doesn't exist*—you think that will really help bring her back?"

＊ ＊ ＊ ＊ ＊

DELL DELLAPLANE HAD taken Bearcat's challenge to heart and was driving back to the roadhouse in his MG sportster, the wind blowing through his hair, humming the tune he'd worked up. It was clear it was a road song, the trees and fence posts peeled by as he climbed the chorus—it could be a driving-along hit, no question. If Bearcat and his band could help him get it in the pocket ... and if they got someone to sing it right.

"O.K., one more time," the Bearcat said an hour and a half later. He was behind a small round floor table, Dell was up on the plywood stage, the band behind him. The roadhouse was afternoon-empty, just Salt setting up the bar and Hosea and Diamondback hanging about. Salt was a very serious-looking man, only a couple years older than Dell, with shiny conked hair, a pair of wire-rimmed glasses stretched down his nose, and an air of dreamy contemplation around him. Hosea was the down-home Bearcat pal, still in overalls and self-snipped haircut, and Diamondback, who'd spent some time in Chitown, was spiffed-up flash in a pin-striped felt suit and bright-red bow tie, even this time of the afternoon. He was a gambler by trade. There was no sign of Sonesta Clarke.

Dell had just honked out the four-bar riff and was ready to do it again. He leaned back, kissed the sax's mouthpiece, felt the music swell from his toes, and *bit-bit-bom, bit-bit-bom-bom* ... got it going.

"I can hear it," the Bearcat said, grin huge on his face. "You're right, *you're right*. I'm there thinking cars, open road, *vroom-vrooom!*" This last sound made the big man's cheeks flutter. "It's moving like that *Rocket 88* song of Ike and Jackie's that went Number 1. Boy, you done good."

Dell preened. Bearcat stood up, motioned to the band, silent behind the young man.

"All right now, Sticks, I want you to give me a straight four, but do that rim shot of yours until the chorus part, then shift into twos and follow the bass line ... *Dum-dum, dum-dum, da-da, dum....*" The band fell right in. "Hear it? That's it. Like tires running asphalt, one of those fast *new* roads. Kind we're just dying for out here." A huge Bearcat snort. "Kind all 'Merica's dyin' for."

Dell gave the big man a look. Bearcat said, "Hey, can't beat 'em, still gotta fight 'em nohow."

Back to the band: "O.K., Clay, put that turnaround of yours in and let's send this puppy home. *Da-da-dum* ... that's it!"

The band worked through the song a couple more times, and then Bearcat turned to Dell.

"Good work, son. You got a bridge for us?"

"Man's never happy," Dell said, though he wriggled his shoulders proudly.

Bearcat stood to his full height. "Yes," said with a cut, "man is *never* happy. You don't get yourself nowhere making yourself happy—you gotta make everyone else happy. That's the job. Now how 'bout that bridge? Something that will take us on out smilin', bring us back laughin'."

"Nothin's come yet."

"Well, boy, make it come! Make it come! I ain't gonna show you every goddamn thing. And it all needs some words." Bearcat cupped his hands around his mouth, lifted himself up on his toes, and went, "*Bee-bee-da-ba, bee-bee-da-ba*. Sticks, you think I could make a scat singer?"

"Sheeit," the long, tall drummer went.

"So, go think of something. *Bee-bee-da-ba—yeah*! O.K., let's take us a break."

The band set down their instruments, but Dell, concentrating, blew a soft riff that went nowhere.

"Hey!"

Dell looked up.

"Here," Bearcat said. He'd undone the ratty leather bag
from his belt and now tossed it to the young man. Dell field-
ed it smooth with his right hand. "All the music in the world's
in there. Just let it come out."

Dell, needing privacy, headed across the roadhouse and
out the front door. On his way, he heard Bearcat's voice
booming, "I feel like we're getting that new thing, right,
boys?" and the band hemming and hawing, not willing to
commit at all.

But they'll get it, Dell thought. It's all gonna come
together. He was outside now, a day just starting to build its
heat. He leaned against the rough wood plank wall of the
roadhouse, fingered his sax. *Beep-beep-beep.* No, nothing
there. He took the leather pouch, his mojo bag, Bearcat called
it—God only knows what was in it; Dell shuddered to think—
and rubbed it up and down his saxophone. The grease, or
worse, on the outside of the bag smeared over the bright
brass. Dell gave a long sigh. He wasn't sure he knew 'bout any
of this, but still the student, he did know not to question too
deeply. He gingerly put the now grimy sax to his lips, closed
his eyes, and started to blow....

The next thing he knew, there was a loud engine rumble right in front of him. When he opened his eyes, they
bloomed wide with astonishment.

It was a pink Cadillac, seemed like it was a block long,
with a silver grill, a powerful snout and blocky shoulders and
fins curved sweet as his horn. And stepping out of it was a man
he recognized from the occasional curious glimpse years
back, both white boys prowling Beale Street, and of course
now from the newspapers. He really didn't know Elvis
Presley, though they were both nineteen. Dell had gone to

East High, home of rich soshes and brainiacs and girls with conservative pleated skirts, while Elvis was Humes High, where souped-up cars and fast girls and serious football reigned. East looked down at Humes, and Humes carried a chip on its shoulder over East. And when the two met, cruising Lamar or hanging at Willie King's or at a football match, fights broke out.

Dell was startled to see Presley now. But what he saw next shook him more.

She was blonde and young—probably 17, at the most 18—and she carried herself with an awkward energy and verve that right then lit up something inside Dell. She wasn't exactly gorgeous, well, she was cute enough, with a pert little nose and full lips, but she was gangly, too, and her shoulders could've gotten her a tryout on the football team. Tall, also, nearly as tall as he was. And determined—he saw something tight and focused in her right off.

A quick stab: Was she Elvis's girlfriend? Rumors even Dell had heard had the singer, who had been a total reject, hanging around now with a bevy of willing girls. Was this vision one of them? A little sheepishly, Dell followed the singer and his retinue into the roadhouse.

"Mistah Cat!" Elvis called out, his voice rising to the exposed rafters of the roadhouse. He had a loose, shambling walk, arms moving, little waltzes side to side; sort of a half-hearted tough-guy strut but not really threatening. "What's shakin'?"

"Well, well, look what the wind blew in." Bearcat said. He gave out an amused smile.

"How ya doin'? You know these guys, right? Scotty Moore. Bill Black."

The guitarist and bass player hung by the door. The blonde girl was a dozen feet in. Dell followed her as if pulled along.

"Last time I heard," Bearcat said, "you were ridin'

round on some Louisiana Hayride, picking straw out of ya teeth. Then I heard you were strummin' 'long at the Grand Ole Opry with a bunch of hillbillies in frilly suits and string ties—"

Elvis winced. Dell had heard how Elvis had recently been received with stony silence in Nashville, and it still must be smarting. But then Elvis lit up again and threw what he could back.

"Yeah, and last I heard you were bailin' Clay here out of jail."

"Well, I gotta do something to keep a band together."

Elvis shrugged. "Same old song, huh?"

"What you gonna do? Things are slow, my man. We're trying to keep the place alive, but I ain't cut a record in years, and we need a singer."

Elvis glanced up the stairs, his pure eyes and untraced brow showing kindly respect. "Where's Sonesta?"

"Well, now, you go down to the 13th Street Baptist Church, you'll probably find her."

"On Monday afternoon?" Elvis said.

Bearcat lowered himself into a chair. "Started out, it was just Sundays, you know. Then she added Fridays, and Wednesdays, now seems like her and her sisters be there most every day."

"She singing there?"

Bearcat, in a sudden roar: "I don't know goddamn what she does there. All I knows, she won't sing for me."

"Damn shame," Elvis said. He looked all empathy, then turned to the cluster behind him of Daisy, Dell, and his two musicians. "Well, I tell everyone, best music I ever heard was between these four walls—right here."

"Tell it to the wind, man," the Bearcat said. He brushed his fingers down the front of his loose coat, flicking away who knew what. "That was back when you were nothin' but a whipper-snappin' pain in my ass, hitchin' and sneakin' out here all the time. 'Causin' us *nothing* but trouble." There was a swell of pride in Bearcat's voice, unmistakable under his rough bark. "By the way, how is yo' mama."

"Oh, my mama," Elvis started to say, and his voice got soft, even reverential. "She thinks all this is wonderful, you know, but it confuses her some, too. Dixie Locke. Other girls I meet—" Dell, watching closely, noticed no nod or anything at all toward the blonde woman "—all this traveling around playin'. She misses me, you know, something awful." A shrug. "I miss her, too."

"We all love our mamas," Bearcat said, glancing up toward the heavens. "Yo' mama, sometimes that's all you ever got."

"Amen, Mistah Cat."

"Amen, Mr. Rocky-Roly Pheee-nom-eee-nonnnn."

Both men slapped hands, laughed hugely.

"I heard you bought yo' mama one of them Cadillacs."

"I sure did," Elvis said. "'Cept, funny thing is, scares her half to death even think about driving, so it just sits there at home."

Bearcat raised himself just enough to look out one of the small windows fronting the roadhouse. "And you driving yo'self a pink one." He shook his head, muttered, "Gracious," as in *What could this wild world show us next?* "And you're ridin' all over the radio to boot."

Elvis was quickly wistful. "It's been awful fast, Mistah Cat, awful fast. Sometimes I—I don't know where it's all going."

"Just hold on to your sideburns, boy. I imagine wheels like that take you just 'bout anywhere you wanted to go."

"You think so?" Elvis young and still so needy it'd break your heart.

"Like I always said, boy, you got it."

Elvis hung his head, but subtly. "Sometimes I—"

Bearcat looked at the greasy-haired kid with the acne-

flecked skin and spoke with deep, adult commiseration. He'd
seen black men feeling this profoundly inferior all his life; he
was a little surprised Elvis, after all that was happening, hadn't
gotten over it.

"No, no, you got it, boy," he said, "and they love it.
They love *you*."

Elvis smiled, lifted his head. And just like that he'd
come back to himself. He gave Bearcat a tight, manly nod of
thanks, then said, "That reminds me, you got yourself a
phone out here yet?"

Bearcat relaxed, gave Elvis the long eye. "Hot water,
too, you wanna take a bath?"

"When I used to come out here," Elvis said brightly to
the rest of the room. He was looking around now, and his
gaze clearly fell on the white saxophone player. Dell
watched for a sign of recognition but got none; he did pick
up on a slight twinge in Presley of challenge—a general
what's-another-young-white-guy-doin'-here appreciation.
But then the singer's gaze moved along, taking in the stained
walls, the beer signs, the tilty tables. He went to the bar and
took himself a Coca-Cola, popped the bottle cap and poured
it down his throat. "There was nothing like a telephone. You
just took your chances. Good thing the Bearcat never left
home."

"I had a heap of work to do, and I done it."

"Not to mention the way you love this place." Elvis
smiled. "Anyway, can Scotty here use the phone?"

Bearcat motioned to the back, next to the toilets. Elvis
decided to unburden himself and took a chair, sitting backward on it, his chin tucked over the bentwood seat back. He
took another pull of his Coke. Everyone else sat down, too.

When Elvis spoke, the sass was back in his voice.

"Thing with these Cadillacs, Mr. Cat, let me tell you,
since I doubt you ever get one of your own—"

Bearcat threw his big head back, gave Elvis the meanest,

darkest hooded look he could. "If I did get me one, wouldn't be no pansy color like *pink*!"

"Hey, hey," Elvis laughed, then curled his lower lip. "Pink's what makes it special. These Cadillacs, they got nothin' on regular cars. No, they got spirits of their own—they like women that way, know what I mean?"

From the back of the room, Dell still had his eye on the girl who'd come in with Elvis. She seemed unawed by being around the famous singer, but truly curious about where she was now, eyeing the ramshackle walls, the hand-lettered signs that read YOU PACKING, YOU LEAVING and TIPS NOT SPIT. Then Dell saw her watching Bearcat and his glinting gold tooth with even more fascination. He also was seeing her more clearly: Up closer, her skin was a little flat, dull in a country way, and her blonde hair looked at best cut by amateur hands. But there was still this huge energizing light in her blue eyes.

"First Caddie I had," Elvis went on, his sharp jaw lifting as he spoke, "it just burned to a crisp, back in June. Day I'll always remember, burned me up my first Cadillac, June 17, 1955." He closed his eyes for a moment, held this private, bemusing memory, then popped his lids up.

So, next thing you know, I decided I better get me *two* of 'em. Now, I told you 'bout the one I gave my mother, it just sits at home with a dead battery." He laughs, a warm glow in his eyes. "So this one, me and the boys are driving along after singing down in Shreveport, heading right into Memphis 'cause we got a gig here tonight, when the thing just quits."

Tsk-tsk noises from everyone else.

"Yep, deader than a doornail. You got yourself a dead pink Cadillac, you got yourself a whole heap of nothing. Anyway, the boys and I get under the hood, but everything's looking sweet. We're by the side of the road, got Bill's bass up top the car, don't dare leave it, but we're obviously going nowhere when—" he gestured toward Daisy "—this little angel appears out of nowhere. Rolls up her sleeves, starts messing with the wires. Tells me to get in the car and start her up. We all think she's crazy, but I get in, turn the key, and the Pink Lady starts on a dime! I couldn't believe it! I asked her where she learned to fix Cadillacs like that, and guess what she says—" He throws his hand again at Daisy. "Tell him what you said. Go on."

Daisy had been walking around the room, and now she was up near the bandstand. "Tractors," she said with a smile. Dell cocked his ear, heard a lilt to her voice, yet a sonorous depth, too.

"Can you believe it?" Elvis said. "Pretty girl like that. *Tractors!* It was like magic. Middle of nowhere.... You got anything that needs fixing?"

"What don't we got!" Bearcat waved a hand around the roadhouse. The door to the bathrooms was hanging on one hinge, the pool table in the back corner had a tear down one side of the baize, and half the Christmas lights on the walls weren't burning. "But the main thing broke's our old Blue Star disc-cutting machine over there." Bearcat pointed to a complicated-looking contraption, half huge sewing machine, half stork. "What I cut all our records on, that baby. 'Course, first I could use me a song that wants cuttin'."

Daisy had left her chair and walked up on the stage, picking up Clay's guitar. She held it gingerly, and when she tried to play a note, she must have hit the volume knob because it fed back through the tweed amplifier with a fierce howl.

"Whoah, little lady," Bearcat said, looking over. "Watch out there now!"

"I know how to play guitar," Daisy said. She had quickly turned down the right knob, and was lifting Clay's wide-leather strap over her stolid shoulders. Even with the heavy guitar hanging from her, her posture was book straight.

"Oh, you do, do you?"

Daisy brought the volume knob up just a tad, then began strumming an open G chord.

"I just haven't played one electric before."

She kept the G going, then filigreed in a sustained C, and began to sing softly. It was a gospel tune, *How Long the Road to Jesus*. Her voice was gravelly but sweet, and soared on the high G notes. Everyone, even Hosea and Diamondback, stopped, fascinated. She sang through a verse with power and rock-solid presence. Half a verse further in, Elvis walked up and started to harmonize with her. The black-haired singer carefully followed her, keeping his voice under hers, but having his voice with hers clearly roused her to new passion. Eyes closed, swaying side to side, she filled the room with the song. *"How long, how long on this lonely road / How long, how long, with this unearthly load...."* Yes, Elvis filled her out, but Daisy carried the song. When they were done the whole room was silent.

It was while Daisy was singing that Sonesta Clarke came home. The older black woman walked in quietly, saw the group around the bandstand, and marched past, paying it no mind. But when she was halfway up the stairs, her curiosity got the better of her and she looked down at who was singing, seeing the young girl with the blonde hair and that boy who used to show out here, Elvis Presley. She immediately brought her hands together tightly and cursed under her breath, saying, *Oh, my, no good is gonna come of this.*

It was in the middle of the song that Daisy saw the black woman looking hard at her from the stairs. Her powerful gaze unsettled Daisy for a moment, but the music carried her through.

Finally Bearcat said softly, "Where on God's green earth did you learn to sing like that?"

Daisy, with the song over, a little awkward, a touch of a blush on her cheeks, mumbled, "Back home."

"C'mon now, I know where this white nigger—" affectionate gesture toward Elvis "—learned it, but where did you?"

"From a ... a very special old woman," Daisy said. She was looking down, as if pained. "I used to sneak out of the regular church and go over there."

"Your daddy's a preacher?"

Daisy's eyes widened. "How'd you know that?"

Bearcat reeled a step back.

"Now that we know you can sing, darlin'," Elvis said, "what else can you do?"

"Oh, I don't know." Daisy shut her eyes, smiled. "I used to be able to shoot a big grisly bear dead with my daddy's rifle at a hundred yards."

Elvis laughed. "I mean songs. What else do you know?"

"Oh, just what we sing back home, colored spirituals, some hillbilly. But I'm ready to learn more. That's why I'm headed to Memphis."

"Well," Elvis said, looking at the Bearcat and seeing the way his mouth was still hanging open. "I don't think you gotta go no further than right here."

Bearcat fixed his former protégé with a startled look.

"Whoa, whoa, whoa!" Bearcat went. "What you sayin'?"

"Hey, you were the one who said you needed a singer."

"Yeah, and I could use a Cadillac, too. You just ordered me one the wrong damn color!"

"Am *I* the wrong color?" Elvis said with heat. "Bill, am I the wrong color?"

Bill Black said, "I don't know. Maybe."

"Sheeit, man," Elvis said. He started grinning broadly, dancing around a little. "What color you think I am?"

"Whatever color you want to be, kid," the big bass player with the hangdog look said.

"Bearcat, you got a problem with *that*?"

The Bearcat was shaken. "But ... she's...."

"Go on, tell us your name again," Elvis said.

"Daisy."

"Pretty as one, ain't she?"

At that moment Scotty Moore came back from the telephone, excited, calling out, "El, you won't believe this!"

"What?"

"We gotta go to New York!"

"What're you talkin' about?"

"I just got off the phone with Bob Neal. The deal. It's done."

"The deal?"

"The motherjumpin' deal! It's RCA, babe! They bought our contract from Sam, lock, stock, and guitar neck. The deal's done, it's ink."

A look of shock yet also preternatural calm went over Elvis's face. It was like he was hearing a private, mythic voice that had been speaking to him for a long time.

"Bob says we gotta be at the airport in one hour. They're holdin' a plane for us now! Bob's worried as can be. C'mon, Bill, let's go."

"I don't believe this...." Elvis said to nobody in particular.

"It's what we've been waitin' for. Get up, man. Your folks are already on their way to the airport to see us off. Newspapers, too. This is the big time callin' dee-rect!"

Elvis looked up for a moment, the bowed his head. "New York," he said, mostly to himself.

"Bob said they paid the highest prite they ever paid for a singer."

"Bearcat, what do you—"

Bearcat, having recovered at this news, walked over to Elvis and put an arm around his shoulder.

"Nothing gonna stop you now. You just don't forget us down here, O.K.?"

"No, man, never ... I could never do that." Elvis gave

his face a scratch, hitched up his jeans, started brushing back his oily hair. He seemed a sudden flurry of nervous tics. "Whoa, New York!" The singer's eyes were huge.

"Come on, boy, come on," Scotty said, leading the way out of the roadhouse. "We gotta get movin'."

The three musicians ran out of the roadhouse, jumped in the pink Cadillac, Elvis at the wheel. He fit the key, turned it, and ... grind, grind.

"Dang!" he cursed. Turned the key again, nothing but that empty, hopeless sound, battery juicing, nothing catching.

"Shit!" Bill Black said.

"Damn," from Scottie Moore.

"I'm trying, guys. Let me give it one more—"

But forcing the key only made the engine sound more forlorn and helpless.

There was deep silence, then Elvis cried, "Wait a minute. Daisy. Where's Daisy?"

He jumped out of the Cadillac, dashed across the dirt parking lot, threw open the door, "Hey, blondie, we need your magic hands. Come on!"

Daisy quickly followed Elvis back to the car. Bearcat, Dell, the band, and the hangers-on followed. A warm wind whisked high-flying leaves.

Elvis popped the hood and raised it, and Daisy dug in. She jiggled this, jangled that, tightened everything, then said, "Give it another turn."

Elvis, back in the driver's seat, obliged.

Grind, grind, grind.

"I think your distributor's shorted," Daisy called.

"Can you fix it?"

She shook her head. "No, I jury-rigged it before, but I think now it simply needs to be replaced. Get a new part, I could have it going in a jiff."

"Bearcat!" Elvis called, stepping out of the pink Cadillac. "Bearcat, you gotta drive us to the airport."

The big man stood there, hands on his hips, a big Chesire Cat grin on his face.

"Just think, he lost his career 'cause of a distributor cap."

"Bearcat, quit joking. Come on! I'll—listen, when I get back, I'll get Dewey Phillips to spin your next record!"

"Yeah, yeah, you just remember, boy, Dewey Phillips was spinning my music 'fore you knew how to tune a guitar." Then the big man's glare turned sunny. "But all right, all right, you boys hop in the truck."

In a flash, Elvis, Scottie, and Bill stripped the pink Cadillac and tossed suitcases and instrument cases, as well as Bill's huge black-leather bass case, in the back of the rusty old Ford pickup truck.

Scottie and Bill joined the luggage in the back, Elvis took the passenger seat, and Bearcat settled himself behind the wheel. Pulled out a key, turned it, and ... nothing.

"Damn!" Bill Black cried.

"Bearcat, what the—" from Elvis.

"Shhhhh," Bearcat hissed. "Quiet."

The Bearcat pulled the key from the ignition, then sat there, back stiff, eyes closed. Everyone was silent. All you could hear was the big man's heavy breathing. Then he began to mumble, "Lucky am I, luck is me / Good fortune's all I see," over and over. The key glittered in the sunlight. When he opened his eyes they glittered, too.

He stuck in the key again, gave it a flip. The truck rumbled to life.

Elvis and his backup players started applauding; Daisy and Dell, Thumper, Sticks, and Clay, and Salt, Hosea, and Diamondback joined in.

"Hold on a sec," Elvis said, and like that he jumped out of the truck's cab.

The singer ran up to Daisy. He was dangling the keys to the Cadillac.

"Daisy, darlin', I don't know how to thank you, but if you can get that distributor cap—get that stupid thing running—running—well, I'd be—"

"El, hey, come on!" Scotty cried.

"Oh, shit, what am I worrying about?"

Bearcat put the truck in gear, slowly started backing up.

"Look, if you fix the car, you can keep it," Elvis said, already moving toward the truck.

"What?"

"I mean it." Elvis jumped on the truck's running board as Bearcat shifted again and started moving forward. "Keep the car, darlin'. It's done everything it can for me. Now it's gotta be yours."

And with that, Elvis pulled open the truck door, threw himself inside as the Bearcat went careering out of the roadhouse lot, kicking up a storm of dust and nearly crashing into a horse-drawn, hay-filled wagon out on the highway. The last anyone heard back at the roadhouse was Bill Black's thunderous *Yee-Haw!*

"I don't believe it," Daisy said softly to herself. She stood there, the Cadillac keys hanging off a rabbit's-foot key chain.

"What?" Dell said. He was about eight feet away from Daisy but hadn't heard what had gone down between her and Elvis—indeed, had felt flashes of jealousy.

"He just gave me his car." She said this so matter-of-factly that Dell didn't exactly hear her at first.

"You said he did what?"

"He said, 'Keep the car, darlin.' " Daisy's voice remained flat, almost as if she were in a trance. ·

"He must just want you to look after it."

"No, no." Daisy looked at Dell now, and started coming back to herself. "He started to say that, then just threw his hands up and said it was mine. Like he gives 'em away every day."

"Working on his legend, I guess," Dell said, half to himself.

"He said I'll be needing it for where I'm going."

"Where's that?"

She looked straight at Dell. "Oh, I got me a few ideas." She smiled wide, then turned and looked down the road Bearcat's truck had disappeared along.

"Do you think that boy's going to be famous? Like, really famous?"

"I don't have a clue," Dell said. "One night Dewey Phillips spun his record on WHBQ, and the next day he was the biggest damn phenomenon you ever saw. But that was just li'l old Memphis. New York? New York's a whole other pail of catfish."

"Still, all that money—just giving away Cadillacs."

"Believe me, money ain't everything."

Daisy smiled at Dell. "Yeah, how would a guy like you know?" Daisy lifted one of her wide shoulders, flirted it Dell's way. "What do *you* drive?"

Dell paused a moment, then shrugged and said, "Oh, I take the bus a lot."

Daisy, mimicking him, shrugged back. "Oh, the bus," she said, and laughed. "Well, that woulda beat me. 'Fore I met that boy, I was walking." She gave Dell a smile brilliant with the full glare of astonished good fortune, then went over to the pink Cadillac and dove back under the hood.

"You know," she said half to herself, "I wonder...." She gave the distributor cap a twist. Dell came over and looked at the engine with her.

"Do me a favor?" she said.

"Sure."

"See if you can get her going." She passed him the rabbit's-foot key chain, and Dell got into the driver's seat.

"Now."

He turned the key, and the engine kicked over.

"How'd you do that?" he called out over the loud thrum.

"Talent." Daisy was standing by the door, waiting for Dell to get up. He put his foot down once more on the gas pedal, bounced it, gunning the engine, then stepped out.

Daisy slid herself in behind the wheel.

"Think I'm going to go for a drive."

"Where to?"

She smiled mischievously, then began to pull out. "Wherever it decides to take me."

"You comin' back?"

The Cadillac went gliding past Dell. Daisy called out the window, "You got a reason for me to?"

Dell, hardly thinking, on instinct only, said, "Yeah. I . . . I got a song for you to sing."

"Song, huh? How's it go?"

Dell still had his sax round his neck, and the mojo bag, too. He brushed the bag, then brought the sax up to his mouth and started blowing his new riff.

Daisy let the car idle, listening over the engine's hum. "I like it. What's it called?"

Dell, finished off the final bars, then took the sax from his mouth. "I don't have a—"

Daisy, impatient, ran the engine.

"But maybe I'll call it—"

Daisy dropped into gear and started to take off. Dell had no idea if she heard what he said next, but the words as they came made perfect sense.

"*Pink Cadillac,*" he sang out, marrying the syllables to his riff. "*I hope I see you . . . comin' back / In your pink Cadillac . . . your pink Cadillac. . . .*"

✳ ✳ ✳ ✳ ✳

IT TOOK COLIN two hours navigating the switchbacks and tangled half streets in the canyons above West L.A. to find

Dell Dellaplane's ivy-hidden, canyon-cantilevered small house. He wondered if Dellaplane's somewhat sketchy directions had been more to deter him than help. Still, here he was.

No one answered the buzzer by the gate on the street for ten minutes—Colin filled with helpless memories of O.J.'s airport chauffeur—but then finally an intercom barked, "Who's there?" and when Colin answered, a tanned, fit man came to let him in.

"I'm Dellaplane," he said, extending a hand. He was wearing an open-collared silk shirt, jeans, and sandals. He had silver hair cut Roman style over a face just beginning to widen with age. He was tall enough, though still a couple inches shorter than Colin, who had to duck slightly to get under the gate's iron frame.

"I'm living alone these days," Dell Dellaplane said, in explanation of the stacks of compact discs, sheet music, and recording equipment strewn around the living room, where he offered Colin a seat on a white leather couch. "Has its pleasures. You have family?"

"Um, no." Colin sat himself so he could see clearly out the picture window, down into a brown-brush arroyo dotted with precariously perched canyonside houses.

"Must make the traveling easier. I take it your music business takes you all over the world?"

"Takes me wherever I have to go, yeah." Colin was watching Dellaplane. There was a tightness around his mouth, skin either surgically stretched or—and maybe this was his romantic imagination—secrets long held. The man seemed friendly enough now, but Colin wanted to proceed carefully.

"And it's brought you here to me. Something about Memphis?"

"Years ago, yeah. When you were starting out."

"That was a long time back. I don't know how much I remember."

"Bearcat Jackson?"

"That's right, you put that CD out on him. I have it—" he waved toward the tilting stacks of thin plastic boxes "—somewhere."

"But that only goes up so far." Colin leaned forward. "To before you knew him, I believe."

"The last record Bearcat cut was in—" two fingers scratching his forehead. "—1953. I didn't know him till late '55." Dellaplane smiled. "Didn't you put out everything on that CD? What was it called, *Hear Me Roar*?"

"Everything I could find, yeah." This was moving along faster than Colin had expected. No reason not to, yet.... "The reason I'm here. Well, I've heard about a *further* recording. Called *Pink Cadillac*. With a Daisy Holliday—"

Dellaplane's eyes narrowed.

"I never heard that." He leaned back in his chair, then blew his cheeks up like Dizzie Gillespie. "Have you?"

That was the question, of course. Colin guessed Dellaplane was lying, but didn't know whether his own lie would help or not.

"I have very strong evidence that it existed. A basic rock number, a white girl singer, raging horns, hot as early Elvis—"

"I would think a song like that would be very famous." Dellaplane brought his palms together in front of his mouth, blew slowly into them. "And Bearcat was involved in this song?"

"It was on his label."

"And when was this?"

"My best evidence puts it in late '56, early '57."

"Bearcat was dead in March 1956."

Colin perked his ears up. "Really, all I've seen is a smudged death certificate."

"I think if you did your research right, you'd know he died in March." He closed his eyes. "March 9, I believe."

"You remember that awfully well," Colin said.

A wary look in Dellaplane's eyes.

"But you don't know anything about *Pink Cadillac*?"

A quick shake.

"Or Daisy Holliday?"

"I don't know. There were a lot of girls floating around back then, but they weren't in the business, you know. They're what later were called, well, groupies."

"People in Memphis remember vividly hearing a song on the radio. *Pink Cadillac*. They heard it, stopped dead in their tracks just like when they heard Elvis for the first time."

"I remember *that*," Dell said, his eyes brightening. "It was Thursday, July 8, 1954. Hot, hot, hot day. I was 17. They played *That's All Right* nonstop on Dewey Phillips's show. I remember hearing it the first time and wanting right then to hear it again, and *he played it right then again*." Dellaplane like that had come to life, hands·waving before him. "I'd been a high school jock, a football player, into that whole scene, but I also played the sax and was listening to people like Bearcat in secret on the radio at night. When I heard *That's All Right*, I knew right away it was a white guy. Told myself, Wow, it can be done." Dellaplane brought the back of his hand to his eyes, brushed them lightly. "Though I was surprised it was Presley, who I knew a little from around—"

Colin had to interrupt. "But you never even heard anything called *Pink Cadillac*?" An angry incredulity was barely hidden in his voice.

Dellaplane lost most of his far-away look; he gave his interrogator a faint, wan smile. "I remember something Springsteen did in the '70s, title something like that. But wasn't that his own song?"

"And you never recorded with Bearcat Jackson?"

A long sigh. "It never got that far. You see, I never knew Bearcat well, just saw him in town now and then, clubs in West Memphis. Besides, this was 1956. I was a *white boy*.

Bearcat didn't play with white people then—he couldn't. The times...."

"Nothing? I'm sure you'd remember, you seem to have a great memory, but I've heard—"

"Listen," Dellaplane said, leaning forcefully forward. "Bearcat Jackson was in trouble in 1956. He was losing his club, hadn't cut a record in years. Fewer people were going out there. In a way, you could say the music had passed him by.

"Now, it wasn't like he might've clued in—probably would've. From what I heard, Bearcat was nothing if not a smart, cagey guy. Did you write the story about the time he gave the Mozart recital?"

"The what?"

"Yeah, it was part of the big man's legend. He took these piano lessons when he was five. His true father was a professional, a lawyer, you know, and Bearcat grew up in relative privilege till his parents were killed in that car accident when he was fifteen."

"I've heard twelve. And that his father was a doctor."

"The joys of mythmaking." Dellaplane smiled. "Anyway, the way the story goes, his mother sent him to piano lessons, with a New England white woman across town, and when he was ten he was trotted out to play Mozart—Sonata No. 15, I think, Köchel 155. 'A Little Sonata for Beginners,' Mozart called it. They supposedly dressed Bearcat in cut-down tails and had him play in front of a garden group—sort of, you train 'em, look what one of the monkeys can do. 'Cept that halfway through it, Bearcat took a deep breath and started playing boogie-woogie." Dellaplane laughed brightly.

"Is that true?"

"Well," Dellaplane said, winking, "seems like it should be, doesn't it? Pretty great story. But there are evidently ... lots of stories."

Colin started to say something, but Dellaplane held up his palm.

"My friend, lots of people saw Thomas Jackson playing Mozart." Dellaplane leaned back with a self-pleased look on his face. "But, of course, that was the end of his classical career. Then after his parents died, all talk of music disappeared."

"I know all that," Colin got in, impatient, though he made a mental note to look further into the Mozart story.

"Then you also know he wouldn't have had enough time," Dellaplane said. "He was dead—"

Colin lifted his head. "What's your story on how he died? I've heard conflicting—"

Now a quickening of Dellaplane's attention. "What have you heard?"

"Stroke, heart attack—"

Dellaplane gave a few quiet nods. "Those true bluesmen lived hard lives."

Colin leaned forward, too. "Also heard things more sinister. That he was shot, for instance. Been talk about money problems, gamblers, *loan sharks*—"

Not a motion in Dell's eyes.

"There's even a story that's got the police killing him—"

Dellaplane flicked a finger along the line of his Roman-cut hair, twisted his mouth. "Pretty hard to cover up murder, wouldn't you think?" he said after a long moment.

"His death certificate, which I did see, is ambiguous. Basically, all it says is—"

"Here lies one dead negro. You see," Dellaplane went on, "that's the way it was in those days. You know, let me ask you a question I often ask people: What was the greatest civil rights problem in the early '50s? What do you think?"

Colin half shook his head. "I don't know, segregation?"

"No, my friend. Lynching. Whites hanging blacks from trees. Strange fruit." Dellaplane cleared his throat.

"You see, you're thinking it's like it is now, but it wasn't then. A man like Bearcat, who was a sort of genius—that's not up for historical dispute, is it?"

Colin grudgingly nodded.

"A man like that," Dellaplane went on, as if he had the upper hand now, "he could pass his whole time in the shadows. Only reason we know of him, really, is 'cause you and a few others like you spent time digging up old discs of his. I bet you never even found metal master discs, did you? Cut that CD from the 78 pressings you could find?"

Colin nodded again.

"And if those 78s didn't exist, then Bearcat wouldn't exist, right?"

"People knew him, heard him...."

"Right, right. People *say* that. People saw him play Mozart, too—"

"Maybe there's some truth to that. I don't think the stories come out of—"

Dellaplane interrupted again. "There's no argument he cut some damn fine records. Sonesta Clarke, I mean, wow. But that doesn't mean people aren't working up what they'd like to hear, right?"

Colin nodded again. "But such vivid—"

"You know how it is. The darker the mystery, the brighter the legend. And wouldn't it be great if it were true." Dellaplane let his eyes open wide. "A female Elvis. Working with a black genius producer in a violently racist South. Creating sounds nobody had even heard before. Then dead before his time, just like you said, shady business, loan sharks, *crooked cops*." Dellaplane shook his head gently. "I mean, imagine it."

"I never said 'crooked' cops—"

Dellaplane leaned back, fanned open his palms. "They're shooting Bearcat Jackson, and they ain't crooked?"

Colin heard the first serious hint of a Southern accent.

He pressed: "So you're telling me there's *nothing* to *Pink Cadillac*? Nothing to Daisy Holliday?"

"Listen, if you can't hear it, it doesn't exist, right?" Dellaplane smiled, almost smugly, then leaned forward again. "Remember, I was there. In Memphis, learning my chops, until late '56. That's when I moved to California—before Presley got here, even." A proud smile. "Those were interesting times. Want to interview me on that? Early Ricky Nelson, Eddie Cochran. And record men like Lew Chudd, Art Rupe—now, those guys were characters. I could tell you stories all day about them."

Colin shrugged.

"Well, my friend, I can tell you're hooked on this fantasy song, yes? But without an actual *record*. Without actually having it in your hands, hearing it . . . well, I don't see any reason to go any further, Mr. Stone. I'm sorry."

Dellaplane stood. It was clear he meant the interview to be over.

Colin just leaned back.

"Daisy Holliday turned up in L.A. later, sang around town some, I hear. You never ran across her?"

Dellaplane shook his head, quick.

"Both of you from Memphis, the Elvis Mafia—"

"I told you I never heard of *any* Daisy Holliday. That there—that there were a lot of girls every—"

"I'm looking for her next," Colin said, standing now himself. He could tell he wouldn't get anything more from Dellaplane. "When I see her, I'll give her your regards. O.K.?"

Dellaplane just gave Colin a tight, touchingly annoyed smile.

"You can tell yourself any ol' story you want," the record producer said. "Just make sure you don't tell anybody else, or print it. Not if it's not true." A tight nod of his head. "Understood? O.K.?"

They left it at that, though Colin was just peeved enough to have a hell of a time backing his car around to get down the hillside. Then he turned the wrong way on Sunset Boulevard. Got lost again trying to find his way back to the hotel.

Secrets. Everybody's got their damn secrets.

What was Dellaplane not telling him? And why? Colin knew in his gut that there had been a *Pink Cadillac* record, even if no one could find it now. And he believed thoroughly that Bearcat Jackson had roused himself one last time and made a great record. Why not Dell Dellaplane right there with him? Colin wasn't convinced that he wasn't. Indeed, though he didn't have a good idea why, Colin was more and more sure Dellaplane was simply lying.

Secrets. Secrets and lies. They all had them. As he drove around L.A., fighting the insane stop-and-go traffic, feeling ever more lost, he couldn't help but think of Daisy Holliday and wonder, if she really sang as great as he was sure *Pink Cadillac* was, what *her* secrets might be.

✳ ✳ ✳ ✳ ✳

DAISY TOOK WHAT was left of her $40 and spent seven of it on a week's lodging in a boarding house with the prominent sign posted: GOOD GIRLS ONLY. The house mistress had been peeping out the window when Daisy pulled up, and when she saw the young girl get out from the pink Cadillac and head up her walk, she decided to double the regular rate, but only if the girl could prove to her satisfaction that she was of pure mind and heart. The car was a particular concern. Daisy, interrogated, said she was just looking after it for a friend who was out of town, then offered her a ride in it.

"What kind of friend?" the widow Sanders asked. She'd led Daisy out for a closer look at the car.

"The kind of friend who drives a pink Cadillac." Daisy

stood there with her hands on her hips, cheeks flared, about to turn around and leave.

Mrs. Sanders batted her eyes at the young girl, then brushed her hand along the pink Cadillac's sleek fender.

"Sounds like a good kind of friend to have." She smiled. "Here, come let me show you your room."

After she was settled Daisy took herself out to an aluminum-wrapped diner for the blue plate special: chicken and biscuits. It was the best she'd eaten in memory, and after she finished one plateful of food, she looked out the wide window at her car and felt so fortunate that she ordered another serving.

There was a HELP WANTED sign behind the cash register, and as she paid her bill—and counted the paltry soiled dollars left in her beaded purse—Daisy inquired.

"It's only part-time, waitressing," the hostess said.

"I'm in Memphis here to be a singer," Daisy said.

The hostess, blonde hair up, chuckled. "Since that Presley boy, you ain't the only one. You have any waitressing experience?"

Daisy frowned, then said bright as she could, "I'm good at all kinds of things, I'm sure I could pick it right up. I got that car out there started earlier today, that boy you mentioned, Elvis Presley, he just gave it to me."

The hostess first looked at her like she was crazy, then peeked through the window and saw the pink Cadillac in the parking lot.

"That really yours?" Eyes wide.

"I hardly believe it, but these keys here fit the ignition. It's what got me to your fine establishment."

The hostess remained dubious. "And now you want to work here, as a waitress. With a car like that?"

"The car, like I said, I just got it today. I don't know what it's all about. But I do know I need some work."

The hostess continued to regard Daisy. "Here, let me look at you."

Daisy stood there as straight as she could.

"You're pretty enough, and you got good wide shoulders, help you carry. Come, walk a straight line for me."

Daisy hesitated a moment, and the hostess drew an imaginary line along a row of the black and white tiles in front of the cash register. "Here."

So she walked it: straight, tall, one foot perfect in front of the other.

"You'll do fine," the hostess said. "Listen, come back tomorrow, we'll put you on. And don't worry, we're very accommodating. You get some singing, we can work around that."

Outside Daisy twirled for joy, then swiftly took in a breath, held it. Was it possible getting this car's changed my luck just like that? she wondered, a little anxious.

✳ ✳ ✳ ✳ ✳

THE BEST THING about the diner job, Daisy found, was the free meals that came with it. Even if she wasn't scheduled, she could drop in and the cook would dish her up a plate of whatever they had a lot of. It was the first time in years that she didn't have to worry about going hungry, and it meant everything.

Driving the pink Caddie got her lots of looks, and she took right to them. Indeed, she was feeling, this was how a star would be received. But Daisy wouldn't let it go to her head. She wore her apron proudly, took all the hours at the diner they could give her, and spent her free time driving around Memphis trying to get a feel for the place.

And thinking about the roadhouse. It was now four days since she'd been taken there by Elvis, and few moments went by when she didn't ponder it. What was holding her back? It was hard to put her finger on it. It wasn't that it was a black man's establishment—she'd been around colored people all her life; liked them least as well as white folks—though she knew if she was too brazen about being out there, any kind of racial hell might break loose. And it wasn't the boy, Dell, and his enthusiasm for her. He was cute enough, and sure could play his music. No, there was no good reason at all not to head back out there, see what she could learn, what would happen. It was just that . . . she wasn't ready.

In a way it had taken everything Daisy had to leave home. Actually packing up and heading down the road hadn't been easy, and even now she worried how her father would take it, if he ever sobered up enough to realize she was gone. She remembered selling her dead mother's jewels to the tinker who'd come past, an impulse that still amazed her, and then with the $40 in her hand, plotting long into the night for months, with her father, when he was home, snoring away through the thin wall, how and when she would go. She was waiting for some kind of sign, but what finally spurred her was too terrible to be called that.

The family tragedy had happened five years back, when she was thirteen. Until then her father had been pastor of the Bent Knee Baptist Church, not a large establishment, but under her daddy, one with ambitions. She'd been the minister's daughter, which gave her standing in the town—which she loved. And her mother had been beautiful, if painfully shy. She almost never left the house those last years, but that was fine by Daisy, who adored her. Her favorite thing in the world was to help comb out her mother's long blonde but graying hair in the evening before bed.

But maybe not beautiful enough. Daisy still didn't understand exactly what had happened, but Marcy Lawrence, one of the choir girls, and not that much older than Daisy, had turned up pregnant, and her father, Hyram Lawrence, blamed Daisy's father.

Her father was a tight-compacted man, with sparkling blue eyes, thick brown hair, and a dashing sense of his own importance. He used to say even from the pulpit that it was God's pleasure to further our pleasures. Of course, he was understood to mean *our* joy in fulfilling the usual pieties: forbearance, chastity, speaking truth before the Lord. But it was well known the reverend liked a tipple or two, and it endeared him at least to the men in the parish to see him hoist a corn liquor jug up on his shoulder and trade them lick for lick.

Reverend Holliday denied everything, and pretty soon the town, even as Marcy kept getting bigger and bigger, was split over whom to believe. Sunday sermons, once the high point of the Holliday week, grew tense, like battles. From the reverend's women defenders there was talk of witches, supernatural impregnation. From his accusers, rumors of times they'd been accosted.

Though the town tried to shield Daisy from the furious scandal, she of course intuited the depth of her father's trouble. And in the way her mother was tense and withdrawn, even more than usual, Daisy tacitly understood that her father had done it.

So far Marcy had held her own counsel. There was even a collection taken up to send her away to Lexington to a special home. But when the witch talk grew, the young girl could keep quiet no more. At the height of the scandal she ran to the steps of the church. From her father, a local deputy, she'd swiped a pair of handcuffs, and she locked herself to the church door. She swore she wouldn't leave until Reverend Holliday did right by her.

That ended everything. Daisy's father was swiftly removed from his pulpit. Marcy Lawrence was sent away from town, and Hyram soon left, too. That left Daisy's mother, who was never the same. She held on for two years, during which she must not have said more than half a dozen words to her husband, and then she took sick and died.

Daisy was sixteen. Her father in the last two years had taken up drink seriously, and found work only as a substitute in the mines, and then only rarely. When he lost his church, he'd lost the nice house that went with it and moved the family to a poorer but respectable house a few blocks back; but then he couldn't keep up with payments on that, and they had to move again, to little more than a tarpaper shack.

In town whispers followed Daisy for the longest time. She would attend school perfunctorily, then dash home; but home was horrible, too, and she began to spend each afternoon and early evening simply out wandering. That's how she found Madame Grosgreen, a religious woman and musician in the black section of Bent Knee.

That man Bearcat reminded her a little of Madame; the electric sense that this person was plugged in to rare knowledge, exceptional rhythms. Madame Grosgreen lived in a small, clean shack, grew all her own food, as well as magical weeds and herbs; she dressed in skirts that were layers and layers of musty, worn purple cotton and wore starched white blouses she clasped tight at her neck, her cracked-leather skin rising above.

Madame Grosgreen must have noticed Daisy more than once, because one afternoon she called out to her, asked her if she'd like a glass of lemonade.

"I don't see any lemons around here," Daisy called out to her, rather sourly she later thought.

"Oh, I have ways, child. And I don't bite—not at all. Come, hie your little body over here, take some of your load off. You look like you carrying the weight of the world."

It wasn't till she began to unburden herself to the wizened old woman that Daisy understood just how hard everything was.

Madame Grosgreen understood. There was nothing Daisy could say where she didn't think that the old woman knew most every word she was going to speak before she did. Usually she kept silent, simply nodding. Daisy let it all out.

Up in a corner of her shack the Madame had an old

twelve-fret guitar. One afternoon she began to strum it and sing an old hymn, in a cracked, hoarse voice. She beckoned Daisy to sing along. Daisy, who had only sung in private before, felt shy, but Madame Grosgreen coaxed her along, and their pleasure was perhaps never greater than when they discovered just how good and pure the young girl's voice was.

Daisy began to come out every afternoon after school and all day Saturday. Her father hardly knew she was gone, and Daisy never spoke of how she spent her time. (She did attend church on Sundays; that was her secret from both her father and Madame Grosgreen.)

At Madame's she followed the old woman into the garden, watching her pick and prepare her weeds and potions. She saw things that beggared all white ideas of the true world. Daisy loved it all so much out there that she started to paint her cheeks dark with mud, wanting them to be dark, too, till Madame Grosgreen told her gently that she could only be what she was, and that that was a quite beautiful young lady.

"But they all hate me," Daisy cried one cloudy afternoon.

"They don't hate you. They don't even *know* you. They just hate what they think they see."

"But that's me."

"They's lookin' right through you, girl. Same way us coloreds always get looked right through. But you don't see us goin' to try and make ourselves white?"

"You could."

Madame Grosgreen laughed. "Well, don't really think so. But if we could, say, just like that, we wouldn't none of us do it anyway. We got what we got. What God gave us."

"What'd God give me?" Daisy raised her voice. "What besides all this trouble?"

"Child, God gave you real talents. More than most. Especially the way you can sing. Come, sing Madame Grosgreen a hymn. Let that music out of you!"

That's when the lessons began in earnest. They worked on Daisy's voice, opening it up, getting her vibrato to tickle each note, get it to bloom into true, original feeling. Daisy slid even faster through her school lessons, kept avoiding her increasingly drunk and surly father, living for the time that nobody knew she spent with the old black woman.

At least nobody in town seemed to know. Truth was, in the town's eyes Daisy Holliday was a lost child, condemned by her wanton preacher father, and nobody plumb cared. At least till her father brought more outrage down around them. Then she couldn't have been doing anything worse than consorting with Madame Grosgreen.

Her father had kept his good looks, sagged and dissipated as they now were, and could still dance out his charms, especially between, say, the second and the fifth drink of an evening. And that was when he won the favors of another young girl.

Sissy Chadstone was a classmate of Daisy's, with a reputation among her peers of being fast. A growing-up-too-quick girl. Which was tolerable as long as she contained her interests to high school boys a grade or two ahead of her. But somehow she fell into the clutches of the former Reverend Holliday.

Who knew the reverend's motivation? It could easily have gone beyond lust of the moment to an impulse to re-create his earlier shame in some perverted hope of redressing that humiliation. At least that was a theory the new reverend in town formulated. But most citizens of Bent Knee weren't able even to pause and think anything out at all. All they knew was that Sissy Chadstone was pregnant, and the story was it was Reverend Holliday's child.

No one was willing to give Holliday any benefit of the doubt this time. Sissy was old enough to avoid the law, but that didn't stop anyone from doing everything they could to shame and hurt Daisy and her father. Tongues wagged, stories of hexing arose again, but this time the finger got pointed at Madame Grosgreen. The child had been sneaking off to the nigger camp, associating with a conjure woman. She was bedeviling the child; maybe the child was bedeviling Sissy Chadstone? The father, drunk and humiliated, was in a way untouchable, but the nigra woman? She must've had something to do with this. There's her conjurin' fingers all over it.

Daisy never saw Madame Grosgreen again. What she did see, tears blurring her sight, was the burned-out cabin and devastated garden. At least Madame had been allowed to flee with her life, if little else. Daisy found the metal tuners of her old guitar amid the charred rubble.

Daisy didn't muster up the courage to leave for another month, each night fingering the eight $5 bills, telling herself they'd be enough—that and her singing talent. Then one morning before dawn, without a word to her lower-than-low father, she left Bent Knee, getting her first ride with a trucker on his way to Bowling Green. The trucker eyeballed her up and down but remained a gentleman. And Daisy was off.

And now with a job, a room, and … a pink Cadillac. Daisy still couldn't believe this good luck; had fine reason not to trust anything that smelled like good fortune, yet each day she woke up and the Cadillac was still there—still hers. She had her voice. And—anytime she wanted, she believed—she could have what Bearcat and Dell offered: a musical sanctuary.

But she was still not ready. Daisy had learned from Madame Grosgreen one more great thing: how to listen to the world. How the world will tell you by *feeling* the right time to make a move. Then how you follow your own inner tides.

This wasn't conjuring, it was just *knowing*. And Daisy was confident she would know just this right moment to further her fate, whichever way it might fall.

✳ ✳ ✳ ✳ ✳

"HEY, BOY, OVER HERE." The thing about Bearcat's voice, wherever Dell was in the roadhouse, it hit him like a Marine drill sergeant had just snuck up behind him and bellowed in his ear. Dell, who had been in the skanky bathroom washing his hands, jumped.

"I got a job for you," Bearcat said when he came out. It was mid-afternoon, and the lunch dishes had just been cleared away. That was one of the things Dell had easily come to love about the roadhouse, the way, like one big family, it chowed down together on the long, red-check oil-cloth-covered tables. The food ran to root stews with the occasional trace of rabbit or a pilfered chicken, spooned up over rice, surrounded by a mound of greens swimming in bacon fat, all bordered by pale yellow corn cakes and dressed with a hot sauce that seared the top of his mouth; and it was tasty food, just what Dell's palate cried out for after the cucumber sandwiches and aspics his mother favored—and there was always more than enough. (Indeed, three pigs out back feasted on what wasn't eaten—before they did their own turns of service.)

Dell had come out each afternoon for a couple days, then moved to the mornings, and finally started crashing on a pallet behind the piano. He eagerly sat in with rehearsals, then helped with whatever needed doing: cleaning vegetables and chopping meat or propping up the foundation on the outhouse outside, all the while wishing his father had taught him more practical things in life like … plumbing. Maybe he could make using the indoor bathrooms not such a potentially heart-attacking proposition (one morning, just sitting there, he got geysered nearly up off the seat). He was taking a proprietary interest in the whole roadhouse, no question, though the main reason he was there, of course, was the music: the way he fit tight with Thumper, Sticks, and Clay;

the way Bearcat, though mostly stern, would occasionally let a small smile steal across his lips when Dell had cranked out a roof-rattling riff on his sax.

"Job?" Dell called now. He was drying his hands on his jeans, there being no towel in sight.

"Yeah, I want you to go help Salt with the empties."

Bearcat was standing next to the bar, and behind it was a teetering mountain of wood crates all filled with empty brown-glass Falstaff beer bottles. Dell knew Bearcat's patrons loved their beer. And the empties piled up.

"What do we do?"

"Salt'll tell you. Basically, you hump these forlorn boys into the pickup, take 'em to the distribution, trade 'em in on some full ones. Think you can handle that?"

"Hey, Bearcat, who fixed your outhouse so it didn't collapse on you at the, um, least opportune moment?"

"Hey, hey!" the Bearcat went. He loved the white boy's sass. "Tell you what, this time, Dell, you do the dealing with the men at the redemption. Play that Salt's just your boy. See if you can get us the *white* rate."

"How much you pay now?"

"Salt'll tell you all that. Now you get these empties loaded in the pickup, get going."

It took Dell twenty-five minutes to lug the heavy crates out to the truck; seemed he did most of the work, the bespectacled bartender acting as supervisor.

When they climbed into the truck's cab, Salt took the passenger's seat.

"Don't worry," he said, leaning back and putting his shoes up on the dash. "I'll tell y'all how to get there."

Dell was about to say something, but checked himself. He knew he was the newcomer, and indeed took it as a perverse expression of respect for him that nobody treated him as anything special because he was white.

"When we're close, we'll swap seats," the young bartender went on. "Like anybody'd believe a white boy'd be drivin' a black one."

Dell smiled. "Don't mind," he said.

Salt fixed him with a look. "Good," was all he said.

For the first ten minutes, driving the back roads, neither of them spoke, the only sound the whistle of the warm wind through the truck windows, the clink and rattle of the empty glass bottles in the back.

After a while they passed a crude hand-lettered sign that read BOLLED PEE-NUTS 2 MILE A HEAD.

"You ever tried them?" Salt said. He was still gazing straight ahead through the windshield, feet planted solid against the dash. He had a long, scholarly brow and a finely fluted nose. There was a quiet intensity around Salt that, though Dell had never really had a conversation with this man close to his own age, intrigued him.

"What?"

"Peanuts." Salt looked over. "P-E-A-N-U-T-S."

"I know how to spell it," Dell said. They went past another sign, this one reading in a different shaky hand, BOLRED PENUTS, 1 MILE A HEAD.

"Don't look like the white people do," Salt said.

"You've gone to school?" Dell asked.

"I liked school. Not too sure it was liked that I liked it."

"What do you mean?"

Salt didn't say anything, then, quick, "Slow down, look, turn in here."

Dell spun the truck off the road into a bumpy dirt turnout, then stopped before a long table next to a grimy black cauldron, steam rising from it.

There was a whole family behind the table, all wearing faded and patched overalls, a round, sallow-faced woman in front of a money drawer, a couple kids spatting about, and a burly guy with a wild black beard stirring the cauldron.

"Howdy," the woman called. "You want yourselves some burelds?"

Salt courteously said to Dell, "After you."

In truth, Dell had never had boiled peanuts. It was a low-class thing, and he just hadn't. But he was curious.

"They good?" he said to Salt.

"Oh, yeah!"

"What're they like?"

"Well," Salt said, pushing Dell forward, "you're just going to have to find out."

The black man walked up to the white folks and said, "We'll take us two, no, make that four bags of fresh 'uns."

"Cyrus, four bags for the folks."

The black-bearded man gave the pot one last stir, then netted out a heap of pale-yellow nuts, all dripping a rich brine.

Salt actually licked his lips, Dell saw.

Dell said to the woman, "How much?"

"Be a quarter, total."

He pursed his brow. "How much for each bag?"

"Each bag be a nickel."

"But—" Then Dell saw Salt giving him a look that said, You can try, but it won't do any good. Salt started reaching into his pocket, but Dell said, "No, no, my treat," and dropped a quarter on the worn-wood table.

Back in the truck the cab quickly filled with the scent of salty brine mixed with an earthier smell. Salt held his bag right in front of him, pulled out a burning peanut, blew on it a little, then cracked it open and sucked each nut into his mouth. Dell, after half scalding his hand, tried the same. The nuts were soft and mushy, and the taste took a little getting used to, but by the fifth one he began to like the way each nut released a spiky flush of flavor into his mouth; though he'd have to say that the peanuts themselves were more fibrous and chewy than he would have liked.

"Like 'em?" Salt said.

"A real treat," Dell said.

"See, you're a Southern boy after all."

"You ever doubt it?"

"Oh, we don't see your kind too much out at the road-house. Some of us aren't sure what to make of you."

"Really?"

"But the Bearcat seems taken, so the rest of us just go along."

Dell considered this. He had been so thrilled to be accepted out there that he hadn't noticed any difficulties or hard feelings. He weighed what to say, then decided just to be straightforward.

"Y'all don't want me there?"

Salt took the peanut shell in his hand, gave it a tiny, almost imperceptible squeeze.

"I'd never say that."

"But you're thinking it? You don't see I'm there just for the music? To help?"

Finally, Salt turned to Dell and said, "Let me put it this way. We're getting used to you." He raised his eyebrows.

"Well, I want you to know that it's like a dream being out there. Best thing I ever did. Simple as that."

Salt chewed that around a little then said, "Bearcat always knows what he's doing, don't he?"

"What do you mean?"

"I think he's thinking put us together here, maybe we'd become some kind of friends, you know."

Dell smiled. "And?"

"Hell, maybe we will."

At that both young men laughed.

"How long you been out there?" Dell said a little farther down the road. They were coming into Memphis now, rows of houses lining the road, sidewalks appearing here and there, service stations turning up on corners.

"Oh, since I left, um, my family." Salt looked away from Dell, out the window. "The Bearcat took me in, taught me things, gave me a real home."

Dell looked over at him, suddenly curious. "How come *you* left?"

Salt half turned his head back, then sighed. "Had me one too many fights with my pa." He was biting his lip.

"Really?" A long thought. "How old were you?"

"Reckon I was fifteen. 'Bout four years ago. When I left home, I had to leave school, too. Nobody wanted to take a nigger in full-time."

"But you said you liked school."

"I loved school," Salt said brightly. "Loved books, reading, stories. Loved mathematics, science. Loved it all."

"And nobody'd help you?"

"Bearcat helped me."

Dell gave a soft nod. "How'd you first get out there?"

"When Bearcat took over the roadhouse it was one sorry mess." Salt lifted an eyebrow. "I know to your fancy-schmantzy eyes it's still a mess, but we're talking fallin' down, crumbled, stairs gone, walls gone, porch stove in, just abandoned. That's why the Bearcat was able to buy it for nigger money. Nobody else wanted it. Too far from town. Too ruined."

"So you helped him rebuild it."

"That's it. Put nails in my teeth, hammer in my hand—" Salt quick laughed, then said, "Sorry." He was referring to an episode with Dell and a broken hammer. "Turned out I was pretty good at constructing."

"But you never went back to school."

The young black man reached up and scratched the back of his neck, tightened his cheekbones. "Well, I read every book I can find, and Bearcat, he doesn't feel 'bout learnin' the way my pa did—that is, he don't whup me for wantin' it—but let's say it's not been a high priority."

"Well, there's a lot to learn out at the roadhouse, trust me," Dell said. "I went to East High, got me the best education they give anybody in Memphis, and it all ain't nothin' compared with what I'm picking up each day out here."

"Yeah, well, we each do what we can," Salt said. He adjusted his glasses. "Right?"

"How 'bout some of the other people out there?" Dell asked a couple minutes later. They were in Memphis now, pulled up to a traffic light. He saw the middle-aged white driver of a DeSoto next to him giving him a curious eyeball—figured it was because he was driving, not the black boy. He just looked down from the pickup's cab at the man and shrugged. "Where they all come from?"

"Like who?"

"Well, that guy always wears the bow tie, what's his name, like some kind of snake?"

"Diamondback."

"Yeah."

"Oh, he's an interesting one." Salt leaned over a little conspiratorially. "You keep a secret?"

"Absolutely."

Salt gave him a long eye. "You swear that on your daddy's grave?"

"My father ain't dead."

"You know what I mean."

And like that Dell did. He gave a low chuckle and said, "Yep."

The light changed, and the truck bearing the clinking glass bottles moved ahead about thirty miles an hour.

"They say that boy's wanted some, down in N'awlins. They say he ran himself a *house* down there."

"A house?"

"Yeah, a house. Gambling, women. *A house*." Salt winked brightly at Dell from behind his spectacles.

"What happened?"

"Well, ol' Diamondback, he was run off, seems some of the moral upstanding white people didn't like a nigger cutting into their business."

"Really? Then what's he wanted for?"

"Well," Salt said, "nobody talks any about it, and I don't truly know, but I think there might've been an al-ter-ca-shon somewhere along the way."

Dell held his fire.

"Like one dead moral upstanding white man." Salt couldn't repress a loud guffaw.

"Really?" Dell said again, this time quieter, almost under his breath.

"Could just be a story, though. Lots of stories out at the roadhouse."

"I saw the sheriff there, he's obviously not dragging Diamondback in."

"Sheriff ain't draggin' anybody in! That's why he's the sheriff."

Dell turned this cryptic comment over for a few moments, then said, "What about the guy who dances all the time, what's his name, Hosea?"

"Hosea it be." Dell waited patiently for Salt to start talking. "Well, what I hear 'bout Hosea is, he was the main nigger on a plantation down the river, but they wanted him to be the house nigger, and, well, it just didn't work out."

"What do you mean?"

"Well, Hosea, they wanted him to be a certain way, and he just refused."

"What way?"

"Boy, where you come from, you got any servants?"

Dell thought of Carl, half smiled. "Well, um, yeah."

"And he's in the house, and he does just what he's sposed to?"

"I don't know. I guess so." Dell thought about the whole

world of blackness that Carl had opened up to him, and added, "But he's his own man."

"Well, some boys out there, they don't have it that way. They have to make a choice. Seems Hosea made his choice."

"What did he do?"

"Well, hundred years ago, he'd be property, and he try to leave, who knows, he get caught, maybe he'd get hung— 'cept probably not, 'cause then somebody'd be out some money. Things are different now, though. Now you get uppity, they just hang you, got nothing else to worry about." Salt gave Dell a cool wink.

"Now I don't know the whole story, but let's say Hosea had himself a grand share of pride, and he didn't want to share it with the white folk. Let's say they wanted somebody round who'd bow and step and fetch, and Hosea wasn't doing any of that. Let's say that these white folks, they have only one understanding of the, um, job description, and they have ways to make sure any, um, candidate, fits in. Understand?"

Dell thought on the older man in his worn overalls and dazed expression, coming to life only when music was playing, and then only to dance his weird, dreamy wiggle-wiggle.

"But he doesn't seem to have anything like pride left."

"Then you don't understand!" Salt said with heat and consternation.

"What did they do to him?"

"They *made* him a house nigger."

Dell shook his head. "I don't—"

"Maybe you ask Hosea, he doing his crazy boy dance some day, ask him to do a striptease."

"A—"

"Ask him to show you his *back!*"

"Oh," Dell said. In his memory he heard his mother yelling at Carl, shrieking at him, heard his friend back away and "Yes'm" his mother till sundown; but he was sure nothing had ever gotten worse than that. And mostly everyone loved the black servant—what wasn't there to love? Was it possible....

"You ask why that man don't have his pride," Salt said, still hot. " 'Cause they took it. They just *took* it from him."

"You're saying that—"

"I'm saying, take yourself a *look* sometime, you see a whole novel written on that sorry man's back. Chapter 1 up top, Chapter 15 down by his bottom."

Dell sighed. He could see the picture Salt was limning only too well now. Yes, there were glimpses here of danger and sacrifice and loss he didn't know, and for a few moments his head was spinning.

"The important thing," Salt was saying, "is that Bearcat takes all these people in. Just like he took you in."

"I don't want to be an idiot," Dell said, humble in a weird, stirring way. "I do understand. It's just . . . new to me."

"One thing you have to understand, my friend," Salt said. "All of us have our own versions of that story. It just goes with . . . everything."

Dell nodded as he took this in, though his imagination was such that he couldn't readily fill in the rest of the blanks about the roadhouse.

"So what's Bearcat's story?" he said. "How long's he been out there?"

"Oh, 'bout six, seven years. Bought the place with money he had saved from playing with the Red Dewey Band—you hear about that?"

Dell shook his head.

"Well, story is he was a hotshot guitar player with them years ago, then he found himself a singer—Sonesta Clarke—and together they found themselves the blues." Salt gestured, then said, "Left turn."

Dell stuck out his hand to signal the turn, then frowned. "So it hasn't always been this kind of music?"

"Bearcat, well, there's lots of stories round him. But

what you gotta know is what he done. He moved in here, made it hospitable, then started making records. They recorded *Cryin' Shame*."

Dell was still frowning. "But that was the *last* record he did, right?"

"I'm sure that wasn't the idea. Think he made himself some money with his own produced hit, with his own produced woman, and he thought it was just going to go from there." Salt winced. "Maybe he reached a little too far."

"What happened?"

"Well, this I'm getting from before my time. Even when I was there, I was just the boy up a ladder with a red bandanna round my head."

Dell pulled up at another stoplight. He found he was cruising slowly now, not wanting to get to the beer-distribution place before he heard what Salt had to tell him.

"Well, Bearcat had his eye on this place right when *Cryin' Shame* was starting to break, but he needed more money to lock it up. So he sold the record to a white man up north. Deal put $500 in Bearcat's pocket, and was gonna put some more of every record sold. Bearcat was flying, thinking he'd scalped the white man." Salt smiled wide to himself. "Turns out it wasn't that way."

"That white girl did the song, what was her name?"

"I can't remember. Tina something. Yeah, man had bought the song—"

"The white guy paid $500 for just the song?"

"Well, there was that damn fine print. You know, the kind the white people type in too small for our cotton-picking eyes to see."

Dell held silent.

"Contract evidently said that the man not only owned *Cryin' Shame* but every record the Bearcat produced."

"Bearcat signed that?"

"Wait, slow down," Salt said. "We need one of these

streets along here. It's a right—yeah, wait, yeah, this one. Turn ... here."

After Dell had spun the growling truck around the corner, Salt went on.

"That's what it looked like. Bearcat cut another side on Sonesta, started to sell it the old way, man's lawyer was up on his doorway, took the master lacquer out of his hands, and that Tina Something had herself another hit."

"Shit!" Dell said. "I'd love to see that contract. Bet it'd never hold up."

"Don't know, don't know," Salt said. "Don't know what Bearcat tried to do, but doubt there was much he could. Not so easy to get a lawyer who's any good for the likes of us. 'Sides, all the man's money went into the roadhouse.

"Still, no question it all took some wind out of his sails. Heard him myself swear he'd never record another record, not if it was just going to that man."

Dell thought for a moment, then said, "I'm sure there's a million ways out of a contract like that. I'd like to see it."

Salt drew in a sharp breath. "I wouldn't want to be the one to ask him about it. Whoa, ho, not me!"

"He might get mean, huh?"

"You've seen that already?"

Indeed, Dell had. A sudden tongue lashing snapped out at Slingshot the bouncer or Clay Booker the guitarist, and worse—much worse—intimated with Sonesta Clarke. Dell himself had come under Bearcat's ire when he was fixing the outhouse and had broken the last hammer at the place. The big man had charged at him, teeth bared, crying things like "You white folk just think you can get away with anything. Be careless, toss us aside," until Sticks and Thumper had interposed, cooled him down. Dell had been calling out all along, "Hey, I'll simply get y'all a new hammer," which he did, but what he remembered was the blind, flashing rage combusting just like that in Bearcat's eyes.

"And you're saying he got his temper because of the record deal?"

Salt was silent a moment. They were in a warehouse district of Memphis, not far from the river; low-slung buildings, forklifts, big trucks jutting halfway out into the street that Dell had to edge around.

"Naw, I think it's more the way he is. Like, you know, you got yourself some trouble growing up, got yourself a mean pop or in his case, step-pop, you can go either way. Turn out mean as a riled skunk, or maybe you don't want yourself any trouble nohow." Quick look at Dell, who held Salt's gaze. "Know what I mean?"

Dell took a moment to nod, but did.

"No question the way the Bearcat went," Salt said, nodding too. "But what did change after *Cryin' Shame*, I saw it, was he got like everything had to be just *his* way. Like if he didn't have every finger jammed into every pie, something'd get away from him. Made some of us a little crazy, I can tell you. Made Sonesta, well, made her find Jesus, you ask my opinion."

"What's going on with her?" Dell asked. "Her and Bearcat?"

Salt was silent a moment, then threw up his hands. "It's been one dark place, down there at the end of the upstairs hall. I don't think nobody see into *that* room." Slight wince. "Don't know if you'd ever want to."

"I don't know," Dell started to say, meaning that at least once each day he was almost stricken with the deepest curiosity of what was going on between Bearcat and Sonesta. He knew, even if Salt didn't seem to, that she had her own room down the hall from Bearcat; what he wasn't sure was how long that had been going on, and how close she and the big man had been. "They're not married, right?"

"Nobody really knows." Salt gave his head half a shake. "Ain't like they's *not* married, know what I mean?" Dell nodded. "I mean, they sure spit and spat like they's married." A quick guffaw from Salt.

"Amen to that," Dell said, thinking of his own parents, though in truth with them it was more a quiet stalemate.

"No, must of us out there, we just let whatever's going on 'tween the king and the queen, well, we let it be."

"Probably smart," Dell said. Then, mostly under his breath, added, "I've seen it look sort of ugly."

"Excuse me?"

"Oh, nothing." Dell looked over. "You think she'll be singing again?"

This was much safer ground, and Salt brightened. "She doesn't, don't know what y'all gonna do." Salt tipped his glasses forward. "Take it a little slower here, place is coming up soon." He rubbed his eyes as Dell crept along. "I mean, y'all sound pretty enough, and you play the sax-o-phone damn nice—"

"Thanks—"

"Yeah, but somebody's gotta sing, know what I mean?"

Dell nodded. He was thinking the same thing, teased by a notion not quite given form, a thought like a bright light out there before him. He was looking out the windshield careful-ly, as if he could see it. What he did see, down at the end of the block they were on, was a large sign that read MCCRUDY'S BEVERAGE DISTRIBUTION.

"Yeah, that's it. That's the place," Salt said. "Here, like Bearcat said, better let me take over the driving, let you look like the master."

Dell was distracted. "You think?"

Salt was nodding his black scholar's head. "I'm also thinking we don't want to make too much, if anything, 'bout us coming from the roadhouse, know what I mean? Like we just got us some empty Falstaffs we gotta change us into fulls, that's all."

"Like I'm not out there with y'all," Dell said, nodding.

He pulled the car over, and he and Salt swapped places.

"Yeah," Salt said as he shifted the truck into gear, "like that's all the story *anybody'd* better hear."

* * * * *

IT WAS SATURDAY NIGHT, a few days later on, about eight, and upstairs in the roadhouse there were three women in a tiny, almost bare room. The room had a monastic simplicity; it was filled only with a single mattress sagging something fierce on an old metal frame, a small wooden vanity table with a slat-back chair, a pine wardrobe in a corner with a smoky eight-by-ten-inch mirror hung on the right-side door, and a lurid blue-and-black picture of a storm-circled Jesus on the cross above the bed. This has been Sonesta's room now for the past six months, and wasn't that a struggle? The Bearcat had taken it personal that she'd taken this room, and things between them had been worse than ever.

" 'Be sober, be vigilant,' " quoted Lil, sitting on the weak mattress. " 'Because your adversary the devil, as a roaring lion, walketh about, seeking whom he may devour.' "

"Amen," cried her sister Lurleen, right next to her.

Sonesta looked on from the wooden chair. She was dressed in a plain black dress, though her two friends had shown up for this Saturday-night prayer session both wearing sateen dresses hemmed barely below the knees, with wide shoulders and frothy frills running up the front. Lil's dress was robin's-egg blue, Lurleen's a smoky purple, and Lil wore a yellow scarf around her neck, while Lurleen's was lilac. But the dresses were flashy enough to make Sonesta dubious that they'd combed their closets for the apparel most suitable for a prayer session with the Lord or, their fallback excuse: "Honey, we just reached in, and this is what come out."

" 'He is despised and rejected of men; a man of sorrows, and acquainted with grief: And we hid as it were our faces from

Him,'" Lil went on, her eyes burning with intensity as she read from the black pebbled-leather-covered book. "'Surely He hath borne our griefs, and carried our sorrows—'" till she stopped at the loud noise. A rough and tumble bass-drum rhythm filled the room, actually shaking the weak walls.

"Go on," Lurleen said. "Pay that no mind."

Lil looked to Sonesta, who after a second, nodded Yes, please continue.

"'The Son of Man goeth as it is written of him: But woe unto that man by whom the Son of Man is betrayed! It had been good for that man if he had not been born.'" Lil had to raise her voice now to be heard clearly over the noise coming through the floor. Besides the drums, Thumper Johnson was dropping a shuffly bass figure into the beat.

Sonesta sighed, concentrated on the scripture. But her mind kept drifting to the music downstairs. She felt her foot start to tap, forced it still. She looked at her sisters. They were sitting ramrod straight, not a trace of the rhythm moving in them. Well, good for them—maybe they were true believers after all.

Sonesta heard herself sigh. She was no longer at all sure how well the full-time Jesus life was working. She'd always been a religious woman; always, when all was said and done, had sung for the Lord—sung in His joy, and to celebrate the boldness and reach of His splendor. Even if sometimes that meant taking life a little on the wild side—meant being anything but churchy and devout.

But all that had changed seven months ago when she first started talking to Reverend Haley Brown at the First Baptist. She had stopped in one Wednesday afternoon when she was in town shopping, hesitant at first, not at all sure exactly why she was even there. Though she'd been raised strict in the church by her parents, all during her music career with Bearcat she wasn't much more than a holiday church-goer at best. But the worries had been with her hard lately,

and the tension with the Bearcat ... simple, it was like a rattling pressure cooker back at the roadhouse, business falling
off, the music not giving her the old thrills, and their private
life.... Well, she was quietly astonished how easy it was to
talk to the handsome Reverend Brown after he'd invited her
into his study, told his secretary not to disturb him, told
Sonesta that he'd seen her perform around town more than
once (glancing upward and saying, "But we won't speak of
that too loudly"), then taking her hand and whispering, "Now
what are your troubles, child?"

She found she could tell the reverend almost everything,
that Bearcat, the man who had discovered her, trained her voice,
brought out every drop of emotion she had ... the man whom
she'd given all her love to ... that man would no longer, well, no
longer seemed to see her as a, well, as ... a ... woman—

"I understand," the reverend said, holding up a hand to
halt her. He gazed deep at her with his hooded brown eyes.

"I ... feel ... so, so ... worthless," Sonesta confessed.

Reverend Brown took her hand again; she flinched at
first, then relaxed in his warm, comforting grip.

"Jesus loves you, my child."

"I know, I know, but—"

"I know you doubt His love is all you need, and I understand that. But what I'm going to tell you is that Jesus *always*
loves you. He loves you unconditionally. He loves you on
your best day and on your worst day. You don't have to win
His love, you don't have to hold His love. His love is always
there."

"But—"

"But that's our comfort. You have to believe that."
Sonesta for a second felt she was actually floating in the reverend's smoky gaze. "It's our faith."

"I'll try—try to believe."

"Oh, you already believe, my child. What you have to
do is *accept* that faith, allow yourself to float within it."

The reverend kept stroking her worn hand, his thumb gentling the soft spots between her fingers, and he held her gaze; and just like that, there it was: She was already floating. A warm bath of the reverend's love and concern. She left him that day feeling new strength, new determination.

That night she began to pray in earnest.

Not that anything changed with the Bearcat, or even changed for her right away. It took her a month until she moved herself into the unused room, brought in the broken-down single bed. And to her dismay things only got tenser with Bearcat. She didn't really understand what was going on with him at all. He still seemed mostly his strong, cheerfully bellowing self, blustering about, running things at the road-house, but with Sonesta in particular (though with the hangers-on, too, she noticed) he could erupt into snapping anger and ripping fists at almost no provocation. It was like he was a tough-as-nuts matchhead dragging slowly along a rough surface; you'd never know at which moment he'd erupt into flame. Sonesta had come to circle him carefully, trying just to get through each day, her new faith and feeling intact.

No one had actually told her she couldn't sing with Bearcat and give her love to Jesus at the same time. It just began to feel so contradictory. She was feeling a small kernel of true peace inside her, and that peace, she believed, had nothing to do with raising her voice and shaking the rafters. What she did have was day-in, day-out consistency—yes, that was the word, *consistency*—the faith that each day would run smooth before her. And yet, and yet—something was missing. Prayer spoke deeply to her, but there was still something wild and unconstrained that needed voice. Another kernel of possibility that at its purest demanded unbridled, delirious *joy*.

Thump, thump, thumpety, thump boomed up from downstairs. Sonesta could hear the chatter of voices now, the roadhouse filling up, though she forced her thoughts back to what Lil, no, actually it was Lurleen now—what Lurleen was reading from the Good Book. " 'For we wrestle not against flesh and blood,' " Lurleen went on, " 'but against principalities, against powers, against the rules of the darkness of this world, against spiritual wickedness in high places.' "

But her words were virtually drowned out by a louder voice, coming orotund and spiky through the floorboards.

"Ladies and gentleman, welcome, welcome y'all to another Saturday night out here in the devil's playground— heh, heh!" It was Bearcat, amplified through the booming lead mike. The stage was almost directly underneath Sonesta's room. "We's gonna get going shortly, so y'all step up to the bar and get yourself a little cheer. It's Saturday night. Want y'all feelin' *good*!"

Lurleen tried to keep reading but couldn't overcome the Bearcat. When he stopped speaking, in the silence that followed, she didn't immediately start up again. Instead she looked to Sonesta, who after a moment's hesitation gave her a nod.

" 'Though we walk through the Valley of Evil—' " she went on.

"O.K., O.K., now y'all settled good," the voice echoed up from below, "got yourself some of that joy juice, what y'all want now?"

A muffled mangle of voices.

"I can't hear you," he called. "What you want?"

"Roar, Bearcat!" It was clear that's what everyone in the crowded room was now crying. The voices filtered upstairs, loud but not yet huge.

"You mean, like this? Grrrrr-rooooaaar."

"Roar, Bearcat, roar!" Downstairs the women were dressed in satin pinks and silk blues; the men in suits from Lansky's on Beale Street, shiny on the knees.

"I'm still not hearin' you. What you want?"

"Roar, Bearcat, roooaaaaar!"

The big man with the shiny head and the short black

hair and the flashing gold tooth leaned into the silver microphone and gave the joyful crowd just what it wanted. "Grrr-raa-rrroooo-roooorrrrrrrr!"

"That's it, Mr. Cat, *rooooaarrrrr*!"

"You mean, that wasn't enough for you?" Bearcat said. "What do you want from me? You want this?"

Dell had given the big man back his leather mojo bag, and it hung from Bearcat's belt. He reached down, gave it a rub, then contorted his face like it was being pressed by a heavenly vise, and squeezed out a yowl that rose black and toothy over the now-vamping band and seemed to burst over the crowd like a thundercloud.

"Grrr-rroooo-raa-roooorrrrrrrrrrrrrrrrrrrrrrrrrrrr!" He wiped his forehead with a red-cotton handkerchief, then gave a huge self-pleased smile. The band softened even more, and slowed till the twelve-bar blues progression took on ballad overtones.

Upstairs all was silence. It was almost impossible to think from the noise coming from downstairs. Sonesta told herself that this was a stupid idea to have a prayer session here on a Saturday night. But her two sisters had insisted. Lurleen set the Bible down closed on her lap, and she and Lil seemed to be listening hard to what was going on below them.

"You got me plumb all wore out," Bearcat said into the mike. "Only so much cat left in the old bear, heh, heh. But we got us a great band tonight, and we gonna make you dance!"

"Roar, Bearcat, rooaarrrrr."

"All right, all right. But it ain't me you really want up here. You want this fine band, and you want some *singin'*."

"That's it!" a voice came from the crowd.

"Yes, yes, that is it. What say we try to get Miss Sonesta Clarke up here. Last time I checked, she was somewhere in the building. You want to hear Sonesta?"

"She's my righteous mama!"

"Let that good lady rip!"

Upstairs, the three women heard this clear as could be but gave it only stony silence. Sonesta glanced at Lurleen, beckoned for her to pass along the Bible.

"O.K., how we gonna do it?" Bearcat hooded his eyes, gazed into the makeshift stage lights. "How we gonna get us our singer up here?"

"Roar for her, Bearcat, *rooaaarrrrr*!"

The Bearcat fixed his audience with a sharp gaze, then said, "You think that's the way to get her? You gonna *roarrr* for Sonesta?"

"Yeah, roar, *rooaaarrrrr*!"

"But I done tried that. What else I got to do?"

"You know how to do it," someone screamed. "Let it *alllllllll* out."

"Hey, baby, I always let it all out. I'm the Bearcat. But what you say? You want me to call her like this?" Bearcat pulled out his harmonica and drew out bent notes yawping deep.

The harp notes curled and spun and rose seductive as incense through the floorboards.

Sonesta set her hands on her knees, a jumble of contradictory feelings.

"That gonna get her? Miss Sonesta, we's callin' to you. We need you to *sing*."

"This is gettin' in the way of our studying," Lil said, her hands planted defiantly on her wide hips.

"You think we can get them to go quiet some if we go down there and ask them?" Lurleen added.

Sonesta gave her two sisters a long look.

"Mama, come on down!"

"I don't see what else we can do," Lurleen insisted. She stood up, a sudden rise of her purple skirt that sent air flowing every which way in the claustral room. "I'm goin' down there and give 'em a piece of—"

"Me, too," Lil said, standing also.

"You want me to go down there?" Sonesta sighed. "You, too?"

"Mama, what else we gonna do?"

"We could just leave," Sonesta said.

Lil glanced at Lurleen, and Lurleen glanced back. "We could do that, but we still gotta take ourselves downstairs."

"Don't seem to be workin'," they heard Bearcat cry. "Maybe we should just go up and get her!"

"Sonesta, hear that, *they's gonna come up here*!" Alarm in Lil's voice.

Sonesta sat stolid and unrevealing. Her breathing was determinedly slow. But inside she felt her resolve weakening. What was she holding out for? What was wrong with her goin' out there and singing? Hadn't she always reached the Lord that way?

"Sonesta?" This was Lurleen, saying, in effect, Hurry! What're we gonna do?

"All right." She stood up, too, and both her sisters radiated pleasure.

"But you ain't gonna sing, are you? They's playing that jungle music."

Sonesta had run out of patience with the two women. And the desire—it was too strong. It was the call of the music, the call of the bright lights, the call of that wonderful rhythm.

The three ladies barely got themselves through the door to the hall, then almost pushed each other over charging down the stairs.

Sonesta slowed, gathered her dignity at the foot of the stairs.

"There she is!" Bearcat called from the stage. "Hey, hey, hey."

"Sonesta, come on, we neeeeeeeeeed you!"

There was laughing and jollying through the crowd, like this was the true high point of their week.

"Roar, Sonesta, *Roooaaaarrrrrrrr*."

The band kept vamping, no tune distinguishable, just twelve-bar chords around and around, but building.

Sonesta walked steady, regally through the parting crowd.

"Oh, girl, what's Reverend Brown gonna *say*?" Lil suddenly cried out, but this was only one last, vain call.

"Oh, Sonesta, we looooovvvvvvvvvve you!"

That's all it took. There she was, up in the one blue spotlight, in front of the silver microphone, and like butter the band smoothed into one of her signature tunes, *Hot-Blooded Mama*. The beat kicked in with a stop-time stutter-step, and Sonesta raised her thick arms and held them in front of her, till Sticks the drummer dropped into a saucy syncopated figure, and she flounced, hip heavy, into a raunchy pose, hip flung out, her right arm crooked there. It felt so good. Before her appeared a swirling sea of smoky colors, women in dresses of burgundy and midnight-blue, men in lime-green and mauve shirts with string ties, patent leather shoes flashing sparks over the floor, everyone's hair done just so, everyone's eyes straining up at her, ready, eager.

Words started coming out of her: *"You figured I was shy / You thought my blood ran cold / But what you saw was just a lie/ You know, my blood runs bold,"* and now she was moving over the stage, strutting past Bearcat, throwing out one leg, then the other, hands back on her hips, then finger-waggling the chorus down to loud cries of "Aah-oooh" and "Ooooh-aaaaaah":

> *I'm a hot-blooded mama, why don't you sit me down to*
> > *supper*
> *Yeah, a hot-blooded mama, melt your men like butter*
> *Ain't their sister—ain't their brother*
> *And you knooooow I ain't their mother*
> *I'm just a hot-blooded mama, and I boil men like water*

She was stepping and thrusting herself into the final verse when she saw a commotion at the door, shouts and alarums that turned heads in front of her. It was hard to see into the spotlight, but by hooding her eyes Sonesta could see that Slingshot the bouncer was having problems with someone, from the looks of it a brightly dressed woman with a black scarf over her head. Slingshot was waving his hands, but also backing up, not touching her. That seemed odd: Sling got his name because he loved to take anyone giving trouble and pitch them out into the dust of the parking lot. Hosea even liked to place bottle caps out there to commemorate some of the Shot's better tosses.

But this time Slingshot wasn't touching anybody.

Sonesta could hear him: "I don't think you's welcome here. Now listen to me. *You's not welcome.*"

And the woman: "I want to talk to Bearcat. Bearcat *knows* me."

Slingshot: "Even if the Man knows you, you's not welcome here, not tonight." He reached toward her, but it was like there was an invisible barrier, his hands just freezing in front of his chest, locked there, palms out. And then, something Sonesta had never before heard, Slingshot actually getting polite. "Pleeeeaaase?"

Bearcat waved the band softer. Sonesta hung there with the mike in her hand, wondering what this was all about—getting, truth told, a little peeved—when Bearcat left the bandstand and went over to the disruption, saying, "Slingshot, what's the—"

At that moment the woman pulled back her black scarf and everyone in the roadhouse drew in a loud, astonished gasp. Her hair was as light and pale yellow as the sun. Everyone but the Bearcat seemed to jump back.

As far as Sonesta knew, there'd never been a white woman at the roadhouse, least not on a Saturday night, or ever, 'less you count that girlie Elvis—

And that's who it was, of course: Daisy Some-thingorother. Now what was she doing here? She looked a lit-tle cleaned up from the other day—she was wearing a plain yellow dress, hemmed below her knees, but with a low-cut neckline trimmed in white lace—but basically she was the same white trash that had come in looking all little lost girl and gone home with that pink Cadillac.

"Bearcat," the girl said. She looked nervous, shaking like a leaf. "You remember me—I'm Daisy. Daisy Holliday."

"You Elvis's friend. Driving that big, beautiful car?"

She nodded. "I still can't quite—"

"But what're you doin' here?"

Dell Dellaplane, the only other white person in the room, had followed Bearcat down from the platform stage. "I told her to come back."

"Yeah, and I—well, I don't really know anyone much in Memphis. I hope—" looking around at the crush of black faces, all gazing at her "—hope it's all O.K."

Bearcat raised his arm, reached out, and swept the slen-der young girl under it. " 'Course it is, sugar. We're glad to see you. Make yourself at home."

A still nervous, sheepish smile from Daisy, yet a hopeful one, too.

"Here," Dell went, pulling out a chair from a table already mostly full of patrons. "All right if she sits here?"

"Sure 'nuff," a big guy with hunched shoulders said. "We'll keep an eye on her."

Bearcat turned back to the band, which had stopped, and gave them a downbeat. They choogled through a whole verse before anyone realized Sonesta was no longer singing.

"Hey, woman, you missed your cue," Bearcat said.

"Yeah, and you missed a lot more than that."

"What you mean?"

"I mean, it's bad 'nuff I'm up here singing. But I'm not gonna be a party to your troublemaking."

"What troublemaking?"

"Don't you got eyes?"

Bearcat fixed Sonesta with a righteous glare. He moved next to her and spoke in a hissing whisper. "Eyes for what? For you giving me lip in front of my patrons?"

"We don't need no white people here. Bad 'nuff we got the sax player, but a white girl, don't you know what that's gonna do?"

"Whose establishment is this?" Bearcat said, then bit his lower lip, hard, like he was holding himself back from something.

"You not careful, it ain't gonna be yours."

Bearcat looked so angry he couldn't speak. He was holding one fist in the other. There was a palpable tension all through the room. Daisy was looking from side to side and fidgeting.

The band kept vamping. Bearcat looked up and gave the audience a big, forced smile. "O.K., let's get the show going."

"No," Sonesta said. "I ain't singing with her out there."

Bearcat looked as if he couldn't believe this.

"First, you ain't gonna sing 'cause you got the Lord ... well, when it suits you. And now you ain't gonna sing 'cause of her? Are you crazy?"

"I ain't gonna take this."

"Sing, woman!" Bearcat's voice rose to a bellow, a roar. Sonesta flinched.

"Godammit, woman, sing!"

And with that Sonesta stormed off the stage.

Bearcat started after her, but Dell reached out from behind and grasped his shoulder. The big man whirled on the young sax player.

"And what do *you* want us to do?" Bearcat said, strained yet quiet.

"Let her sing."

"Who?"

"Daisy."

Bearcat's brow sagged. He looked perplexed.

"Remember her voice?"

"Oh, I don't know," Bearcat said, soft to Dell. "Maybe Sonesta's right—I don't know if she should even be here."

"But you got a club full of people. You just gonna—"

"Has she ever sung with us before? How you think she's gonna—"

But Dell was determined. He reached past Bearcat and beckoned to Daisy.

She didn't seem to see him. Her gaze was on the back of the roadhouse, where Sonesta and her two sisters were climbing the stairs back to her room. At this moment Daisy looked extremely nervous.

The crowd began to stamp their feet and call out, "Hey, come on, it's Saturday night!"

And now Bearcat started moving.

"C'mon, Missy, we heard you sing," he said, down at her table now. "C'mon up here and see what you can do."

Daisy eyes were crossed. "I only came out here to—" she started to say, but then it was clear that all eyes in the house were on her.

"C'mon and sing, little girl," Bearcat said in his most soothing voice. "We neeeed you."

"But what about that woman ... she was so *good*."

"What can I say," Bearcat said, a little wistful. "Sonesta Clarke's got her own ways now. Don't always know what I can do about 'em."

"But nobody wants to hear me get up and sing that church song."

"Don't worry 'bout that, just follow me now. We'll start you slow, and then drop you down."

"But I don't know enough—"

Dell stepped forward then, letting his sax swing to his side, and took Daisy's hand. She flinched at first and gave him an ambiguous look, but when he pulled her arm, she followed him toward the stage. Dell gave Bearcat a big nod.

You could hear the crowd swallow its breath as Daisy took the stage.

"We're all gonna have us a little experiment here tonight," Bearcat said, back at the mike, in his most commanding voice. "Gonna do us a new, new thang." He gestured toward Daisy, who was standing there, her knees pinched close together, her arms knit tight to her chest, looking like a little schoolgirl about to shoot up her hand for a bathroom pass. "Goin' to try us a new singer."

Sticks hit a rim shot.

"Yeah, yeah, give us 'nother one of dem."

Crack!—Sticks hit the snare's circumference again.

"Well, hey, hey!" Bearcat was pushing it now. "I'm not sure exactly what to say, but let's give the little lady here a big, encouragin' round of applause."

The whole crowd, every milky white eye in every black face, was focused on Daisy, and not a soul clapped their hands. All that rose up to the stage were nervous titters, the rustle of neighbors elbowing neighbors, and then a low-level thrush of rampant whispers.

"Hi, y'all," Daisy said, her face brightening into the blue spotlight. She was forcing a big tight smile, white teeth gleaming, but so constricted and fragile, one quick move and her jaw might break.

Sticks rumbled a low six-to-the-eight shuffle, and Thumper shoved up bass notes against him.

"Now you all, you listen up here," Bearcat said, stepping in front of Daisy and facing the still stunned audience. "I know what you're thinking. But the Bearcat wants to try something new—he *gotta* try something new."

Attention now.

"I know, I know, y'all thinkin', Has the Bearcat lost his *mind*? What's he doin' bringin' a—" and though he couldn't bring himself to say it, everyone saw his lips move over the two words *white girl* "—into this place. But the Bearcat's telling you, wait till you hear this voice! This is a voice that shook the heavens here just one week ago."

Palpable curiosity now, people leaning forward, looking at Daisy, waiting for something, ears up.

"Now I know you ain't sung much in front of people," Bearcat went on, soothingly to Daisy now, "but you said you been doin' it in church, and this ain't nothin' but the other side of church." A big smile, then an angry bark up the stairs. "Right woman?" Then back to Daisy: "You ain't gonna have no trouble goin' cross that line, are you?"

Daisy looked like she didn't hear Bearcat's question. She'd begun to sway back and forth to the drum-bass rhythm, eyes half closed, a dreamy expression floating onto her face. Her blonde ponytail brushed her shoulders. She nervously kept flouncing down her wide skirt, but all in all, you'd have to say she was looking more at home.

"Well," Bearcat said, "you ready?"

Daisy's eyes popped open, startled. She leaned up to Bearcat, put a hand on his shoulder, and whispered in his ear: "Oh, I was just thinkin' 'bout being home, 'membering when I used to dream of getting up in front of an audience." A slender smile. "Used to dream that dream a lot, Mr. Jackson." A blush. "Feels like I'm *still* dreamin' it."

A big Bearcat laugh. "Well, it's 'bout to get real—*really real*." He glanced behind him. "Boys?"

Sticks and Thumper picked up the beat. Clay scratched some guitar chords. Dell, who'd been sort of shadowing Daisy as if she might suddenly faint, let the music go without him. He leaned forward though, whispered, "Go get 'em."

"O.K., O.K., looks like here she comes. Miss Daisy." A pause. "Miss Daisy—"

"Holliday." Daisy said, shrugging.

"That's it, like we're on a *sea cruise*." Bearcat was all confidence now, all certainty that he was doing the right thing. "Come on, now, get those bugs out of your eyes. Put those hands together, make this little doll feel *welcome*. You can do it." Bearcat turned to Daisy and began to rhythmically clap his huge hands. "Come on, let's it hear it for Miss Lazy Daisy—We All Gonna Be Goin' on a—Holliday!"

And now Daisy stepped to the microphone. Leaned in too close, took in a breath, and as she let it out, the thing shrieked feedback.

She jumped back. Dell put a hand gently on her shoulder. Without thinking, she reached up and patted it.

Diamondback, in his stud tie and flared pants, jumped up to the stage and adjusted the mike. Blew into it. Feedback gone.

"This is all new for me like it is for you," Daisy, back before the mike, said softly, tentatively. She still looked startled by the way her amplified voice echoed around the large room. "And I know I got some huge shoes to fill. But—" same longing look toward the stairway "—I'm gonna give it a try."

"And y'all gonna let her," Bearcat chimed in.

"Now, let's get this thing *movin'*."

The band suddenly doubled the tempo, and Dell leaned forward and blew a mighty sax intro. The tune was recognizably the one she'd sung with Elvis, *How Long the Road to Jesus*, but fast now, pumped—all Saturday night.

Yet when Daisy started to sing, it was all wrong. The tone was there, round and luscious, but her voice just hung there like a ripe peach—she couldn't find the beat. Sticks and Thumper heard her and made a quick adjustment, and though the rest of the band fell into the new rhythm, Daisy had just then sped up and raced past them. Then her voice went shrill.

The band stopped first, then scattered groans rose from the crowd.

"I'm sorry y'all," Daisy said.

Bearcat gave her a sudden disapproving look, his eyebrows hanging heavy.

"I think maybe this isn't, well—" she went on, taking a step back from the mike and glancing up with a forlorn look of dismay.

Dell was by her side. "Listen, I know you can do it," he whispered into her ear. "You've got magic in you—I heard it, it's there. All you got to do, Sugar, is just relax and let it out."

Daisy's eyes roamed the packed roadhouse, all those eyes back on her. "But—"

"Bearcat," Dell said, a quick sideways whisper, "give me the bag."

The big man nodded right away, then reached down, undid the fetid leather mojo sack, and held it out to Dell.

"Here," Dell said. "Put this round your neck. I know, I know—smells like a dead possum. But it's gonna relax you, bring what's true out of you."

Daisy looked down at the skanky sack with utter cool dispassion. Finally she said, "Are you sure—"

"You don't know what magic it's got. Trust it. And don't worry, I'll be here, right behind you. Trust me, too—"

"Oh, I know 'bout that sack more than I know 'bout—"

Dell laughed. "Well, look out there. Think you got any choice? There's a hungry school of fish looking at you like you were a tasty worm. Got me?"

Daisy, still with shiny-as-chrome eyes, turned to face the room again. She was pinching her knees together, looking wobbly. Bearcat's half-skinned mojo bag hung around her neck, contrasting with her clean, almost prim yellow dress. At Madame Grosgreen's she'd come in contact with much worse than this, but she was wearing the fanciest dress she owned and dreaded the way the greasy bag was going to smear animal juice all over it. Then Dell fingered a downbeat to Sticks, who started in with brushes on the snare, nothing else, and there was no time to worry. It was an easy, sinuous rhythm, and Dell, still holding Daisy's shoulders, got her swaying to the easy beat.

"Now breathe," he said. "Fill your lungs, let the air ride in and out on the beat, yeah, that's it, it's nothing, it's just lettin' go to it."

She sort of wobbled but then it was as if the music was a gentle wind and her sails were out—she floated.

"Good, that's it, now just like that, and you let the words out, don't think 'bout nothin', it's like you're back home ... and you're just having fun."

Daisy's eyes were tight shut, and it looked like easeful pictures were playing behind her eyes. Dell flicked his head toward Thumper, and he married his bass again to Sticks.

It was that kind of bright-breeze, flower-petal-floating beat that made any ol' body sway like the slenderest of stalks. From up on the bandstand the whole audience was flowing left, then right—and that didn't hurt at all.

When Daisy started singing, she was on top of the rhythm like petals and leaves. Her tone was crystal-bell clear, the words dropping just right.

She started off the first chorus singing *"How long the road to Jesus,"* but it just didn't work, and the next time she sang it—and through the rest of the song—she was without thinking changing the words, and the chorus rang out, *"How long the road to love."*

At that Dell stepped back, a smile on his face. He went low with his sax, under the melody, blowing low, growling notes that just seemed to push Daisy along.

The amazing thing was, you were in that audience and closed your eyes—and almost everyone had their eyes closed by now—you were dead sure that it was a negro lady up there singing. There was that husk and depth, and that pain and all-powerful release, and you were thinking, It's like Bessie, but newer; like Ruth Brown, but saltier; like a young'un you'd heard recently, Etta James, yeah, just an awful lot like her.

But that wasn't just it, because there was a sweet country fizz on top of everything, sunny day, hay wagon—this picture you got was this black, black woman with this white, white hair ... and a big polka-dot kerchief tied round it to boot. This was your inner eyes playing tricks on you, and so you opened 'em, and this is what you saw: A blonde-ponytail-swaying, slim, plain-cotton-clothes-wearing, rosy-cheeked, obsidian-souled girl, couldn't have been over 20, with a voice that sounded like passed-down ebony, singing so powerful it was like she was pulling it all up from a bottomless well.

Bearcat clapped his hands and doubled the beat, the drums seeming to jump ahead, and the rest of the band careering along, and Daisy went right with it. *"How long,"* she shouted. *"How long ... the road to love?"*

Bearcat kept speeding up the song, and everyone hung on with it; and when finally, five minutes later, Sticks went *doot-doot-doot-doot* and crashed down on his cymbals, the whole crowd broke into hoots of excitement and jubilation.

Daisy glowed lantern bright as the applause rose up to her.

"Well, now, you see," Bearcat went, his face as luminous as the moon. "Looks like we got ourselves a new singer."

Dell tooted his sax in jubilation. He was bent over backward, blowing to raise the roof off the joint, when a loud knock came at the roadhouse door—heavy, metal on the wood.

Bearcat looked over, beckoned to Slingshot, who was about to pull the door open when it swung back.

In a flash Bearcat beckoned to Dell to grab the still glowing Daisy and get them both out the roadhouse's back door. Dell, catching a glimpse of a gray peaked hat, wasted no time.

"Come on, sugar, we gotta *mooove*."

"But I'm—"

"Come on, girl, *go!*"

They were barely out the back when the sheriff appeared.

"Hey!" he called after Dell, whose arm was still visible in the room. But Dell scampered out.

"What's going on, Sheriff?" Bearcat said, moving over to meet the lawman.

"I thought I warned you 'bout mixing it up in here."

"I don't know what you're talking about. We're just doing what we always do come Saturday night. Little fun for the local folks."

"You can't pull no wool over my eyes," the sheriff said, drawing himself up. "I saw that Dellaplane here earlier ... now wasn't that him just going out the door?"

"Well, Sheriff, that boy's a musician. We don't think here musicians are either black or white or green."

The sheriff just nodded.

"You got stamps on all those liquor bottles, Jackson?"

"Sheriff, I took care of you *last week*. What you doin'?"

"All right, party's over." The sheriff swept up his arms. Everyone was suddenly sheepish; they knew this was a fight they couldn't begin to win. "Come on, everyone out of here. Party's over for tonight."

"Now Sheriff—" Bearcat cried.

"Listen, Jackson. Didn't I warn you?"

"Sheriff, you never done nothin' in your life 'cept warn me 'bout something. And with your hand out, I might add."

"Shhhhh." The sheriff mockingly brought a finger to his lips, then he laughed. It was a constricted sort of guffaw, not a whole lot of fun in it. Truth was, he didn't look like he had much problem letting people in this place know he could be reached.

"So what is it this time?" Bearcat said.

"How well you know that boy who's up on the stage with you?"

"What boy?"

"*Ransom Dellaplane's boy,*" the sheriff said, rolling his eyes.

"Why, you got something you should tell me 'bout him?"

The sheriff moved over so he was right next to Bearcat, then he touched his breast pocket twice. "Well, now, that all depends on you, my friend."

Bearcat faced the sheriff for a moment, glaring angrily, then reached into his pocket and pulled out a wad of single dollar bills. Ostentatiously, in full sight, he began peeling them off.

The sheriff held up each one of those bills, and took the longest look at it.

"Dollars?"

"Dollars always—"

The sheriff held up a hand, choking off his words. Then looked down his long nose, fixed the Bearcat with a look of distaste and dismissal, before he slipped the pile of dollar bills into his pocket.

* * * * *

THE MOON WAS a full pumpkin orange, with a bright yellow corona, and big enough tonight to flare out over the eastern sky; it hung pendulous across the wide, muddy river, itself oil-green and viscous under the oddly electric orange-yellow light. They were sitting on a levee, an easy drive for anyone—a drive easier still when you got there in a pink Cadillac.

"Does the sheriff always bust up the place like that?" Daisy asked. She was leaning back on the hood of the Cadillac, head on her folded hands as if she were moon-bathing. She still had Bearcat's mojo bag around her neck like it belonged there. Next to her lay Dell's sax.

"I doubt it. I think usually there's, well, an understanding."

"Was it because of me?"

"How'd he even know you were there?"

"You're right," Daisy said. She was breathing in the night air deeply, then blowing out her breath straight at the hovering moon, trying to scoot it through the sky. Gentle waves lapped against the mud-sucky shore. "Was it *you*?"

Dell didn't say anything. He was down by the riverbank, skimming rocks across it. He was up to a consistent three bouncer, the rocks *whisp, whisp, whisping* white cowls before glugging down to the deep.

"I sort of smell my father." Dell pitched another stone. This one skipped four times.

"Really? Why?"

"Oh, he's probably got the sheriff after me, drag me out of there, get me away from the 'bad element.' "

"You're from a nice family, ain't ya?"

"Nice? I wouldn't call it nice." Another stone. This one hit all wrong and went straight down.

Daisy waited.

"Oh, we get along, I guess, when I play the game," Dell went on, "but I just—." He bent over, searching for a perfectly flat rock, then changed the subject. "Well, why'd you leave home?"

Daisy's sigh lit up the air. "Well, it's the longest darn story—"

"We have all night."

Daisy laughed gentle. "Yeah, we do, don't we. 'Cept I got to go to work tomorrow, do the lunch shift."

"You got a waitress job?"

"And lucky for it."

Dell nodded, then, fingering a perfect rock, sent it skipping five times over the viscous water. He gave himself a pat on the back, then walked up to the Cadillac.

"So, tell me, what was it?"

"Why I left home?" Daisy put her hands behind her and

hoisted herself up on the Caddie's front end. Dell followed her, both of them sitting there, tapping their heels against the luscious pink paint job. "Well, there was...." Daisy paused a moment. "I haven't had an easy life, really. It wasn't a 'nice' home."

"Mine wasn't either, once you got past the tall white portico."

"Yeah, but sounds like you least have money."

Dell half-shrugged, then didn't say anything for a long minute. Finally, he asked again, "So why did you leave?"

Daisy leaned back. "Well, I just—I had me a calling, guess you'd say." She brightened. It was like she was telling out loud a story long held in silent privacy. "I just heard myself singing. Heard my voice out there, everywhere, you know? People listenin', feelin' what I'm feelin'. Making everything a little better—"

"It's funny what we hear," Dell said. He still had a rock in his hand, and spun it over and over. "I used to come down here and play my sax all night long. I'd sit here, play to the moon, try to get it to sound like all those cats I was hearin' on Beale Street."

Daisy shifted on the hood of the Cadillac, then tilted toward Dell.

"There was a woman where I come from, old negro woman. She was supposed to be one of those conjurers who used black magic and all?" There was a question in her look, and when Dell gave a gentle nod, she went on. "She was strictly off-limits. You can imagine—"

"I can indeed."

"Well, like you, I used to steal down to the crick where she lived, and I'd get her to sing for me. I'd help her dig up roots and pick greens and stuff, and I'd think, Now this is the most beautiful voice I ever heard. I'd heard lots of music— they was always singing in Daddy's church—but this voice ... this was a voice that truly came from heaven."

"Like yours."

Daisy smiled, threw back her hair. "You don't have to pay me no compliments. I'm not that kind of girl, you know."

"I meant it," Dell said straight at her.

Daisy blushed. "Well, anyways, I went down there much as I could, got Madame Grosgreen—that's all anyone called her, Madame Grosgreen—to teach me all that I could learn. I don't know how much stuck, but that was all I ever wanted, to sing like that. Whooeeee! And did I pay for it." Daisy shifted again on the Cadillac's hood.

"How?"

"Oh, my daddy. It was bad 'nuff I was singing out of church, I mean, not those hymns from his leather book, but then I was singing like a nigger, and then he found out I was gettin' it from a nigger, and one with conjurin' and all. Daddy, he would whup me something awful—"

"And that's why you really left?"

"No, no, I took the whuppings, they was worth it. Like I said, I left when I was ready to follow my calling."

"Your daddy was a preacher, you said?"

"Well, he *was* a preacher. He had a little problem, they took away his collar and his church." Daisy looked down at the ground; Dell couldn't see her face at all. "He worked in the mines some, too, when he could see straight."

"He drank?"

Daisy looked up then, held Dell's concerned gaze with force and heat.

"Oh, he had sinnin' comin' and goin'!"

"And your mother?"

"My mother died a while back."

Dell leaned toward her, set a hand on her shoulder.

"I'm sorry."

"Nothing to be sorry 'bout. What is, is what is." At that, Daisy slid off the car's hood and reached back to pick up Dell's sax. She looped the cord over her neck, then held it to her chest and ran her fingers desultorily over the keys. "I loved my mother, though—really miss her sometimes."

Dell gently patted her shoulder. "Must've been hard."

Daisy was silent a moment, then said, "What about you? I've told you my story, what's yours?"

Dell looked down at the ground. "It wouldn't interest you."

"If it wouldn't interest me, I wouldn't have asked." Daisy faced him straight on. "Right?"

Dell held her clear gaze but still said, "I don't know what to say."

"You don't get along with your daddy, how come?"

Dell was kicking his heels in a faint, nervous tattoo against the Cadillac's fender. "We just see the world different, I guess."

"Nobody sees the world like their daddy," Daisy said. She was still fingering the saxophone's keys. "But that don't mean you can't get along."

"I guess."

"Boy," Daisy said, suddenly animated, "getting something from you's like squeezing turnip juice." She shook her wide shoulders, fresh and blithely, like a horse in a river shaking off water. "Come on! I told you 'bout me, and it wasn't a pretty story. Now I want to know about you—*I do!*"

"Well," Dell said still looking down. "I don't—I'm never—hell, I'm just not sure what my father wants." Kick kick kick against the pink car. "Just don't seem like it's me."

Daisy leaned in with vivid interest. "You got any brothers or sisters?"

Dell started to shake his head, then said softly, "I had a brother, Jason—he was older."

"*Had?* You mean, he's—"

"Yeah, he's dead. Died in Korea, Unsan. Going up a hill. They say he was a hero."

"I'm sorry."

"Yeah." Dell looked out across the river, tracing its undulations. "But what is, is what is, right?"

Daisy just kept looking at Dell, ignoring his iteration. "What was he like?"

"I think he was a good guy." Dell spoke slowly, stoically. "I mean, he was my older brother. I looked up to him. He—well, you know how older brothers are."

"I'd probably have to guess, you know."

"Wouldn't make any difference. Jason died, and my father—"

"He can't forget him."

"I don't know," Dell said, turning right to Daisy now. "I do know I tried. Went out for football, was All-City. Did some hunting, fishing—Jason was great on that stuff—and I, well … what I really loved was music." He reached out, ran a finger down the side of his golden saxophone, only inches away from Daisy's breasts. "All my father saw was some boy he kept calling 'dreamy.' "

"Nothing wrong with being dreamy."

"Whatever that is." Dell snorted under his breath, then pitched out the black stone he'd been holding all this time. It skipped twice, then sank. "You know, when he looks at me, he just doesn't *see* me." A look over. "That make sense?"

Daisy leaned in and patted Dell's upper arm.

"It ain't over yet, you know."

"Oh, yeah!" Dell said, abruptly sliding down off the car's hood. "Wait'll he hears what I'm doing. He'll understand that real well. Hah! Now instead of 'dreamy' I'll be 'a nigger lover.' "

"You are, aren't you?"

Dell looked startled. Didn't speak for a long moment.

"Maybe." A difficult smile. "Guess I am. Guess he'll never love me now."

"You never know," Daisy said consolingly. "He's not a drunk, is he? Or a lecher?"

"Who knows," Dell laughed, "but I doubt it. He seems consumed with work to me. I hardly ever see him."

"Well, maybe one day he'll see something you've accomplished, and he'll get it. Something only you could do."

"That's a pretty thought," Dell finally said.

"At least you got yourself a chance," Daisy said, then shook her head. "I never even had that. Never had anything easy—" She said this without any trace of self-pity, just firm and definite. Yet her voice tolled a ringing sadness that pulled Dell out of his own thoughts. It was a voice much older than this lovely young woman seemed. Not resigned so much as steady, clear. It suddenly seemed immensely important to him to find a way to ease her troubles—so much more so than worrying about himself.

"Don't expect I ever will," Daisy added.

Dell knew just what to say. "Oh, I don't know 'bout that."

"What do you mean?"

"I mean, look at this here." He waved his hand along the sleek fender of the pink Cadillac. "That didn't come too hard."

Daisy raised an eyebrow, then smiled. "It *is* a damn nice drive," she said, and a pealing laugh erupted from her.

Both of them were silent as the last of her laugh faded into the warm night. The pumpkin moon hung above them rich and full. The air thickened between them.

Anything could have happened, but what did was she moved the saxophone directly in front of her. She wasn't quite looking at Dell, but not looking away either. The instrument's golden skin picked up the moon's light. A large question hung above them.

A moment later Daisy put the reed to her lips and started to blow. She blew into it nervously, and not much came out but a grumpy, choked-off squawk. She tried again, and it just sounded worse.

Dell, eyes rich with the question, was simply looking at her. Daisy laughed, then began to take the strap off from her neck. "Well, *this* damn thing ain't gonna come easy."

"Wait a second," Dell said, moving right in front of her.

"Yeah?" Large eyes at Dell.

"There's a few basic things you got to learn." Dell's voice was all business, yet he was only inches from her.

"Like?" Eyebrows up now, but it felt like she was concentrating only on the instrument before her.

"Like, you just got to make sure the reed's nice and wet."

"Oh, yeah?" She tilted back her head. "Nice and . . . wet. How do you do that?"

"You do it with your mouth."

Daisy smiled, then licked her lips and brought the mouthpiece up.

"Like this?"

"No, watch." Dell slid over so that he was right behind her. He leaned his head half over her shoulder, got her to raise the sax up, and then moved his mouth over the reed and wet it all over.

Daisy flinched, back against Dell. "God! Then what?"

"You just purse your lips, like this—" he put the mouthpiece back between his lips "—and place the reed in your mouth."

Daisy, still holding the bowl of the sax, moved it over to her mouth. *"Like this?"*

Dell's mouth was right at her ear. He gave a gentle laugh. "No, like this."

They passed the mouthpiece back and forth, trying it out for fit. The reed glistened with their saliva. He kept his head next to hers, his mouth half buried in her hair. Daisy, though, was concentrating full on the golden sax.

"Better," Dell said. "Now you slowly breath into it, real steady, like you're givin' it life."

Daisy took a huge breath then blew into the instrument with a constant stream. The sax issued a low moaning sound, low and flat, like it was rising off the river itself. Daisy kept blowing, pushing out more air than anyone could imagine, and the note sounded louder and louder until it seemed to fill up the sky. Finally, she began to stagger back, determined to use her very last bit of air.

"Wow!" she said, swooning. Her eyes were nearly as bright as the moon.

"That was great," Dell said in admiration.

"Yeah ... can we do it again?"

"I want you to try something." Dell leaned back over her shoulder and put his arms around her again, setting his fingers on the sax keys. "O.K., exhale again."

Daisy pursed her lips, then blew just right into the mouthpiece. As she did, Dell moved his fingers, playing a whole string of notes.

"Oh, man ... that was nice."

"That's the song." Dell leaned away from her now, against the Cadillac's haunches.

"What song?"

"The one I'm writing for you. Here, let me do it."

He took the sax from her and blew it all himself. It was the basic melody he'd come up with with Bearcat, but this time it launched into an eight-bar middle section that sent shivers up both their spines.

"I got the bridge, too," Dell said.

"That's wild," Daisy said. "But what do you mean it's for me?"

"Bearcat and I been trying to get that right all day." He played the song again, and this time locked it down cold. "Damn!"

"What's it called?"

Dell slowly took his lips from the sax's mouthpiece, then softly said, *"Pink Cadillac."*

"Liar!"

Daisy lifted off Bearcat's mojo sack and playfully tossed it to Dell. Dell caught it one-handed, then lifted off the sax strap and replaced it with the bag. He wedged the saxophone carefully into the Cadillac's wide bumper. Then it was all attention to Daisy. He gave her a smiling, slanted kind of look, then sidled up next to her and lifted his arms to her wide shoulders, this time face on.

Daisy smiled at him, but before anything happened, she let out a long, worried look that seemed to be saying, Do you really know me? Are you sure you want to get involved with someone as troubled as I am?

Dell, in his own urgency, let any intimations slide past.

Then Daisy's spirit kicked in, and she threw her blonde head back with a saucy, I'm-ready look. She pressed herself against Dell, letting her whole body go. Together they leaned back on the Cadillac's hood and kissed the night away.

✳ ✳ ✳ ✳ ✳

DAWN BROKE OVER them a few hours later, pink and yellow-blue over the river.

They woke in each other's arms, on a blanket Daisy had found in the Cadillac's trunk, their clothes mussed but fully intact.

"Sweet," was the first word out of Daisy's mouth. She breathed it gentle and cottony, a benediction to the morning.

Dell stretched his arms beside her, then quickly popped onto his side, propped up by his elbow. His determined look startled her.

"What?" she said.

"I want Bearcat to hear our song."

"It's *our* song now?"

"It was always our song."

"Oh, men. Whoever says women got all the soft thinking."

"What's soft about me having written you a song?"

"Oh. You mean?"

"I mean, we got to come up with some lyrics. I was thinking earlier, chorus should go '*I don't care if I never look back / in my Pink Cadillac.*'" He sang the melody softly.

"You mean, like somebody taking off?" Daisy yawned, brought a hand to her mouth. "Sorry," she breathed.

Dell was looking direct at her.

"I mean, like the Cadillac sets you free."

"Is that what you want, freedom?"

"Doesn't everyone?" Dell said.

Daisy yawned again. "Damn," she said, "being up this early, makes me think of the summer I was twelve. I spent it at my Aunt Ruth's slopping pigs." She grimaced.

"So what do you think?"

"You mean—*what*?"

"Lyrics."

Daisy took a deep breath. "How about, '*You can keep the magic in Bearcat's mojo sack, I'd rather have my Pink Cadillac*'?"

Dell frowned. "That doesn't sound like any pop song."

"Just a notion."

"No, no, pink Cadillac, think wheels, moving, getting yourself *along*—" Dell tooted the melody. "That's what the music says."

"I see."

"Come on, help me with a verse. What's the story gonna be?"

"O.K., how about this," Daisy said. "Girl comes to town, girl gets Cadillac, then the girl meets a boy—" Wide, playful eyes up at Dell.

"Then what?" Bright young smile.

"Well, if it's storytellin' like out in Hollywood, after the boy gets the girl, he's got to lose her, then—"

Dell looked suddenly chastened. "I don't know if that's the right story—"

"Why not? You're the one who wants it to go, 'I don't care if I never look back....'"

Dell jumped up and said, "The important thing is that I've got the whole melody. We gotta get Bearcat to hear it. Come on, we'll think up some kind of lyrics on the way." When they were both standing, Dell waited for Daisy to pick up the blanket and fold it. Then he went over and climbed into the driver's seat.

Daisy, blanket clenched before her, stood next to the open window.

"Come on," Dell said, "get in."

"Aren't we, um, forgetting something?"

"What?" Dell said, consternation in his tone. "You got hours yet till you got to get to your waitress job. Come on."

"No, silly," Daisy said, standing firm by the driver's side window. "Whose, um, Cadillac is this?"

"You mean, you're gonna *drive*?"

"Hey, somebody's gotta take us where we gotta go. Remember Elvis?"

Dell glowered for a second, then scooted across the wide leather seat. Daisy got in and fired up the car with one turn.

As she pulled away from the river, she punched her foot on the accelerator and the car burned down the road.

"Whoeee!" she cried. "Maybe you are right, we ain't *never* gonna look back!"

* * * * *

WHEN THEY GOT to the roadhouse both Dell and Daisy were surprised to see Bearcat sitting on the front porch. Sticks was on one side, young Clay the guitar player on the other. They were playing an old blues song, a version of Robert Johnson's *Stones in my Passway*:

I got stones in my passway, and my road seems dark as night
I got stones in my passway, and my road stretches forever night
I have pains in my heart, they have taken my appetite

Bearcat was leaning back and drawling mournful notes from his harp when Daisy and Dell walked up to the porch. Their enthusiasm, especially Dell's, was bubbling.

"Hey, I finished our song," Dell cried. He pulled Bearcat's mojo bag from his neck and tossed it at the older man. It fell unnoticed in Bearcat's sprawling lap.

Nobody looked at him. Dell cocked his head. "Hey, our song. I'm callin' it *Pink Cadillac*." Glance back at Daisy's car. "It's done!"

Nobody even looked up. Sticks was drumming soft on the stripped-wood porch floor, Clay shooting a bottleneck up the neck, ringing and ringing, and Bearcat blowing the harmonica as if only for himself and his God.

Another verse:

My enemies have betrayed me, have overtaken the
    Bearcat at last
My enemies have betrayed me, have overtaken the
    Bearcat at last
And there's only one thing certain, they laid these stones
    all in my path

By now it was dawning on Dell that something wasn't right. Daisy already had a concerned look on her face, but feeling so new, she kept quiet.

"Bearcat, what is it? What's goin' on?"

From Bearcat, nothing but the blues.

"Dell, what's that?" Daisy was pointing to a long sheet of heavy paper stapled to the roadhouse's front door.

Dell leaped the steps and went over to the placard. He read:

SEIZURE OF PROPERTY FOR TAX DELINQUENCY
PROPERTY TO BE AUCTIONED DECEMBER 31, 1955

His eyes beaded tight. "They've closed the place," he said.
"Why?" Daisy asked.
"It looks like taxes, but I'm sure—"
Bearcat went into the bridge of the song:

*I'm cryin' plea-ease let us be friends
And when you hear me howlin' in your pathway, rider,
please, plea-ease open that door and let me in*

"Bearcat, talk to us." Dell was away from the door, facing his mentor. "When did this happen? Who did it?"
The Bearcat turned huge white eyes on Dell. For just a second there he looked haunted, just returned from sepulchral fields. "Maybe you'll tell me," he said, then got up and went into the roadhouse.
"I don't have any idea," Dell said, following him.
Bearcat spun around and said, "What I hear, a man named Dellaplane's behind this."
"That's my father."
"Oh, is it?" Bearcat took a seat at the bar.
"You—you don't think *I* had anything to do with this?"
Bearcat took up the mojo sack Dell had tossed back to him and rubbed it gently between his large paws. When he spoke, it was as if he were talking to the bag.
"Now, do we believe in coincidences or don't we?"
"But he doesn't even know I'm out here." Then Dell remembered the sheriff the night before. "I don't think so—"
"Oh, somebody knows you're here. *We* know you're here."
"Is it the sheriff?" Dell was pacing now. "The sheriff, he'd tell my father he saw me. Sheriff'd do that."

Bearcat raised an eyebrow. "So you think this is about you being out here? Simple as that?" Then Bearcat turned to Salt behind the bar. "Whiskey."

"It could be," Dell said. "Could be indeed. My father could get the city council to vote any which way he wants, and if he knew I was out here playing with you, he might just get them to issue an order for spite. Damn him!"

"That simple?" the Bearcat repeated. He threw down a shot glass of amber liquid.

"Why, what else?" Daisy said.

"Oh, I think it's bigger than one white boy playing with the niggers. I think, that was the problem, they's easier ways to fix it. I think we're talkin' that ol' clover leaf again."

"I got nothin' to do with that!"

"But your father does. That's what I heard. Ol' man Dellaplane—he's building the highway out here. And where there's one highway, soon 'nuf there's gonna be more of them. There's gonna be *clover leafs*, just like I said." Bearcat swung out a hand. "You see them oaks and hickories, over there— there's gonna be restaurants and gas stations, hotels and motels! It's a new world a comin'." A snort. "Man gets ahold of land pretty as this, with the new world rollin' out this way, no tellin' how well he'd do."

"But *you* own the land," Dell said. "They can't take your land."

"Well, that's where you're wrong, my son." Bearcat stretched out his hands. "I been talkin' to a lawyer in town, a *colored* lawyer. What he tells me, if the county wanted, they could bring down on me something called eminent domain. *Em-i-nent do-main* means they just grab your land for the good of everybody."

"But—" Dell interjected.

All this time Daisy had been in the roadhouse, too, but paying only partial attention to the two men. Now she was off in a shadowy corner, fiddling with an old, rusted contraption that looked like a combination professional dough kneader and sewing machine.

"I know," Bearcat said. "That ain't what they're doin'. That's what I'm not figurin'. The note up there says they gonna seize this place 'cuz we ain't paid enough taxes. Well, I paid my taxes—I'm no fool, I always pay my taxes. But looks like I'm being 'sessed taxes I didn't even know I owed."

"And do you have the money?" Dell said.

"Say what? All I'm making out here comes from folks' Saturday-night four bits, and whatever beer they drink and the hooch I gotta pay an arm 'n' a leg for, come from some white trash up the hills. I ain't had any other income since I had me a record out—and that didn't bring much more 'n nothin'."

Dell's eyebrows were pursed; he looked like he was thinking fast.

"But I'm with you now."

Bearcat cocked his big black head. "So?"

"So, I'll come up with—"

Just then a screechy noise buzzed loud through the roadhouse.

"Hey!" Bearcat called out across the room. "What the hell she doin'?"

"Daisy, what're you up to?" Dell called down to the singer.

Daisy ignored them. She kept focused on the machine. She was also singing to herself, just loud enough for the two men to hear.

"If I wan't looking right at her, way she moves a tune, I'd swear she was black as tar," Bearcat said.

"What's that she's fussin' with?" Dell asked. "That what I think—"

"It's our old record cutting machine. Right there, that's the in-stru-ment we cut Sonesta's *Cryin' Shame* on. Made us a master, went top 10 on the race records chart—"

"That's it!" Dell shouted. "We'll record."

"Say what?"

"We'll record. We got the band, we got the voice, and now we got us a song. I even know some big music people in Nashville, I bet they're just dyin' to cross over."

Bearcat rubbed his neck. "I know all about recording with white people. Oh, yeah, been down *that* route before. What we gotta do is get more people, paying more money, into my club here."

"But we can do that, too," Dell said, all excitement. "The record'll bring attention, and attention will bring a crowd."

"Same ol' poor crowd."

Dell was pacing now. "No, no, we can get us a new crowd. A Daisy Holliday kind of crowd."

Bearcat frowned. "Sonesta already thinks I'm a fool for messing with you white people. Think what everyone'll think if that happens?"

Dell walked right up to Bearcat. "Make me your partner."

"Make you my *what*?"

"Partner. Sell me a piece of the roadhouse."

"Oh, yeah," Bearcat said. "Now I see—"

"No, no, this is nothing to do with my father. This is *against* my father."

"Tell me about it. Tell me 'bout blood—"

"Thicker than water," Dell said fast, "but what isn't? But it's not thicker than what we got here. Not thicker than the music."

Bearcat was rubbing the double folds of his wide chin. "I don't—"

"Here," Dell said, going over to the bar and ripping away a rough piece of paper sack. He looked around for a pencil, and Salt pulled one out of his shirt pocket. Dell drew a circle on the paper, tearing it in parts, then divided the circle. He went over to Bearcat to show him.

"You'll keep the majority," Dell said quickly. "I just need a piece. Just enough to go talk to anyone who needs talkin' to." He pointed to the napkin. "Just enough to be able to raise us some money."

"They's just squiggles to me, boy," the big man said.

"No, look, this is your share—"

The Bearcat didn't even bother to look at the napkin chart again. He folded his arms before him and let his eyes fall hooded.

"You're not going to take advantage of me, are you?"

Dell looked startled. "How can you say that?"

"Oh," the Bearcat said, "I have me some experience with promises from white people—even white people with music in 'em."

"No, no, I just want to help you." Dell swung a hand out, encompassing the whole roadhouse. "Help us."

Bearcat looked at him with huge, full intensity. "You know, I'm not edycated, not much. I started out to be but—but things happened. All I ever really learned was music. You hear what I'm sayin'?"

Dell, silent now, gave a soft nod.

"Tell me what I'm saying."

"You're saying that like anybody, educated or not, you make a deal, you have to be careful."

Bearcat shut his left eye, gleamed in with the right at Dell. He looked surprised by what he'd just heard, as if it was more incisive than he expected.

A moment later the big man gave a slanted, shrewd smile.

"Twenty percent?" he said.

Dell took a step back, muffled his own surprise that they were now dealing.

"I'm going to be doing a lot out here, and it's going to be just what you need. Forty."

"Never."

Dell pointed again to his napkin, then realized it cut nothing with the Bearcat, and made a show of crumpling it up and tossing it aside.

"You'll still be in charge," he said. "You'll be the Man."

"Twenty-seven."

The way Bearcat whipped the figure out, and that it was so precise, made Dell grin. It *was* dealing now, and he was starting to enjoy it.

"I don't think I can do it for less than—"

"That's my offer, you come in with me, bring enough money to make this tax problem go away, we'll go see my colored lawyer friend, draw us up a contract…. Twenty-seven percent."

Dell stepped forward, stuck out his hand. "Thirty-three, and it's a deal."

Bearcat eyeballed the young man, then broke into a wide grin. It was clear he was enjoying the horse-trading, too. "O.K., Thirty-three, but no way thirty-three and a third."

Dell nodded, winked.

"Deal!" Bearcat bellowed, and shook the young man's open hand.

"All right!" Dell threw his fist into the air.

Bearcat gave a long, unreadable smile.

"I just want you to know one thing," he said. "I'm taking you on your word, boy. Now, nothin' ever happened to me makes me think I should trust *any* white man, no matter how well he blows his horn. But here I am, going to trust you—"

Dell started to speak, but Bearcat held up his huge pink-palmed hand.

"Just that one thing. You fuck me and I'll kill you."

Dell, looking up at the older man, stood his ground, didn't say a thing. But his face went pale just like that.

"Just one thing," Bearcat said, then went over and put his meaty arm over the thin boy's T-shirted shoulders. Gave him a smothering hug. " 'Nuff said?

Dell said softly but distinctly, "Yes, sir."

Bearcat smiled, then let go of Dell and stepped back. He had a wide grin on his face, a look that feigned a kind of simple bemusement but in truth was forceful and intense.

"Who knows," he said distractedly, as if to the air. "They say life's got a lot of surprises—"

Dell, who had quickly recovered, said, "Opportunities."

"Oh, yeah, oh, yeah," Bearcat chuckled. "White people call 'em *opportunities*, we call 'em *surprises*." He went over to the stage, where he picked up Clay's electric guitar and began to strum it. "But what I'm really thinkin' is, O.K., this white boy appears out of nowhere, seems to prefer the company of poor ol' black folks to his rich, powerful father, who seems to wanna own my place, but this boy, he can play some mean sax, which means maybe he ain't just a poser, which means that as long as he understands the *nature* of the agreement—" Bearcat raised his eyebrows— "and I can keep him to thirty-three percent, well, maybe we can do some business—"

"Bearcat—" Dell started to interrupt.

The big man took a hand off the guitar, held it up. "And maybe I'm sittin' here with a woman who's a true talent with a boundless soul but who's givin' it all now to Jesus, and then who should show up at my door but a white girl with true talent and a boundless soul, and she's *lookin'* to sing. Maybe I can get my head around that—"

"But—"

Quick shake of Bearcat's head. "And maybe I can get my head round the idea we go with the times and turn ol' Bearcat's joint into a *mixed* club, even though people like me get lynched for much, much less. Maybe I sense something in the air, though, something gonna make that ... possible."

"Yeah, but—" Dell went again.

Bearcat shook his head again, meaning, You're my partner, you show me respect.

"And maybe all of a sudden we got us a song to sing,

good song, *rockin'* song, and maybe the white boy tells us he got us *opportunities* in Nashville. Maybe I believe all that, that all that don't count as *surprises*."

"But—"

"But I still say we got us one in-su-per-able problem."

"What?"

"That record cutter over there ain't worked in years."

Daisy looked up at that, with her own thin, sly smile. She stepped back, and the disc on the machine started to spin. From a large, blooming horn speaker came the phrase, *Maybe all of a sudden we got us a song to sing, good song, rockin' song.*

"What the—?"

"She fixed it, Bearcat," Dell cried. "Damn, Daisy, you got it working!"

The next voice that came from the machine was Daisy's, and it was her singing. The words were perfectly clear. They all heard:

> *Where we're going, no one can know*
> *'Cept it'll be a long, long road*
> *Yeah, where we're goin', we'll never look back*
> *In our Pink Cadillac*
> *Our Pink Cad-il-laaaaac.*

Part Two
Misfortune

COLIN STONE SAT IN HIS West L.A. hotel room, the phone in front of him. No more hesitation. He punched in the numbers.

The phone on the other end rang and rang. Colin kept waiting for an answering machine at least to pick up, but nothing did. He was about to hang up when a click and then a voice giving a cheery female "Hello" startled him.

"I'm sorry," the woman went on, "we were playing tennis, and I had to run in from the court."

"No problem," Colin said, sweet as he could. "I'm just trying to reach a Miss Daisy Holliday."

Colin heard the quick intake of breath on the other end. "You're asking for Daisy ... Holliday?"

"Yes, from Memphis many years ago. My name is Colin Stone, and I'm the president of Blue Moon Records. Perhaps you've—"

"And you're trying to reach ... Daisy Holliday?" The voice was rich and smooth, unruffled though undercut, Colin thought, with uneasiness.

"Yes, I want to talk to her about her music career. Years ago in Memphis. It's important."

"How could it be important?" the woman said.

"Are you Daisy Holliday?"

A pause. That startled her. Colin read the situation: She's married, nobody's called her by her maiden name for years, she was never expecting the past to suddenly rise up on her. Go gentle, he told himself.

"I don't know what you want," the woman finally started to say, "but I don't think you should peddle it here."

"What?"

"You heard me, young man."

"But I just want to talk to ... you. A few questions."

"No."

"You are Miss Holliday, aren't you? Listen, it's about *Pink Cadillac*. About Dell Dellaplane and Bearcat Jackson. I'm a record man, and I'm looking—I'm desperate to hear a copy of—"

"There's nothing anyone can tell you about that here." This time clear, disdainful anger.

"But you are—or maybe you were—Daisy Holliday, right? You do know what I'm talking about? If you'd just let me—"

"No."

"I—I won't take much of your time, and I'll come to you, in—" Colin checked his notes; all he had was a phone number, and he'd looked up the area code. It was 602, the Phoenix area, but he didn't know which city. "—in Arizona."

"You set foot in this state, my husband will shoot you."

"But, Miss Holliday, it was so long ago. Almost forty years. I just—"

"I'm going to hang up now."

"Please, don't." Colin took a deep breath. He didn't understand why this woman on the other end, if it truly was Daisy Holliday, could be so riled up. It *was* forty years ago. Why wouldn't she talk to him. "I can tell you're upset, but I have to tell you, I don't know why. Wasn't I clear? I'm searching for information on a historical event of exceptional import. I've been talking to people, and from everything I hear, you were at the center of it. Could I just—"

All this time Colin was trying to imagine her from her voice on the phone. It didn't sound that old, it was still forceful and smooth, and Colin was seeing a woman—well, she'd only be in her upper fifties—who might not yet even have the silver mane of the Southwestern matron. She could be well preserved in the dry air. She could still be beautiful.

"Who have you talked to?"

"I talked to Dell Dellaplane."

An inrush of breath. She hung up.

Colin hit redial, held his breath.

The phone rang and rang.

Finally, he put it down. Stared at it. Felt a powerful desire run through him.

Colin knew a few tricks from a reporter friend of his, the first of which was to simply let some time pass and call again, especially at an odd hour. You could easily catch whoever you wanted in a different mood. They'd have been thinking, that low hum of the past you'd been asking about rising up in them and buzzing furiously. Sometimes, the friend said, they broke just like that, the whole story already nearly perfectly formed hissing out. But you couldn't count on that. And then you had to go to the next level: Go see them. It was easier to hang up a phone than turn someone away from your door; one of those human rules, the friend said, without which we wouldn't have newspapers worth reading. Just show your face. Smile. And be persistent. We all have stories, he insisted, and most of us spend an embarrassing amount of time actually waiting for someone to come up and ask all about them.

Colin eyed the phone again. Tapped his fingers lightly on the dimpled keys. The idea that had just been a low-level thrum in the back of his thoughts sprang to him full-blown: He knew now he had to see Daisy Holliday. He let the jumble of pictures and sounds shoot through him, bright and loud as fireworks, and when they settled into a definite plan, he simply called an airline and booked a flight to Phoenix.

* * * * *

THE RECORDING of *Pink Cadillac* that played through the hallways of Old Gold Records in Nashville was scratchy and with almost rhythmic pops and clicks—the actual disc cut by Daisy and Dell and Bearcat the week before in Memphis, with a hand-drawn Bearcat label stuck on the black shellac—and when Cuth Starks heard it drifting out of his secretary's office, where it was spinning on the portable 45 player on her desk, he called out through his office door, "Turn that nigger music off."

"Mr. Starks," the secretary, Babs Kieusewski, said, "it's Mr. Finkelstein of Decca Records in New York."

"I don't care, we don't do nigger music, *turn it off*!"

Babs lowered the volume on the machine, then looked again at the eight-by-ten glossy photo that had come with the disc and laughed and laughed.

In his office Cuth Starks, president of Old Gold Records, picked up the receiver and said, "Yes, yes, Mr. Finkelstein, how are you, sir? Yes, Christmas, I mean, *holiday* greetings to you...." Cuth bit down on his tongue; those New Yorkers.

Finkelstein spoke for a while, and then Cuth said, "Well, I do think I've got a few artists you might be interested in ... well, yes, sir, they *are* country singers, but they have some of that new 'beat thing' you say you're looking for.... Yep, they all move pretty good.... No, no, haven't actually seen them do that 'shake-a-leg' thing, but I'm sure they could learn it. I mean, anybody can do that, right? Heh, heh!... No, no, they'd *all* be gentlemen, yes, sir...."

Cuth Starks had his feet up on his desk by now, was leaning back in his executive chair shipped all the way from Chicago. He was nodding to a long question on the other end of the phone.

"Well, now, Mr. Finkelstein, there just aren't a whole lot of women right now. You got the Miller Sisters and Barbara

Pittman, but they're signed to Sam Phillips on that Sun label in Memphis, and, frankly, they ain't that great. . . ."

He shifted his feet.

"Yeah, Sam Phillips, he's the one with that Carl Perkins fella, you're right. Well, he might be interested. I know Sam, he's a deal maker, sure enough. But remember, sir, the word on the street is RCA *overpaid* for that Presley fella. . . . That's what I say, too—'flash in the pan.' Ab-so-lute-ly. Yes, yes, much too crude. . . .

"Yes, sir, I'd definitely stake my career on that. What we're gonna find for you are good singers, nice people, but ones those kids'll love too. . . . Of course I understand. I'm not much older than the kids myself, and I come from Memphis, too. But if I may say so, Nashville is still the only place down in the South where records that are going to last will be coming from. Yes, sir. . . ."

In Babs's office the acetate had run down. She'd left her desk and was standing just outside Starks's office.

"Yes, I understand, girl singers. . . . Well, yes, yes, that *might* be a good idea. I know, something different, a novelty. . . . Oh, you don't mean a novelty, you mean. . . ." Cuth pursed his brow, frowned down at the phone. "Sir, if I may be frank, I wouldn't put much faith in a woman in that way. Sure as shootin', you're not going to find one who does the leg-shakin' thing—not here in the South."

From his office door Babs was beginning to gesticulate, pointing at the picture she was holding. Cuth shooed her away.

"Well, I'll try, I promise you that. I know, I know, it burns me up, too. But as I said, flash in the pan, flash in the pan. Yes, sir. Yes, the first thing I hear. . . . Right, best to the kids. And I'll tell my father you said hi. . . . O.K., bye."

With a long sigh Cuth reached out and dropped the phone dramatically back in its cradle. Then he turned to Babs.

"I'm sittin' here playin' kiss-ass to my best contact in New York City, he's got some crazy idea we need us a female Elvis, and you're playin' *nigger* music at me? What's got into you?"

Babs just stood in the door, holding out the shiny photo.

"Yeah, so what's this?"

Just stood there. Smiling. Laughing behind the smile.

"You gonna show it to me?"

A few strides across the room.

Cuth held the picture out at arm's length, squinted down his eyes. "You ain't tellin' me the girl lyin' on this Cadillac was the one singin' on your player?"

"You tell me, Mr. Boss."

"Where'd this come from?"

"Memphis."

"Memphis? And they sent it on acetate? What are they, in the dark ages? Where's the letter?" Babs handed a large manila envelope over, a sheet of stationery carefully clipped to it. Cuth peered in at it, then cried, "Ho, ho! Not Prince Dell Fuckin' Dellaplane."

✳ ✳ ✳ ✳ ✳

IT WAS A MOMENT of pure thrilling exuberance that had caused Dell to wrap up the copy of *Pink Cadillac* they'd grooved on the old record cutter—the recording they'd blown through that same afternoon, Daisy stepping right into the beat and gutting out her own lyrics when Dell was coming up shy. Though none of the musicians had seemed too eager, they were at bottom Bearcat's employees, and the big man wanted to give it a try. When they kicked off into the wailing-sax opening, the music had quickly taken them over: Sticks had never hammered steadier, Thumper banged his bass right down there with him, and Dell soared over that husky yet silky voice with his golden sax. When they played the recording back, they all sat there, Bearcat, too, with their jaws low and their eyes wide.

"We done it," the big man finally said. He was standing in front of the stage, facing Dell and Daisy, who were sitting on its lip, and the musicians still in place behind them. "This says *hit*, well as I can tell."

"It is," Dell said firmly. "It's gonna be a smash."

Sticks, behind his drum kit, raised an eyebrow, shot a sidelong glance at Thumper.

"What?" Bearcat said, not letting a thing get past him. "You still don't get that rocky-roly, Mr. Skins?"

"Didn't say that, boss."

"Then what you thinkin'?"

The drummer shook his head, then looked down.

Bearcat turned to the bass player. "Thumper, what're y'all thinking?"

The bass player zipped his right pointer finger across his own lips.

"Talk to me, right now," Bearcat said.

All the musicians stayed mum.

Dell nodded his head toward Salt, leaning on his elbows on the bar. "What's going on?"

The young man flicked his goatee. "I think they're wondering who's gonna play it on the radio?"

"That it?" Bearcat said.

Thumper looked from Sticks to Clay the guitarist, then gave a solemn nod.

"Least we're gettin' somewhere. And why won't it get played, it got *hit* writ all over it?"

"Boss," Sticks finally opened up, "it's like Sonesta done said. They hear about who's played on this, all hell's gonna break loose. I mean, *look at us*."

"But they just gonna hear the—"

"Yeah, they hear this *Pink Cadillac*, they'll like it, sure— but then there's gonna have to be a story."

Bearcat was shaking his head. "They like it, they's not gonna care how it come to be. Right, Dell?"

"You're right, Mistah Cat." Dell was still smiling, half smirking, high on the whole session. "Gotta believe this is our chance. That the music's gonna sweep everything 'long with us."

"That's it, that's it!" the big man cried, waving his meaty arms. "You boys just gotta have faith. 'Sides, if anybody cares, we just paint you boys white. Or paint the little lady here black. Or paint you all with polka-dots. Heh, heh!"

At the mention of Daisy, everyone turned at that moment to her. She still looked shaken by the whole recording experience; during playback she'd been the most astonished.

"I still can't believe that was me" she said softly.

Dell leaned over and grasped her shoulders and gave her a friendly tumble and shake. "You just listen," he said.

"I—I really don't know where it came from." Her eyes were wide. "Y'all—" nod back to the band "—it don't matter who you are or what you are, when you started playing, it was, well—" she rolled her eyes with pure amazement "—with y'all behind me, it was just *there*."

"Magic," Dell said. He got up, went toward the Bearcat. "That's what we got here. We got us the color of magic."

Nobody on the stage, no matter what they were thinking, said a word.

"Bearcat," Dell went on, a quiet, more serious smile on his face. "You were holdin' that mojo sack the whole time, right?"

The Bearcat looked down at the stained leather bag and lightly brushed it. Everyone else's eyes were on the mangy bag, too. Everyone in the room, from Salt, Diamondback, and Hosea to the musicians to Bearcat and the two white kids, they all looked, at least for that moment, as if they were ready to believe.

"So what do we do now?" Daisy finally said, breaking the silence.

"We get you on the radio, make you a star."

Daisy shook herself then, half pushing away Dell's playful hands.

"Yeah, right, like everybody else who thinks they can sing."

"I don't know just what I can do," Bearcat said. "My connections, well, they's pretty worn and tattered by now. 'Sides, they was with race records."

"How 'bout with Sam Phillips?" Dell said.

Bearcat shook his head. "Sam's a genius, no question, but he demands lock, stock, and your mama's next grandchile. And the people he deals with up north, they's just worse. 'Less we're willing to shit in any pail they stick in front of us—sorry, darling—there ain't no way he's gonna just distribute us."

"Even though it's so good?" Daisy said, waving away Bearcat's crudity with a flick of her hand.

"No, we gotta cut our own river here, can't just sail in someone else's. What we'd do, we had enough money, is we'd press up some discs, then get somebody to distribute—"

"Money?" Dell said. "First, we got this tax thing hangin' over us—partner."

Though Dell was smiling, the Bearcat wasn't. "Yeah," was all he said.

"Hey," Dell said, brightening even more. "I just got me an idea. There was this old friend of mine, least he was my friend for a while.... Anyway, from what I hear he's in the record business in Nashville, been working as a scout. You know the song *Pretty Lady*?"

Not a blink from anyone.

"Well, it was sort of sappy, but this guy, Cuth Starks, he got it up to Dot Records in New York, and they got it on the charts."

"And he likes the blues?" Bearcat said, dubious.

"He's gonna like a hit." Dell jumped up, started pacing. "And he ain't so big he's gonna skin us. Just come up with the money to get the song recorded proper, then released—hell, maybe even up north."

Dell's eyes were wide.

"We're not gonna cut somebody else in," Bearcat said.

"But what else we gonna do? Guys, it's just the ticket."

"You want to send him our only recording?" Daisy said.

"Yeah, we gotta move fast. We need another one, we'll just record it again."

"I don't like it," Bearcat said.

"What can it hurt? He don't hear what we hear, well, that's that, we just shake and say so long."

Bearcat shook his head. "No."

"What do you mean—"

More emphatic. "I mean, no. I've had me experience with white men getting records, you ain't. We're just gonna hold on to that disc for now."

Dell looked dismayed. "But what if I—"

"N-fucking-O."

"Daisy?" A look from the old man to her.

"I think we gotta trust Bearcat."

Dell shook his head. "But how we gonna get things going?"

"We get the place going first," Bearcat said. "We got a lot to do here. We gonna have us a show, got to get this place *ready*."

* * * * *

BEARCAT WAS RIGHT: There was a lot to take care of, so Dell kept his secret plans to himself. First he went to talk to an old friend of his, Dick Spring, who was in his second year of law school, and found that the kind of order Bearcat's roadhouse had received could be easily stayed with the payment of the taxes—even if the taxes weren't really owed.

"What if we fought it?" Dell asked.

"Cost you more than paying it," was the crew-cut law student's quick answer.

It turned out to be only a couple hundred dollars. Dell's arrangement with his parents was that they gave him a small allowance, passed to him by the maid each Saturday morning after he mowed the back lawn, just as he'd had to do when he was ten—his father was still trying to create "character" in his son. Other than that, Dell came and went as he pleased, and tried not to get in anyone's way.

So coming up with even a couple hundred dollars wasn't that simple. Still, he was a Dellaplane, and he thought the banks might help. Old George LaCrosse at the First National, who had been to Dell's christening and admitted with a hey-hey raised eyebrow to winning a tidy pot on the East-Humes football game when Dell had captained his team to victory, bubbled with pink-faced joy to see him but became increasingly taciturn as he heard Dell out.

"And you're living out there with the nigra?" A high-flying eyebrow.

"No, not living—just spending time." Dell smiled though he knew already things were hopeless. He'd been bright and giddy with the musical breakthrough at the roadhouse and his deal with Bearcat, and he didn't realize he was heading into such a chill wind. "Keeping an eye on my investment."

"Your *investment*." A hand under the banker's chin. "Hmnn. And what does your father say?"

Dell took a moment to answer. "He doesn't say anything."

"I'm not surprised," LaCrosse said, leaning back in his wooden banker's chair and folding his hands before his chest smugly. "Frankly, if he did know, I think he'd be appalled."

One more shot. "But you have to listen to the record," Dell cried. He'd brought the acetate of *Pink Cadillac* with him.

"I don't like music."

"Mr. LaCrosse, this music's worth a million bucks. You heard 'bout that Presley boy, he just went up to New York?"

LaCrosse pulled a long face. It was exactly the face he would have made if shown definitive evidence his wife had been sleeping with the devil. "Sorry, Dell," he said. "You know I respect and honor your father, but I can't imagine what made you think an upright establishment like ours would fund a nigger establishment like that." The belligerent way these words were spoken was no different, Dell thought, from a high school invitation to a fight out back.

Dell did the only thing he could: He gave the banker a slant-eyed look, then simply got up and left, not even reaching out for the older man's hand.

And headed back to the roadhouse, feeling low and worthless. Yeah, I'm going to be a big help, he was thinking. Bringing the Dellaplane fortune to the table. And all the glorious power of the Dellaplane name.

It was mid-afternoon, and the only people in the roadhouse were Salt behind the bar and the bow-tied fancy man Diamondback nursing amber liquid in a cheap glass.

"Bearcat around?" Dell said as he came in.

"Nope."

"Know where he is?"

Salt shook his head. "Didn't say. He tell you, Mr. D?"

Diamondback had a way of squinting his left eye before he spoke. It was an elaborate maneuver, in which he squinched it up tight as a sponge you'd be wringing out, then let it blossom. Took Dell a few moments to realize the eyeball was glass. "He went out in his Sunday suit, no telling what mischief that boy getting into," Diamondback said in a high-pitched, nasally voice. The bright-browed man chuckled, then did his scrinchy eyeball thing again.

"You think he's off about the taxes?"

"Don't know where he'd have the money for 'em," Salt

said. "Isn't like we've been pulling much in here lately, without anybody singing."

"I know," Dell said. "I was just trying to raise some money, ran into a brick wall."

"You lookin' to borrow?" Diamondback said.

"Looking to get it anyway I can, this side of legal."

"Well, you know—" up went the eyebrow, down went the eyelid, around went the eyeball "—I think ol' Mr. Bearcat, he's probably tapped out. But, son, pardon my speaking, you're fresh meat."

"I am," Dell said, smiling. "That's the point, isn't it?"

"So, what I'm saying—" Diamondback suddenly leaned back, stretching himself back so far on his bar stool that he was almost horizontal. A moment later he bobbed back up, then swooped up his glass and tippled back a grand swallow. "So what I'm saying is, maybe I know some people who can help."

"You do?"

"D—" Salt said with a definite note of caution in his tone.

"Oh, yeah. You be knowing Beale Street, son?"

"Absolutely." Dell was nodding widely. "Been there a thousand times."

"Oh, yes, I'm sure you have." The gambler leaned back again, bobbled around, then did his eye thing. A jeweled stick pin glittered on the lapel of his formal black suit. "Sure you have. Well, I'm going to send you to a couple old com-pa-tri-ots of mine. You know that word, *com-pa-tri-ots*?"

"Friends of yours."

"Well, friends in a way." That way-up-there, blithely wheezing voice. "A special way. Friends in the war, son. Friends in the only war worth fighting. War of the *dice*."

Dell said, half impatient, "I'll do it."

Salt turned to his new friend. "Dell, you sure? I know the kinds of guys Diamond spun with. I'm not—"

"Tha's good, tha's good," Diamondback said, hushing down the upstart young crow. "Just one thing you gotta promise me."

"Yeah?"

"You don't breathe yourself one word of this to Mr. Bearcat."

Dell leaned forward. "Why?"

Diamondback puffed up his bantam chest, inhaled so loud and wheezy it sounded like a bellows. "Well, let's just say they had them a little problem once upon a time."

"Problem?" This was Salt, curious now, too.

"Little not seein' things eye to eye. There was hot words, then there was guns—"

"Guns! Over what?"

"What you think?" Diamondback looked to be thoroughly enjoying himself.

"Money?" Dell said.

Diamondback gave him a theatrical hooded-eye glare. "Money? Money fixes money."

"So what was it?"

"Well, question is, Who was it? And that I ain't sayin'."

"A woman?"

"I ain't sayin'!" Diamondback practically shouted. "But you mark my words, Bearcat finds out any money's coming from Beauregard T. Washington."

"Beauregard T.—" Dell started to say.

"Washington. And the T, it stands for Teee-nacious. Beauregard Teee-nacious Washington—"

"Sounds like a statue down by the courthouse," Salt said.

Dell gave him a wink.

"Well, you just remember, Bearcat find out you gettin' money from Beauregard, he won't take one red cent, and he might have to even redden up the man who made him remember, you understand?"

"Fine," Dell said, backing off a tad. "I promise. Not a word to Bearcat."

"Never! Never a word to him. Nor where you heard this. Or where the money come from. *Promise!*"

Dell was nodding over and over. "I promise. Just tell me where to find this ... Mr. Washington."

Diamondback still had the most furious glare on him, but he was definitely calming down a little. Still, he looked the young white boy up and down, clearly assessing him. He looked like he was checking the odds on a certain jack coming up straight from a deck of cards. Finally, he did an elaborate self-winking eye dance that culminated in his reaching out and shaking Dell's hand.

Dell shook it firmly back.

"Well," the gambler said, seeming to be mollified now, "like the song says, 'You go lookin' high, and you go lookin' low'—this case, I think low's best."

Dell scraped his leather heel against the floor, almost like he was pawing it. "Just give me an address, even a name."

"Well, the address you want, it's a jump from Lansky's and a hip from the Pig's Foot Inn, you know that, and it's up some rickety stairs."

Dell half shut his eyes, tried to see Beale Street. "I sort of—"

"Well, you look for the Indian, the wooden Indian, that's where you go in."

"Right."

"And you're looking principally for Mr. Beauregard T. Washington, you understand." Diamondback said. "He's the one. He'll help you, for sure. That man, he's made of money." And there was just a hint of envy there, a whiff of sad air rising from the older man's beautifully pressed black coat, his bow tie and glittery—but hardly a diamond—stick pin.

"I'm on my way," Dell said.

"But you don't forget your promise," the gambler

insisted. "Not a word to Mr. Bearcat. Not a word—ever!"

Dell nodded again as he flew out the door and jumped into his Triumph, zooming off to town.

Turned out that Diamondback's friends, especially Beauregard Tenacious Washington, weren't wholly unknown to Dell, a fact Dell realized when he found the wooden Indian, asked inside for Mr. Teee-nacious Washington, heard the old man there say, "You mean Snake Eyes? What's a young boy like you want with him?"

Dell didn't answer the question, just thought to himself, Snake Eyes? Oh, and probably the other gentleman's his pal Bullfrog. Dell smiled to himself. A couple years back on a dare he'd followed an older high school friend, Chick Strong, down here for a poker game. Dell had pretty much hung in the background, but Chick, through his own tenaciousness, had actually walked off a small but substantial winner. For two weeks after that both Dell and his friend kept seeing out of the corner of their eyes a couple sloe-eyed, slinky guys that Snake and Fish had sent, no doubt to waylay Chick and rob their money back. Dell, totally pissed, finally headed back to Beale Street and confronted them. "And what I don't get," he finished up, "is that I didn't even win the money myself, not that my friend didn't take it legitimately."

Pshaw, pshaw, pshaw, you just 'magining things, they went, but when Dell left he knew he'd won their respect—along with a promise to get Chick into another game a week following, where he lost back half what he'd made, and both boys figured, O.K., now we all call it quits.

There was another story about Snake Eyes and one of his East High classmates, a terrible, murky tale that Dell in his determination about the roadhouse had put out of his memory.

This afternoon Snake Eyes was the only one in the third-floor rooms, spread out on a chintz-covered bed. Snake had eyes near sewn shut from a spell as a boxer, as well as half his nose broken away from the other half; his face was a big, black, mangled thing, the overall impression was dozy looking, but Dell knew, get too close, he could strike out like a whip even if he was asleep. Right now he was wearing nothing but a silver-threaded vest and Western boots, and was propped up on a pillow, with a naked young girl tucked under his left arm.

"Is that a white boy I see in my room?" he called out. He rubbed his eyes. "White boy don't look completely strange to me?"

"Dell Dellaplane," the saxophone player called out as he walked in.

"Oh, yeah, oh, yeah. Boy that thinks he knows something 'bout cards."

Dell smiled, brushed back his mop of blond hair.

"Howdy, Mr. Eyes."

Snake Eyes raised himself in the bed, letting the naked girl slip out of his crooked arm, then glared at Dell as if he were looking to see if he was being disrespectful. "Yep, in the back of my head, my son. You here to try me?"

"No, no." Dell threw his hands up as if such a thought would only be that of a madman. "Like to do a little business."

"You got that sax'phone of yours up in hock again at the Jews?"

"Sort of—matter of speaking." Dell had decided to be deliberately cagey here. Even with Diamondback's referral, no telling what lines of business with Bearcat might lie crossed in past history.

"How much you need?"

"I think three hundred'll do it."

"Sax only worth $125."

"Let's say, it's not just the sax, it's what makes it work."

"What do you mean?"

"I mean, this is important, Snake."

"And you can cover the vig?"

"How much slack can you cut?"

"When you 'spect to start paying?" Snake Eyes asked. The girl next to him stretched. Dell could see a perfectly formed breast rise and fall.

"After the first of the year."

"That's a month away."

"Got a lot of work to do on your investment."

Snake Eyes leaned back. His hand went back to cupping the girl's perfect breast.

"Tell you what, I'll give you till that first of the year, but after that, we're gonna be talking fifteen percent—a week. And money is due when money is due. Understand?" Dell nodded. The club, the record, they were sure things, weren't they? "Honey, get up and get me my wallet. It's over there with my pants."

The naked girl was tall with a black bush that startled Dell. He averted his eyes, thinking he should be respectful.

"You want a taste?" Snake Eyes said.

"You mean—"

"We can make it $325," the loan shark said. "Less if I get to stay here and watch yo' white ass."

Though the girl was more than attractive, and with a smoky heat Dell could feel as she handed him the six $50 bills after Snake had counted them out, he demurred; he pocketed the money, thanked the gambler, then walked out with the payment warm in his back pocket.

Here was his plan: Not wanting anyone at the tax assessor's office to know where the money was coming from, he decided to get Daisy to deliver it. He checked his watch, should be just about time for her to get off from the lunch shift at the diner. He tooled by, then pulled up across the street.

And when she walked out in her pink uniform, her cheeks flushed from the warm-stove diner atmosphere, her wide shoulders moving purposefully, her hips strong beneath the seersucker pink skirt, he had a sudden vision of the tall black girl on Beale Street; and when Daisy saw he was there and ran across the road waving and stood next to him, saying, "Dell, what's up?" well, it took him a long minute to catch his breath and tell her.

She was totally game, though she insisted they go in her car.

After waiting around twenty minutes at the county office Daisy laid out each bill carefully on the clerk's desk, then demanded a receipt that said all was solid with the road-house property—and that the auction would not go forward.

Dell, waiting for Daisy a couple blocks away in the pink Cadillac, had had enough time to calm himself. He was sitting in the passenger seat—she still insisted on driving every-where. Dell tried to get her to take side streets when she could, it was so degrading being driven about in a pansy pink car by a girl, and more than once he slid down so all anyone could see was his growing-out hair. Only problem was: He loved being with her.

There hadn't yet been another moment like that one by the river, when he'd wrapped his arms around her and kissed her, and only kissed her, Daisy demurely keeping his hands away even from her breasts. Indeed, after making the record, Daisy'd said they had a business relationship now, and so they should be all business. Which made some sense. At least Dell found himself agreeing. He kept telling himself it was all about the way she was singing his, well, *their* songs, which meant that whatever was getting stirred up in his heart was being stirred because of the music, which meant the music should be enough … that's how his rationalizing thoughts ran on. And really, come to think of it, that pumpkin-moon night by the water had been about his saxophone and the song *Pink Cadillac*, and that was business, so maybe business *was* all it was.

Except that he couldn't quite stomp down the notion that he was really sweet on her.

Daisy, though, was hard to read. She seemed focused one hundred percent on the music, and though it thrilled Dell how well they played together, it frustrated him some, too. They were so busy taking hammer and nails and paint to the roadhouse, then rehearsing with Bearcat's band, as well as starting to sketch out new songs and planning the New Year's Eve opening—well, it just seemed they were too busy for any distractions, and well as Dell could tell, anything more than business with him was right now a distraction and a half.

Which wasn't so bad, since the more he worked with Daisy, the more it felt something strong and real was going down between them. The music was powerful as romance and sex, and almost as satisfying, at least for now. Nothing like having a focused-on-together purpose.

Dell was a little worried about the Bearcat, though. He was being a good sport, couldn't deny it, but he was still getting flak from the rest of the roadhouse about messing with white kids. Sonesta Clarke most of all let it be known she simply thought they were calling hell and tarnation down on themselves, and when she started in, Bearcat just went, "Hush, hush, woman, you don't know nothin' 'bout it. Come on, we're sounding great—one more time through." And everybody would play to beat the band, though the Bearcat himself never quit slipping off to the side with his harmonica and speaking his heart through it; and the music that Dell heard was worried music.

But Dell remained all optimism. And whenever anyone's spirits really flagged, he played the acetate they'd cut of *Pink Cadillac*, and when the music jumped out of the old horn speaker, you just couldn't keep their feet from moving. Hosea always leaped up and did his half-bare-assed barnyard scratch across the sawdust floor, Diamondback cawed brightly, even Sonesta, the few times she was there, was seen clattering her black-shoed feet on the sawdust floor. That record was their hope and their promise, and it got them through. So much so that when Dell insisted the new version of the roadhouse be called the Pink Cadillac club, even Bearcat went along.

The record would also be their salvation, and Dell without telling anyone set about on his own to do what he could with it. The acetate and the photo went to Nashville.

* * * * *

EVERYTHING WAS SAILING bright till Christmas Eve. Dell's mother stopped him in the hall and, her eyes pixillated, told her son that he was expected at Christmas dinner the next day.

"You sure?"

"Yes."

"But ... father."

"He'll be there, yes, he lives here, too."

"I haven't spoken to him in—"

"That's all right, son. He wants to talk to you. He asked me to make sure you were going to be with us."

Actually, Hosea out at the roadhouse had shot a couple turkeys and there was going to be a big feast there. Dell had even begun anticipating, in the looseness of a holiday and a big meal, seeing if he could move things a little off the all-business footing with Daisy.

"If I have other plans?"

"Your father has instructed me to make sure you will be there." His mother was blinking more than was natural, but her voice was steely. "And you will be there."

"He wants to talk to me?"

"I think it has to do with his business. But I don't meddle. You'll find out tomorrow."

Dell was on his way back to Bearcat's, wondering about his father. They'd hardly spoken in the last couple of years, since Dell had graduated high school. As Dell had told Daisy, when his football success didn't seem to make any difference with his father, and Dell had taken up the saxophone in earnest, well, there didn't seem to be anything much to say.

If there ever had been. Even when they were the model family, his father was off most every night on what his mother called "bizness negotiations," even all through World War II when his friend's fathers had gone off to fight. Seems his father had something wrong with his eyes, or maybe it was his leg; occasionally in public Dell saw him limp. There were also, evidently, a lot of sudden war widows with farms and no way to run them, and Ransom Dellaplane was there to help.

It was a public service, the least he could do; and nobody said too much when the deed ended up in his back pocket. One farm led to another, and of course there were right-of-way concerns, but Dellaplane could make problems go away just like *that!* Pretty soon he owned huge tracts of land; and when the soldiers who hadn't died flooded home, they needed places to live, and Memphis was ready to grow, and thank God there was a man with the smarts to have everything in place to further this growth and provide these men with homes to raise their families in. Or so the Chamber of Commerce put it in a tribute Dell had been forced to attend while still in short pants. His father, it turned out, "was a man of singular vision." As the toastmaster said, "Many men showed us how to win the war; it is the rare man like Ransom Dellaplane who has showed us how to win the peace."

Both Dell and his older brother, Jason, hadn't seen too much of their father, but when they did, at least it was special. What Dell most remembered was how he'd wait up for his father most evenings, propped up in his bed, Jason sleeping soundly in the same room, and finally the front door would open and Dell would hear his father's heels clatter along the wood floor his mother would spend much of her time polishing. It wasn't that fancy a home they were in then, but it sparkled, and when his father wasn't out on business, the family would gather round the big, black Philco radio and listen to favorite shows like *The Shadow* and *Amos and Andy*.

Dell, his breath hushed, would reach over and shake Jason, who'd raise his head and give his brother a dirty look—though he never went right back to sleep. Both boys would be nearly holding their breath as the steps got closer to their bedroom door. Dell knew exactly how long it would take, and would count, silently, the seconds till his father would be there. One, two, three, four … he should be there by five. And there he was, without fail, the handsome, cigar-smoke-smelling, still black-haired man slipping the door open a crack and leaning in and saying, softly, "How're the little tigers tonight?"

And Jason, then Dell, would cry, "Great, Pops."

The Dellaplanes moved when Dell was seven. The new house was a mansion, with two stories, a white portico out front, and acres of land. Jason and Dell each got their own bedrooms, and it was after that that the nocturnal visits stopped. They had a butler now, and when the front door opened, Dell, who kept himself awake, heard Samson say, "Evening, Mr. Dellaplane," and then his father's heels clattering up the white-marble staircase. His counting wouldn't begin until he heard the footfalls leave the noisy marble and hit the carpet in the hallway. In this house it took his father seven seconds to get to his door, six … seven … eight … nine. The door next to him would open, and his father would call out, "Jason, you sleepy tiger, how're you tonight?"

Dell never knew what he'd done. But as he held his breath waiting for his father to stop for him, the younger boy began to wish he could hold his breath so long he would simply die.

After Jason did die, in Korea, when Dell was fourteen, the younger son tried to believe that there was something other than contempt in the way his father treated him. Even after Dell's glory season of high school football he was never sure. But now that he'd chosen not to go to Ole Miss, well, it was just a good thing the estate was big enough that Dell could move to the quarters above the carriage shed a quarter of a mile away.

Though their paths rarely crossed, when they did, Dell could see a look in his father's eyes that said, simply, I'm a paragon of forbearance to let this son of mine still dwell on my property.

Dell chose not to give words to the look in his own eyes.

Thinking about it now, Dell realized they hadn't actually had a full conversation in over a year. He wondered what it could be. The roadhouse? But did his father really know about that?

His father was civil through cocktails, even told a couple stiff, unfunny jokes as they sat down to dinner, and kept his own counsel through the meal. Of course, there were twenty people there, mostly business and political cronies of his father's. But when the last plate had been swept from the table and the gentlemen were adjourning to the smoking room, his father said, "Now, Dell," and led him into his oak-lined office.

He pointed Dell to a heavy, leather-covered armchair, and the son, feeling more of his father's power than he wanted to, sat right down. He sat on his hands, feeling them tense underneath him and wanting to make sure he kept them under control. Ransom Dellaplane had grown a puffed-back mane of silver hair; his nose had turned red, and his lips were thicker than they'd been, though still dark and unrevealing. The rich man perched himself on the edge of his large, hand-tooled desk.

"I'm not going to beat around the bush, son. I know exactly what you've been up to, and I've been remarkably tolerant, if I do say so myself." Dellaplane paused, pulled a cigar from a humidor, and looked down its long expanse. He flourished forth a small knife from his pocket and flicked a switch on it, and a three-inch blade popped out. His father blithely clipped off the end of the cigar.

"You're listening to me?" he said.

Dell gave a tight nod.

"Good. Now I have a very simple proposition. I know you've become involved in, well, in a place outside of town I wouldn't dignify by mentioning normally. You do know that your presence out there is bringing embarrassment to the family—"

That was it, the roadhouse. Dell was startled. He understood in a second that it was his own illusion that his father was totally ignoring him, letting him go his own way; and a quick flame of anger ran up both his cheeks. After all his father's seeming indifference, he was spying on his son as a matter of course.

"How do you know that?" Dell said softly.

His father paused for just a second, and Dell could see the words, "What was that?" form on his lips, but instead his father just held up his cigar and gave it a contemptuous flourish.

"But that's not why we're here, son. It's hard to remember a time when you weren't, well—"

Dell felt his hands clench; yes, he was right to be sitting on them. The word *embarrassment* was echoing in his head. His father took one last cool look at the tobacco roll, then pulled out a silver lighter and fired up the cigar's tip. Puff, puff, and it glowed brilliant red in the crepuscular den. Dell turned his head away, but the acrid smoke caught him anyway and made his throat burn.

"We're here to talk about how you can help me."

Dell got out a tight shake of his head, leaned forward. He was hearing a ringing in his ears. "There's nothing I can do to—" he started to say, but up went the cigar's tip, waving Dell back into the chair.

"*Son.*" A tight, crisp word devoid of any emotion. Ransom took another carefree puff; in all this he seemed to be enjoying himself. "I'm according you the honor, *son*, of proposing a business arrangement to you. I hear you've been making some business deals of your own—"

Under his breath Dell said only to himself, *None of your fucking business.*

"Well," his father swept right on, "this will be a whole different arrangement—between gentlemen." Ransom's pink face crinkled with a kind of pleasure. "Indeed, the terms to you will be rather fair, if I do say so." A swift, slicing motion with his ring-bedizened right hand, inexplicable until his next sentence came out. "I will not be known," he said sonorously, "as someone who scalps his only son, no matter how wayward."

Dell heard this as a direct attack. It was harder not to speak now, but he didn't want to dignify his father's pompous approach. Instead he was thinking of all those nights waiting alone in his bed, this now jolly-seeming man simply walking past his room.

Dellaplane's mirth increased, but Dell was so deep into his angry memories that he hardly heard him. "One could even say I've already done things right. I mean, isn't it a remarkable coincidence in my favor to have you where you are? Especially since I've decided I have to proceed, um, quietly."

What was that? *Where you are?* Meaning…?

"I can see you looking curious. O.K., O.K., here's what I'm proposing," Ransom said, puffing now on the cigar, sending blue-white miniclouds to the ceiling. "If you agree to help me, not only will I let you continue to live on here in the carriage house—a comfort that will, of course, be in jeopardy if you refuse—but I'll add a significant amount of funds to the trust we set up for you when you were born. And these monies—significant monies—will be *immediately* available. To help launch you in a business of your own, say. A music establishment that will be all yours. Maybe even enough money to start your own record company—"

He's threatening me, Dell heard through the ringing in

his ears. He's trying to bribe me. The hot anger on his cheeks spread, down his neck, up his forehead till his scalp seemed to be burning. How fucking dare him?

Right then Dell knew he should simply stand up and storm off. The tight anger in his hands radiated through him. But ... this was his father! There was some vestige of Honor Him down there, and yet there was this searing rage running through him, too; and now these loud, conflicting voices were clanging through the ringing in his head: *What's wrong with you? Just get up and go*, and then, *Or at least tell him to take his bribery and shove it*, and then, smaller but knife sharp, a voice whispering, *Daddy, Daddy, why didn't you ever love me like you did Jason? ...*

All these voices rang out amidst the raging anger, and later when Dell was dismissed by his father and walked out so furious yet stunned that he knew he wasn't seeing straight, he realized he didn't actually know what his father's proposal had been. He only hoped that his father had taken his furious, distracted silence as refusal ... though the more he thought about it, he simply didn't give a flying fuck what his old man thought.

* * * * *

SHE WAS IN LOVE, and the power of her love scared her. Well, the object of her love scared her a little, too, but how could she not be absolutely gaga? Except that it wasn't a man, it was a car. Not just any car, of course, but her pink Cadillac.

When she wasn't waitressing or at the roadhouse, she spent far too much time just driving around in it, through the streets of Memphis, down Poplar to Third, then back out Union, all the while tooling slow, loving the way people would stop on the sidewalk and gawk at her; and then out into the countryside, where she could jam the pedal to the floor and feel the beast inside it leap down the road. More than the actual car itself, Daisy loved more and more the *idea* of it—the idea of her, Daisy Holliday from Bent Knee, Kentucky, owning and being known in and talking to and dreaming out her life inside her pink Cadillac.

There was something magical about it, no question. Here she was, this backwoods, hick girl, and the car made her so ... glamorous. No other word for it. Even though she was all unconfidence and nervous newness to Memphis and to singing seriously, in the pink Cadillac not a trace of anxiety was betrayed.

Indeed, one afternoon, after a rehearsal—and with the opening of Dell's Pink Cadillac Club less than a week away—Hosea was pulling out of the parking lot in Bearcat's truck, on his way to the dump, and he grazed her bumper.

Daisy flew out of the Cadillac.

"Look at this," she cried, pointing at the chrome bumper and seeing the way the scratch broke up her reflection. Then her voice went up five or six notes. "I don't know what I'm doin' out at this sorry place. You all ain't got no class."

Dell had walked over to look down at the bumper. "Don't *have any* class," he said, a joke to try to lighten things.

"No, *no class*!"

"You don't really mean that." He realized she was serious.

"Goddamn right I do." Daisy started marching around the pink Cadillac, her hands flying every which way. "Here I am, giving my whole life over to y'all, and what do I get? People all the time sniping at me, making me feel I don't fit, they don't know what I'm doin' here even when I'm saving their sorry asses." She stomped a bit more. "O.K., O.K., so I don't get no respect? I can live with that. But then they bang up my goddamn *car*!"

Hosea, who'd gotten right out of the truck, tried to say he was sorry, but Daisy wouldn't even acknowledge him.

"Daze, it was an accident," Dell said, moving in and looking at the bumper. "And you can hardly see anything." He rubbed the dinged spot with a wet finger. "Little silver paint, never know it happened at all."

"I'm gonna know." She glared all around her, mostly at the hangers-on now come out of the roadhouse. "Gonna know what you all think of me. Gonna know just how well you know the meaning of the word *respect*."

"Daisy, what're you—" Dell started to say, but right then the Bearcat banged out of the roadhouse, coming over and interposing his large body. He gave Daisy a long look, but when he spoke, it was to Dell.

"Daisy's just a little nervous," he said, "she got a big debut in a few days. I think we're gonna let her cool down some."

"Nothin' wrong with me!"

"Now, now. Nobody meant nothin' by this. It *was* just an accident."

Bearcat spoke with such authority that Daisy didn't say a thing, just stood there stamping her foot.

"Sweetheart," he went on, "why don't you take your car here out for a drive? Really, nothin' wrong with it at all. And that always settles you."

Daisy looked over at Bearcat, sudden, as if she weren't sure exactly where she was for a second. She blushed, feeling like a strange fever had broken. Without another word she hopped in her car and peeled out of the parking lot.

And the driving did its job. It took her ten, fifteen minutes, but then the way the car eased through the curves then barreled full force down the straightaways ... it was sunset now, and she found herself headed west, into the sun, rolling through some sorry cotton fields, the sun a huge gold ball of promise in front of her, streaming along in her beautiful pink car, bearing down on the sun, heading into it, devil take heed, flooring the gas pedal, almost lifting now, hotter and faster and more glorious ... until she and the car flew along so perfectly she knew there was no way anything could ever get in her way and stop her.

* * * * *

LATER THAT AFTERNOON Daisy came back, ashamed and apologetic. Dell was at his parents', Sonesta was at church; it was just Bearcat and some of his brood hanging round the place.

"Where is everybody?" she asked, after pulling into the lot and carefully parking the pink Cadillac.

"Off," Bearcat said. He was sitting on the porch, watching the sun set over the moss trees.

"Oh!" Daisy said. She squinched up her cute face, looked disappointed.

"You have something you want to tell us?"

"Like what?"

"Like—" Bearcat went and waved open his huge hands.

Daisy was about five feet away from him, standing there with her legs crossed, a blush creeping up on her face.

"Like I'm ... sorry."

"Like, that would do, for a start."

"Does Dell hate me?"

"Dell doesn't have it in 'im to hate you."

"And you?" Daisy's blush spread. She kept standing there, just a few feet in front of the Bearcat.

Bearcat laughed. "Hell, I'm the one made the excuse for you. Remember?"

"Yeah, thanks. I was—I don't know. All crazy there for a second." Daisy, seeming to be aware of her blush, glanced down.

"Here, c'mon, have a seat," Bearcat said. "Let's have us a talk."

Daisy came up and without brushing away any of the

dust and soot sat right down on the porch step next to Bearcat.

"I've been noticin'," he said when she was settled.

"Yeah?"

Bearcat cleared his throat, the sound just like a cement mixer. Then his voice got serious. "You know, you got it—got the talent good—and you're comin' right along, with the electricity behind you and all." He stretched out his hands, cracked his knuckles. "But I also can read your mind."

"Yeah?" Daisy smiled, a little saucily in spite of herself.

"Yeah. You're gettin'—gettin' some ahead of yourself."

"Like what?"

"Like expecting it's all gonna turn over and happen like *that*."

Daisy was silent.

"You know, you gotta love it, you gotta make it the thing you do no matter whether you goin' up or you goin' down."

"No problem with that."

Bearcat looked at her. She was a beautiful young girl, no question. He loved the way she lit up everything around her, including his old bones.

"You say that a little too ... easy."

Daisy went to protest, but Bearcat held up his hand and stopped her.

"I know you do love the singin', the reaching down inside you and being 'stonished with what pops up, yeah, I knows that." He threw a long eye at her. "But what I don't know's how you gonna do when no one else knows it."

"But nobody else knew it my whole life, 'cept for Madame Grosgreen, till now. And I really do love y'all, and not just 'cuz you love my singing. Means the world to me."

"But you ain't been tested yet," Bearcat said. "Tha's all I'm saying. Nobody in this business ain't had to pay their dues somehow."

Daisy leaned back, let a playful look into her eyes.

"What 'bout that boy gave me the Cadillac? It wasn't two years after he made his first record, he's *givin'* 'em away!"

"That Elvis was comin' out to see me since he was fourteen. Been hangin' round Beale Street soaking everything up. Been getting razzed and spit on in his high school 'cuz he dressed funny. You ask Sonesta if Elvis didn't come out here bawling his boy tears day after day there."

Daisy suddenly got feisty. "Yeah, and I didn't take my daddy's paddle on my rear end 'cuz I was spending time over at Madame Grosgreen's learning everything I could? I didn't basically get run out of town, and not even my fault?"

"Hey, I'm just cautionin' you," Bearcat said. He looked surprised that Daisy had torn into him like this.

"And I—I appreciate it," she said, clearly trying to cool things back down. "I'm out here to learn, for sure. And I'm learnin' lots." She stood up, took a couple steps back. "But couple days from now, it's gonna be me up there—up there all alone. Winning over a crowd of people ain't even gonna know what they're seein'. You don't figure I gotta do whatever I can to get past that?"

"And that's all, huh?"

"What else is there?"

Bearcat shrugged. But what he knew was that he didn't see any difference in the light that fired up Daisy Holliday's eyes. The same light he'd been watching now for weeks, the same one that flared at all of them when the bumper was scratched. It was a light he knew well, because it was the same light he'd had when he started out. The light trained dead-ahead on fame and glory. That light so focused it don't always see what's sneaking up on it till it's too late.

* * * * *

THERE WAS AN INVITATION in the letter to the New Year's Eve opening of something called the Pink Cadillac Club, where, Dell had written—and Cuth even on paper could hear his voice, way too much the proud rooster—the blonde chickie on the pale Cadillac was going to be singing; and when he'd gotten through Christmas, then cleared things away, Cuth Starks decided to head to Memphis a few days early, see his parents, catch up on the old neighborhood. Because he wanted time to think, he set out driving all night in his black Cadillac to get there.

All the way he was thinking about Dellaplane. Once that boy had been a good buddy, when his family had moved in a few houses down when he and Dell were seven, and they'd spent hours bulldozing dirt and playing tag or stick baseball. But as they got bigger, Dell got into a kind of roughhousing Cuth didn't really care for, and he spent less time with Dell; which Dell hardly seemed to mind, making new friends, then going on to high school and hanging with cliques that Cuth wasn't invited into.

Tight little groups of nose-in-the-air kids that Cuth knew he was easily superior to. He didn't know why they didn't like him; assumed it was because he had better manners, was more sensitive, quieter, simply more refined. (Cuth's hero even then was the movie star George Sanders.)

Dell (for reasons Cuth never bothered to know) went out for football, and though Cuth didn't really like the sport much, he had to say that, hey, Cuth Starks had his own natural athletic grace—he was pretty damn graceful at everything—and when Dell made the team, it was a kind of jealous envy that made Cuth try out, too.

That's when everything came to a head. They were runners, and it was natural for both to go out for halfback. Their coach was a beefy guy named Swanger, and Coach Swanger seemed to love pitting the two of them against each other. He kept switching the criteria for the job. First it was how fast a forty—Cuth took Dell by a few seconds. And danced around, rubbing it in like acid. But Coach wasn't through. How far could they push the tackle dummy sled? How many catches in a row could they make at twenty-five yards? Then, how early would they show up on a Saturday to help him with yard work? The position seesawed back and forth, each the more fired up when the other was given the nod. The coach kept saying their competitive fire fueled the rest of the team. (What neither of the boys knew was that that was just pretext; what Coach told his friends was that it simply did his heart good to see young bucks like these tangle horns.)

Cuth won the first-game position by a hair but in the game didn't do anything spectacular. Coach Swanger put Dell in the next game, and he rushed for 138 yards and made two TDs. Then he got even better. Dell held the position for the rest of the season, as well as Cuth's smoldering enmity.

And now the ol' boy was reaching out to Cuth for help. Was Dell Dellaplane so obtuse he didn't know how Cuth felt about him? High school wasn't that far back, but much had changed. Cuth, feeling a kind of glorious release, graduated and found that with his father's money he no longer had to conform to the silly dictates of everyone's coarse expectations. What did Cuth want to do? Music seemed to offer the most ... freedom. Through his father, but then, of course, through his own damn good ears, he had started Old Gold Records and made a success of it. You could say he was just farm league down there in Nashville, but he'd pulled up a handful of local hits and had even sent a couple to the majors in New York. And since Sam Phillips had taken Southern music national, the big boys like Finkelstein were calling all the time.

And now Dell Dellaplane wanted something from him. *Hah!* Cuth didn't know much about what Dellaplane was doing these days; just that he'd dropped out of Ole Miss and moved back home. The music angle surprised him, though he remembered Dell playing saxophone in the school band. He was sort of glad that Dell's football hadn't gone anywhere. But his music?

Well, he sure wasn't driving the all-nighter to Memphis to help out ol' Dell Dellaplane. No, it was the girl on the Cadillac. Back in high school, when he didn't understand himself quite so well, there'd been a chick named Mindy Phillips (second cousin of Sam's), who Cuth had had a huge, dreamy crush on. He'd nursed the crush from afar through his sophomore year—he'd had a photographer blow up her freshman yearbook photo, and he kept it over his bed, along with the pictures of some of his musical heroes, like Nat King Cole, Ray Price, and Johnny Mathis—but after making the football team, he was finally ready to make his move. The funny thing was how tongue-tied he was around her—around all girls. He simply seemed to expect that they'd see how wonderful he was, and if they didn't, he wasn't sure what to say or do next.

But with Mindy Phillips ... well, he'd asked her out for a soda after school. Sorry, she said blithely, I'd love to, but, you know, I have a date with Dell Dellaplane.

Cuth hadn't even known they were together; actually, didn't think they were more than a casual thing. Thinking about it now, he was certain that Dell never went out more than a couple times with Mindy Phillips. Cuth would bet Dell probably wouldn't even remember her. But, curiously, Mindy Phillips was the spitting image of the girl on the pink Cadillac. Cuth called up a memory of that dreamy picture of Mindy up on his wall next to Nat King and Johnny. The two girls had the same fly-away blonde hair, heart-shaped faces, and, at least in the Cadillac picture, a long damn pair of colt legs.

The letter said her name was Daisy Holliday. After seeing the picture, Cuth had listened three times to the acetate Dell had enclosed. Listened close. It still sounded like nigger music to him, and no way was he going to walk *that* road, but he also heard something pure and mountain-runnel clear in her voice—a tone that actually made hairs on the back of his neck dance—a voice that certainly with the right coaching could sing anything.

And who better to coach her: A weasel like Dell Dellaplane or the suave owner of his own Nashville record label; a man more than ready to put this pie-tin town behind him and take the North by storm?

* * * * *

THE LEATHER CHAIRS were blocky, the oak table long, the air smoky, the ashtrays full with half-inch blocks of wispy gray ash. There were three men in the room, looking down at a model landscape as detailed with bushes, shrubs, winding roads, and tiny houses as a classic HO-gauge train set.

The tallest man, with thick silver hair and a long, aquiline nose, held a stick pointer, tapping its rubber tip at a place where two roads intersected, and a flood of tiny Monopoly-like houses rose away.

"What about the other route?" a younger man, with short black hair and a fine suit, said. He had his own pointer, and he moved it half a foot away. "We could get that property a lot easier."

"Easier 'cause it's a goddamn swamp, Tom," the third man, named Jim Tucker, said. He was older, with a wide, red face and a belly hanging over his tailored pants. "Ransom, what was the figure on that? Six million dollars to drain the goddamn thing?"

The tall man nodded.

"And we just need that one property?" Jim Tucker pushed away the pointer in Tom McNair's hand. "That's the key one left, right, Ransom?"

The tall man nodded again. Kept tapping the first intersection.

"I have to say, I'm surprised we don't have it yet," Tucker said. "It's just a bunch of niggers, right?"

Ransom Dellaplane nodded. "I'm a little surprised, too."

Tom McNair awkwardly twisted his pointer in his hands, then tapped its tip against the floor. He gave Jim Tucker a sideways look.

"Didn't you have us using the sheriff, Jim?" McNair said. "Wasn't that your idea? How'd that work out?"

Dellaplane in effect stepped between his two underlings. "Sheriff said he'd have things under control by now, but he hasn't." He looked from Tucker to McNair. "I've come up with another way."

There was a long pause, then finally the red-faced Tucker said, "Your son?"

The stick in Dellaplane's hands fluttered. "You know about that?"

Tucker glanced at Tom McNair, who kept a poker face.

"It has gotten around, Ransom," Tucker said. "People are talking."

The tall man was silent for a long moment.

"Do we trust him?" McNair finally said. He had a slim mustache and it rose in a way that accented the question.

"He is my son—"

"Yes, but—"

"Oh, boys, don't worry so. It's just a nigger. If my son can't get him to dance—" Dellaplane held that thought.

"We have other ways," Tucker said, stepping in front of McNair to finish Dellaplane's sentence. There was something beady and overzealous in his eyes.

"Of course we have other ways." Dellaplane pursed his silver eyebrows, looked from one man to the other. "But don't you think it would be better if Dell did it all for us?"

* * * * *

THEY WERE DOWN to three days before the New Year's Eve opening, then two, then one, Bearcat an on-and-off sort of crew boss, taking all of his brethren, the slick ones, Diamondback and Walter, and the farm boys, Slappy, Hosea, and Scruffy, and getting them all mops and buckets and paint brushes and setting them to work in earnest. Anyone who complained, anyone with doubts—they fell into line under the lash of his words, the urgency in his eyes. Dell was busy in his own regard, and everything he was doing—Bearcat was eagle-eyeing him throughout—seemed to help the road-house. He was contacting the local radio stations and rehearsing the band; and then he was spending money, buying paint and supplies, printing up cards and fliers. His final act was to call in a sign company. In the early evening dusk that December 31 he and Daisy (who'd fully apologized to Dell for the other day) and some of the rest of the crew gathered out in the parking lot when Salt threw the switch, and there above them, letters, flowing along the unmistakable silhouette of a long, sleek car, bright in neon pink, read out PINK CADILLAC CLUB. They couldn't help themselves: Everyone applauded wildly.

On the porch Bearcat, who knew nothing about Snake Eyes and the loan—indeed, had only his own speculations as to where Dell's money was coming from—sat quietly looking on.

He was keeping to himself more and more. No word against Dell's transformation came from his lips, but there was something different about the great man. He was edgier, yet definitely quieter, more diffident, less of a whirligig presence. He looked to be keeping his own counsel, and, oddly, his silence made him seem larger, more of the man-beast than even before. It was something to do with his aura; and it was not uncommon for one of the hangers-on to fly right into him and then go bouncing off as they were scurrying about with their paint cans. It was like Bearcat was both more there, yet also less so, and it was a curiosity to all.

Later that night, Sonesta came in. She hadn't been around much the last few weeks, spending more time at her church in town, and with her two girlfriends. Tonight, though, she was alone.

Daisy was rehearsing with the band. She'd picked up confidence enough that if not running the show, she was at least making sure the band was behind her the way she felt most comfortable. It hadn't taken them long under Dell's tutelage to get that jumpy-thumpy rock 'n' roll backbeat going, and along with *Pink Cadillac*, they had a couple other new songs, as well as a whole host of covers of the day like *Tutti Frutti*, *Tweedledee*, and *Shake Rattle and Roll*. Bearcat blew harp from time to time, but often just looked on from the floor, no expression anyone could read on his stolid face. And Daisy cut her looks directly back at Sticks and Thumper now.

Daisy was still on stage, just finished with a singularly convincing version of *Roll With Me Henry*, when Sonesta came through the door. She hadn't been home since Christmas, a particularly ambiguous affair.

"Well, *now* look what the cat's dragged in," Bearcat said, rising from where he'd been sitting in the shadows. "Where you been, woman? You still having it off with that slim new preacher in town?" His voice was sharp and bellowing, and everyone stopped what they were doing and looked at him and his former star.

Sonesta was wearing a black dress with a tight white collar high up as it could go, and a hem that knocked about her ankles. She had an old rabbit fur stole wrapped around her to ward off the post-Christmas chill in the air.

"You ain't been home for five days," Bearcat went on. "Gonna 'spect me an explanation."

Sonesta looked wary. "I just gotta get me something from upstairs."

She headed toward the staircase, but Bearcat was over on her in a second.

"What you mean, get you something?"

"I mean just that, Jackson."

"You mean, you movin' out?"

"I got me some work—some honest work."

"What you mean, *work*?" The Bearcat's voice was so loud and sharp it near tore the new paint off the walls.

"I mean an honest job," Sonesta said. She stood there, and she looked a sad picture. Her shoulders were drooping, and she quick dabbed a kerchief at her eyes. "I mean, I'm a maid now, working at the Peabody."

"You what?"

"Working honest. Getting me a room there, too."

"And you just—" Bearcat was bellowing. "You just come in here like this and tell me this, and that's that, and you're gonna be off, and that's all this Bearcat gets to know?"

"I was gonna—"

Bearcat reached out and slapped her. It wasn't hard, but it was loud and resounded through the roadhouse.

Sonesta whirled on him, her face reddening.

"It's not the same out here, Jackson, you can't see it, but I can. This place is going to hell in a handbasket, and you the big bull moose in the caboose—"

Another slap. This one Sonesta half saw coming and pulled back, the palm of Bearcat's fist barely grazing her. She was florid. She stepped right into him and shouted, "You ain't gonna pull that shit on me no more, I don't *need* you."

"You can't—"

"Oh yes I can, Jackson. I can say my mind. You runnin' this place pucker-lips into white-boy heaven, but you can't see the coon for the tree. The whole firmament's gonna come down on you."

Then his fury broke. He started out cuffing her, right hand, left hand, right hand, but then his slaps turned to blows.

Sonesta threw her hands over her head, scrunched down. She was crying now, everyone could hear it.

Dell and Daisy, at the same moment, leaped off the stage and ran to Bearcat and Sonesta. Dell cried, "Bearcat, stop hitting her!" Daisy, whose angle was better, jumped at him and tried to grab his arm. The first time she missed, but the next she got a good grip and held tight. He lifted her off the floor about four inches as he swept his hand forward. But Daisy kept him from touching the older woman.

"Bearcat, let her go this second," Daisy cried. "She doesn't mean anything. She's—"

Dell was close enough now that he could grab Bearcat's hand and pull it off of Daisy. Sonesta still cowered in front of him, but Daisy saw her look longingly up the stairs, and Daisy read her mind. Though with her eyes Daisy was saying that Sonesta should just skeedaddle this second, she was also gesturing up the stairs to make it clear to the older woman that she'd get her belongings later and take them into town. Sonesta saw the promise and her eyes lit quickly with thanks.

Bearcat shook off Dell, too, but there was a new look in his eyes, a trace of embarrassment and shame behind the fury, and he took a step back from Sonesta. He had never hit her before that anyone but his minions were there to watch him, and it confused him having the two white kids there. At that moment it was clear the fight was out of him.

Sonesta wasted no time getting out of there anyway. But not before she stopped at the doorway, tears gleaming down her cheeks, and called back, "You're goin' down the wrong, wrong road, Mister Man. You don't know what they're sayin' 'bout you in town, but you gonna find out. And I ain't gonna be doin' nothin' but cryin' for you when that happens." She was sobbing now. "Cryin' for us all."

She slammed the door behind her.

A huge silence filled the roadhouse, everyone stiff, staring mostly into the distance, not at all looking at anyone else. Finally, after a couple awkward coughs, Bearcat strode to the stage and tried to get the rehearsal going again. It was clear nobody could get their heart into it; the beat was sluggish, the players distracted. Bearcat himself looked as if his thoughts were a thousand miles away.

Dell had taken his place on the bandstand but couldn't bring himself to actually blow any notes. Bearcat gave him a dark look, but it was Daisy who was the real trouble. She stood rigid, her arms pushed into her side, her fists tight in front of her chest. And she wouldn't sing.

"Come on," the big man said. "That's your cue."

She looked both fragile and furious.

"Sticks."

The drummer tapped out a wan beat.

"*Sticks!*"

Something was building in Daisy, and finally it blew. She walked over to the big man and asked point blank, "Why'd you hit her?"

Bearcat shook his head, like he wasn't sure what he was hearing. Daisy was staring straight at him, as if she could bore the words out of him. Finally, Bearcat fixed a look on her. "That's 'tween me and her."

"No it isn't."

"Yes it is." He was turning a harmonica over and over in his meaty hands. "It's all 'tween me and her."

Bearcat was looking straight ahead, and it was clear he wasn't going to say anything more on the subject. Instead, he demanded, "Are we going to rehearse now?"

"Not me," Daisy said, stepping down from the bandstand.

"Daze—" Dell went.

She shot him a look.

The Bearcat was looking shaken, confused . . . and older than they'd ever seen him. He drew in a deep, rattling breath. "If we ain't gonna work, I'm going to bed."

"Tomorrow we go on," Dell said, almost plaintively. "Tomorrow this place's gonna be filled with people—" He looked out into the bare roadhouse as if he were already imagining it filled, with an audience demanding and vocal, staring right up at them all.

Daisy went over and gently took his hand.

"It's enough," she said. She turned to the players and added, "O.K., guys, we're going to kill 'em tomorrow, but that's it for now."

There was visible, noisy relief among Thumper, Sticks, and Clay. They packed up quick and got out of there. Bearcat watched them go, then said, not really to anyone, "Good night." Then he lumbered to the stairs, and gave a long look at them—a long, pausing, wondering gaze—before he pulled his bones up them and disappeared.

Dell and Daisy were alone. The night was suddenly all around them, crickets clattering in the distance, a silver-gray moon rising through an upper window.

Daisy saw the look in Dell's eyes and said, "I had to say it."

He took a long moment before answering, "I know. I just don't know if it does any good."

"Why not?"

"Meddling."

"Oh, no," she said. "He smacked her. We all heard it. And she was crying—"

"I know," Dell said. He looked as if he didn't want to be having this conversation. "And we stopped it. Sonesta got out of here safe."

"So—"

"So, it's still between them, isn't it?" Dell's voice was rising a little. "I just don't—"

"I won't stand for that," Daisy said. She spoke with absolute conviction. "I just *won't*."

Dell looked at her, silent for a moment, then said, "All right."

"Then—"

"But we still have to go on tomorrow night. With Bearcat. And with you. And me—"

Daisy smiled at that. "I know we're going to knock 'em wild."

Dell nodded. "All I was saying is, the more we rehearse the better."

"But we have it down. We nailed it with the record. And it's just gotten better—"

It was right then that they both realized she was still holding Dell's hand. It wasn't much of a grip, and not at all caressing, but her fingers were laid across his, and the heat of her palm was now vivid to him.

Involuntarily, he pulled his hand away.

She gave him a curious look, but when Dell started to say something, she went, "Shhhhhh." She took a suddenly free finger and put it to her lips. She was looking Dell straight in the eyes. Then she took the finger from her lips and placed it back on his.

This time he didn't flinch. Instead he took her hand and led her over to one of the wooden tables. They sat across from each other, a stretch of wood between them, a left-behind bottle of hootch standing sentry between them.

"Do you realize," Daisy said in a whole new tone, "this is the first time we've been together alone since ... since that night by the river?"

"I know," Dell said after a moment. "We've been so busy—"

"Good busy, though, right?"

Instead of answering Daisy right away, Dell got up and fetched a glass from the bar, then picked up the bottle.

"This isn't to try to get me drunk now, is it, Mr. Della-plane?" Daisy said with a fey laugh.

Dell gave her a long look, then tipped his head at the single glass he'd brought, meaning, This is for me.

Daisy looked around and saw a used glass sitting on the next table over. She leaned there and got it.

"Here," she said, taking the near-empty glass, tipping

the dribbles that were left on the floor, then running the bottom of her blouse around the edges. She pushed forward the glass. "Why don't you pour me one."

Dell cocked an eyebrow. "You ever had this before?"

"Oh, sure, lots of times."

"Yeah?"

"Yeah, I mean, my daddy, he knew his way round a bottle."

Dell didn't believe for a minute she knew anything about drinking, but he poured Bearcat's glass full. Something about her sudden launch into flirtatiousness, if that's what it was, well, it put a sharper edge on him.

Daisy took the bootleg, gave it a long look. She squinched up her face, then held her nose and threw down a gulp of the firewater. And spit it right up. It went spraying across the table.

"Oh, my God!" Daisy said. "Sorry. Gee whiz, how embarrassing." She got up and dug out a rag from behind the bar, then swabbed the chipped table down.

When she was settled, Dell sipped tentatively at his own bootleg, letting the fiery liquid seep down his throat. In truth he too almost never drank, but it was going to be a badge of honor not to let Daisy see that; to imbibe as if he were putting back shots with someone as experienced as his old man.

The booze burned, and when it hit his stomach, made him flinch slightly, but he was pretty sure he squelched any evidence of gagging.

Daisy thought not. "Hah!" she cried. "Look at you."

"Look at me what?"

"You're turning red!" She laughed. "Mr. Suave and Sophisticated, huh? You think we didn't get Clark Gable movies in Bent Knee? We got 'em. Clark Gable never drank pussy-foot like that!"

Dell gave her a wicked eye, then picked up the glass of booze and threw down a mighty swallow. And held on, even as backyard-still firewater went swirling and tilting through him. Like being on a boat he thought, just balance and ride it out. He was surprised, though, when a burp popped out. But ... a manly burp.

"O.K.," Daisy said, "better."

Dell winked at her.

"Oh, now look at him, so grown up, so—"

"Shhhhh," he went, and like lighting got up and went around the table and kissed her.

"Whoa!" finally came out of her, but not until she'd held his kiss for a mindlessly long time.

Dell, standing half bent over, sort of awkward above her, sidled back to his own chair.

"You're just gonna leave it at that?" she said.

Dell thought about that for a moment, then said, "Come here." He pushed his chair back from the table and gave his upper thighs a pat.

To Daisy's credit she didn't hesitate. Walked around the table and lowered herself as politely and daintily as possible onto his lap.

He turned her to him, a wide smile of a kind of victory on his face. Then he brought her head forward until their lips met. He kissed her straight on, and she kissed him straight on back, and it wasn't more than a few seconds before their breaths were pulsing loud and fast.

Finally, Dell pulled away. He gave her a big, serious smile. "Maybe you are right," he said.

"Right?" Slight alarm from Daisy, whose face was still only an inch or two from Dell's. "About what?"

"What you said the other day, you know, to not mix things up right now."

"Dell! What are you—"

"Daisy, I'm *agreeing* with you." Dell had one hand around her waist, the other over her wide shoulders, but the way he held her was suddenly more friendly than romantic.

"We got us plenty of time—*plenty* of time. I think we ought to just focus on the show now. That's the important thing."

"You're gettin' me all confused."

"And that's my whole point, Daze." Dell leaned back even further. "We don't want you confused—or me, either. Bad enough we got this thing going on with Bearcat and Sonesta. But we got to have us all ready for your debut. Can't get anything in the way of that. It's only one day away—"

"Dell, I don't—"

"Listen, I'm the *guy*. If I can put business first—"

Daisy distractedly nodded, but evidently Dell had proved his point. She lifted herself off of him and took a hardback chair from the next table and set it before him. She seated herself on it backward, splay-legged around the seat's ribs, the wooden back like bars between the two of them.

"Listen," he said when she was settled. His tone was noticeably more businesslike. "Did I tell you? I went ahead and sent our record off a few weeks ago to that old friend of mine Cuth Starks. He's got his own record company. I invited him here for New Year's Eve."

Daisy's eyes went wide. "But Bearcat said he didn't want you to—"

"But, Daze, I had to do something."

Daisy took a deep breath. Dell could see the idea growing with her.

"Is he coming?"

"Truth, I haven't heard back, but I got a feeling he's going to be there. Hell, I don't see why not. We were good friends as kids."

"A record man, right in the audience?" she said. She involuntarily rattled the chair from side to side, legs clattering on the wooden floor.

"That is what we want, isn't it?"

Her eyes stayed round. "Gee whiz, me singing for a record man."

There was such youthful enthusiasm in her voice that all the tension just fled the room. Dell's shoulders relaxed. He smiled again.

Now it really did seem all business.

"It's going to happen, Daze."

"You think it?"

"I *know*. It's not only Bearcat's got auguring, I got it, too." Dell winked. "And it's all lined up. Long as we keep our eyes focused—"

"Like we's keeping 'em focused now." Daisy bulged her eyes slightly, like she was making a face.

"Right on it."

"Right on tomorrow night."

"No, look, it's *tonight*," Daisy said. She pointed to a clock above the bar. It read 12:05. She looked at him then, and he couldn't quite read her look. It was both firm yet liquid, closed off from the way it was before yet not without some welcoming. "Gee whiz, it's late. I better get going."

And now Dell surprised himself with a big, gulping swallow. "Seems pretty late to head back—"

"You're saying?"

"You could stay here."

"Oh, I bet I could!" Daisy made a gesture of straightening out her clothes, then gripped the chair back in front of her. "Talk about confusing a girl!"

"No, no, you take Sonesta's room. It's sure she ain't coming back tonight."

"You don't think Bearcat would mind?"

Dell thought about that for a moment. "I think he'd think it was better to have you here all day tomorrow. You did take the day off work, right?"

Daisy nodded, then said softly, "Sonesta Clarke's room." She looked at Dell. "Where do you sleep?"

"Oh, I've been bunkin' behind the bandstand nights I stay here." His eyes gestured in that direction. "Got me a pallet there. No great shakes."

"Sounds pretty uncomfortable."

"And now *you're* saying?"

"Oh, I ain't saying nothing!" Daisy suddenly jumped up, started flapping her hands over her dress like she was brushing brambles off it.

They stood there for a minute, the silence thick around them, then Dell smiled. "Tomorrow—today—it really is a big night." He lifted his right pointer finger, touched his lips, then brushed the tip against Daisy's. "Good night, Daze."

She stood there for a long moment, a sadness on her faintly, like a touch of dew; but then her irrepressible light showed through it. "Good night, Dell," she said. With a flush of enthusiasm, she added something she remembered reading in a magazine about what theater people said to each other, "Break a leg, eh?"

Dell simply smiled and said, "Yeah."

DELL'S FLOOR PALLET was a straw mattress, and though it prickled him terrible through the T-shirt and briefs he slept in, not to mention his bare legs, he'd been there often enough now that it felt far more comfortable than his feather bed at his parents' estate—it felt simply like home.

His hands were behind his head on a moss pillow, and he was staring up into the beams of the roadhouse ceiling, listening to the cicadas singing wildly outside, the chill, late-December wind cracking against the thin-paned windows. He nestled down deeper into the wool blankets he'd brought from home and thought about what had just happened.

In particular, he was thinking about Daisy's enraged, emphatic reaction to Bearcat's striking Sonesta. Now no way would Dell argue for what Bearcat had done, and he didn't have any true understanding even why it had happened—wrote it off to the mysteries of grownups and their relationships—but what held his thoughts was Daisy: What in her past had caused her to react so strongly?

She hadn't said much to him about where she'd come from except for that night by the river, when she'd talked about 'whuppings.' She'd laughed, whistling whatever it meant into the air; but Dell wasn't a fool and tried to imagine what living with her drunk, abusive father might've been like. He did wonder for a second, Was it worse than his own father's perfect disdain? But he wasn't thinking about himself now. He pictured the wild, lovely, excitable young woman. And shuddered at the thought of what might have happened to her before she came into his life.

Dell was young enough, and his dreams in ways even younger, that he quickly envisioned himself as her savior—her knight in shining armor. And would that be what Daisy saw in Dell?

He rolled his head to the side so that he was looking up the stairs, to the living quarters, Sonesta's room, Daisy, asleep ... or not. Had he shown her enough what he felt toward her? Made it clear that he understood, or wanted to understand, what her life was like? He remembered the long kiss when she was in his lap, the simple warmth of her, the way her hair fell tickling over his nose, her eyes wide and amazed when they finally pulled their heads back a few inches. Most of all he remembered the steady way she kissed him, no flirtatiousness then, no games, no half-heartedness or self-consciousness. Instead, simple, steady, firm desire. Though he'd kissed at least dozens, he'd never kissed a girl like that, so much herself—so certain and strong.

The great thing was it didn't scare him at all, because he felt from Daisy all they had together: their song, *Pink Cadillac*, for sure, but more, the way his sax climbed her voice, leading it, but also being lifted by her passion, even as he pushed her into greater exuberance and ferocity.

He felt the strongest wash of desire, stretched and rubbed his legs under the blanket, felt his forehead burning, thinking how close he was to the stairs, and how she was up there, and how maybe she was thinking very similar thoughts, and how much he'd give to know. Could he just go ask her? Have a few more words? He started to rise up under the thin blanket, like a spirit from a woolen bog, his eyes shining, the febrile touch on his fingers ... but—

No, no, it wasn't a good idea, was it? Complicate everything hugely, wouldn't it? And what if she weren't—O.K., he'd been right. Keep the focus on the first public performance. Nail that—nail the music. After that ... anything was possible.

So finally he floated back to his pallet, took a deep breath and blew a silent, protective kiss up to her. Sleep well, Daze, he thought. And let us both trust the music—the music will get us through.

✳ ✳ ✳ ✳ ✳

AFTER THEY'D REHEARSED so much the next morning that Daisy was almost hoarse, Bearcat waved everyone silent and said, "O.K., O.K. let's let it rest. We're on. No problem. Everybody blow off, don't think about nothin', and we'll be seein' you here at eight." Though Dell asked Daisy if she wanted to take a drive, she demurred, remembering her tacit promise to Sonesta after Bearcat had struck her. Besides, she felt she had to be alone before her debut tonight.

She had to sneak up to the second floor to gather up the older singer's things, which weren't many, a little plain jewelry, a few funereal dresses and coarser stockings and underthings than Daisy expected—Daisy wondered where all her show clothes were—as well as her well-worn Bible and a small bottle of John the Conquerer oil. She found a valise in the wardrobe in the small room that passed for a closet and carefully filled it. Then she was off to town in her pink Cadillac.

She had never been to the Peabody Hotel, never been anywhere with valet parking before, and wouldn't give up her car to the uniformed attendant: She parked it herself on the street. She turned a few heads when she went into the plush, plant-lined lobby; made the desk clerk's jaw literally drop when she said she was there not for a room but for Sonesta Clarke.

"We don't have anyone by that name staying here," the baldheaded man said.

"She isn't a guest, she works here."

He pursed his brow. "You mean, that new maid?"

Daisy nodded, and the clerk looked as if it was beyond his comprehension why such a lovely young white woman would be asking for the help. Then a faint light in his murky eyes: "Oh, she was your mammy, right?"

Daisy quickly said, "Yes, sir," and the clerk waved her down the hall to an officious woman with a clipboard who told Daisy that Sonesta Clarke was turning beds, but she had a lunch break coming up in . . . 22 minutes.

Sonesta, when she was called down, seemed surprised to see Daisy. She was wearing an ill-fitting uniform, large on her bosom, pinched around her wide hips, but striped in a pink that actually flattered her black skin.

"Child, what're you doin' here?" The older woman's eyes were wide, maybe lifted in a little comic enhancement for the benefit of the supervisor.

"Miss Sonesta," Daisy said, playing along, "I just came down here to bring you those things you asked about?" She held up the valise.

Sonesta read the scene immediately. "Well, thank you." A turn to the supervisor. "Can I take my lunch break with this young woman?"

The woman glanced at her clipboard, then said, "You have twenty-six minutes. That time is your own, at least here at the Peabody."

"Thank you," Sonesta said in a neutral voice. Then she led Daisy down a hall and into a nondescript room with linoleum floor, a refrigerator, and some knock-about tables. Fortunately, it was empty.

"Well, thank you," the older woman said. "This is a surprise."

"You saw me, didn't you?" Daisy said, taking a seat across from Sonesta. "When you were leaving, after ... after Bearcat, he—"

"He hit me, that's what you're gonna say?"

"I—I couldn't believe it. Dell and I, we did what we could to stop him—"

"You shouldn't've done nothing. Could've got hurt yourselves."

"You think?"

Sonesta was by the refrigerator, which she'd just opened. She reached in and took out a sandwich in wax paper.

"You don't mind if I eat while we sit?"

Daisy shook her head, fine.

Sonesta took a few bites of the sandwich. Daisy could see it was peanut butter and grape jelly. The older singer looked tired to Daisy, a little worn out. It was in the way her shoulders sagged, her jaw muscles slowly chewed over the sticky sandwich. After a few moments of silent eating, a thick purple glob stuck on the corner of Sonesta's mouth. Daisy debated whether to say anything, but finally did.

"Thank you," Sonesta said. She reached up and with a long finger spiked away the stray jelly. These were the first words in over a minute, and they emboldened Daisy to pick up her earlier question.

"Would he, do you think, I mean, would he really have—"

"Hurt you?" Sonesta said. She stopped chewing.

"Would he?"

"There's no telling. That man sees red, he sees *nothing but red*."

Daisy involuntarily flinched. "I'm not surprised you left him," she said after a moment.

"Oh, I am." Sonesta gave the younger woman a slow smile.

"You are?"

"Even now I don't—" A look down at her sandwich. "It's not easy."

"But you just—"

"I know, I have the church, and the reverend, even if he does have his eye on the younger gals, and thank the Lord, I got me this job." She set down the uneaten rind of her sandwich, then brought her hands together. "I'm givin' it a try."

"I don't know what it's my place to say," Daisy started to say, and at a curious but not cold smile from Sonesta, went on with, "but I'm proud of you."

"Doesn't hurt you any much, though—"

"What do you mean?" Daisy said.

"Oh, with you singin'. Get me out of the way."

Daisy looked appalled. "*I would never—*" she started to say.

"I know, I know." Sonesta shook her head. "And here you doing me this good turn, bringin' me my sorry stuff."

"I could never do what you do?" the younger woman said. "I wouldn't have any clue how to try. But it's just . . . what Dell and I . . . that song we do—"

Sonesta held up her hand. "We don't have to go into that. What's done is done. And it ain't 'bout you I left the place. We all do know that."

Daisy had to work to calm herself, but she did. She wanted to be on the good side of the older singer, and so she didn't say anything for a few moments. Sonesta got up and poured herself a glass of some fruit-looking beverage, took a couple sips.

"I really want to—well, I'm wondering how you got together with him?" Daisy said.

"Bearcat?"

She nodded.

"Oh, my, there's a story. You sure you want to hear that sorry tale—"

"Not so sorry, I'm sure. I mean, you had yourself a hit record."

Sonesta's eyes lit up. "Oh, well, sort of. You don't know the story behind *Cryin' Shame* either?"

Daisy leaned back in her chair, looked at the maid expectantly.

"Well, all this took place long time ago. I was just a girl. How old're you?"

"I'm eighteen."

The older woman rolled her eyes as if something that young was beyond her ken, but it wasn't, for she said, "I was eighteen, too, and like to say just as pretty as you are—" Daisy gave her a smile "—and, gotta say too, probably as headstrong and blind," and the corners of Daisy's mouth drooped just a wiggle.

"Now don't go making faces. Maybe I just got a little envy in me, I mean, that young, starting out all over again."

"I want," Daisy said, "to hear how you did it." A concentrated focus. "I do."

"Well," Sonesta started. She looked then at the young woman, holding a question, but there was such a respectful, and needy, look in Daisy's eyes, that she went on. "That was more years ago than you have." She shook her head at the absurdity of it. "I was a, well, quite a proper young woman growing up in Charleston. Big family, with some money, all things considered. My daddy was a deacon in the church, a powerful man, and I was a sheltered, Christian girl. Only the best negro schools, too." A quick wince. "You should've seen the way I looked: Those starched skirts with the crinoline, God, it'd take me and my sisters hours to get ready to go anywhere, and on Sundays—Lord!" A hand to her head.

Daisy, thinking of her own parched upbringing in Bent Knee, listened with a kind of magical envy.

"Funny thing, though, none of it was enough. Only part of church I liked was the singing, and I was in every choir that'd have me. Wasn't long before I knew only life I wanted was music, and not just gospel, either. Any kind of music that moved me.

"I was lucky to have a lot of friends—I was pretty popular—and some of them had records at home." The older woman shut her eyes and smiled with an unabashed joy. "When I run through the list of those 78s I would listen to on long, drizzly afternoons, my golly. There was Bessie, of course, and Sippie Wallace and Alberta Hunter. There was Ethel Waters, from up north, and the mama, Ma Rainey. Chippie Hill, Lillian Glinn, Bobbie Cadillac, Monette Moore. I loved those women. Loved 'em!

"I had me a voice, too. It could go pretty in the choir, but, you know, child, it could soar and rasp and bark when it had to, even if I had to take that kind of singing, well, downtown.

"Anyway, I got me through enough school, and then I heard this band was coming to town, the Red Dewey Band, and that there was going to be a talent tryout." Her hand went to her wide forehead. "I was *ner-vous*, but I had to do it. *Had to!* Went down there, wearing this crisp chartreuse dress, with ruffles all over, looked like some kind of carny doll, but my voice was great—one special appreciator later said that he thought my voice could *scald paint*."

There was a lift to her voice when she used that odd phrasing, *special appreciator*, that made Daisy think immediately: Bearcat.

Sonesta must have seen the light in her eyes.

"Yes, it was Thomas Jackson, and he was a picture back then. *A picture!*" She told Daisy that he was this tall but still thin piano player with the Dewey Band; mid-20s but with all the airs of a boy who'd seen some of the world. He couldn't have dressed sharper, wide-lapeled suits, bright-yellow or fuchsia shirts, bold-colored ties, and an endless stash of marijuana hung in a bag around his belt.

At Daisy's raised eyebrows, Sonesta said, "Well, he was a musician, child." Then as her eyebrows stayed up, "But these days he got some kind of hoodoo-voodoo thang in that bag, Christian woman like me don't want to know." A loud, contemptuous snort.

"Nobody called him Bearcat, but he still had all that around him. You should've heard the stories going. They said that beautiful man, he was descended from African princes, said he had a touch of royal British blood, something to do with some prince back there who went to Africa. They said he'd turned down scholarships to a Northern medical school to play music instead. Boy, they said lots of things. Have to say for myself, well, I'd never met anybody in Charleston quite like him."

This was almost a Hollywood story, and Daisy was appreciating it like the movies she'd grown up on. And Sonesta capped it when she said, "And, Lordy, he seemed to be noticing *me!*"

She didn't get hired, though. "Get this, they said I sang too church for that Red Dewey sound! I mean! All they saw was this girl who was just the picture of primness and rectitude. In that crinkly chartreuse dress." Then a wink. "But Thomas, he noticed everything.

"Jackson set up a meeting that night, said he wanted to talk about my career. Well! First time anybody ever used that word with me. My ears was burning. *Ca-reer!* I can't tell you!"

But of course the older woman didn't have to. Daisy knew the siren song of that word just as well.

"First thing he said was that he loved my singing: 'You had those willy boys *tap-dancing* up my spine,' he told me in his big, sweet voice.

And what did I say to him? 'I just opened my mouth, Mr. Jackson, 'n' that's what came out.'

"And I meant it. Didn't know quite what I was doing. He said, 'Now sing me again, but sing it like you never saw a church in your life.'

"I opened my mouth and Thomas played some chords on his piano right there and I sang, and sitting there with him in front of me, well, that voice just kept getting darker and darker, and heavier, yet bright as a copper penny, too. It was like watching him watching me sing, well, I was singing better than I ever done, and it made him shimmy with pleasure, and so I rang it up higher, and he loved it more, and … well, then he jumped me."

"*He what?*"

"Well, he was a man, child. And I moved him. No small matter. So he gave me the long eye for a second's warning, then he pounced on me."

"What'd you do?"

"What would *you* do?"

"I don't know." Daisy looked shaken. "Scream?"

"That was it! I screamed. Then I jumped up. Thomas, he said, 'Listen, child, anybody sings like that, I don't care what you look like, you're an *animal*.' " And though there was immense satisfaction in Sonesta's voice as she said this to Daisy, she quickly added, "But he was wrong. I wasn't. I was sweet and cultured and innocent more than half. I really *was*. Deacon's daughter. And that man—that man plumb scared the living daylights out of me!

" 'Course, by not giving in, I made him totally crazy about me." A big smile.

"He wrote to me from the road, but I didn't write back. Called my house, but he only got my momma, and, boy, did she give him a piece of her mind. 'No Clarke is going to consort with musicianly riff-raff. No Clarke is going to be a singer. This little girl is on her way to marriage, to a good man, a serious man, an older man, a *pharmacist*.'

"Delmore Manwing," Sonesta went on. "He *was* a very good man, with a *very good* position. And he was ... somewhat older." A playful smile. "Honey, if my voice could make paint scald, that man could make paint run down off the wall and jump back into the bucket, just to get away from his smiling good cheer." She gave a visible shudder. "Girl, that man was so good he had the angels taking bets on what damn stupid thing he'd say next. Finally, it got to a point where I couldn't take it anymore.

"The Bearcat's letters kept arriving, thank God, and he always noted the Dewey Band's itinerary, half bragging, half hoping; and one night, it was in Boston, well, that man he looked out from behind his piano, and there I was.

"Yeah, I just left. I was old enough, and I packed me a bag and took a train, and next thing you know I was in the North. And I knew what I was doing—I was ready for any—well, *almost* anything." Sonesta struck an uncompromisingly prim note. "But that's how we put it all together.

"Bearcat, he was staying in this liberal colored establishment where they understood musicians, and he had no problem sneaking me into his room." Daisy leaned forward, and Sonesta's eyebrows flew up. She raised a finger to the younger woman. "Not that that did him any good! I mean, we all knew I was there with him because I'd just jilted my fiancé, shocked my family, run away from home, but was I gonna...." A shake of her head. "Well, not that night.

"But I *was* there to sing, and Thomas, bless him, he knew just what to do." Sonesta's eyes softened. "He had this way, he'd be at his piano, and he'd play a few notes, then like magic he'd be reaching right into me and pulling out this big glow of music. Child! That man had the touch, made me feel ways of singing notes I'd never imagined. We played around with some show music, played around with some big band, but finally we just went back to the songs he'd known growing up, after his parents died. Took us both to the *blues*."

Daisy gave a quick, sympathetic nod.

" 'Cept we took those old songs and made 'em jump."

Daisy, who'd had Dell play *Cryin' Shame* and other Sonesta Clarke recordings for her, smiled warmly.

"*The true jump*," Sonesta went on, eyes closed, head swaying just a little as if the rhythm were in her then and there. "And I was with him all the way. We got ourselves a combo, got the beat just right, and when it was time . . . we cut ourselves a damn doozy of a record."

"But you—" Daisy started to say, then blushed. "You never—with Bearcat. . . ?"

Sonesta didn't answer for a moment. Then she said simply, "Well, truth was, child, there was a lot of traveling together. After a while. . . ." She half-smiled. "Can't say it didn't make things any easier, though." That secret smile was there even as she wagged her head. "Just was no way around it. Even a girl, she sometimes gets the hunger. You know what I mean?"

Daisy was smiling to herself even as she blushed. It was just what she'd been thinking: It wouldn't make it any easier, even if sometimes it just had to happen.

Sonesta turned her head to the side, gave the younger woman a look out of the corner of her eye.

"You want to tell me 'bout that white boy?"

Daisy started.

"What boy?"

Sonesta gave her a who-you-kidding look.

"You mean, Dell?" A half-hearted shake of her head. "What's there to tell?"

"Oh, plenty, from the looks of you two." Sonesta rested back, her arms still before her chest, not a wall now so much as a well-built shelf she could lean into. "Now *you* mixing business with music?"

"Not—not really." But Daisy couldn't help but think of Dell's kisses, and that special, silent understanding they'd reached the night before.

"Tell it, child!"

"I don't—" Daisy swallowed. "I mean, he's cute and all—"

"Cute—"

"Well, yeah. And we have—we got the music together...."

Sonesta leaned back now, with a definite air about her of You said it, not me. Now don't say you don't understand.

"What?" the younger woman said.

Sonesta simply smiled.

"The music—is that what you're smilin' at?" Daisy looked abruptly concerned. "Something funny about that?"

The older woman kept smiling. "It ain't the music, child. It's the jump, like I said. That's what you two got, ain't it?"

"I—I don't know."

"Honest?"

"I really—" Daisy's head was spinning, just like that. She hadn't actually defined anything with Dell yet, was just letting it play out. "Maybe it's too soon to say—"

"Sugar, that's how I was with Mister Thomas Jackson. Oh, yeah, I just didn't think I ... knew." Light shake of her head. "Then I did." More vigorous. "I had it—had it once, and I had it good. Gracious! Honey, you get yourself that *true jump*, there's never going back. You understand?"

"I think so, I don't know—maybe I'm too young."

"You're not too young."

Daisy mulled this over for a minute, then said, "But you're done with him now? Bearcat, I mean. That's what you said."

"Child, *done*?" Sonesta gave almost a whinnying shiver. "I don't know nothin' 'bout *done*. Done's in the grave, if then." She stretched herself out, like a cat on a rug in sunlight. "But, yeah, I've left. I'm here. Got my job, got my own room. Woman needs her own room, you know—"

Daisy waited; noticed she was holding her breath.

"But about the *jump*," Sonesta went on. "Woman gets to a certain age, she tells herself she don't need the jump no more. She put herself beyond all that. Oh, indeed-y." A long sigh, then a silent nod to herself. "And that's what I'm telling myself all the live-long day. Got me the Lord, help me tell it to myself. Got me that cute preacher at the church help me tell it, too. We're all tellin' it, *we are*! Hmmmnph!"

In the quiet that followed, Daisy heard her loud exhalation flood the room. What a girl I am, she was telling herself. She didn't know quite what to make of all the turns of Sonesta's confession. She also told herself, But how much I want to grow up!

"So, you still want to hear 'bout our record?" Sonesta said finally, having to change the subject. *"Our hit record?"*

Daisy was surprised how glad she was to let the conversation go back to that. She nodded vigorously.

"Well, after a bunch of not-quite-readies, we cut *Cryin' Shame*. We knew it was something, and it took right off up the charts—right up 'em. The Bearcat was moving discs he'd pressed himself, but the funny thing with a hit, if it's the right size, you can do fine, but if it gets too big—and you ain't big enough—well, that's a problem. We started getting this huge demand, and Jackson couldn't satisfy it himself, so he started looking around for help. And what he came up with, well, the next thing we knew *Cryin' Shame* was climbing the charts all over the country, but it was sung by *that white woman*. That Tina Scott."

"God!" Daisy went, hardly able, as new to all this as she was, to imagine someone stealing her own music, her own *voice*.

"That wasn't the half of it." Sonesta brought a hand to her eye. "Seems that Jackson signed himself a contract. And that contract, well, it put what the Northern folk call the kibosh on things." A deep shrug. "We just sort of buried ourselves out here. Played Friday and Saturday nights, filled the roadhouse, got by. But, wan't till you children came along that it even looked like—"

"But you, you don't seem to even want us here."

"Well, you brought the Bearcat back to life, that's something." A long sigh. "But, I'm not eighteen, darlin'. Not close. It just—I know it's just trouble."

"But the music—" Daisy leaned forward. "You were talkin' about the music, the *jump*, you called it—"

"Honey, music may be closest us mortals come to the Lord himself, and it may be worth everything in our lives and our god-almighty souls, but that don't mean you bring it into the world, it don't got the devil all mixed up in it. And what Jackson's doing, he's trifling with *all kinds of devils*—"

"Like—"

"Like white devils he can't even imagine."

It didn't take Daisy more than a moment to nod slowly, thinking of Madame Grosgreen and her burned-out house, the lady herself disappeared without hide or hair.

"None of us want any trouble," Daisy said. "We just want to make music. We just want ... a hit."

"Like I said, get yourself a hit," the older woman said sagely, "and that's when the trouble *truly* starts."

There was a long silence then, Daisy turning this over and over in her head. She didn't quite believe the older woman—she *was* only eighteen—but the notion planted a seed that perhaps made a difference later that night.

"But I know I'm not gonna shake you children any," Sonesta finally said as if she were reading Daisy's thoughts. "I know you're just hoppin' and leapin' with the excitement you're 'bout to cause."

"It *is* a good song, isn't it?"

"Yeah, you got me." The older woman looked like the weight of eternity had just dropped down on her shoulders. "I think it's a fine song. A credit to you. And I'm sure you'll do fine tonight."

"Will you be there?" Daisy asked point-blank.

"*Me?*"

"It would mean the world—"

Sonesta suddenly stood up, started beating her hands around her.

"Honey, it's *your* night. And I gotta get me back to work."

"Sonesta—" Daisy realized as she said her name that it was the first time she'd spoken it straight to the older woman. She wasn't sure what that meant.

"I wish you all luck, darlin'. And I thank you deep for bringing me my things."

And with that the older woman went back off to empty ashtrays and turn down beds.

Daisy, with all this to think about as she drove back to the roadhouse in her pink Cadillac, found that pretty soon her thoughts went in just one direction: Her debut performance later that night. She was nervous, yet also deeply calm, and as she drove along, she let the whole evening play out in her mind; and of course, she got it all wrong.

✳ ✳ ✳ ✳ ✳

HE WASN'T READY FOR the heat in Phoenix, but once Colin loosened up enough to buy a gaily-patterned baggy cotton shirt at a K-mart near his motel, he not only felt loose and cool, he felt like he fit right in.

He'd tracked down the phone number through a reverse Internet search to an address in Scottsdale, and after a good night's sleep, he drove out there first thing in the morning.

He skirted the foothills, past land-gobbling resorts and water-gulping golf courses, turned up a street with an Indian name, unfurled the map, took a left, then a right, and pulled up before a low-slung, sprawling ranch house with what looked like a five-car garage. A cactus garden bloomed beautifully in the front yard.

Deep breath, up the walkway. Rang the bell. No answer. Rang again. Faint scurrying of quick feet, then a loud bark. Half-consciously, Colin dropped into a vestigial stance from childhood karate lessons. A flick of the latch. Tense.

It was a short Hispanic woman in a pink candy-striped maid's uniform. She held a metal chain leash attached to a huge Doberman, tugged backward.

"Hi," Colin said, "I have an appointment to see Miss Holliday."

"Who?" the maid quickly said. The dog was under her control, Colin pretty much believed, though with its front paws it was still wildly scraping across the black-and-white tile floor.

"Daisy Holliday."

The maid cocked an ear.

"Señora Daisy?"

"Yes."

"Oh, no, she's not here." Wide consternation on her teardrop-shaped face. "*Tiene un* appointment?"

"Well," Colin said, "not exactly for this moment." Bright smile. "She just asked me to stop when I was in the neighborhood."

"Oh, but Señora Daisy is not here."

"Do you know when she'll be back? Or—" quick inspiration "—where I could find her now?"

"Oh, she's probably at *el* club."

"And which club is that?"

"Oh, it's one of the clubs. *Bajo*, Soldier, *bajo!*" The Doberman had taken a big leap forward, tugging the maid four feet over the floor. Colin backed up so fast he landed in a tall barrel cactus. The cactus's needles pierced his K-mart shirt. He flinched, bit down on his lip to keep from crying out.

The maid reached down and whacked the Doberman on the head, but that didn't do much good. He was growling loudly now at Colin.

"If you could," Colin said, pulling himself off the cactus without getting too close to the dog, "give me the name of the—"

"Oh, just a second, Señor. Soldier, *mal perro!*" Another swat at the lunging dog, and then the maid pulled back and slammed the door shut.

Colin waited ten minutes and was about to leave, figuring he'd just come back in the late afternoon—beat the husband home from work, he was thinking—when the door opened and the maid, relieved to see Colin still there, handed him a slip of paper with the words Lagunitas del Sol, and an address on Hayden Road.

* * * * *

YOU CAN HEAR IT from half a mile away, a dark, plangent thumping, like the earth breathing in and out. It's a cool, bracing night, dipping into cold, and you have the windows mostly up and the heater on the Buick you borrowed again from Dad blowing, but still, there it is, a sound that first comes to you as something huge and deep and primeval. Closer, you can begin to separate out the instruments, first the kick of a bass drum married to the whomp of that new-fangled electric bass; then, as you swing the Buick into a wide turn and catch a trace of a distant pink glow hanging in the trees—how strange!—you can hear, muddying down the middle of the music, an oozy organ, churchy and soulful at the same time; and then, even closer, there's the razor-bright electric guitar, blistered by a wild sax—all snapped home by cymbals cracking steady in the hot night air.

It's still dark on the road, shadowy and blue, not much moon, but there's that pink glow, and when the music is all around you, you see through the long leaves a multicolored thrum, out there like a pulsing thing, brighter than anything you can imagine. This place is so different from the first time you snuck out here a couple months back; indeed, what you thought just your secret has now become The Pink Cadillac Club, and the rumors chasing hopes chasing thrills round the high school campuses, malt shops, and record sections of appliance stores are saying that something really new is brewing out there—a place for the new music, run by a young rich boy only a couple years older than you, who plays mean sax himself and ... runs with niggers.

That's what they say, and you can barely believe it, even though you got your own memories. What they're saying is that this white boy, Dell Dellaplane—could it be the same guy you saw out there last time?—has taken over an old nigra roadhouse outside of town, home of Bearcat Jackson—that must be the huge man-beast with the gold tooth—who put a few hits up on the race chart when you were in grammar school. You can also remember your older sister mooning to a song called *Cryin' Shame*, but that was sung by a white gal out of New Jersey name of Tina Scott.

Now it makes some sense in the way new things are happening that this rich white boy up and bought himself an old broken-down nigra roadhouse, fixed it up, and hung one of those brilliant neon signs out in front—and it's pretty damn exciting to think that he's hep to the new music and is gonna make the joint *rock*—but it beggars the imagination what the rumors have been whispering: that the nigra Bearcat Jackson is *still* out there. Playing. With his nigra band, with this rich boy Dell Dellaplane sitting in with the group.

Nothing like this has ever happened, least not in the

South, not so you know, at least, and you can't imagine it. It's one thing that that Elvis *sounds* like a nigra, but to actually play with them...?

But whether it's true or not, there have been meetings at the high school, parents discussing rock and roll music in general—heathen music, they call it, nigra jungle bunny sex music, except they don't use the word *sex* because they don't want anyone to think about sex, even though you do all the time. *They* call it rhythm music, because it makes you *moooove*, but that's what you love about it; the way that drum backbeat makes your feet start slip-sliding and your shoulders bob, and next thing you know, your legs are out there and they're going crazy!

The parents and the churches are getting up in arms. They're talking about taking action to defend innocent youth against the wanton seductions of the heathen music, except they don't use the word *wanton* either. Too suggestive, though the very idea of wanton, as in a wanton, uninhibited, blouse-bursting, do-anything girl makes you ... stiffen. Which makes you a little crazy, and that makes you want to hear that new music more, and dance to it, and maybe get Sue Ann Ryan or Peggy Starks to take a drive with you in Dad's Buick—and who knows what will happen? Except you do know, they're good girls, and they'll just say something like "I don't like foreign boys." And you'll go, "But I'm red-blood American far back as you can go." And they'll say, "Then why do you have Roman hands and Russian fingers?"

Which is why you don't believe the final rumor at all. No, it's just not possible. That there's a beautiful girl—a white girl, a *blonde* girl!—out there singing rock and roll with Dellaplane and the nigras and all. No, you'd first believe they got a monkey from the zoo out there singing.

But what if it were true? They say they got a song called *Pink Cadillac*, which is why the club's called Pink Cadillac, and all that's because Elvis Presley himself gave this girl one of his *own* Pink Cadillacs. Which sounds like a fairy tale. They make up something like that just to get people into their new club? Well ... there you are, turning into the parking lot. And there's the car itself, parked right out by the road: long, a little fat in the haunches, sparkling with chrome, and pink as a baby's bottom. You drive by slow and marvel.

This close you hear a singer, too, but it ain't a girl and it ain't like any white person who ever lived, no matter how much he'd been listening to WHBQ and caught himself the boogie woogie flu. This is one deep, growly, animal roar. This is a man singing, must be the big gold-tooth man himself, and all you can hear are the words "Nineteen Fifty-Six." And there goes a loud bunch of voices shouting back, "Nineteen Fifty-Six."

Wow! The parking lot must be full, there's a wiry nigra man with a flashlight waving you to park the Buick down the road. Then you have to walk along a dusty lane till you turn and get your first good glance of the club and your eyes bomb open and your jaw drops. That place is lit up! The PINK CADILLAC sign glows huge above you, and strings of white lights sway in the trees, but the joint itself! Your first thought is, This is something else. This is from another world. Everything's blue and yellow and red and white, and glowing, and spitting out raucous music, and jammed with kids both black and white, spilling out on an old porch and peering in through smoky windows, and you have only one weird, funny thought: It's like the flying saucers have finally landed. Billy Lee Riley was singin' it right! That's what this place is, all glowy and loud. This place is out of this world. Yeah, anything—*anything*—can happen here. The Martians have landed, and they want nothing more than to rock and roll!

Your heart's pounding something like the wild beat, and you're trying to slip your way into the club itself when you're elbowed aside by a guy all duded up in country clothes, flared Western shirt, slant pockets, embroidered collar, string tie,

tight pants and boots—you don't see that too often round
Memphis, it's a Nashville look, and a little prissy to boot. This
guy is shouting and pushing and insisting he has to get in; you
look back and see he just got out of a long black limousine, no
one probably ever saw one of *them* out this way. There are
kids still in the doorway, and about fifteen more waiting to get
in, guys with Elvis sideburns and front-curled hair—style you
still think looks pretty peculiar—and girls in skirts that look
ready to spin up their legs, but this dude is ready to move 'em
all aside. Yeah, he's Mister Important, that's what he is. As he
comes alongside you, you let an elbow slip out just a tad and
. . . you jam it into his gut.

"Hey, fuckface!" he says, just like that. Nasty bark.

You turn on him and say, "You looking for trouble?"

He gives you a long up-and-down look, and you don't
like at all what he sees. He sees a high school senior with a
flat-top haircut and a letterman sweater, in track. He sees
somebody he can just push aside.

"I said, 'You looking for trouble?'" you say, chest out.

"Don't waste my time," he says, and you don't know
how he does it, but he cuts like a hot knife through the crowd,
and you don't see him again till forty-five minutes later when
you finally get into the room, but by then all the action's over.

* * * * *

"NINETEEN FIFTY-SIX," the Bearcat cried into his mike,
then turned it around, pointing out at the astonishingly
crowded room and sending the crowd into a paroxysm of
echolalia: "Nineteen Fifty-Six, *Nineteen Fifty-Six, NINE-
TEEN FIFTY-SIX.*"

"Hey, hey," Bearcat went, then took back the mike and
turned to the band, tamping them down, setting them off on
a vamp through the eight-bar blues progression. "Well, now,"
he started in, talking over the scratchy guitar and softly honk-

ing sax. "I want to keep tellin' you how all this got going. Like I said, it was me and my friend Dell here, we was talkin' 'bout how we're sitting out here in Nineteen Fifty-*Five*, and we's playing the best music of our *lives*, and ain't nobody come hearin' us. We blowing the blazing roof off this joint ev'y Saturday night, there not be more than a couple lost souls out with us contemplatin' it all.

"So I says to my friend Dell, I says, we gotta get us a new beat. Got to get us a beat that represents—" And he holds out the mike again.

"Nineteen Fifty-Six!" shouted the crowd.

"Yessir, Nineteen Fifty-Six. We gotta get us a Nineteen-Fifty-Six beat. Beat like that crazy boy Li'l Richard got down N'awlins, and our own swivel-hips Mr. Elvis Presley has right here in Memphis."

"Elvis!" a couple voices called.

"Yessss, Mr. Elvis Presley, the man who gave us our new name, yes he did. Mr. Elvis Presley hisself. Hey, hey.

"So we got us this new beat, didn't we, Dell, and it goes like this."

And like digging the spurs into a horse, the band kicked off into the opening riff to Dell and Daisy's song, *Pink Cadillac*.

After a minute Bearcat tamped them down again.

"Now, we got us a new beat, that Nineteen-Fifty-Six beat, but what we don't got is a Nineteen-Fifty-Six *singer*. We still using the old jalopy—" glance toward the staircase, even though Sonesta was in no way there "—the crank-up-the-engine . . . the Nineteen Fifty-*Five* singer. Hey, hey. We need us something sleek, something with tail fins make you weep, something pink and shiny and glorious . . . a pink Cadillac of a singer. Now what you say 'bout that?"

"*Nineteen Fifty-Six*," everyone yelled, laughing with heady joy.

"Yes, indeeeee-dy! Now where we gonna get ourselves

one of these new models. We gonna go down to Bud Crenshaw's car lot, gonna order us up one of those new models off his showroom?"

"*No!*"

"You're right, you ain't gonna do that. Ain't gonna order a new singer out o' no Sears catalog, neither. No, it's gonna take a bit more magic than mail order to conjure up what we need. And that is—"

"*Nineteen Fifty-Six.*"

"So what we gonna do? Well, me and my friend Dell, we put our heads together real tight—his nappy ol' black head, and my head blond as a waterlily. Hey, hey! Dell said, 'Bearcat, what's that sack hangin' down your waist?' " Bearcat dropped his gaze, and there was the skanky leather mojo sack on his belt. "And I says, 'What, you mean my *mojo bag*?'

"Well, Dell, you can see, he's a black ol' nigger, he don't know 'bout mojo sacks, and so he says—" and here Bearcat drops his voice so deep it's like it's coming out of a well "—'Yeah, my white-boy friend, what is that?'

" 'Well,' I tells him, 'why don't you rub it, and we'll just see.' "

Dell had moved over now, scraping close to Bearcat, and he leaned down, his hand fluttering there for just a second, and then he gave the mojo bag a squeeze.

"Whoa, my!" Bearcat went and danced his thick legs up and back. Everyone laughed good-naturedly. "Yeah, he done squeezed my sack, but you know, nothing happened. I says, 'Dell, how we gonna get us a Nineteen-Fifty-Six singer, you can't squeeze no better than that?' So he reaches over and squeezes my sack again." And Dell reached over and did just that.

"But nothing happened again." Bearcat gave a lubricious shimmy, his girth jostling and shaking. "Hmmnnn, this mojo sack, it ain't workin' so good. I say, 'Dell, maybe we need us some conjurin' to make it work,' and Dell goes,

'Mumbo jumbo, mumbo jumbo,' and I goes, 'Dell, what kind of nigra conjurin' is that? Here's what I'm talkin' bout. Give us a 'Rah, rah, sis-boom-bah! Let's go, let's go ... Bulldogs.'"

Bearcat let out a huge chortle, but the crowd, at least the white kids, didn't immediately laugh along. Indeed, they looked more than half bemused.

"Well, well, guess I gotta say that wasn't the right conjurin', either. Nosiree!"

"*Nineteen Fifty-Six*," someone cried. "*Nineteen Fifty-Six!*"

"Yeah, yeah, I'm gettin' to that. Gettin' to that. Well, now, we got us one dead mojo bag—we don't know what to do with that sorry thang." Bearcat reached down and unhooked the bag from his belt, held it up in front of him, looked at it. It was just like a dead opossum, gnarled black-gray and smelly. He rattled it, and if you were right up close, you could hear a sound like old bones knocking against weathered stones. "We don't know what to do with it, that's the truth. We lookin' at that sack, turnin' it this way, that way, when all of a sudden that sack, like its got a mind of it's own, it leaps up in the air and, what do you know, it jumps smack dab into Dell's sax!"

And like that, with an unnoticeable feint of his meaty hand the bag flew away from Bearcat and dropped smack into the bowl of Dell's saxophone.

"*Whoeeee!*" Bearcat yelled. "And then, my blackest of black brothers, what came out?"

Dell moved to the front of the stage, leaned back, and blew huge the opening riff to *Pink Cadillac*. The notes caught the crowd, jumped them forward.

"Well, we's almost there. It's late in Nineteen Fifty-Five, we got us the mojo, we got us the music, all we's need's that ... *Nineteen-Fifty-Six singer*."

Bearcat held his hands over the bowl of Dell's sax, Dell blew hard, and like that the mojo bag popped up and into his grip.

"You got some more conjurin' in you, Mr. Bag?" Bearcat said to it. "You gonna find us a *singer*?"

He held the bag up in front of him, talking to it. "We got the song now, we gonna find us some words to have you bring us that singer."

The bag was mute.

"Oh, come on, Mr. Bag, Mr. Bag, help get us a—"

And then there came a spine-chilling sound, not really singing yet, more like keening, notes soaring up and down, wild melismas; a sound far more black than white, but not categorizable at all. It was a voice like a thickening mist, gathering form, weight, depth.

"Whoa!" Bearcat went. "Where'd that come from? That you, Mr. Bag, that your special voice?"

The sound continued, but more human now, more like singing, rough and rattly, smoky and piercing and going right to the hot points in the audience's brains. There was a deep silence, like whatever they were thinking was just sucked out of them and all they could do was listen to this voice—this astonishing black/white voice.

"Is that it, the sound of Nineteen Fifty-Six?" the Bearcat said. "What's that voice look like? You want to see it? You want—"

Out of the silence came the chant again: *"Nineteen Fifty-Six, Nineteen Fifty-Six, Nineteen Fifty-Six!"*

"Hey, hey!" Bearcat went, and there was a bright flash, then a cloud of theatrical smoke. The audience jumped back, oohing and aahing, the smoke billowing over the stage, too thick to see ... but then, with one of the spots Dell's money had bought right on her, there was Daisy behind the mike.

Bearcat stepped back, a huge, man-eating grin on his face, and cried out, "Let me introduce you to Miss ... Daisy ... Holliday!"

It's safe to say the white kids in the audience let out a loud, ringing cheer, while the blacks, Bearcat's longtime customers, seemed more nonplused. They wore faces that said, What kind of conjurin' you doing, Mr. Big Man? They wore faces that were straight-up *show-me* faces. Nonetheless, Daisy took the stage with presence and command.

And dropped right into the new song, *Pink Cadillac*.

> *When you got the jump and you got the quick*
> *Ain't nothing gonna move you like your gear shift stick*
> *Ain't nothing gonna thrill you like the midnight ride*
> *When you get in that Cadillac and slide and glide*
>
> ***Chorus:*** *Yeah, where we're going, nobody's gonna know*
> *Till our star burns bright out on Catfish Row*
> *Yeah, where we're going, ain't never lookin' back*
> *From our pink Cadillac, our pink Cadillac*

She belted, growled, mean-moved the song over, let her hair fly side to side, her hips wiggle, wrapped her legs round the microphone pole, dropped down, shook her way up it, threw the blonde hair again, held out her hands trance-style, wiggled her fingers, whipped her arms back, threw out her hip, then screamed out the chorus, all the while letting her gaze pierce the audience. A quarterway through the song there were white kids dancing, and halfway through the song there were black men moving, and three quarters through the song there were black women shimmying, and when she whooped the chorus down over and over for the last time, "Our pink Cadillac, our pink Cadillac, *our pink Cadillac*, OUR PINK CADILLAC," there wasn't anyone not dancing and clapping in the place.

Up on the stage behind Daisy, Dell was blasting along on his sax, rhythm-honking behind her singing, then running notes up past her voice at the end of a phrase, carrying them both as high as they could get. After one dizzying riff she glanced back at him and gave him an ecstatic smile. Dell winked. She was nailing the song, and the crowd was loving it. It was going to be a hit—*had to be.*

Near the end of the song Dell noticed the Grand Ole Opry–dressed guy over by the bar, blinked, wondered who could be here looking like that, then recognized his old amigo Cuth Starks, though Cuth looked different: hair oiled back, a mustache, an altogether more vulpine countenance than Dell remembered from high school. But, hey, Cuth had come!

Honk! Let that high B riffle curl his spine.

When the song finally came to its crashing end, Daisy gave Dell a quick glance, and he gave her back a widely encouraging nod. She quickly tucked right into a slow ballad Bearcat had recently taught her, *What My Eyes Have Seen.* It was a blues of cruelty, dismay, and ultimate endurance, and she sang it ripping up from her gut. *"I can't tell, I can't ever tell you … what my eyes have seen,"* she sang, then took the microphone in her hands, swayed the base round and round, clutching it as she would a mast in a roiling storm.

The black part of the audience, finally roused and cheering through *Pink Cadillac*, were back in silent contemplation; and yet as Daisy pulled sounds out that surprised even herself—*what had she seen?* the song made everyone wonder; and how after that could *anyone* prevail?—the crowd started swaying slowly side to side; people clutched the hand of the partner next to them, closed their eyes, began the long catalog of their own trials; then, to Daisy's impassioned voice, warmed to a glow of possibility.

There was a sax break halfway through the song, and again Dell soared up over Daisy's rising, tremulous voice, catapulting the melody into a silvery realm of pure sound.

But when the solo ended and Daisy eased into the third verse, Dell laid down his sax and went into the audience.

"Hey, man, haven't seen you since high school," Dell said after sidling up to Cuth Starks. He must have caught the record man by surprise because Cuth jolted, just slightly but noticeably. "The football team, Coach Swanger. Remember old 'How's It Swinging' Swanger? Don't that seem a million years ago?"

He was giving Cuth a shoulder-swagger thing, that high school bop-a-lu, but when Cuth turned to Dell, the dark-haired man seemed tight, almost prissy in his remove.

"Hey," Cuth said, but kept his eyes on the stage.

Dell felt something was off but couldn't adjust his track. Figured he might as well get right down to business, he was feeling so proud of their performance. "Don't you love her?" he said, gesturing to Daisy who was wrapping up *What My Eyes Have Seen*. Cuth's gaze was still there. Finally he turned to Dell with a look he couldn't cover up fast enough that said, How much can you know?

But it was the businessman who spoke to Dell a moment later.

"She seems to have some talent," he said over Daisy's singing.

"Some?" Dell was holding an imaginary sax in front of him, lightly fingering its invisible keys.

"She's a little raw." Cuth pursed his mouth just so. "Where's she from?"

"Some hamlet in Kentucky."

"Seems it," Cuth said.

Dell gave him a look that said he was tumbling to Cuth's ploy.

"But she has it, right?"

Cuth kept looking at the stage, where Daisy, launched now into a light cover version of *Tweedledee*, was openly looking at the two men. Cuth gave her a wink, which Dell saw.

Cuth turned to the sax player, opened his hands.

"Let's cut right to it, O.K., old friend." His eyes were ungodly bright right then. Dell felt oddly creepy but didn't understand why. "I'll be honest with you," Cuth went on. "She's got a little something, anyone can see that, and it might turn into something more if the right man works with her long enough, and if she takes the instruction well—"

"We've—"

Cuth held up a hand, stopping his old acquaintance. "But what I'm seeing here, it just ain't possible."

Dell blinked. "What do you—"

"Well," Cuth said, and he was back on his heels now, fingers fiddling with his string tie, "the *Cadillac* song's all right—you wrote that, yes?"

"We did."

"Yeah, right, you and.... Well, it's not bad, got a beat and all, but no way any major label in this country's gonna release a song with a white girl singin' coon music with coons playin' behind her." The yellow and blue lights above the stage were reflecting off Cuth's forehead right into Dell's eyes; made it hard to look up at the man. "Ain't ever gonna happen."

"But—" Dell swung his hand around to take in the black and white crowd.

"I'm surprised at you, Dell. Think about it. How you gonna promote? How you gonna tour? I think you've been spending too much time out here with the nigras, you've plumb lost your senses."

The look on Dell's face was not fully readable, though it clearly mixed anger with a kind of hapless persistence.

"But what about Little Richard? What about Chuck Berry?"

"But those *are* nigras." Cuth held his hands open as if what he'd just said was so self-evident it seemed beneath contempt to even mention.

"And Elvis?"

"That Humes boy's just a flash in the pan." Cuth took a step toward Dell, put an arm over his shoulder. "What you have to understand, my friend," he said, mock whispering into Dell's ear, as if he were imparting hugely privileged information, "is that all this rock 'n' roll stuff is gonna blow over real soon. It's a fad. Give it six months, maybe a year, then who's gonna be listening to it?"

Dell started to protest, but Cuth pinched his shoulder tighter.

"Now what I'm willing to talk to you about is, we bring that pretty filly down to Nashville, put her with es-tab-lished musicians, get her behind a good piece of product—"

"I don't—"

"Now, Dell," Cuth went on, his voice rising above Daisy's next song, "I'm not promising nothing, but I think it might be worth a try. Get her in a studio, see what comes out." He raised an eye to the stage, where Daisy was clearly looking over at them, wondering what was going on. "She does got the look."

It was Cuth's leer that finally set Dell off.

"I'd prefer that you just sent the acetate back."

"Her doing that nigra song?" Another wink toward Daisy. "If I can find it."

Up went Dell's voice: "What do you mean, *find it*?"

Eyes back on the sax man. "C'mon, Dell, you know how many demos I get every day." Cuth was bumped then by a black couple dancing by; he looked down at them with an unbridled flash of anger and contempt.

"But that was our only copy—"

But Cuth was smiles when he turned back to Dell. "Well, what say I take the filly up to Nashville. Maybe as a favor I'll have her do 'nother version of your *Cadillac* song, sing it right."

Dell suddenly looked like he was about to punch Cuth.

Bearcat, all this while also watching the two young men, left the bandstand halfway through *Tweedledee* and came over.

"Gentlemen, talking a little business?"

Dell, unsettled, said, "This cat here, he's got our demo and won't give it back."

Bearcat looked down with long eyes at Dell.

"What we doin' with carny men anyway?"

"You remember, I said I got a friend—"

"And I thought *I* said—" There was a quiet fury to Bearcat's voice, but then he held fire, clearly thinking it's not smart to show division in front of strangers. "He don't look like no friend to me."

Cuth was suddenly all effusive eagerness. He stuck out his hand and said, "Mr. Jackson, it's an honor. I'm Cuth Starks."

"From Nashville?"

"The Music City itself."

"And you've got our record?" Bearcat leaned forward.

"What I'm doing, um, Mr. Jackson, is trying to tell Dell here that we might be able to use this, what's her name?—this flowery Christmas lady—use her in Nashville, get some players behind her there—"

"We not good enough for you?"

"No, no," Cuth said, looking up at the big man. "It's just the way the market is." He shuffled from side to side. "We wouldn't have a *place* for what she's doing here, things just ain't like that."

"So you can't help us?"

"I can only help you if you'll help *me*."

"That's what I said. You can't help *us*."

Cuth was trying to stand up to the Bearcat, toe to toe, but tall as he was, there was no question who was in control.

"I think you should leave, Mr. Carny."

Cuth didn't budge, but he did send a vivid glance toward Daisy, stepping down now from the stage.

"I think I should be able to talk to Miss Holliday."

"You got her name right that time," Dell said.

"I just want to have a few words with her."

"Not a chance," Bearcat said. He beckoned to the door, where he caught Slingshot's eye. "Not a goddamn chance. Now I think it's time you leave."

A more frantic glance toward Daisy, who now was looking with the strongest curiosity at the three men talking. Cuth
caught her eye again, but it wasn't at all clear what kind of
acknowledgment she gave back.

"You won't let me have just one word with her?"

And Dell blew. "You fuckin' snake." He cocked his arm.
"Get the hell out of here."

Bearcat smiled, then restrained the younger man.

"I think our Mr. Slingshot here's gonna help our pretty
Mr. Carny out into the parking lot, where he'll get in his car
and head back to that fabulous Music City. Sling?"

Slingshot gingerly took Cuth's arm. The bouncer, too,
had a few inches on the record man, as well as twenty pounds
of muscle. Cuth's mouth twitched, and he looked for a second
as if he wanted to step in and slug Dell, but he really didn't
move at all. Just turned and walked with Slingshot to the
door.

He turned there and mouthed words that they couldn't
quite make out, though Dell's best interpretation was, This is
just starting, asshole.

"Who was that?" Daisy said, over by Dell and Bearcat
now.

"Some clown come to the wrong circus," Bearcat said.
He gave Dell a look.

"He did look sort of funny in that getup," Daisy said.
"What was he doing here?"

"Nothing," Dell said.

"You're not telling me something?"

Both men were silent.

Daisy gave a silent nod. "He was the record guy Dell
wanted to send our disc to, right?" A glance between the blues
man and the sax player. "What did he say?"

Both men shuffled back and forth and didn't say
anything.

"What's the matter, didn't he like me?"

Dell, hearing plaintive insecurity in her tone, crumbled. "No, no, he liked you just fine. You were great. Truly great!"

"Then what was the problem?"

"It wasn't going to work out," Dell finally said.

"Damn!" Daisy threw back her hair. "What did he say?"

"Just that it wasn't going to work out."

Daisy pursed her lips. "You're still not telling me something."

"Daisy," Dell said, "you were fabulous tonight. You took this crowd and spun 'em round your little finger—"

"But we aren't going to get a record deal, that's it, truth?"

"We got a lot of other possibilities," Dell said, hand to chin.

Daisy nodded silently to herself.

"Like what?"

"That's just what Bearcat and I was working on."

"Oh, the men." Daisy shrugged her wide shoulders. "You'll let me know when you got my *caa-reeer* worked out."

"*Daze—*"

But Daisy had started to walk away. The band was still up on the stage, but Daisy wasn't going back there. Instead she headed toward the door.

"Daisy, where you going?"

"We're having a little intermission," she said. "Going to do some thinking. In my car."

Dell looked at Bearcat, who looked back at Dell. Both men shrugged. Then Bearcat said to the band, "O.K., everyone, we're taking a break. But Miss Daisy Holliday will be back with you in twenty minutes. Bar's over there, Salt's ready to set 'em on up. Have yourselves a great dang ol' time."

✳ ✳ ✳ ✳ ✳

LAGUNITAS DEL SOL took up at least a mile of roadside, but as Colin drove along it, and back, and back again, he just couldn't find the gate. Finally, he saw a wide though unmarked opening, and feeling both annoyed yet desperate, Colin turned into it. It led him on a curved road that zigzagged alongside a golf course for a half mile. Finally he came upon what had to be the office, and pulled into a space in front of a sign that said VISITOR PARKING 30 MIN.

A picture: Would he even last that long before security guards clapped him up and heave-ho'd him out of there?

He realized as he walked into the painfully air-conditioned office that he didn't know Daisy Holliday's current last name. *Señora Daisy*, the maid had called her. Not the most common of names. Would that work?

All confidence, even bluster, Colin went up to a short blonde woman in a starched white shirt and high-cut khaki shorts behind the front desk.

"Hi, I'm Daisy's nephew. I just popped into town. Is she here?"

"Daisy?"

Keep looking straight at her.

"Yeah, yeah, Aunt Daisy." Huge glabbering smile.

The woman looked at him closely. Colin kept smiling back. With her shiny, wide-open sunburned face and unlined forehead, what Colin sensed was that she was less security guard and more golf-pro assistant pulled in to take over the front desk.

"You know, I think I saw Daisy Cooper down at the snack bar just a little while ago. With Mrs. Randall. They'd just finished their tennis."

"And the snack bar is—"

"Maybe I should have her paged for you."

"Oh, but I'd really like to surprise her. You see, she doesn't know I'm here—doesn't even know I'm in the States."

"You're English?"

"Yes, a sort of distant cousin. Here for business. And I was told at her house to come look for her up here."

The girl looked a little concerned, but Colin could tell his story was working. Finally, she brightened and said, "Everyone loves a good surprise. You'll find the snack bar down that corridor."

"Thanks," Colin said and quickly scuttled along.

There were eight women in the snack bar, grouped around white tables; two were young, two more were alone, leaving two twosomes, both of which were roughly the right age.

Colin went up and bought a cup of coffee from an attendant, and as she was ringing up his purchase, turned and surveyed the room. He told himself: If my intuition can't pick out Daisy Holliday from this group, I will leave right now and forget the whole thing. The four possible women were all white-blonde, well-tanned, wearing tennis togs over reasonably trim bodies. Two had very short hair, the third shoulder length, the fourth a ponytail down below her shoulders.

Ponytail, ponytail, he thought. Looked more closely. Her eyes were blue. He checked her companion. Green eyes, a dyed pixie cut. O.K., he liked the blue eyes. Looking closer. That ineffable … he read privilege in all the women, of course, but not born-to wealth in Miss Ponytail. A way in which she both tried harder, yet didn't have to. A natural grace missing from—

"Daisy Cooper," he said, walking straight up to her.

The woman with the ponytail was reaching behind her head to undo her hair; it fell to her shoulders. She looked to her friend for a moment, but Colin quickly saw the look wasn't: Oh, you want *her*, but instead, What does this strange man want?

She was silent, waiting for what Colin would say next. But he didn't speak at all. Yeah, he could see it. With her hair out of her ponytail, Daisy Cooper looked older than she first had—the age she was supposed to be—but still looked very good. She had a lightness, a delicate grace. He wasn't wrong about that, either: There were definite correspondences to—

"I've been looking for you—actually for Daisy Holliday."

The woman's skin tightened around her eyes.

"Oh, yes," she said, politely for her now curious friend, "you must be the gentleman who called the other day."

Colin smiled. "I decided to take you up on your kind offer to visit. I—" glance to Daisy's friend "—hope I'm not intruding."

"No, no," Daisy said. "I'm just a little surprised to see you *here*." She kept her smile bright. "From what you said on the phone, I didn't really . . . expect you."

The friend was squirming with curiosity now.

"Oh, Samantha, this is Mr.—"

"Stone. Colin Stone."

"He's here, well, he says he wants to ask me some questions about when I was in show business. Isn't that right?"

"Exactly."

"And so I guess, Samantha, maybe I should go talk to Mr., um, Stone for a few minutes. Can you excuse me?"

The friend brightened, said no problem.

"We'll just be a minute." Daisy floated her eyebrows. "I'll be right back."

She led Colin to an unused massage room just down the hall. Nearly pulled him in. Spun on him.

"What right?" she shouted. She breathed fire. "What right do you have to sneak up on me like this?"

"I've been researching Bearcat Jackson's recordings. I run a record company, Blue Moon, and we put out old records. That's all." Colin leaned against the massage table, as nonchalantly as he could. He had decided he had to be truthful with Daisy. He believed the truth would be enough. "And I'm going around the world looking for any trace of the song *Pink Cadillac*."

"I told you on the phone. I told you about . . . my husband. Why are you here?"

"Because I'm convinced there was a *Pink Cadillac*. That Dell Dellaplane wrote it, Bearcat Jackson's band played on it, and *you* sang it." Colin stared at her, gently but firmly. She must have really been a looker, fine blonde hair curved behind her ears, wide, barely traced forehead, a finely cut nose, large mouth and eyes. There was also a weariness about her that went far deeper than just having played a tennis match, something heavy and worn; and yet still, below that, Colin was sure he saw the flame of more than a little sex. It was no trouble to imagine how she would have burned herself into a microphone 40 years before.

Perhaps it was enough for Daisy to see the way this young Englishman was looking at her, but there was a new light in her eye. "But why do you care?"

"Why do I *care*?"

Daisy's shoulders relaxed just a touch. A trace of curiosity swept her face.

"Yeah, why do you care about an old, stupid record."

"You don't know, do you?"

"Know what?" Daisy took a step back, leaned against the wall.

Colin hoisted himself up on the massage table, crossed his legs before him.

"There are those of us who see *Pink Cadillac*, which, mind you, we've never actually heard, as the great lost record in rock 'n' roll history."

Daisy laughed. "Rock 'n' roll history?"

"Which you were a part of."

"Hey, now, brother, I haven't admitted to anything."

Colin hooked an eye at her. She smiled, almost flirtatiously. At least, he thought, she's starting to enjoy this.

"So go on," she said.

"Go on how?" A touch of being miffed in his voice. Let her come back on that.

"About how this ... this record ... is some huge historical thing."

"Simple. What I understand is that you were going to be the female Elvis."

"Yeah, right."

"That when *Pink Cadillac* was played on WHBQ the phones lit up—just like when Dewey Phillips played *It's All Right Mama*. That when *Pink Cadillac* was playing at Bearcat's club, kids fought to get in. That when you sang, everyone went *wild*."

Daisy looked at Colin with a hint of disbelief and more than a trace of unease. But when a moment later she closed her eyes, he knew he had her.

"It existed, didn't it?"

She didn't say anything for a moment, and he didn't say anything again. He could see that she was remembering, casting herself back those forty years, which she might not have even thought of in twenty. He let her go.

Finally, he prodded again. "It was a great record, wasn't it?"

"It should have been," she said. She kept her eyes closed. "It was going to be the goddamn best."

"So it existed."

"Oh, yes," Daisy said softly.

"And?"

"It was on the radio, just like you said."

"But was it ever *sold*? I've talked to people who've heard it, but nobody ever had a copy. Do you know what happened?"

Daisy kept her eyes closed but looked perplexed, as if she were trying to dig something out of the very long ago and lost past. "I'm not sure, really."

"Not sure?" Colin heard himself, loud at this older woman, but he knew he had to push her now. "Why not?"

Daisy Cooper, née Daisy Holliday, opened her glaringly blue eyes.

"Because." She was staring right at the record man. "Because, Mr. Colin Stone of Blue Moon Records, because I made the biggest mistake of my life."

* * * * *

"DAMN!" DELL CRIED OUT. He was sitting at the bar of the Pink Cadillac club, the black phone stretched to the end of its wire in front of him. He slammed the receiver down.

Bearcat said, "Like the wind, huh?"

Dell shot him a glare. He was in no mood for anything like humor, gallows or otherwise. Not only had Daisy not come back after she'd gone to the parking lot "to think" the night before, there was no tracing her today. There was also no digging up Cuth Starks. Dell had no evidence for what Daisy had done after she left the bandstand, but with each passing minute—and each desperate phone call—he surmised the worst.

No sign of Daisy at her rooming house. No sign of her at the café where she'd been waitressing. Then he'd tried the Peabody Hotel. No sign of Cuth Starks, though he had checked in there the day before. And checked out now? No, he was still registered, but he was not in his room. "And, no, we really can't comment on our guests' whereabouts, you understand.... Oh, yes, Mr. Dellaplane, I guess I could tell *you*. But, sir, we haven't seen him since last night when he drove off around nine. No, sir, but I'll be happy to take a message."

"You could always call Sonesta," Bearcat said from his corner of the bar. He was smoking a cigar. He rarely smoked, but was puffing away like crazy on a Havana now. Seeing the visible distress Dell was suffering, he'd held back from lighting into him for his transgression: The boy had been *told* not to send their record to anyone and had plumb gone ahead and done it. It was clear whatever was going on with Daisy was on his shoulders; the only redeeming thing for Bearcat was that Dell knew that, was taking everything badly. Still, this affront to the Bearcat, even if it wasn't so unexpected, he knew he wasn't going to be forgetting it easy. "She says she's working at that hotel now. She could tell you if she seen your carny man."

Dell held his finger above the phone's rotary dial.

"Get her involved in this?" Dell was frowning.

"You could."

"No, you call her."

Bearcat threw up his hands. "Hey, this is the pie you baked, son." A quick grimace. "'Sides, I ain't callin' that woman for nothin'. She's gotta call me."

Dell didn't say anything for a moment, then sighed. "O.K.," he said, and dialed back the Peabody Hotel, but the operator told him it was hotel policy not to transfer phone calls to the help while they were on duty. He could leave a message, though, which he did.

No sign of Cuth either at the Starks mansion, down the road from the Dellaplane establishment. Indeed, Cuth's father seemed almost alarmed to hear from Dell Dellaplane, but Dell couldn't stop to think what that might mean.

He finally dialed the last call he could think to make, Cuth's record company office in Nashville, but all the secretary would say was that Mr. Starks was away from the office and she didn't know when to expect him back.

"Is Cuth still in Memphis?" Dell pushed.

"Sorry, sir, he's just out of the office. Um, I have another call." And like that the secretary hung up.

Dell slammed the phone back in its cradle.

"Well, she always had a kinda *glint*," Bearcat said. He took a long pull at his Havana, sent a blue cloud of smoke above him. He was thinking, Even if the boy had brought the fisherman, it wan't like the fish wasn't looking for some bait. "Something any minute might go flames in her eyes."

"I can't believe it," Dell said. His head was sunk down in his shoulders; he hadn't shaved and had blond fuzz over his cheeks and chin. He pushed his hands back through his hair. "What could she have done?"

"Well, like I was saying, 'bout that *glint*. It was eyeballs maybe looking for something to *burn*."

"Bearcat, quit speaking in riddles. Where in God's hell is she?"

"She's with the carny record man *you* brought here, you know that."

"What would she be doin' with him?"

"Listenin' to his sweet words, I don't doubt." Puff, puff. Bearcat's end of the bar was clouding up fast.

"I can't believe. . . . She—." Dell, thinking of his oily old acquaintance, shivered. "No, I know her better than that. She wouldn't desert us, would she?"

"What if she didn't see it as deserting? If she sees it as furthering the *music*?"

"But Cuth Starks is a talentless snake."

"Then why'd you send him the only damn copy of our record?" Furious puff, puff, puff.

"He was a friend of mine! In a position to help us, I thought."

"And then invite him here."

"I know, I know, I screwed up. Damn!" Dell jumped from his seat, started pacing "I still can't see—I mean, I *know* her."

"Dell, nobody ever knows anybody, truth." Long, slow inhale. "But certainly you didn't have time to know Miss Daisy yet, not really. *Did you?*"

Dell deflected the obvious question. "You're wrong, Bearcat. She couldn't have sung my—*our*—song like that, if she wasn't true."

"Oh, my boy, my boy." Bearcat waved his Cuban expansively. "You don't know yet how the music business can be nothin' but a lie." The tip of the cigar glowed red. "I ain't heard nothin' from nobody in years ain't been a lie."

"But the music, Bearcat. You play the harp, I play my sax, that ain't no lie. Daisy singing, *that ain't no lie!*"

"And she runnin' off with your snaky carny friend ain't no lie, neither." A bright, perversely pleased puff, puff, puff right then. "And you know it."

"So, I know it." Pace, pace. "No, I *don't* know it." Pace, pace, pace. "O.K., dammit, I do know it. But why in tarnation you so bent on making me 'knowledge it? Don't you know what it does to me?"

"What you don't know is what it does to *me.*"

"What do you mean?"

"You so busy feeling sorry for yo' little white self, you don't think one minute what it does to the roadhouse."

"Yeah?" Dell stopped his pacing, looked at Bearcat.

"Yeah, like it puts us back where we was. 'Cept we got a shiny new 'stablishment here. We got us a pink sign lights up near miles round. We got us a whole roomful of paying patrons goin' home saying, 'I had me the most fabulous time last night, yeah, new place, Pink Cadillac Club, yeah, down in the woods, I know, I know, but that's what makes it special ... that and this new singer I saw, name of Miss ... Daisy ... Holliday."

"The roadhouse," Dell said soft. He stopped moving. A quick thought to the gambler Snake Eyes. The deal with him had been: The new year comes, Dell starts paying back what he borrowed; it was January 2, and at that moment he could almost hear the vig start ticking.

"Yeah, and if we don't got Daisy, we ain't got a draw, do we? And if we don't got Daisy, well, at least we could have that record of hers, 'cept you gave the only copy of our record to that carny man, and *we ain't got that, too!*"

"I thought we'd just record us another take, when we got goin' here." Dell looked even more crestfallen, if that were possible. "Go downtown, get a proper studio, make a proper release."

"Need a singer to do that." Puff, puff, puff.

"We don't—" Dell was moving again, swift kicking strides, going nowhere fast "—we don't know that for sure now, do we?"

Bearcat set his stogie, burned near the butt, into a glass ashtray; balanced it there. Then he pulled his leather mojo bag off his belt.

"Want we should consult this?"

"I know, Bearcat, you got all that mumbo-jumbo shit down. You the Conjurer Man. But you gonna tell me you can predict the future? You gonna tell me that bag's gonna tell us just where Daisy is?"

Bearcat took the smelly sack and held it up before his face. It was, Dell realized for the first time, just about the same color as Bearcat was, with about the same type of lines to its skin. The big man held it before him for a second, and Dell could swear that he felt something coming off it. Either it was that, or it was coming from Bearcat, who always exuded his own sense of power, except that this was different, not really like a halo or an aura, but some definite excitement of the air around the mojo bag, a way you could just tell—even if you couldn't actually see—that the molecules were jumping and slanting in a different way; and yet it wasn't simply that but also the way the bag made you *look* at it different, or look through it, or look anywhere at all. Up to now the bag had seemed like a neat trick to Dell, something to goof on, have a little fun with—ooh, ooh, hoodoo voodoo. But he had never really *felt* it, not like this. He was staring at it, and for a second felt half-hypnotized, as if this worthless piece of unmentionable animal flesh with its rotted animal legs and crumbled plant stuff and ugly little rattly stones and bones inside it, as if this bag actually could bring the world into some kind of order that the world wouldn't be in if the bag wasn't out and hanging there and doing its spooky hoodoo-shit thang.

And when Dell was so locked into thinking all this that he was thinking that, who knew, anything was possible, and this bag might....

Well, the door opened, and Daisy was there.

He didn't see her right away, just felt her, first thinking this was some new emanation from the *blooming bag*, as if the bag really were playing him, making the room ripple and warp from it, and it was just this kind of rippling and warping that made Dell feel that someone new was in the room, and he actually wondered if the bag itself were now conjuring up the *spirit* of Daisy Holliday, making him feel it, when he turned and there, in a kind of morning silhouette in the doorway, was her almost-all-known shape, and then into the room were her arms, her breasts, her legs—all of her.

Dell blinked.

"Hi," she said softly.

"It's you?" Dell said, voice tinged in awe.

"You expecting anyone else?"

"No, no." Trying to quickly recover. "Where were you?"

Daisy took a deep breath. "The only question, dear Dell, is where I'm going."

Bearcat meanwhile had set his mojo bag down on the bar and taken up his cigar butt. He was having trouble getting it lit again. "Where *are* you goin', sugar?" he said.

"Well, I'm only gonna know that when I get there."

"You're leavin' us?"

"Dell, I'm sorry, but—"

Dell jumped up, angry. But he couldn't keep something tender out of his voice, too. "What're you tellin' us? You're goin' off with Cuth Starks?"

"I got me a deal, Dell." Daisy was far enough in the room now that Dell could see she held both a paper bag and a letter-sized white envelope. She held up the envelope. "It's a signed contract with Old Gold Records. I'm goin'—goin' out on the road."

"With Starks?"

"Dell, it's only business."

"Oh, Daisy, I was worried sick about you."

"I know, I know. But . . . Cuth, he insisted. He said it had to be a clean break. But I—"

"What's in the bag, li'l girl?" Bearcat said.

"That's what . . . that's what I insisted on. It's our record, our acetate of *Pink Cadillac*. I wanted you to have it."

Bearcat reached out, and Daisy handed him the paper sack.

"I got somethin' for you, too, sweetheart."

Dell was nonplused. He didn't know what to say. He wasn't going to mortify himself by trying to argue her out of it, but he couldn't just let her go, could he? What he wanted was to stick a knife right up Cuth Starks's too-tight Western shirt.

"Something for you. Dell, please."

She was hurting, that was clear to his eyes, and this confused Dell. She got herself a record contract, why wasn't she jumping for joy. Oh, you mean she's got some feelings for us? Me and Bearcat, took her in, taught her everything we knew, got her up on a stage, got her knockin' that crowd *dead*! Feelings?

What was she holding out? It was small and silvery and glinted in the filtered morning sunlight.

"It's like a promise," she was saying. "That I won't forget you. Both of you, all you done. And that—well, that—" He thought he saw a tear fall from her right eye, but the way the light was, well. . . . All he was sure of was that she shrugged, hopeless in the face of saying anything more. "You'll treat it well?"

There was still nothing Dell could say. He saw the set

of keys in her hand, and he knew what they were to. But he didn't at all know what that meant.

"He'll treat it like his own, darling," Bearcat said. "Here, you just pass that shiny bit of joy over here."

"No, they're for Dell. Dell?"

He wanted to walk over to her, of course, but knew that if he did, he'd want to embrace her; and he knew he couldn't bear it if she pushed him away.

"Dell?"

"I thought we—"

"Dell, *this is business*! Please, understand. This is everything I ever dreamed of. I'm gonna make a record—for a real label. With distribution! And I'm gonna go out and play—"

"But what about—"

A loud honking came from the parking lot.

"Is that him?"

"No."

"What do you mean?"

"He didn't want to come out here. He just sent me in his limo."

"His limo?"

More loud honking, impatient.

"Dell, I gotta go. Right now. Here, I want you to have the Cadillac, keep it for me." She held up the keys again, then tossed them at Dell. The throw was good, and Dell caught them easily, right hand floating up and nabbing the keys, though it looked as if the catch was in spite of himself.

"Bearcat, thanks for everything. It might've, but...." A thin pointer finger to her blue eyes. "Well, I'll never forget you guys. I—I love you. Both of you."

Another honk. Daisy stood there for a second more, biting her lip, still and frozen. Then she dashed out the door.

Dell stood looking after her. Finally he said, "What a chicken."

Bearcat was silent, just raised an eyebrow.

"I'm gonna kill him, I ever see him again."

"What about Daisy?"

Dell started pacing again. "She'll be back," he finally said.

"Yeah, and how do you know that?"

Wheeled on Bearcat. "Talk to your bag, Mr. Conjurer Man. Talk to your goddamn bag."

Part Three
Redemption

LATER, DAISY'S RESPONSE to him resonated hugely with Colin. By that time he was already on his way to Memphis; and already with his heart creeping up in his throat. *Because I made the biggest mistake of my life*, she'd said. *The biggest mis—*

Yet the mistake with Robin seemed so little. No one even called it that; the only word anyone used was *accident. The tragic accident.* But there hadn't been a day gone by since the ... well, since he'd lost his wife that he didn't achingly replay the last minute, demand from himself what he could have done differently, why he hadn't reached out and saved her.

In the high-pitched whine of the Delta jet to Memphis it only got worse.

He'd met her there four years ago while he was working on the Bearcat anthology. He was staying at a Holiday Inn, had a good rate befitting a record producer who hoped to unearth and market the life's work of a man who must have sold fewer than 4,000 records in his day, and someone named Robin Longworth was singing in a club off the hotel lobby hopefully named The Delta Stops Here. The first two nights he'd hustled past the lounge, thinking, Right! The Delta Stops Here Club in the Holiday Inn—isn't that where Howling Wolf was discovered? But his third night there, after a long day of interviews that left him sure that the next morning he'd finally turn up the original acetates of Bearcat's recordings, jet lag and busyness caught up with him, and he decided to stay in. He kicked off his boots, raided the mini-

bar, flipped on the cable box ... and it didn't take more than
fifteen minutes of hopeless dial spinning to send Colin downstairs in search of *any* real-life diversion.

So imagine his surprise when the Vegas-y head shot of
the blonde on the placard outside the Delta Stops Here Club
turned out to be this lovely, down-to-earth woman bent over
a shaded-top Gibson guitar playing bottleneck Robert
Johnson, Charlie Patton, and Blind Willie Johnson songs.

He didn't realize how quick-smitten he was till later;
first he was simply intrigued, surprised that some of the real
Mississippi Delta had actually worked its way into the not-
very-dark, squeaky-clean banquette-lined club with the
fishnet-stocking-clad hostesses. He heard a rousing, kick-it-
out version of *Pony Blues* followed by a growlingly soulful
Milk Cow Blues and a haunted, moaning *Dark Was the Night,
Cold Was the Ground* that might've made Ry Cooder spin his
head. The blonde woman's fretwork was impeccable, her
voice gripping. When her set was done, Colin hung around,
then caught her as she was leaving, offering to buy her a
drink.

She looked past him, said she didn't drink with
customers.

Colin insisted he wasn't a customer.

She gave him a wry look, What do you mean?

"I'm a record producer," he said.

"Oh, right, right," Robin chortled. "But isn't that
worse?" But then she heard his English accent, and that
seemed to catch her. She asked where he was from, and after
he told her, asked why he was in Memphis.

"I'm almost afraid to say anything," he said humbly.
"But I'm here—well, I'm putting out a CD on a guy nobody's
ever heard of named Thomas Jackson, and—"

"Bearcat Jackson?"

"You know him?"

Robin gave him a look that read, Are you nuts? You

think I can nail Furry Lewis and not know the Bearcat?

"You getting Sonesta Clarke and Clay Booker, all of them?" she asked.

"I've been promised that tomorrow I'll be shown a complete set of Bearcat's recordings," Colin said softly. Even the thought of it still left him in a quiet kind of awe.

"The original ones?"

"A collector in town has them. Guy Davenport."

It was half-said as a question, but this lovely blonde singer shook her head.

"You ever hear of Daisy Holliday? Dell Dellaplane?" Colin asked then. He held his breath. Another shake of her head. *"Pink Cadillac?"* A thoughtful purse of her brow but finally another shake.

"What's that?"

"A song rumored to be cut by Bearcat but by a white girl, back in '55 or '56."

"A white girl, singing with Bearcat Jackson?" Robin gave her head a quick shake. "That would be amazing!"

"Yeah—it's sort of my Holy Grail," Colin said.

"Really," the blonde singer went. "Tell me more."

And he did. Talking late into the night, and after her show the next day, a DAT tape of the acetates of *Cryin' Shame*, *Booker's Boogie*, and all the others finally in hand, playing it for Robin, watching her listen intently, then lightly finger her guitar to the tape, adding a soft yet piercing accompaniment to the forty-year-old recordings.

Was that when he knew he loved her? Or was it a few minutes later when he kissed her for the first time and whatever they were doing was immediately much more about the present than the past?

He stayed in Memphis a week longer than planned, and when he left he had a bride on his arm. It hadn't been easy to talk her away from Memphis, where she'd grown up, where her family was, her job, but when it all looked impossible, she'd simply cried out, "It's an adventure! What kind of wuss am I? I love you, Colin Stone. I have to do it!"

They were married down the road from Graceland. Tried to honeymoon in Heartbreak Hotel but ended up in the Love Me Tender Inn. And flew off together to England.

Where they lived in a joy the dweeby man who'd dedicated his life's work to tracking down obscure, mothballed music couldn't have imagined. Robin quickly found work on the folk-blues circuit; Colin put out the Bearcat CD to acclaim (and with no *Pink Cadillac*, not that many sales); and all went fine for three years.

Robin, in her mid-30s now, was getting a little tired of the road, being away from their home; and there was urgent talk, then action to try to start a family. No luck yet, but they were in town one afternoon to see Robin's doctor when they decided to stay in London for dinner. It was about 4:30, and so they had a couple hours to kill. No good news yet from the doctor, but Robin had told her husband that she had an intuition that next month she'd conceive.

Though he hoped so, all he'd said was a quiet, "We'll see."

"No, no," Robin said. "I can feel it." That shoulder flick with her hair, the wide eyes that still got Colin cold. "Haven't you learned to trust my instincts by now?" She was in high, expansive spirits, skipping along the crowded West End sidewalk toward Piccadilly Circus.

"Whatever you say, dear," he said, half-distracted by thoughts of the work he'd missed that day, half just husbandly mollification.

It was the last thing he ever said to her.

She ran ahead of him, came up to a light, and in a moment that way back in his mind he later realized he'd actually dreaded ever since he'd brought her to England, he watched her like a Yank look left to cross the street instead of right, then step off the curb directly into the path of a speeding chrome-grilled black taxi.

He remembered calling to her, thought he reached out for her, but she was just a few feet too far away. There was the squeal of the taxi's brakes, the whine of its tires, but it was too close. The cab sent her flying fifty feet. Sirens seemed to start howling immediately, to flash up out of nowhere. Shoving men in uniforms, barked commands, a stretcher, an oxygen mask....

Colin stood there in a shock so profound he knew he'd never feel anything else in his life again; didn't even know if he'd ever speak. He saw her look left, and after a second it registered that she was *only* looking left, and he cried, "Look right! Look right!" and reached out, his fingers huge but ineffective before him, fluttering like wanton butterflies, and he reached to her and called to her ... and with truly no warning she was swept away.

She never regained consciousness.

He buried her a week later, yet to this day couldn't believe she was actually gone. He found himself still ready to ring her up to tell her something interesting, or waiting for her call after a gig in Cambridge, or—certainly now—wanting to give her every detail of his search for that "amazing" lost 45.

The search that was now taking him back to Memphis.

There was no way to duck it, and indeed, there was a faint hope that going there might—well, he didn't really know how—but might somehow make things make more sense. The thought of Robin's family crossed his mind. He hadn't seen her parents or her younger sister, Seely, since the funeral. Should he look them up? A long sigh. Well, he'd just have to see how he felt when he got there, he guessed.

He looked to his wristwatch, decided to make the time shift from Mountain Time to Central Time. Colin wore an old-fashioned windup watch, and the sound of the gears softly spinning the hour ahead soothed him. O.K., to the business at hand. He had to find the record. He wasn't foolish enough to think that *Pink Cadillac* could make anything easier with Robin's death, and yet the focus and dedication toward trying to find it over the last week … well, it was something to believe in, wasn't it?

Besides, he thought as his thoughts turned back to Daisy Cooper, there were new mysteries enough there to pre-occupy anyone.

Back in Arizona, she had never really explained what her mistake was, though she'd said enough that Colin got a pretty good idea: She'd left Bearcat and Dell too soon.

"But you came back?" Colin had said to her in her country club.

No response.

"You must've come back."

"Why do you say that?"

"Because I heard somewhere that you were there at the end."

"End of what?"

"When Bearcat died."

Daisy Cooper tilted her head up. "You heard that *somewhere*?"

"I—I can't remember. The whole death is a mystery. I've heard—"

"All kinds of things." A small smile. "I can imagine. What did Dell tell you? How is he anyway?"

"I couldn't say," Colin said. "Looked healthy. But guarded. *Very* guarded."

"I can imagine."

Colin's ears went up.

"Imagine what?"

"That he'd be—he'd be, well, like you said."

"Guarded."

Daisy looked suddenly very uncomfortable. "Listen, I can't believe—*cannot believe*—I've been talking to you like this. I haven't even thought of any of these things in years, I can't tell you. But I—I better get back to Samantha. She'll be wondering—"

Daisy got up, and Colin stood, too, trying not to be so rude as to actually block her, but in truth doing just that.

"So what did happen back there in Memphis?" he said as gently as he could. He was right in front of her.

Daisy gave him a long, unknowable look. Her face was pinched, strained. When he looked into her eyes, they were swirling a long-ago smoke. One word came to Colin: *haunted.*

It was clear she wasn't going to answer; finally she gave him an unreadable flicker of her eyes, then brushed down her tennis skirt and took a big step around him. Colin spun and was about to follow her when halfway to the door she stopped and turned.

"I'll say just one more thing to you, Mr. Stone. The story is more complicated than anyone can imagine, even you." Though her voice was tight, she gave him a coy smile. "For what you really want to know—what you're here for—I can honestly say I wasn't there. *I really wasn't.* But other people were. They're the ones you want to talk to."

"Like who?"

"Put that imagination to good use, Mr. Stone. Think it out."

✳ ✳ ✳ ✳ ✳

IT WASN'T THAT he was actually scared—or at least, could admit that to himself—it's just that suddenly he felt consumed by being *wary.* That is: Who is that man who seemed to be following him, the tall, skinny guy behind thick dark glasses, one day wearing a blue watch cap over his orange-conked hair, the next with a brown felt fedora shadowing eyes even warier than Dell's? The same man? Any man at all? Dell truly didn't know; he just felt watched. Of course he knew why: It was well into January 1956 and he hadn't made one payment to Beauregard T. Washington, a.k.a. Snake Eyes, a.k.a. Teeee-nacious, a.k.a. the man who held the marker for $300 Dell didn't have and now that Daisy was gone, didn't know how he'd get.

In the last week Dell had remembered the rest of the other story he knew about Snake Eyes; the story about Dell's East High classmate who'd borrowed from the gambler a few years back.

The guy was named Kenny Morris, he was a lineman on the football team, and he'd gotten his girlfriend, Linda Sue Fenner, pregnant. Not the only football player to knock someone up, but Kenny panicked. Talked to everyone he knew, and someone—it wasn't Dell—sent him down to Beale Street for help. There he found a wheezy, gray-haired doctor who said he could take care of Linda Sue for $100 and no questions asked. Here was Kenny's thinking: There was no way she could have their child; they were just kids themselves. He wasn't sure how much he even loved Linda Sue, and besides he was dead set on joining the Navy after high school and starting his life then.

A hundred dollars, though. Kenny's piggy bank at home had $22. He didn't have any job. He knew he couldn't go to his parents, and telling the Fenners would be suicide. The doctor suggested he look up a gentleman named Snake Eyes, and after a fretful week Kenny did. The loan was just for $80. Kenny was sure that by working hard mowing lawns, driving a truck after school—anything he could get—he could pay it back with interest. He was desperate, and he made the deal. Snake Eyes gave him three weeks to start handling the vig.

Everything Dell remembered about the episode gave him chills: What happened to Linda Sue in the backroom clinic (she died after a hemorrhage the doctor couldn't stop), and what happened to Kenny when in his grief and caught up in the investigation he forsook his payments: He disappeared from school for four weeks, and when he finally came back, he was hobbled on crutches. Though he never admitted what happened, the story was that the loan shark he'd borrowed from had broken both his knees.

And who was that man with the dark glasses Dell kept seeing?

Though there'd been no overt word from the gambler, Dell knew it would come. And for a week now he'd been turning over his options. Three hundred dollars wasn't that much, but he didn't have more than $35 to his name, and the grudging allowance from his father—only $20 a week—was hanging by a thread.

Dell was sitting on the porch outside the roadhouse, bundled in a shearling coat, watching his breath mist before him. Staring out into the nearly abandoned parking lot.

He eyeballed his own car, the Triumph his father had bought for him when he graduated high school (and hadn't even stuck around to be thanked), but it turned out Dell never saw the pink slip. His father's real estate company, Wm.Dellaplane, Inc., held the title, and Dell had no doubt that if he sold the car, his father would have him arrested for grand theft auto.

It was a gray, icy day. Dell sighed but didn't want to go back into the roadhouse, where Bearcat was even icier than the gray skies out here.

He furrowed his brow. So, how else could he get the money? No way he could go to his father. Dell had left their meeting in such a rage that he never wanted to see the man again; and though he'd cooled some, he didn't know what his father was up to and didn't want to know. No, no answer there. And his mother? She might be helpful for clothes or burgers, but he could never borrow anything serious from her. No, he wasn't coming up with anything except the one plan he'd always had: The roadhouse hits; we make enough to press up *Pink Cadillac*, and *that* hits; calls come from New York for Daisy Holiday and her blazing band; Dell follows the swivel-hips guy onto television; and he never sees his goddamn father again.

But Daisy was gone.

Plumb, devastatingly *gone*. Gone with Cuth Starks, who Dell had brought in to help them—don't think he didn't feel terrible about that; and how did it help to constantly feel Bearcat's silent anger over his mistake?—and though in his mind's eye he kept hearing a car pull into the parking lot and seeing the blonde singer with the wide shoulders step, a little hesitant, sure, but clearly contrite, freely admitting her error and right then saying something like, "I can't sing with anybody else but y'all; I open my mouth, *nothing* comes out. I missed you horrible! I'm back, really back, and all I want to do is sing with you. Set that mike up, let's do a whole blooming record!"

But as his gaze swept the parking lot, there was only a reminder of Daisy: the pink Cadillac, sitting in a corner of the lot, these January days a sheen of frost on it, looking as cold, abandoned, and forlorn as Dell Dellaplane's heart.

Only true reminder, that is, but one. A sudden spark. What about the acetate of *Pink Cadillac* they'd recorded? Dell had lost it to Cuth, but Daisy had brought it back. What if we...? But Bearcat had taken the record and spirited it away. Still, as he sat there, puffing mist balls in front of him, that was all Dell could think of: that platter of black lacquer. And the more he did, the more it looked to him like black gold.

✳ ✳ ✳ ✳ ✳

THE BEARCAT HAD other ideas, and they focused on, of all people, Sonesta Clarke. Yes, she was back, lured away from her job at the Peabody, moved in again upstairs in her small room, ensconced there with her Bible and her two "sisters," Lil and Lurleen.

Speculation around the roadhouse was that Bearcat had got her back with one of those sweaty-palmed shakes of his mojo bag, but according to what Sonesta gave out, it had

something to do with her *church*, of all things—something
there gone wrong. Least that's what she told everyone. She
said, "I discovered that the Lord—*my* Lord—wasn't living in
that house. That was a house that had not what I loved." She
was still talking in that God-smitten voice, and that was a
drag, but when all was said and done, everyone, Bearcat
included, was happy to see her.

Sonesta had smiled a mystery smile when she was told
that Daisy had run off with Cuth Starks.

"So she went with the man that drove the longest, baddest car," she said, sounding much more her sharp-tongued
self. "Don't really surprise me."

"Sonesta," Dell told her, exasperated still, "*Daisy* drove
the longest, baddest car—Elvis's pink Cadillac."

"Then why'd she go off with this cracker record man?"
she snapped.

Dell closed his eyes, remembered standing in the doorway to the roadhouse watching Cuth Starks's long black limousine gliding over the newly paved parking lot, then out on
the rutted road, disappearing for good. He involuntarily
sighed.

And was surprised by the older woman's rough maid's
hand smoothing over his.

"Listen, I'm sorry," Sonesta said, as consoling as she
could be. "She was a good girl—you know I had my problems with her. Thought the whole thing out here was crazy.
But—" She let a memory steal across her eyes. "She *was* a
good girl, even if her voice was sort of thin—"

"*Thin?*"

A smile while the skin around her eyes crinkled. Patted
his hand again.

"Dell, all I can say is, I'm sorry she did this to you—
broke your heart. Truly sorry."

At that moment Dell felt emotions for the older woman
he couldn't remember ever having had before.

What happened to her at her church? Bearcat had his musings.

"She learned where the true Lord lie," he told Dell on a Sunday afternoon, eight days since Daisy had left. Sonesta had been back three days and was already running the house like always.

"Oh, yeah," Dell said, eyebrows up, like he had an idea what Bearcat was going to say, "and where's that?"

"Righty here."

"Yeah, sure."

"You surprise me, Dell. You been brainwashed 'bout that? They got you thinkin' only place the Lord sets his big ass down is in them pointy-top white clapboard buildings?" Bearcat's hands went spiraling up. "You think Mr. Lord, he goes flying o'erhead, he sees a joint like ours, goes, 'Nope, ain't gonna set myself down there, they's playin' music! They's havin' *fun*! They's celebratin' life in a noisy, noisy way! Nosirree, ain't gonna let *nobody* catch my hide in a 'stablishment like that.' That your white-boy idea of the Lord: 'No, I want a place where everyone go *hushed*—I got my hearing ta worry 'bout. And I want a place everyone got their heads bowed down, 'cuz I'm one sneaky motherfucker, and I don't want 'em seeing me creepin' in. And I want a place where everybody got their collars buttoned tight up their necks, 'cuz I don't want 'em breathin' too much of God's beautiful air!'

"You think tha's the Lord? Sonesta, she think that. I say, 'Mr. Lord, you welcome here *anytime*. You show up here, we put the *jump* back into ya.'"

Dell was smiling. "Bearcat, you oughta be a preacher yourself."

"Don't think I didn't think it. I *did* think it, 'specially when I was gettin' beat by that man my mother married. Get me the Lord behind me, *smite* that motherfucker." A loud Bearcat chortle. "But when it all comes down, I say, where you want to do your preachin' from? One of those polished-wood, hushed-up church kind of places, or a place where the wood goddamn *breathes*!"

"Reverend Bearcat, I'd follow you anywhere," Dell said, half mocking, but more than serious, and followed that up by putting his hands over his head and bowing exaggeratedly like some Egyptian courtier.

"Yeah, right now you 'bout to follow me to the poorhouse."

"Yeah," Dell said, his blithe mood washed away in a sudden thought of Snake Eyes, "don't I know it. What're we gonna do?"

What they were talking about was the night before, the Saturday night a week after Daisy had gone. Word of her performance had streaked through young and nascently cool Memphis, and by nine the place was packed—with even more white kids than before. (And one tall, cool-looking black gentleman in the back wearing shades?) The white kids were shouting, "Where's Daisy? Bring on *Pink Cadillac*!" It had come down to Dell to make the announcement that Daisy Holliday was ... no longer there.

"Huh?" went the crowd of young men.

"Kick it!" Dell yelled to the band, and though they played for all they were worth, Bearcat's harmonica-honking blues was just too different for the newfound audience. By the end of the first set the crowd was down about two thirds, and halfway through the second there wasn't a white face to be seen.

"We gotta get us a new singer," Dell answered himself after Bearcat kept quiet.

"You mean, I just rub my bag again, and another talent likes of which nobody's yet seen walks in through that door, motor oil up to her elbows?"

Dell was up now, pacing. "We got the song—they love *Pink Cadillac*. How 'bout we hold a talent scout?"

Bearcat rubbed his droopy eyes. "Told you, don't think it works like that."

"Well, how's it going to work?" Though Dell tried to keep the anxiety down, it certainly rang loud to him. He hadn't yet told the Bearcat word one about the deal with Snake Eyes; intuition told him to keep it that way, at least for now.

"Well, you know," the Bearcat said, "We can always go with proven talent."

It took Dell a second to get it, then he threw a glance up the stairs, to where Sonesta was presumably sleeping in. She'd gone off with her Lil and Lurleen last night before the music started, and Dell hadn't seen her come back. "You mean—"

"I think she's been hintin'."

"Oh, yeah," Dell said, "*hintin'* meaning there we were, rockin' our souls away last night, we never saw one hair of her or those creepy women with her. *Hinting* meaning she seems sort of *glad* Daisy's gone."

"Son, you don't know her. I tell you, she's been hintin'."

"How?"

Bearcat looked right at the young man, boring in, as if a deep lesson were on its way. "It's in her eyes. Don't ever leave, really. 'Member, we got her down here before." Bearcat wiped a handkerchief over his forehead. "And nobody kills a song like Sonesta Clarke. That's what we need—*a killer*."

"That was years ago." Dell looked dubious. "We're talking 'bout a whole new sort of thing. We're talkin' *Pink Cadillac*."

"Let's give it a try." Bearcat stood up, like it was all settled. "Come on, son, have a little faith. What if I'm right—what if we got the Lord right here where we need 'im?" He went over to the stairs and shouted up them, "Hey, you ol' bag of sleepy bones, we need you down here!"

But Bearcat wasn't right. When Sonesta finally did appear, right before Sunday supper about 4 p.m., Bearcat took her back upstairs, where he threw all his charm, as well as promises and cajoles he'd never admit to (and probably didn't for a second mean), at the older singer, and she let him beg and grovel and swear up and down on his mother's grave things were gonna be sweet. It was pretty soon obvious to both of them that he'd get what he wanted. Sonesta Clarke was a singer, and she was born to sing. The only problem? She wasn't born to sing *Pink Cadillac*.

This all came clear the next afternoon, the band in place, Bearcat kicking 'em off. But no matter how they started, Sonesta took Dell and Daisy's song, all up-tempo scatted rock 'n roll, and smoothed it out and made it soulful. Her rendition was stirring in its way, but it wasn't the song—and it wasn't what was getting on the radio.

Dell and Bearcat had a powwow over a smoke in the parking lot.

"She doesn't hear the backbeat," Dell said.

"That's true."

"It goes right past her, clippety clop, clippety clop."

"Too true." Bearcat lit the butt of one of the cheap Cubans he carried loose in his pocket.

"And when she hits that upper register, might as well be singin' gospel."

"True, too. All that time with that reverend back home."

"So what're we going to do?"

Bearcat had a sudden fury in his eyes. "We're gonna make her sing it *right*."

But it just wasn't going to happen.

"Ba-baba-ba-baba-ba—you can hear that?" Bearcat was still smoking the cigar, indoors now, which he knew always annoyed Sonesta. He was standing next to Thumper, having him lay down the *Pink Cadillac* bass riff.

"Of course I can hear that, old man. You think we never cut a tune before?"

"But the beat goes skippety-skippety." A wave to Sticks Miller, who cracked his snare.

"I know where the goddamn beat is." Sonesta was up in front of the microphone, stiff, shuffling from side to side, her head with its black lacquered hair jutting forward nervously like a hungry chicken.

Bearcat went over to Dell, right next to him. "You think she's sassin' me?"

Dell raised a noncommittal eyebrow over the mouthpiece of his sax.

"You sassin' *me*?"

"I'm just trying to get you to let me sing your goddamn song!"

Sonesta made a little show of setting her two stolid, black-shoed feet right before the microphone, then facing it as if she were facing a firing squad. Salt was over ready to work the disc-cutting machine, except they weren't ready to cut anything yet.

"But you singin' it like you in goddamn church!"

"Yeah, and what's wrong with that? That's the way I sing."

"But, um," Dell said softly from beside her, "this isn't a church song. This is a get-yourself-a-Caddie, hit-the-open-road, jam-your-foot-to-the-floor, ain't-*never*-going-to-look-back song."

"Yeah, and where'm I gonna get me a Cadillac?"

"You sing the song right, you gonna be swimmin' in Caddies," Bearcat said cooingly, trying flattery.

"Yeah, just like *Cryin' Shame* was gonna get me swim-min' in furs. Swimmin' in ermine, swimmin' in mink!" She gave Bearcat a hooked glare. " 'Stead I was just swimmin' in *tears*."

"She is, she's sassin' me," Bearcat cried out. "Y'all hear her, she's sassin' me something fierce."

Sonesta sent a cool glance over at the Bearcat, who was suddenly wary.

"Now let's just try it this way," Dell said, stepping

between the two of them. "You have to think driving, driving, driving. Just let go, feel the beat."

"I am the beat, white boy."

"Whoa!"

"And I know what you want. You want me to sing this song just like that white gal."

"No, we don't," Dell said. "But we gotta.... Well, think Ruth Brown. Think Little Richard."

"They ain't white."

"That's what the boy's sayin'," Bearcat said, moving around Dell. "Sticks, give us that beat again. That rocky-roly beat. Come on, woman, *hit it*!"

But it truly wasn't going to happen.

They tried everything. Sticks slowed the beat, got it rolling tumpety-tumpety, just like a semi's big wheels cruising the highway, and they tried to ease Sonesta into it, then bring it up to tempo; but though she grooved there beautifully when the beat was slooooow, she just couldn't catch the back-beat when Sticks shifted it into rock 'n' roll. Bearcat even went up and swung his mojo bag in front of her like he was trying to hypnotize her, but all Sonesta did was swat it aside and say, "Get that stinkin' piece of coon meat out of my face!"

Finally Dell said, "You know, Bearcat, maybe we should just let her do it *her* way. Least we'll get something down on wax."

"Might as well get the Mormon Tabernacle Choir to do it."

"Hell, I do it my way, pour that true Southern soul on it," Sonesta said, "you know white folks gonna be coverin' it—they gonna get the hit out of it."

Bearcat pursed his wide black brow. "I feel a change, woman. I think you put 'nuff of that rocky-roly soul on it, I can sell it like flapjacks. But we need us *real* rocky-roly soul."

"You and yo mama!"

"She's sassin' me again!"

Dell just laughed. It was a loud, guffawing laugh as

much of frustration as anything, but laugh he did. "Come on, children."

"Who you—" Bearcat went, but at that moment Slingshot the bouncer came in carrying a small Japanese transistor radio and shouted, "You hear this?"

There was a song playing on the radio, but it was tinny, and it wasn't till Bearcat saw the look in Sling's eyes and shushed everyone still going at it that anyone could make out what he'd heard.

Then, unmistakable: *"I don't care if I ever look back / In my pink Cadillac, my pink Cadillac."*

"Goddamn!" Bearcat went.

"What is that?" Sonesta said. "That your song?"

"Sure as shit and Shinola, it is. Who's that singing?"

The fidelity on the radio was so shrill it was hard to make out the voice.

"That somebody coverin' our song already? How'd that—"

"It's Daisy," Dell said, half to himself.

"What you mean, it's Daisy?" Bearcat stomped around. "How the fuck is it Daisy? Wait—don't tell me. She's recordin' the song already with that carny fellow, and they got it on the radio. Hot damn!"

They all listened as quiet as they could. It was Daisy, and they all heard her whooping through the final verse, then driving the chorus home: *"Never look back, never look back / My pink Cadillac, my piiiiiiink Cadillac."*

"That sounds like you, Dell, playin' that sax," Thumper the bass player said.

"Yeah, and that sounds like me on drums," Sticks said. "Hard to make out, though, but—"

Dell was smiling, but quiet, as if he were listening as if his life depended on it.

When the record ended, Dewey Phillips came on, crying, "Hoo-*gaw*! Listen to that li'l diamond of spinnin' wax. I think that record have 'Hit!' written all over it. But you gotta tell *me*, I got the phone lines wide open. Till I hear from you, why, we're just gonna play it again!"

And he did.

Halfway through the second playing, Dell was dancing, his feet doing giddy shuffle steps over the roadhouse floor.

"Boy," Bearcat called, "what you know about this?"

"Um, nothin'," Dell said.

"BOY!"

Dell was smiling wide 'nuff to beat the band.

"It's our record, ain't it? What you doin' to me? You didn't learn *nothin'* from your carny friend?"

"We got ourselves our hit, Bearcat. You heard Dewey."

"But how'd he get our record? Last I saw, there was only one copy of that *Pink Cadillac* acetate, the one Daisy brought us back, and I had it upstairs under lock and key."

"Not much of a lock." Dell shrugged.

"You took it!"

"I got it where it'll do us some good. Where people can *hear it*."

"But we decided it was too rough."

"Don't sound too rough right now, does it?"

Indeed, it sounded damn good to them as it played over the little radio, Daisy's voice swelling over the final *"Pink Cad-il-lac, pink Cad-il-lac"* shout-down.

"So what you got goin'?" Bearcat finally said.

"What do you mean?"

"I mean, *What you got goin'?*"

"Nothing."

"Yeah, you just walked our record down to Daddy-o Dewey, that white man?"

"I had to do *something*."

"But Dewey Phillips? You know 'bout that man, don't you? I couldn't go get that record from that man if his hair was on fire and I had me a long, loose hose." Bearcat snorted.

Dell looked at the big man quizzically.

"That man," Bearcat went on, into a riff now, "he like to *play* blues and hollers, and when he plays 'em, he does us all a world of good. But there be folks at that station just not so quick to *deal* with them who make 'em." Gave Dell a long look. "Know what I'm sayin'? For me that disc might as well be in China—or Nashville."

Dell took the dig silently for a second, then said, "Bearcat, he's the man everybody listens to. You know that. Remember what he did for Elvis."

Bearcat thought that over for a minute, then said, softer now, "Still, you didn't trust me enough to ask me?"

"I—I didn't know what you'd say."

Bearcat fixed him with a quick, furious glare. Dell squirmed visibly, shuffling side to side in little, mincing steps.

"You ... didn't ... know ... what ... I'd ... say?"

Bearcat was big and scary, and Dell was tongue-tied.

"YOU WANNA KNOW WHAT I'LL SAY?"

Dell swallowed loudly.

"Well." Deep scowl, but there was more than a touch of play in his voice now, and Dell found himself starting to relax even before he heard the next sentence. "What I say is, We got us a hit! We got us a motherjumpin' hit record!"

When they were all finished leaping around, it dawned on them what they didn't have: Any kind of distribution deal. Or even the singer herself. Dell shook the worry off.

"The song's out there, we got that—people are going to love the version on the acetate. So we just put that out."

"What're we gonna do for money?" Bearcat said.

"Money for what?"

"Press that record. Distribute it. Get it into folks' hands." Bearcat rubbed his meaty thumb and middle finger together. "*Moooo-neeeey.*"

"Dewey keeps playin' it, well, we'll find some way to get it out there," Dell said, thinking, What could be more bankable than a record getting played over and over on the radio? "How much of a problem could it be? The hard part's comin' up with a hit, ain't it? And this is gonna be a big, wild hit! Why you worrying?"

The big man muttered something like, "You're so young." Sonesta walked over, patted his arm. He looked lost in thought.

"But how you gonna sell it without Daisy being here?" Sticks said from behind Dell.

"Well," Dell said. He went tight-lipped, and the silence just hung there. "Well, we got the record. We just do it."

"That's another thing," Bearcat said, looking up but still glowering. "What if she beats us to it? What if they hear Dewey's breakin' *Pink Cadillac*, that carny man gets her into a big studio, and the next thing we know...."

"Oh, I wouldn't worry 'bout *that*." Dell gave everyone a big, sunny, boyish smile. "That's one cut I'd love to hear."

"What you mean?"

"I mean, Bearcat, those white folks who play for Cuth Starks, oh, yeah, they got the true rocky-roly soul *deep* in their bones."

✳ ✳ ✳ ✳ ✳

IT WAS *COOOOLD* UP NORTH. Colder than she'd ever been, snow blowing on the streets and icicles hanging down like spear tips, and even when she was inside and swaddled in the fox fur that Cuth had given her, the cold stuck with her, got way down there deep in her marrow ... and stayed.

Not that it wasn't worth it. She was singing two sets a night in a club in Buffalo, the Tin Spot, with a tasty piano trio behind her, learning songs in the afternoon, and trying them out that night to a room of patrons who actually listened closely and never failed to give her applause.

This was what Cuth called wood-shedding, he loved the

term, would lift his mustache, pucker his lips, and go, "Babe, be patient, we're just *wooood-sheddin'*. We're getting everything right 'fore we take you to New York."

"But why Buffalo?" Daisy would ask. "It's cooooooold up here."

"Babe, that's the way the bizness works. We gotta get you close enough to the Apple people'll hear of you, but not so close they can come see you. Buffalo's perfect."

Well, perfect for Cuth, who took the train up Friday night for New York City and stayed through the weekend. Not so perfect for Daisy, who had what seemed like a whole hotel to herself the rest of the time. Buffalo, it turned out, was nobody's idea of a vacation place in January.

Or February. You could say the thrill was, um, wearing off. The singing, well, she had developed poise on the stage, and through lessons Cuth had arranged with a former vaudeville singer, she'd gotten her pitch spot on, and through practice in a mirror she'd shaken off a few of her Tennessee mountain pinched-throat vocal mannerisms—she was starting to sound like a regular American. But the nights dragged long after a show; and the days, gray at best, blizzardy at worst, were longer than the slowest church meeting her father'd ever conducted.

But when Cuth showed up at the Tin Spot toward the end of her last set on Friday, well, everything came to life.

He'd shake the snow off his fur-collared Chesterfield coat, then pull out the roll of hundreds in his pocket, tight under a gold-and-diamond clip, and casually drop one with the bartender and take care of the room. He'd always have a gift for Daisy, perfume or jewelry or the sheerest black stockings, that he told her he'd spent half a day looking for in New York.

"Don't they have you workin' down there?" Daisy would say, the gift resplendent before her.

"The music biz, Babe. We keep, ah, flexible hours."

Cuth had arranged an office for himself with Decca Records and was handling Old Gold's business long distance while he groomed Daisy. It seemed a pretty grand life, and Daisy was dying to get to New York City.

"We're getting close, darlin'. Each Friday I come up here, I surprise myself all over again how great you're getting. But there's still—" Cuth hesitated; he was about to bring up a sore spot between them "—still a little of that, um, roughness. They ain't gonna like that in New York. That ain't gonna get you on *Arthur Godfrey* or *Hit Parade*."

"Ain't—*ain't* gonna like it? You're a big help to me, Mr. Cuth Starks, talkin' like that. You funnin' with me again?"

Cuth reached over and touched Daisy's heavily powdered cheek.

"You just trust ol' Cuth, Baby, we'll get you down to the Apple and blow that town right open!"

The powder on Daisy's cheek—so much that sometimes on stage she imagined she could hear it crack—was part of Cuth's "makeover," the way he was grooming her for stardom. Sometimes she wondered what he needed with the real Daisy Holliday at all, he was remaking her so thoroughly: her accent, the singing lessons, and personal instructions when he was there on how to walk, hold herself, move her arms, smile—just be this *winning* performer. And then there was the, as he constantly put it, the rep-er-*toire*.

Cuth could always be counted on to tell her how much he loved her voice, that it was one in a million—much too good to waste on even hillbilly music, not to mention that nigger stuff she was doing when he found her (one time he let drop the word *rescued*). No, they didn't understand that music in Buffalo, let alone New York City. *In New York, up at Decca, they want sophisticated songs, clever songs, or simply lovingly funny songs. You know, like Rosemary Clooney, Patti Page—glamorous but wholesome. We'll get you there, you got all the right equipment, Babe—one classy chassis.*

Classy chassis or not, well, at least so far Cuth Starks was being the perfect gentleman. No, she had nothing to complain about there. Except that even *that* was starting to make her edgy a bit. She didn't in any way *want* his advances, she was just, well, surprised that he could be so businesslike all of the time. Even though she didn't want to think about it, Daisy was missing the easy, flirty, fun way it had been with—

No, no reason to think about Dell. Or Bearcat or Sonesta or.... That was history, she'd only been there a few months out of her whole 19 years, they were just a way station on her journey to ... Buffalo? But she had to remember that everything up here in this northern town was so new, and so different; I mean, she hardly knew what she was feeling any special time of the day, her emotions just jumping and heaving like *crazy*. It wasn't exactly that she was homesick—well, she *was* homesick, even if she couldn't admit it to herself. There were even mornings after she woke up when she spent hours under the covers, remembering that time between arriving in Memphis and meeting Cuth. Well, it had felt awfully natural and comfortable and sort of kick-back wonderful there with the Bearcat and Dell, but maybe that was just a fluke—and 'sides, hadn't it simply gotten her what she always wanted? Got her the attention of a true record man. Got her a career going to take her soon to the Apple. Where Elvis went right after he gave her the car—.

Sometimes, strange as it was, that's what she missed most, that huge gleaming pile of pink metal. In Buffalo she didn't have a car, didn't need one, Cuth said, able to walk from the hotel to the Tin Spot and back, and dine in the hotel or at a diner along the way. So what she had to pull on every piece of clothing she owned just about, and tilt her shoulder into the icy wind or snow to get anywhere. It was just that the car was so ... beautiful. The chrome grill, the bold, haunchy fenders, that white leather upholstery.... She had dreams about the car, about blasting down a back road, the wind whipping her hair, her foot challenging the gas pedal to take her faster, faster—and the Cadillac leaping ahead. Dreams in which birds circled overhead and the sun was always shining. Dreams with soundtracks, just like the movies, but instead of violin schmaltz, thumpy, churning, *driving* rock 'n' roll.

And sometimes the dreams overcame her when she was onstage. Working through *How Much Is That Doggy in the Window*. Working through *Que Sera, Sera*. This wouldn't happen usually till a Thursday night, long into the week without Cuth, but she would close her eyes and just see it, the Pink Cadillac, almost feel the wind in her hair, and there'd be just a little hump in the music, a little slip-back to what she used to sing, hint of a growl, she couldn't control it, and she'd look out into the darkened room to see if anyone noticed, but nobody ever did. Then she'd have to get a grab on herself, because she would want to spin around and say to her trio, "Hey, guys, there's this song I used to do, it's pretty easy, just three chords, but it moves a little different from *Doggy*. More of a beat. Song about a car I used to own. Think I could teach it to you?"

But she wouldn't say that, and the next day Cuth would pull in from New York, walk in bold as could be, his mustache bristling, then buy the room drinks and lead the applause for her final set; and then even though she was tired and more than a little lonely, he'd take her up to his room and have her walk back and forth for an hour with a book on her head, have her practice saying things like "Mr. McGillicuddy was muddy, but Billy was silly, and they all shilly-shallyed with Lally and ... Wentworth," stupid phrases he'd make up, then he'd have her sit in front of him and move her mouth up down and sideways so it no longer felt like *her* mouth at all.

When she could barely see straight, when she was so tired her head kept falling onto her wide shoulders, her face so sore from bending and stretching it felt like she'd been all night at the dentist, Cuth would lean back in his chair and say, "Daisy, you're a lot of work. A ... lot ... of ... work."

What fiery glare flew from her eyes?

"Now don't you look at me that way. You gonna thank me when I'm done. 'Cuz when you're ready, we're goin' to New York, sweetheart. And Ed Sullivan, he's just gonna love you."

When the fire melted from her eyes, as it always did, there'd still be some warmth, some interest there. It was just because it was so cold and she was so lonely, but the look, even if she wasn't sure she actually meant it, wasn't hidden, she thought.

But nothing happened. Cuth would lean over and pat her golden-haired head and say, "Lot's more work tomorrow, Babe," and then he'd tell her to sleep tight and not let the bedbugs bite—and there probably were bedbugs; *something* was nipping her arms every morning—and head off to his room in a whole other hotel down the street.

A full weekend of this, and then on Sunday afternoon he'd pull on his fur-collared Chesterfield and be gone again for the week.

✳ ✳ ✳ ✳ ✳

IF NOTHING ELSE, it was an object lesson in *humidity*. (Well, perhaps humility, too, but all of his life seemed to be that.) At the moment Colin's first thoughts were on his sticky shirt, mop-wet hair, clammy forehead. It was not nearly as degree hot where he was now, but it was a lot closer to Hades than Arizona had been. As he drove away from the airport looking for a motel, he thought, But still, there is something about this place. It feels right, like I've been away too long. He was finding that even the thought of Robin here was more a comfort than a worry. Yeah, feels like I'm back home.

In Scottsdale he'd called an acquaintance at *Living Blues* magazine, in Oxford, Mississippi, and together they tried to piece together the Bearcat Jackson band that would have played on *Pink Cadillac*. David Brown, the friend, said that Sticks McGhee must've been there, but that he'd died in Chicago in 1968. Thumper Johnson probably was on bass, and he lasted till 1989 and went right in the Mississippi Delta town of Indianola, where he'd been born, leaving two great-grandsons already with their own blues band. Sonesta Clarke? Colin doubted she was even there when *Pink Cadillac* would've been cut, and remembered that he hadn't been able to find her when he'd put together the Bearcat CD. That left the guitar player, Clayton Booker.

Brown was pretty sure Booker was alive. He had played in bands at least up through the '80s; Brown just hadn't heard much about him since.

"I have to talk to him," Colin said into the phone.

"Let me ask around, see what anybody knows. Where you going to be?"

"Not staying here, that's for sure," Colin said. "Not ready for golf yet, even if Alice Cooper lives for it. I think I'll head on to Memphis." Colin had decided that just that second, but it made sense: One, as a likely place to find Clayton Booker if he was still alive; and two, because all along he'd known he'd have to see again the place where the record he now knew really did exist had been made.

And of course, there was Robin.

"Call me from there," David said. "I'm sure I'll have something for you."

And he did. Clayton Booker was going strong. He worked as a bartender at a place called the Palm Bar. The evening shift, 7 p.m. to closing. Which gave Colin, after he'd found a room, the afternoon free.

And though his hand shook as he dialed the phone, no good reason not to call the Longworths. Robin's mother answered. She didn't seem surprised at all to hear from Colin, or to learn that he was staying in the Skyway Motel in town. No, she was all classic Southern hospitality. "I insist," she said, "that you drop everything and come see us."

"I'm here on business—" he started to say, as if actually this close he could simply beg off seeing his in-laws.

"Oh, I know 'bout business, and I'm having nothing of it. Do you remember the way out here? It's easy. Just get yourself on the ring road, get off at Walnut Grove. Then here's what you do."

The funny thing was Colin remembered exactly how to get to the Longworths'. Robin had brought him home only the second day they'd been together; and he'd taken meals with her family almost the rest of the week he was courting his wife. Yet he was still surprised how easily he made the turns, how familiar the overhanging oaks were, the signs by the road—it was as if nothing had changed.

He parked by the curb, stood for a second by the screen door gathering his nerves, then rang the chiming doorbell. Nobody appeared for almost a minute, and then he was totally disarmed by what he saw. He was looking through the screen so everything was slightly blurry, but there was a figure coming toward him who had the shape, the gait, even as she got closer, a shimmering vision of the face of his wife.

His breath froze in his throat.

"Colin," the woman called out. "Sorry we didn't get the door right away. We're setting up a barbecue out back." And now the woman was right by the door, and he knew who she was. "Hope you'll be able to stay. It's in your honor."

For a second her name escaped him, but then he remembered—Cecilia, called Seely. The younger sister, but only by a couple years. A ... what was she? Nothing to do with music; doctorsomething, or—research chemist, that was it. Married, no kids. And seeing her now, finally up close, he remembered that she didn't really look that much like Robin. Close enough in bones to tell they were sisters, but the coloring was different. Robin had had sparkly green-hazel eyes, Seely's were brown but equally bright. Seely had auburn hair, and it had been cut very short, while Robin's had been past her shoulders and blonde.

The curious thing now, though, was that Seely's hair seemed much lighter, and it was definitely grown out so it was almost the length Robin's had been when he first saw her.

"A barbecue," Colin said. "Well—" He blinked as Seely pulled the door back. His quick image of himself: a startled animal. She really did look much more like his wife than he remembered. "That's lovely. I do feel honored. I—I have an appointment later, but it's not till tonight."

"Great." The slender woman ushered him in. "So, I'm sure you're not in town just to see us. What's up?"

"Oh, it's interesting—I think." Colin was trying to remember if Seely had any musical interests, and then he remembered Robin telling him how they always were singing together as kids, harmonizing. Indeed, hadn't they had a singing group together in high school? "I'm here for work, actually. Chasing down a lost record."

"Really!" Up went her voice, and with its flash of enthusiasm it mimicked Robin's. He shook his head again. "You'll have to tell us all about it." They stepped through the kitchen, then out into the backyard. "Look, here's Mom. Dad should be home from the office in—" she looked at her wristwatch "—about an hour—"

At this point Mrs. Longworth came up to him. Colin was attuned to any possible hesitation; he had, he knew, been the man who not only took her eldest daughter away, but who also couldn't—*didn't*—reach out to pull her back as she stepped to her death. But the kind-looking woman with the lightly frosted champagne hair and sweet, round smile didn't miss a beat. She threw open her arms and pulled Colin to her, then said loud as a bright bell, "It's such a pleasure to see you again. I thought—well, with you in England and all—that I'd never lay eyes on you again. But you're here!" She was still holding his hands, smiling into his eyes.

"Come, let me make you a drink. You're still a rum and Coke man?"

They couldn't have been more hospitable. Mother and daughter treated him like family, like *true* family, and pretty soon he was sitting there more relaxed than he could remember. Even when Mr. Longworth showed up, looking exactly like Colin remembered him—short, wiry, intense, with close-cropped gray hair—well, he was a guy, and so he wasn't all beaming ebullience, and maybe when he gripped Colin's hand there was a twinge of extra squeeze, a hint that he hadn't simply been sitting around for nine months waiting for his daughter's husband to show up and flood them with memories of their lost girl; but even Harold Longworth seemed genuinely not to *blame* Colin for anything—at least that's what the record producer came to feel.

He was more and more curious what Seely was doing there, and finally while they were all drinking and waiting for the grill to get hot, he came right out and asked.

She blushed, as prettily as Robin ever had.

"Well, let's not beat around that bush. I'm separated. From Davis. It's—well, I'm back home for a while." A tight smile. "Licking my wounds, I guess."

"I'm sorry," Colin said. He was trying to remember if he'd ever met Davis—was that a first name or a last?—but knew he hadn't. Could he remember anything about him? Just that Robin had never liked her sister's choice in mate.

"Well, I'm not. I'm relieved. But—let's not talk about that. We want to hear all about what you're doing here."

"Well," Colin said, "that's a good question. I'm—I'm here on a sort of wild goose chase, I'm afraid."

"Oh, don't be *negative*, Colin," Mrs. Longworth said to the half-frowning man.

"Mother!" Seely went.

Colin smiled from Seely to her mother, took a quick sip of his rum and Coke, then told them about his search for the

lost 45, meeting Dell Dellaplane, Daisy Holliday, and how he
hoped to be connecting with the guitarist Clay Booker that
night. Behind him Mr. Longworth had set the steaks hissing on
the grill. Mrs. Longworth listened politely, but Seely leaned in
with particular interest. When he was finished, she surprised
Colin doubly. First, she remembered that Colin had met Robin
while in Memphis getting material for the Bearcat CD.

"Right," he said.

Then she said, "We saw her, about eight years ago."

Colin's eyebrows went up; he shifted forward. "Who?"

"That woman, the one you mentioned, the older
singer—"

"Sonesta Clarke?"

Seely nodded broadly. "Yeah, Robin and me. She was
playing in a club somewhere in town, I don't think it was on
Beale Street." She squinched up her pretty features.
"Might've been."

"You and Robin?" Colin's head was swimming. "Before
I came here."

"Of course. Years before. Robin knew Sonesta Clarke's
music, what was it, *What a Shame*?"

"*Cryin' Shame.*"

"Yeah, yeah," Seely went, catching Colin's excitement
now. "She was pretty old, least that's how it seemed to us
then—we were just kids. But she had a voice on her! I remember Robin paying particular attention, even singing along
under her breath. She was trying to learn everything she
could."

Colin closed his eyes, his imagination swelling for that
moment with the picture of his wife in a smoky, probably run-
down club, Sonesta Clarke up on the stage, singing the songs
she'd done for Bearcat at his roadhouse. He could almost
imagine the black singer, but he saw his wife perfectly: the
tight intensity of Robin's upper lip, her left, better ear tilted
forward, all her attention on the singer; doing her best, he just

knew, to relive the older woman's life through her own imagination. He savored the picture; it resonated within him in ways he knew he might never be able to—or even want to—explain.

When he came back to himself, he said, "Do you think she might still be around?"

Seely looked at him for a moment, her head tilted to the side just so, and for a second it was his wife looking at him. He started. But of course it wasn't.

"I don't have any idea. I haven't seen her name in the *Commercial Appeal* or anywhere else, not that I pay that much attention. It's not like I'm dating again or anything." A wry, in-turned smile.

Colin was wondering if he could find Sonesta. That couldn't hurt, could it? He'd ask Clay Booker tonight when he saw him. Booker would probably know where she was, if she was still alive.

Mr. Longworth forked the steaks and flipped them over; flames shot up.

"Harold, how *are* those steaks?" Mrs. Longworth said.

"Oh, you know," the gray-haired man said, "no steak before its time."

"Harold's deepest intuition has to do with the doneness of meat, right dear?" Robin's mother said with a chuckle. "I'm going to go freshen up. Seely, you want to freshen up, too? Colin?"

"No, Mother, I'm fine."

"Thanks, Mrs. Longworth."

"Call me Dorothy."

Colin gave the older woman a smile.

After the steaks had flamed up for the last, perfect time, and after they'd all eaten heartily, leaving meat juices glazed over the china plates, Seely asked Colin if he'd like to take a walk. The Longworth home was at the end of a dead-end street, and there was a thick pine grove behind it. It was still light enough out that they could find their way easily. Seely led him in.

They didn't speak for a while, the only sounds being their shoes crackling over pine needles and a breeze sweeping through the branches.

"It's good to see you," Seely finally said. "You're looking good."

"Thank you," Colin said. He was feeling surprisingly calm. "You, too." He smiled ahead at the young woman. "I wasn't sure, you know, whether I should—" Was this the right thing to say? He held his tongue a few seconds longer.

"Oh, I think we're all glad you came. You know, none of us think. . . ." A pause. "I mean, it wasn't—" Now Seely held her tongue. She stopped, turned, and faced the Englishman. "Listen, Colin, it wasn't your fault, nobody *ever* thought that."

"I wasn't asking."

Seely looked down a moment. "I know."

"But I'm glad, well, glad to hear it. And very, very happy I came. You've all been wonderful."

Seely gave out a long sigh. "I can't say I don't miss her. I mean, it was hard when she went with you to London, but at least we could write, talk on the phone. And besides, my life was, well, busier, fuller—"

"I miss her, too," Colin said into the hush.

"Of course you do." Seely looked right at him. "Do you think ... have you given any thought ... well, this search you're on, for this record, does it have anything to do with Robin?"

Colin hesitated, then said, "I don't think there's very much I *don't* do that doesn't have something of Robin in it." He held up his hands. "This? It just amazes me to think this record is out there and nobody's heard it in over forty years. That's what it's most about."

"I can see that." Seely was looking right at him. Her

brown eyes, not Robin's hazel, still had a shape and intensity in them that was remarkably similar. Colin felt himself deeply moved. Startled in a way he couldn't explain to himself.

"Yeah, it's—" But his sentence just died there.

They both shuffled back and forth for a few moments, not really looking at each other, but not looking anywhere else, either.

Finally, Seely sighed. "It's getting pretty dark. Better head back, O.K.?"

Colin nodded silently.

On the way to the house, Seely said, "You have to let me know what you find out. Promise?"

"Sure."

"No, I mean it." Her pretty voice rose. "I've felt—well, I'm really interested in this *Pink Cadillac* record. I'm *dying* to know."

"I will."

"You promise?" There was a lot buzzing around inside her, Colin could feel it even if he couldn't explain it.

"Yes." He laughed. "I'll call you for sure."

Now Seely was quiet.

"But yes, I can tell," Colin started to say, nervously now, just to fill up the silence, "that you are interested." He heard himself kicking pine needles. "I mean, you saw Sonesta Clarke perform. That's more than me. I have to—well, that's amazing!"

"And she was great," Robin said then. "A great singer. A great night."

That was it. There was nothing more Colin could say. But all the way back into town, and even when he was lost trying to find the Palm Bar, pulling over to the side of the street and fumbling with his map, only to look up and see the neon-outlined palm tree and the words PALM BAR hanging there in neon yellow and blue—all that time he kept thinking not just about Robin, but also what a nice time he'd had with her family.

∗ ∗ ∗ ∗ ∗

LATER THAT NIGHT, when all the excitement of hearing *Pink Cadillac* go rocking out of Slingshot's transistor radio had died down, Bearcat and Dell found themselves sitting at one of the oil-cloth-covered tables, a bottle of bootleg between them, trying to decide what to do next. Salt was swabbing down the bar, the overalled Hosea had curled up in one corner with a bottle, and Sling the doorman was listening to his radio soft in another.

"We have to get the record out there," Dell insisted. "I mean, I didn't really know when I gave it to Dewey what he'd do—but he's playin' it. Over and over. Now we gotta get it out there—"

"And I say again," the Bearcat said, soft-popping his thumb and middle finger, "*M-0-N-E-Y.*"

"Whatta we got? Anything we can use as collateral?"

"You're talkin' to one busted-up negro," Bearcat said but with no diminishment of pride. "You the Mr. Rich Pockets white boy."

"Right."

"Don't give me that." Bearcat frowned. "You did us fine before when we needed money for the club. Dropped a bucket, look what all came up!" He swept his hands out to take in the fancy decorations, still bedizening the walls and ceiling. "Ain't that a well you could dip into again?"

Dell, thinking of Snake Eyes and how he knew he couldn't tell Bearcat about that, simply shook his head.

But Bearcat didn't buy it, pushed on: "You tellin' me there ain't no more money where that came from?"

Dell shook his head again. Of course, there was money in Snake Eyes, but no way Dell could see any of it coming to him; hell, he *owed* Snake Eyes the $300 and didn't have a clue how to get it back to him. Then there was that shadowy guy with the prison eyes and orange conked hair Dell kept seeing everywhere. And the promise to Diamondback. Yet there was such insistence in Bearcat, Dell felt he had to play him along.

"How much would it take?"

"Press that sucker up, get it out there—" The big man squinted his left eye down easy. "Wouldn't be more than a couple, three, four hundred bucks, I'd say."

"Hmnn, only a few hundred." Dell looked lost in thought.

"That's all! Must be easy for a boy like you to come up with that kind of money. Hell, that must just be pocket change to you, right, white boy? Ain't that just *al-low-ance*?"

So that's what Bearcat was getting at. Good, he really didn't have any idea where the $300 had come from. Thought it was from—yeah, that made sense. Dell, whether out of pride or not wanting Bearcat to blow up on him, he would never be certain, still didn't want to confess that he'd gone to Beale Street and Snake Eyes for the money the first time. Maybe he did in some way want Bearcat to think he had the obvious source of income—that he was, how'd the older man put it, Mr. Rich Pockets.

"Yeah, I get an allowance," Dell said deadpan. "I get twenty dollars a week."

Bearcat cast a glance behind him, as if out to the parking lot.

"And I don't own that car, either. Barely mine to drive. I sell it, the real Mr. Rich Pockets, he'll have my ass in jail so fast it'll make that bag round your waist jump up and shout, 'Hi-di-ho!' "

"Fifteen dollars," Bearcat said. "That ain't much." He fixed Dell with an intent gaze. "That the truth?"

Dell nodded. "Barely pays for gas and burgers."

The old man's eye was hooked now. "And that explains the way you're always lookin' so sharp?"

Dell looked down at what he was wearing: buckle-bright leather jacket, J.C. Penny's wool shirt over a white T-shirt, black jeans, and thick engineer boots. "I wouldn't call this sharp, but, yeah, my mother now and then gives me a few bucks for clothes." Dell looked back to Bearcat. "But that's not where the money came from."

"Where was it, then?" It was hard to read the Bearcat's tone. He was obviously asking direct, but there was a way in which he wasn't asking, too; a way where the answer was no longer of any consequence to him.

"Um, I'd rather—"

"You'd rather keep it your own secret, eh, paaaarrt-nerrrr?" Bearcat drawled out the final word.

Dell heard what he was saying. But he couldn't answer him, simple as that. It had to be his own secret. Later, though, Dell would ask himself, and ask himself again, if it would have made any difference to the tragedy that followed had he simply admitted everything to the big man. *I went down to Beale Street, gentleman there you have a feud with, name of Beauregard T. Washington, a.k.a. Snake Eyes, a.k.a. to you Snake in the Grass, and he funded us. I'd go talk to him again 'cept that he's got a shadowy guy gunning for me 'cuz I haven't been paying the vig on the first amount.* He could have said it, and Bearcat could've said, *How dare you go to my mortal enemy behind my back?* Or he might have said, *Hmmnn, that's an interesting development. Been looking for a reason to reconnect with that bad man. Hell, maybe I could take care of ol' Tee-nacious Washington for you—might be a pleasure.* But Dell didn't speak up, and that was that.

Curiously, Bearcat wasn't waiting for an answer. It was like he had his fixed idea and wasn't brooking any other explanations. Or that wherever the first money had come from, they desperately needed another $300, and that was the only true issue at hand.

"Well," the Bearcat said, looking around the room, "we got no money, we got no record. Right?" He spoke as if uttering a biblical truth.

"I know it," Dell said right up, simply glad the subject had been pulled off of him.

"Salt?"

"You're right, old man."

A glare at the kid, but then Bearcat spun around. "Hosea?"

The layabout stirred from the corner where he'd taken a brown bottle of hooch and said simperingly, "Whatever you say, boss, whatever you say."

"You see, it's the truth." Bearcat did his lucre finger-pop again, then turned to the far corner. "Sling?"

Nothing. The huge bouncer had the tiny pink radio up by his right ear, already cauliflowered from his younger years in the ring, so it looked like some weird atomic-energy mutation.

"Slingshot!" Top of the big man's lungs.

"Huh?"

"They still playing that dad-burned disc at Dewey's?"

"What, boss?"

"Take that goddamn thing out of yo' ugly ear for a moment." The bouncer obliged. "I say, they still playing our record, Sling?"

"Oh, yeah."

"How many times?" Dell asked.

"I'd say five, seven or so."

"One after the other?"

"No, 'bout every four or six they drop the needle."

"It still sounding O.K.?" This was Dell, thinking, All I gave the radio station was our sole acetate. And it wasn't made to stand up to too many playings.

"Seems fine to me, Mr. Dell."

"But it ain't gonna hold up much longer, you know that, right?" Bearcat said.

"I'm worrying."

"Damn!" Bearcat hit his hand on the table. "And that damn girl ran off with the carny man."

Dell winced, and hated himself for it.

"Got to get us that money," the old man went on. "Salt, anything we can sell quick?"

"Yo' mama," the bartender said.

Bearcat raised his hand in eruptive astonishment at the young man's effrontery, but it was only a mock gesture.

"That sweet woman still with us, I might go out and sell her. Hey, hey. But we ain't got nothin' else?"

Salt held out his hands, spread them, opened them to the roadhouse around them.

"Yeah, and you know, we go lookin' for money legitimate, even with that record, well ... anybody we'd *want* to talk to, we're just laze-'bout niggers. Anybody else, well, you'd be crazy."

You see, Dell told himself. That's what he thinks of Snake Eyes. But ... it was clearly time to bring up what he'd been thinking all along: Why not sell the record? His eyes flashed for a second, then he lowered them; he hoped Bearcat hadn't seen it, but of course he had.

"What you got?" the old man insisted.

Dell shook his head.

"I said, You thinking of something. What you got?"

"I got nothing."

"*Nothing?* That's all I'm hearin'. But goddammit, *nothin'* ain't enough!"

"O.K.," Dell went cautiously, figuring he knew by now what the older man would say. "How about we try one of those northern labels? Chess? Modern?"

"That's your idea?" Bearcat started breathing heavily.

"Yeah, what do you think?" Dell heard Bearcat's flush of anger, but, he was thinking, what was the alternative? It was a last resort, sure, but having the record just die there, limp on their own sad vine.... Hell, if they couldn't press up and sell *Pink Cadillac*, he was sure somebody else would jump at the chance. So what, Bearcat had been burned before. This time Dell would make sure they had a good lawyer, except that a lawyer would cost money, too, maybe more than pressing up the—

"*What do I think?*"

"Yeah." Less certain.

"You ain't learned nothin' since you been out here? I ain't taught you anything? *Your own blinkin' eyes ain't taught you anything?*"

"I know, I know, you had some trouble with *Cryin' Shame*—"

"And we had us some more trouble with your carny man—"

"Yeah, but this time we do it right, go legiti—"

Bearcat slapped the table again, halting Dell in his tracks. The sound was loud, and everybody flinched. Then the big man stood up.

"Listen, we're keepin' this one with us. This one's goin' out on Bearcat Records, and it's comin' back on Bearcat Records. You understand? Even if I gotta sell my soul down where the two roads cross, this record's stayin' with *me*."

"Us," Dell said.

"What was that, white boy?"

"I said, 'Us.' "

"Yeah, well, you go wash out your white-boy mouth, you talkin' 'bout them Jews in Chicago or L.A. You say 'Us,' you mean *'Us!'* "

"You're right," Dell said. "Us." He stood up, too. "O.K., I'll come up with something. Just give me some time."

"Time for what?" That slant-eyed look again. "See maybe you can go renegotiating that 'lowance?"

Dell shook his head, then started to say, "Time to—"

Then he froze. Bearcat did, too. A loud crash stopped them both—glass breaking. All eyes turned to a window in the front of the roadhouse, glitteringly shattered, pointed shards jutting out from the frame, unimpeded moonlight flowing through. Slingshot, the closest, ran to it, ducking down as he went. He bent, picked up a smoothly gray stone, held it up.

"What the fuck?" Bearcat said.

"Do you see anybody?" Dell asked Slingshot.

The bouncer went bent-legged to the window next to the broken one, peeked his head up, then shouted, "Three men, running down the road."

"Three?"

"Yeah, they're almost out of the parking lot. Right by the Cadillac. Come on, let's get 'em!"

Dell was first out the door, followed by Salt, then Slingshot, and finally a lumbering Bearcat.

Dell went hauling through the lot, came to the road, saw three figures in the moonlight hell-bent to get out of there. He could tell they all were white, probably about his age, maybe the one in the middle a little older, wearing jackets that flew behind them and hunters caps with flaps pulled down over their ears and concealing their faces. He could tell he wouldn't be able to make out any particular features.

The three men had a good lead, but Dell dashed down the dirt road after them, then saw them disappear around a curve, which, when he came to it, showed him nothing but a gray DeSoto scattering dust and gravel as it peeled away.

"Damn!" Dell cried, but a moment later his pulse jumped. Daisy's pink Cadillac pulled up next to him, Bearcat at the wheel, crying, "Jump in!"

As he climbed into the car Dell saw emblazoned in red lipstick along the car's passenger door the words NIGGER LOVER.

Bearcat gunned the Caddie, and it flew with its own dust and gravel cloud behind it; he went charging into a curve, wheels almost sliding off the road, but hit the brake in just the right way and kept the car going.

"Didn't know I could drive like that, did you?" he yelled

above the whirring engine. Dell was in the backseat, Slingshot in the front next to Bearcat.

"Who do you think it is?" Dell asked.

"Trouble," the Bearcat said.

"Yeah, but who?"

Bearcat turned his head a second. "Don't matter. Only got one name: *Trouble*." Looked back at the road. The gray DeSoto was still in sight but wasn't losing any ground to the Caddie. When he spoke again, his pitch was slightly higher. "You got *yourself* any idea?"

"Faster!" Slingshot shouted, drowning Bearcat out.

"Faster! I'm going fast as this goddamn car can go. You ever get it tuned up after Daisy left with the carny?"

Nobody said a word.

"It just been sitting there, we're lucky I got it started. Hell, lucky I had the keys hung up underneath the bar."

Dell, who had passed the keys to Bearcat after Daisy had left and he felt so stupid and guilty, hadn't had a clue where they'd ended up. But now he made a mental note. Indeed, as they ripped along in the pink Cadillac he was noodling a new idea. It was bright before him, and it was ... making sense.

The gray DeSoto flew around a curve, and when the pink Caddie followed, the car they were pursuing was nowhere to be seen.

"Damn!" Bearcat went.

"Where the hell did it go?" Dell said.

Bearcat shook his head. "They know some trick?"

"The highway," Sling said, "ain't far ahead. Maybe they just made it there."

Bearcat pursed his brow.

"Anybody catch the license plate?" Dell asked.

Neither Bearcat or Slingshot spoke for a moment, just looked at each other; then Bearcat said, "You think that'd do any good? What, we phone it in to the sheriff?" Bearcat's voice minced up. "'Mr. Sheriff, some loutish white boys just broke our window! Yes, yes, only one window. What—you're sendin' your boys out *to break the other one?*"

"I just asked," Dell said.

"Damn!" Bearcat went, seething. "I can't believe this."

"You see what they did to Daisy's car?" Dell said. The lipstick inscription was on the passenger side, and Bearcat shook his head. "Pull up. You won't believe it."

Bearcat stopped the pink Cadillac in the middle of the dirt road, and he, Sling, and Dell got out. They read the words over: NIGGER LOVER.

"Damn! *Damn!*"

"What do you think they want?" Dell said. The moonlight hit the lipstick in such a way that, against the pink background, it looked not red but midnight black.

"They want to fuck with me, is what." Bearcat paced back and forth, more steam blowing from him than from under the hood of the pink Cadillac. *"Want my goddamn soul's what they want."*

"I don't know," Dell started to say, but then stopped. He had been shaken by the rock attack, the writing on Daisy's car. Didn't know what to think. It just seemed a bad, dark omen. And yet there was that bright new idea. Yeah, that could be a long shot, but still what did they have to lose?

"Listen, we gotta get us the money to make that record." Bearcat stopped pacing, spun on Dell. "That's the only way to show 'em, we make the goddamn record. Stuff it down their fuckin' bigoted faces."

"I'm with you," Dell said.

And like that Bearcat was right over him, in his face.

"Are you?" he cried. "Are you with me?"

✳ ✳ ✳ ✳ ✳

DELL'S IDEA BLOSSOMED as they were driving back to the roadhouse, and as soon as they got there, he began to put it into action. He volunteered to clean the vile words off the Cadillac, and then suggested to Bearcat that he take the car in to have it tuned up, get an oil change, whatever it needed. Bearcat gave the keys a long look but handed them over to the sax player. And the next day, bright and not too cold even though it was late January, Dell drove it to town.

His idea was so obvious he was surprised he'd overlooked it: the pink Cadillac itself. There it was, the song's namesake, sitting forlorn in the parking lot, just waiting to be of use.

Dell had earlier rejected any idea of selling it; though Daisy had in effect given the car up, *abandoned* wasn't too strong a word. Dell knew in his bones that if he sold the Cadillac, it would lead to some kind of certain disaster. The Cadillac had brought them Daisy, brought them the song, *the record*, but if he lost the car, no telling what might follow. But more than that: The pink Cadillac was the only thing he knew for sure would bring Daisy Holliday back to them.

But that didn't mean it couldn't be put to use.

This was the first time he'd actually been behind the wheel of the car, and as he tooled into Memphis, he felt the magic in the machine. His Triumph sputtered and kicked and raised a god-awful noise as he hit ninety on a back road, but this Cadillac was something else: It glided, floated around curves no matter how tight, swam elegantly past traffic, hummed lovingly; and it was high up! Driving this mutha, you were lord of all you surveyed. Light beamed off the chrome head ornament, glinted off the trim, and you were up on your throne, taking it all in. At bottom, Dell realized, the car delivered ... peace. A profound peace that said this world is just the way it should be, and you were in just the right place in it. He was amazed such a beautiful thing had just been left to sit in front of the roadhouse. This car was their salvation! How come nobody had seen that before?

And if he loved the car, just think about someone like Beauregard T. Washington.

He took it sort of quick up Beale Street the first time, starting at Front Street, then headed up to Fourth Street, then back down. Slower this time, letting the sunlight bomb along the chrome bumpers and splinter off the fender ornaments. He wanted to catch people's eyes, and he saw he did. It wasn't that they didn't get Cadillacs from time to time here on Beale Street, it was just that they didn't get *pink* Cadillacs. And the denizens, in their black suits with red piping, their pink silk ties, seemed particularly attuned to this car. Dell saw jaws open, fingers get raised and point— and jaws drop further when they saw it was a white boy driving.

That be Elvis Presley? That's what they were saying. That boy made all that money singing our music? He come down here showing off his gains? But, no, Dell didn't look enough like Elvis to fool anyone; and he wasn't trying to. He just wanted to cause a stir, get Beale Street excited.

And by the time he passed Lansky's, then the Pig Foot Inn, and parked next to a store with a wooden Indian out front, he had a cluster of folks around him.

They were a little distant at first, grouping a couple feet back from the car, their dark visages faintly reflected in the now weather-streaked pink enamel finish, their brows pursed as if they were seeing something almost magical. Finally, one skinny guy with a huge cherry-red birthmark on his neck stepped forward and with a tacit look at Dell made a motion with his hand, Can I touch it? Dell nodded, Of course, and with a flutter of bony fingers the skinny guy ran his hand over the Cadillac's left haunch. That was enough for everyone else; they crowded forward, swiping their hands over the finish, lifting kids up on the fenders, generally treating the car as a circus—which was Dell's plan.

The jabber rose, too.

"Sweet set of wheels," one older man said with reverence.

"This one of them Elvis cars?" a young girl in pigtails asked right up by Dell's window.

"Once upon a time," he said.

"Sure a beaut," a late-teenaged boy said, his eyes saucer round. "How fast it go?"

"How fast you want it to go?" Dell said deadpan.

"Wow!" the kid went. "Like that?"

"Better," Dell said. He was thinkin,: So this was what Daisy was enamored of, the attention, the sense of being part of something of unmitigated loveliness. And yet ... she gave the car up.

With a kind of quick anger he turned his head to the door next to the wooden Indian. Nothing yet. But traffic was backing up, horns honking behind him, the crowd burgeoning on Beale Street. The cacophony should be loud enough. He knew that if this were going to work, he couldn't do anything overt. All he could do was wait—

And there, the blue door opened. Out came Mr. Snake Eyes himself, the short, beetle-browed tough, followed by a new young squeeze, followed by his partner, lanky Elbert (Bullfrog) Johnson, followed by an even taller, thinner man with a midnight-blue watch cap over his orange hair.

"Hey, what's all this *noise*?" Snake Eyes said. He didn't speak particularly loudly, but the crowd around the Cadillac swiftly grew quieter, pulled back a little. "You're ruinin' a man's sleep. *Man's gotta sleep.*"

As the gambler walked toward the Cadillac the sea of pink shirts and red dresses and overalled kids and porkpie-hatted older gents and hospital-stockinged women parted. Snake Eyes stepped around the front of the car, looking right into the windshield. Because of the sun's reflection he couldn't see in, but Dell could see every flicker of fascination over his remarkable face. Snake was appreciating the car, that was clear. His lips pursed, his tongue darted covetously out, his bullet eyes widened, his conked hair seemed to actually rise up higher over his forehead. Dell noticed each gesture and loved it.

"Whoa, nelly!" the gambler cried when he was around the front and right by the side window. "Am I seein' ghosts?" He turned to his retinue. "Bullfrog, Shike—" Shike had to be the orange-haired man "—*am I seein' ghosts?*"

The tall Shike came up and looked right at Dell. His eyes were unearthly, least they seemed that way to Dell; a pale yellowy white, with fine pinpricks of pupils, and a way of staring at him that looked like death itself.

Dell felt his heart start hammering his chest.

"Ain't a ghost," Shike said. His prison eyes were stone cold. "Yet."

Bullfrog Johnson let out a guffaw, then said, "Boy, you got balls."

"If it ain't Dell Dellaplane." Snake Eyes had pushed aside his compatriots and was stepping toward the window.

"Hey!" Dell went.

"You gonna step out, let us talk about this like men," Snake Eyes said.

Dell's hand flew to the handle; he let the Caddie's door glide open, joined the others on the street.

"So maybe you've come with our money, maybe that's why you waltzed yourself right up here."

"No money," Dell said.

"Yeah, Shike's been tellin' me he ain't seen much evidence of cash flow, you and that duplicitous nigger out at your roadhouse." He rubbed his hands gleefully along his satin pants, let his gaze lower to Dell's crotch. "Boy, Bullfrog says it true."

"I got better."

"What you got?" Dark curiosity

"Can't you see?"

Snake Eyes took a step back, and then it dawned on him.

"You're bringin' me the car?"

"You like it?"

A long consideration, then: "What's not to like?"

"Exactly."

Snakes eyes grew bright with mirth. "O.K., I'll take it."

Dell felt the breath fly out of his chest. This was moving a little too fast for him. He wasn't planning to *give* Snake Eyes the car. He looked beyond the short gambler at the tall enforcer, Shike. There was a bulge in his right front pocket that meant either he was one fortunate fellow, or he had his knife right there at the ready.

"Well," Dell said after a quick moment's consideration, "why don't you settle in here, see how you like it."

He held open the door, and Snake slid in. He was too short to reach the gas pedals, so Dell leaned down and adjusted the seat. Snake had a hard time seeing over the steering wheel, too, and kept bouncing up and down.

"Key's in the ignition, give it a turn," Dell said.

Snake fired up the Caddie, leaned down enough to jam his foot on the accelerator; the engine growled hugely and a cloud of untuned-engine smoke blew out the back, starting a flurry of coughing among the crowd.

"Back it up," Bullfrog Johnson said, pushing away the crowd with open hands. "Back it up, let the man through."

It wasn't easy for Snake Eyes to drive; he had to slink down far enough to jab the gas pedal, then bounce up to see where he was going. The car lurched backward, then he shifted into DRIVE, and the car lurched forward. The crowd, quickly seeing what was going on, scattered to safety on the sidewalk. Snake Eyes kept at it. This was one nearly out-of-control pink Cadillac humping and jumping down Beale Street.

"Whoeeee!" Snake Eyes let out. "*Whoooeeeeeee!*"

He drove the car out of sight, Dell's heart beginning to sink, but then a few minutes later, it came back into view, heading toward him the other way on Beale. Pulled up right next to him.

"O.K., loan's taken care of," the gambler said.

"Um, not so quick," Dell said.

Shike was right there, and Dell could feel the enforcer's ears perk up.

"Not ... so. . . ."

"Quick," Dell said. "How much you figure this pink Caddie's worth."

"Least $300."

"Least a lot more than that."

Snake was silent a moment, but he couldn't deny it.

"So what are you sayin', white boy?"

"Sayin' this gotta be collateral."

"Collateral?"

"Yeah, meaning you loan me another $300, and I don't come up with the full six in, say, three months, the car is yours."

Snake Eyes didn't speak right away. Shike moved closer.

"You know, rights says we take the three from you anyway we gotta. Take it in *pink flesh*, you know, we don't take it in pink paint."

"I know," Dell said. With Shike next to him he knew he could only agree. "But you got a reputation for fairness, you—"

Snake Eyes snorted; Bullfrog Johnson did, too.

"Fairness?"

"O.K., listen, here's my idea," Dell said, quick uptake. "This car gotta be worked up some for you, don't you think? You know, personalized—"

"What're you sayin'?"

"Personalized. Made just right for you."

"You sayin'—"

"No, no, just that if you're gonna own it, you want it, um, right for you."

"Bull, he making fun of me?"

"I'm not," Dell said. "Just saying, give me the three more long, and if I don't get you back six in three months, then this car'll come pulling up in front of your place here, and it'll be so personalized the keys'll be attached to a tag says SNAKE EYES on it in jewels."

The gambler gave him a long sideways look up from the driver's seat.

"And no games?"

"Car'll be all yours."

"Three months?"

"Time for spring driving weather. April showers, May flowers—"

"And we won't have to send Shike after you, you come to us."

"I swear."

"On your father?"

"I swear on … my father. But," Dell said, thinking, Damn, that record better be a hit, "I come up with the six long—"

"Six long," Snake Eyes interrupted, "plus two more for the vig."

Dell swallowed hard. "O.K., three months, eight hundred bucks. Then you're a happy man, right?"

"Hey, I'm always a happy man," Snake Eyes said, eyes dancing. He had let himself out of the Cadillac now and looked longingly down its spectacular pink length. "But, O.K., you got a deal."

Dell heard his breath rush out of him. Snake Eyes reached back, pulled out three more hundred-dollar bills, slapped them into Dell's waiting palm.

"Now, you don't do nothin' to hurt this beauty till then, you hear?"

"It's gonna be better than ever. I'm takin' it right now for a tune-up and a lube job."

"And don't think we won't have our eyes on you," Snake said, with a nod to Shike.

"Thanks," Dell said. His heart was pounding too hard, he couldn't bear being there another moment, so he threw the car into gear and drove smoothly away.

When he turned right on Third, then started heading south, he found after a few blocks he had to pull over and just sit there till his breathing slowed and his heartbeat grew regular. It took longer than he thought. God, he said to himself, what have I gotten into? Then he patted his wallet, thickened just a few fractions of an inch by the three hundred-dollar bills, but thickened immeasurably nonetheless.

As he started up again, he flicked the radio on. "Hee gaw!" he heard the disc jockey, Dewey Phillips cry. "Here's that song you can't get enough of, Lazy Glazy Dai-sy Holliday doing *Pink Cadillac*. Don't know why it ain't in the stores yet, but that ain't gonna stop *me*. I say it *still* got that true jump. Let it rip, boys and girls!"

✳ ✳ ✳ ✳ ✳

AS COLIN HEADED into the Palm Bar, he had a quick flash of nerves. This, he couldn't keep from saying to himself, was his best hope to get the full story. He had to play it cool; *had* to make it work. The record had to be out there somewhere, and Clay Booker was possibly the only person left who knew what had happened.

Then he thought of Robin, and Seely, and how they'd gone to see Sonesta Clarke, probably less than ten years back, and he felt calmer. Maybe Sonesta was still alive; maybe he could find her, too. And yet that wasn't the only reason he felt a sudden wave of confident peace as he walked past the indoor palm trees into the track-lit bar; no, something else was changing deep inside him, though he didn't have a grip on it yet.

He recognized Booker right away, tall, thin, filled out but with the same narrow, hook-nosed face from the smudgy photo Colin had reproduced on the back of the Bearcat Jackson CD. He was wearing a sequined jacket and a bow tie that looked like it was tied too tight. Gray flecked the hair above his ears. Then Colin recognized even more: That he'd seen this man back in the early '90s at a blues festival in Holland, playing guitar behind a contemporary Delta bluesman. The recognition of the face startled him; he'd been in Amsterdam well before he'd started on the Bearcat album, and he'd never made the connection. But this was clearly the same guy. The rest of Colin's nervousness fled. He'd been thinking that being direct hadn't worked with Dellaplane and Daisy, but now he had his opening.

He ordered a beer.

Booker poured it expertly, leaving two thirds of an inch of foam, and slid it over to Colin, who immediately drained half of it.

"Know any good place to hear music?" Colin said, sending his English accent out thick.

"This is Memphis, ain't no *bad* place to hear music," the bartender said. "You try Beale Street?"

Colin pursed his brow. "I was hoping for something more, um, authentic."

Booker smiled. "You mean, a place where the boys still carry knives and guns?"

Colin thought: Do I go wide-eyed doofus, or do I let him know I mean business? He took another pull of the beer, then said, "No, really just a place they're not playing only for tourists."

The bartender wiped down the bar with a white terry cloth towel. "Well, these days that's not so easy to come by. Seems everybody's a tourist. You from England?"

"Yeah."

"I played there a couple times, back ten, fifteen years or so."

"You're a musician?" Colin said. O.K., wide-eyed had its place.

"When I'm not earning me a living," Booker laughed. "What's your name?"

"Colin."

"Colin, I'm Clay." He held out his hand.

Colin shook it firmly, then raised an eyebrow. "Clay? Clayton Booker? Guitar player?"

The bartender's eyes hooked up just a fraction, then he gave Colin a slow smile. "Well, now, you're not your run-of-the-mill tourist, are you? How you know that?"

"I saw you in Amsterdam, 1991."

"No lie!" Clay turned his smile inward. "Ah, Amsterdam. That be one sweet city. Girlies in those little red windows. Delights on *every* street corner. You caught my set, eh?"

"You were great. Playing with Lonnie Pitchford and R.L. Burnside. I thought you rocked."

"Hey! We rocked." Bright amusement now in Clay's eyes. He took his towel and hung it over his arm, then reached for Colin's glass. "You ready for another one? On me."

"Sure, thanks," Colin said.

As he poured Colin's beer, Booker said, "Yeah, it's funny 'bout all that. Man spend his whole life making music, playing in what all them tourist promoters rightly call the Cradle of the Blues, but when it comes to making yourself any kind of penny, you got to go overseas. Got to leave your wife— God rest her soul—and kids and go someplace they don't even speak your language." He shook his head in gentle amazement. "And people love you. Everyone loves you. They think you *rock*." He topped off the beer, getting the head perfect again, and slid it over to Colin. "I think I made more playing Europe a couple times than I made my whole life playing here."

When the mug was in front of Colin, he said, "But you're not from Memphis, are you?"

"Well, I don't know." Clayton dropped his hands onto his slim hips. "I been here so long, might as well be."

"You were born outside Yazoo City, right?"

The bartender's eyebrows went up. "How you know that?"

"Oh," Colin said. "I got this guidebook here." He reached quick into his bag, pulled out a paperback novel he was reading, careful to keep the cover from Booker's gaze. "Says here, 'Clayton Booker. Blues guitar player. Born in Yazoo City, Mississippi. Played with Floyd Cadmon and the Silver Bullets for two years. Recorded by Ike Turner in Clarksdale in '51. Did time for bootlegging in '52—'"

"They got that bootlegging in there? What kind of book is that? Let me see it?"

Booker reached over, but Colin pulled the book back close to his chest. He hoped Booker wouldn't make out the picture of a large hand flourishing a silver gun on the cover, or the slinky woman in the black miniskirt.

"Hey, it gets better," Colin said, rushing ahead. "Here, let me keep going. 'Booker moved to Memphis in '54—'"

"It was '53," Clayton said. "Remember it like it was yesterday."

"Well, you know these books." Colin hopefully repeated Booker's last sentence to himself.

"So what else that book say?"

"Um, well," Colin elaborately used his pointer finger to find his place back in the paperback. "Here it is: 'In Memphis, Booker played with Bearcat Jackson's roadhouse band until Jackson's death in '56. Cut two instrumental sides for Jackson that charted on the R&B charts. Booker was reputed to have played on the fabled session for Jackson's crossover hit, *Pink Cadillac*—'"

"What's that?" Alarm in Booker's tone. "Let me see that thing."

Colin grasped the paperback tightly, but Booker had

big, fast hands, and he somehow slipped it out of the record producer's grasp. He read, "*The Long Goodbye*? What's going on here, man?"

Colin held out his hand.

"My name's Colin Stone. Ring any bells?"

Booker shook his head.

"I own Blue Moon Records. We put out that disc a few years back on Bearcat Jackson. Used your two instrumental cuts—"

A new wariness in the bartender's eyes. "There ain't no problem with 'em, right?"

"Of course not."

"And we done all the money stuff correct?"

"Clay," Colin said, leaning forward across the bar, "I'm here for *Pink Cadillac*."

"*Pink Cadillac?*" Booker's eyes widening again.

"Daisy Holliday. Dell Dellaplane. You played on it."

"How you know that? That in that *book* of yours?"

"I just came from Arizona, where I talked to Daisy Holliday."

"Miss Daisy?" It was odd, but Colin noticed that Booker's tone was changing, an Old South drawl stealing in.

"She's doing O.K. Got herself a rich husband."

Clay nodded his head. "I'm not surprised." Then, eyes wider. "It ain't Dell Dellaplane, is it?"

Colin shook his head. "Saw him, too. He's in L.A. Living off movie money."

"And I'm tending bar."

Colin took a deep breath, held Clay's gaze. "I can change all that."

"What do you mean?"

"If I can find *Pink Cadillac*, if you'll help me, I'll try to make it so that you never have to work like this again. Not another day in your life."

"What are you saying?"

"*Pink Cadillac* could be the most important lost record in history. Think about it, Daisy Holliday, first white woman to record with a mixed band. It won't stop with the record. TV will be all over it. Might make a good movie, too—"

"And that's what you're here for, that record." Booker had folded his arms in front of him, stood there more composed, even stolid. An older guy down the bar raised his hand and gave it a wave, and Booker said, "Excuse me. Customer."

When Booker came back, he said, "I don't think I can help you."

"Don't *think*?"

Booker hung back. "What do you want?"

Colin said it quick: "The record."

The bartender took all the time in the world nodding this to himself. Then he said, "And what else?"

"You mean, from you?"

"Yeah."

"Anything you can tell me, Clay. What really happened. Any part of the story you know."

Booker took a deep breath. "I know the *whole* story. I was there."

"I'll make it worth your while."

"For the *story*?"

"For any help you can give me."

Booker looked up and down the bar, then gave Colin an agreeable nod. "Well, all that's gonna take us a while. You can wait till I'm off?"

Colin, all brightness, said, "I'm not moving an inch."

Booker gave his head a shake. "Well, I'll see what I can do. Things slow down, maybe I can get away a little early."

Colin lifted his mug. A glance around the room. "I'll be right there in the corner. You serve food here? Want to send over a waitress?"

* * * * *

ALL THE WAY BACK he was trying to decide whether to stop and get the three hundred-dollar bills broken. What would be more impressive? Fan out a sheath of fives, tens, and twenties or just drop the three Franklins on the table? Dell kept concentrating, thinking of the Bearcat, his deep, sunken brown eyes, his eyebrows curving thick like Tootsie Rolls, his alligator skin, trying to figure what would jazz him most. Whoosh: All those bills laid out there. Or, Smack!: One, two, *three* crisp Bens, each commanding its own space on the oil-cloth-covered table.

He just couldn't make up his mind, and finally decided it didn't matter. All that counted was that he had the money. They were on their way: No reason they couldn't press up and start selling *Pink Cadillac* immediately . . .

. . . If that was the best plan. He had no experience in all this, and didn't know how long it took to set up a pressing schedule; how long it would take for the beautiful black discs to get into their hands; and what to do then. But Bearcat knew. What Dell was sure of was that there should be a tight little dance between taking the disc from Dewey Phillips and getting it pressed: They couldn't afford to lose any more radio time than they had to. But once all the pressing-plant plans were made, well, that'd be easy.

So he squirreled his Triumph into the parking lot, sending up a storm of dust, then flew into the roadhouse and . . . found nobody downstairs at all.

"Bearcat," he cried up the stairs. "Bearcat, you up there?"

No answer.

This was odd. It was three in the afternoon, Dell could tell by the Falstaff Lager clock hung canted on the bare-wood wall, and even assuming the clock was set incorrectly, there was no good reason nobody should be around.

Dell went to the bar, pulled out a cold bottle of Royal Crown Cola, flipped the cap, and settled back.

And didn't have long to wait till the front door popped open and the clatter of boots and shoes roused him.

He turned, saw Bearcat, Slingshot, Salt, the guitarist Clay Booker, even the layabout Hosea all trudging in.

"Hey," Dell called out. "What's going on?"

Bearcat looked distracted: glowering, in-turned, and not quite put together. He went right to the bar and poured himself a shot of homemade, then threw it down. When he finally seemed to notice Dell, he gave a start, almost as if he'd seen a ghost.

"Where *you* been?"

Dell couldn't contain himself with his good news. "Oh, you'll see," he said with a bright laugh.

But Dell's high spirits were going right over the big man. Bearcat threw down the rest of his shot, then shook off his black, moth-nibbled greatcoat and dropped into a seat next to Dell with a huge sigh. He looked sunk deep into his own thoughts.

"So, where were you guys?" Dell said, first to Bearcat, who ignored him, then to anyone else. "What happened?"

"They came at us again," Salt said, hanging his lighter coat up on a post by the bar.

"Who?"

"Whoooo?" the Bearcat went. He looked a little crazy, Dell thought, spooked now himself. "Whooooooooo? Listen to Mr. Owl here."

"We don't know," Salt went on. "Hosea was the only one who saw 'em clear. Two guys this time. Said they were carrying cotton rags and bright-red gas cans—"

"Jesus!" Dell leaped up, started pacing. "Gasoline?"

"That's what Hosea saw."

"I did, I saw 'em," the overalled man cried. "They was gonna burn us out!"

"You think?" Dell to Salt.

The mustached bartender was shaking his head, What

else could it be? "They were there for sure, two white crackers running like hell. We ran after them, and I caught a glimpse as they turned a corner, but I couldn't tell what they had with them. They'd jumped into a pickup, were getting the hell out of here."

"They'll be back," Bearcat said. He sounded more grounded, less crazy. And though Dell couldn't tell how much he'd been following the conversation, the way he said this riveted their sight.

"Damn," Dell said. "Well, we just gotta move fast." He took the seat he'd left a minute before, took a pull from his bottle of RC. "Bearcat, look!" He pulled out the three hundred-dollar bills, held them up before his face, spread them out so the old man was sure to see the denomination.

"What's that?" Bearcat wasn't even bothering to look closely.

"Frankins," Dell said. There was clear pride in his voice. "Three *good-looking* Uncle Bens."

"What?" Bearcat still looked a little like he had bugs flying around his brain.

"Money," Dell said, thinking it was that Bearcat didn't know the lingo; but then, realizing where the phrases came from, not wanting to push the issue. With the hand not holding the bills he did the same lucre-snap as Bearcat had the other day. "Three … hundred … dollars. More than enough to press up *Pink Cadillac*."

Yes, he was beaming, and why shouldn't he be?

The Bearcat *was* focusing now, his eyes hooded, jumpy. Dell didn't know how to read them.

"Where'd it come from?"

Dell caught his breath.

"I have it. It's real, here it is." He waved the three bills. "Want to see 'em?"

"I … want … to … know … where … they … came … from."

A longer, deeper inhalation. "I—I can't say."

Bearcat stood quick, with one of those flourishes of his that made it feel like the whole room had just jumped a few feet.

"*You … can't … say?*" Loud now.

An even deeper sigh. Dell was a little lightheaded. The Bearcat towered over him.

"I'm sorry." He was shrinking back in his chair, much as he didn't want to. "There're promises. And, trust me, it doesn't matter. There aren't any strings—"

"There are always strings," the big man bellowed. "That's m-o-n-e-y you're holding there, *lee-gal tender*? Then there're always, always strings."

"No strings we gotta worry about," Dell said. He hadn't yet, and couldn't bring himself, to even begin to imagine what his life would be like if in three months he didn't have the eight long for Snake Eyes. *Eight hundred dollars!* You could buy a whole car for that—a *nice* car. No, couldn't think about the eight hundred. They had the record. That was—it had to be—money in the bank. "No strings that at least *you* gotta worry about."

Bearcat was giving him the longest look. He started to say again, "Tell me where it—" but he dropped the question halfway through. It was like a response had come to him just through the air; like he had his own answer, and it was all the answer he needed.

Instead he said, "No, all I gotta worry 'bout is riled up crackers trying to burn me out. *Burn down my roadhouse.* Do you understand?"

"We'll get the record out," Dell insisted. "And we can. We got the money now. Why don't we just call up that place, whatshisname, Buster Williams, guy who presses them up. Three long must get us some priority." Dell stood up, too, couldn't bear it any longer being seated and having to gaze up at the big man. "You know all about this—you've done it before. You said all we needed was the money, and we got that now. We'll press up *Pink Cadillac*, get it out there—we gotta!"

"That gonna stop 'em from burning us out?" This was Salt, from over at his bar.

In truth, of course, Dell didn't know, hadn't a clue. He was so bent on selling *Pink Cadillac* he couldn't see beyond that. Still, he said, "How could it hurt? Man, you know, everybody loves a success."

Bearcat was looking down at his young white friend with a look that said, You don't know one fucking thing, do you? Dell saw it but didn't know what else to do but keep saying what he already had.

"We gotta get the record out, you know that. And now we can. I got the money." He waved the bills again at Bearcat. *"I got us the scratch."*

Bearcat kept looking at the young man, but his countenance was unreadable. What Dell did see didn't look at all encouraging. He was frankly baffled.

"Hey," he went on, starting to walk around the room, though all the while keeping his gaze on the Bearcat. "I thought you'd be thrilled. We're on our way! Gonna get the record out. It's what we talked about—" His voice got shriller, and his head was spinning.

Bearcat held Dell's gaze, then looked toward the window that had been broken the other day, now covered with cardboard and black tape, then back at Dell, then at the money still held up eagerly in the boy's hand, then right into the young man's eyes.

"Bearcat, why you lookin' at me that way?"

The older man was silent.

"I don't—I don't under—this doesn't make any—"

With a quick strike Bearcat reached out and grabbed at the three hundred-dollar bills in Dell's hand.

Dell was faster; he yanked them back.

Bearcat fixed him with a withering glare.

"I thought the money was for *us*."

"Of course," Dell said, though he kept the bills tight to his chest. "But us, you and me *together*, we'll call up Buster Williams—we can call him right now and make the arrangements to have *Pink Cadillac* pressed up. That's what I'm thinking. Then we can go get the acetate from Dewey, I mean, we wouldn't want to get it too soon, not till all the arrangements are made, we want Dewey to play it as long as he will, you know, keep the *Pink Cadillac* fire burning.

"But then I—I mean, we—we can go get it back from Dewey, when the timing's right, that is, and take it to Buster's. They oughta be able to strike a master or whatever they do—hell, you know this better than me—but strike a master lickety-split, then we can take the first pressings back to Dewey, and they'll be fresh pressings, no worn-down acetate, and I'm sure he'll keep playing it, 'cept now he can say it's gonna be on sale any day—" Dell was almost out of breath. He quickly finished up.

"Then people'll buy it, and we'll have our hit. Bearcat, that's all we need, *we need us that hit!*"

The older man hadn't said a word or made a gesture during Dell's long, breathless spiel. He just kept looking at him, then looking at the three hundred-dollar bills pressed to the young man's chest, then back at his angular, handsome, rich-boy white face.

But all the while any meaning Dell could read seemed to be draining out of the big man. He didn't know what the Bearcat was thinking, or even if he'd been listening to him. Was it just the assholes with the gasoline? It felt like something bigger than that; Dell made a note to ask Salt what he thought later. But right now he had to get through to Bearcat, had to get them going on pressing up the record, but the big man simply looked like he'd lost all interest. How could this be? What was he thinking?

"Bearcat, come on, we can have our hit!"

But Dell had lost him. Bearcat, with his thoughts looking miles away, and a few of those bugs back flying around his
brain, simply turned his heavy body around and walked away,
trudging up the stairs, disappearing into the netherworld of
his own quarters.

"Salt, what?" Dell said, turning to his friend, who was
swabbing down the wooden bar.

Salt just shook his head.

"But I got the money! What are we going to do?"

Salt lifted his hands, half shrugged, then said,
"Remember, that man's seen things—things we couldn't even
begin to imagine." He gave the bar another swipe with his cotton cloth. "Just let him be. He'll come around."

✳ ✳ ✳ ✳ ✳

AND HE DID SEEM to come around. That night when Sticks
counted out his one, two, three, *four!* and Thumper lowered
himself into the beat, and Clay filigreed above it, then Dell
honked his sax to raise the roof, the Bearcat put his tiny silver
harp to his huge pink mouth and skirled all-colored notes
around the room like a fine wind blowing autumn leaves.
After their traditional opening instrumental, there was
Sonesta, singing high and strong, and rousing the half-filled
house as well as she ever had.

Through the set Dell kept his eyes on Bearcat, looking
for any trace of the hesitation, distance, even bemusement of
that afternoon after the gasoline-can incident, but the musician was rock solid. Indeed, he played with a firm determination and led the band with all the majestic certainty he had
had when Dell first showed up. Dell shook his head. Since the
Daisy fiasco he'd gotten used to half running the show, picking numbers, leading count-ins, but this night Bearcat
brooked no competition, didn't even seem to remember that
he'd ceded some authority to the white boy; this was the

Bearcat Show at its richest, with that Finest of Purveyors of Bluesy Vocal Stylings, Sonesta Clarke, singing right by his side.

And what a show it was. The roadhouse had been hopping, the success of *Pink Cadillac* on the radio having freed them all, it seemed, to just play their hearts out. Sonesta was piping the blues in trashy, brilliant guttural moans, soaring on a freedom she probably hadn't felt in years. It was music to sway the gods, even if it wasn't the newfangled rocky-roly; but nobody was thinking that—they had a burgeoning hit on the radio, and tonight they could play what they wanted ... or at least, without Daisy, play what they could. Dell had taken the roof off with his sax, emptying his lungs time and time again, until he fell to his knees at the tail end of Mama Thornton's *Hound Dog* and literally couldn't get up.

When things finally wound down about three in the morning, it was Bearcat who went around putting the roadhouse to bed, an unheard-of gesture. He flicked off the lights downstairs and was about to climb upstairs when Dell, his head resting on hands interlocked behind him, called out from his pallet behind the stage, "Hey, Bearcat, we were great tonight." Dell had been thinking this all through the set, figuring that having *Pink Cadillac* on the radio, and now the money to press it up in hand, had set them free in a remarkable way.

"Hey hey," the big man went. He was at the foot of the stairs. The roadhouse was dark except for thin moonlight through the windows besides the boarded-up one.

"And now I got the money, we can get on with *Pink Cadillac*."

No response from the Bearcat.

"Hey," Dell said, "how many you think we should go for at first?"

Still nothing from the Bearcat. Dell raised himself on his elbows to make sure the big man was still there. He saw a large shadowy outline about six steps up the stairs, the shadow's head cut off by the bottom of the floor above.

"*Bearcat?*"

"We'll talk about it tomorrow, hey, Dellaplane?"

Dell thought that odd, couldn't remember Bearcat calling him by his last name. "I'm just lying here thinking. You think 10,000 will be too many?"

"Tomorrow, Dell. I'm heading up." Dell saw the shadow move.

Dell sighed, fell back on his mat. *Sure*, he said to himself, *tomorrow*, then fell asleep, totally exhausted.

And probably could have slept all day if he wasn't awakened by the crack of a loud engine backfiring right outside the window above him. His head swam up, he blinked into the pale gray first dawn light, wondered who was shooting off what. His first, dire thought: the two or three white men, back with explosives. He waited a moment, but nothing blew up, nothing shook. Then another notion: It was the sheriff, back with deputies and writs and paddy wagons for 'em all. But when he looked out onto the parking lot all he saw was Bearcat's old mud-spattered truck, and as it drove past out onto the road, the old man himself at the wheel. Dell shook his head, blinked. Where could he be going at dawn? They'd all hit the hay just … three hours before. Which meant he'd barely slept at all. Hmmnnn. And the look on his face, eyes hooded, jaw tight, staring determinedly out the windshield. Dell shook his head, then sagged back on the straw.

He woke up again a few hours later, roused by a clatter of pans in the kitchen. He stretched, knew he wouldn't get back to sleep, didn't particularly care. *Sleep when I die*, he told himself, smiling. He craned his head over and saw Sonesta, wearing a navy-blue housecoat with yellow piping, cracking eggs into a peach-colored bowl.

"Oh!" she cried, and took her hand to her chest. "Dell, you startled me."

"Sorry," he said. "I fell asleep over there. It was too late to go home." A half-embarrassed shrug: He was wearing just a towel, and Sonesta was giving his skinny bones a long appraising look. "I'm going to go take a shower," he said, sidling by. A nervous grin, met by her wide smile. "You were great last night, by the way."

"Thanks," she said. "Yeah, it was ... well, I guess it's still inside of me, no matter what I think." A faint blush on her brown cheeks. "Hey, hurry on back, I'll make you some eggs."

"Sounds wonderful."

The shower at the roadhouse was a cold-water pipe out of the wall out back, with a rusty spigot on it that dripped more than anything else, but, as Bearcat always pointed out, it sure beat things before they got running water. There was an icy frost on the ground, but Dell was thinking he was pretty smelly, so he traipsed to the spigot, got the water running—it almost never froze—and stepped in. *Brrrrruuggggh!* He shook the cold, cold water off his back, soaped himself much as he could, flapped around like a wild duck, rinsed off fast, and beat the frayed cotton towel all around him to get dry. He did feel better, though. Dressed fast, put on his boots, and clambered over to the large, four-doored outhouse a couple hundred feet from the roadhouse's back door.

When he was back inside where it was warm and cozy, there was a heap of yellow-and-white scrambled eggs and grits waiting for him, and a steaming mug of thick coffee.

"These are delicious," he said, digging in. "Don't get eggs like this where I come from. My house they come in cups and wear little tutus."

Sonesta gave a curious look, then said, "And you thought I wasn't good for nothin'."

Dell gave her a long look, not sure how to take this. Didn't she know how much he'd loved *Cryin' Shame*? But he decided just to smile and keep eating.

"You have any idea where Bearcat was rushing off to this morning?" Dell said after a minute.

Sonesta looked over at him, her fork frozen for just a second in front of her.

"He took off?"

"You didn't know?"

Sonesta just looked down at her own plate of eggs. It didn't take more than a couple more seconds for Dell to realize he'd asked a difficult question. He hurried on: "Seemed hell-bent on something."

Sonesta sighed. "You never know nothin' with that man."

"I hope he gets back soon." Dell spooned up more of the fluffy eggs. "Got a lot I want to do today."

He waited a moment for Sonesta to respond to his enthusiasm by asking him what, but there was a faint trace of embarrassment around her wide lips, and a certain tilt to her head, and Dell went on to answer his own implied question: "Gotta get moving on our record."

"You still dreaming 'bout that?"

"Not dreaming!" A slug of coffee chasing the eggs down his throat. "Got us the *mon-ey.*" Couldn't help himself, did that lucre finger-snap just like the Bearcat.

"You did?" Sonesta stood up, turned away from Dell so he couldn't see her expression, and took her half-eaten plate of eggs over to the sink.

"Yeah, and I want to get us going on pressing it up, getting the record out there."

When the older woman turned around again, she had a pained look on her face.

"What's wrong?" Dell said.

"Y'all are goin' through with this, ain't you?"

"Of course we are, what do you mean?"

Sonesta shook her head. "Nothin'."

"Something's bothering you," Dell said. He was attacking the rest of his eggs.

"I don't—"

"C'mon, you're feeding me. 'Sides, I need to know everything I can about all this. Got a lot of questions."

Sonesta sighed loudly. "I just hate to see y'all go through all this again."

"Why?"

"Well, after last time."

"This isn't gonna be the same as with ... your song," Dell said. "It's going to be different—"

Sonesta wheeled and said, "What you know about it?"

Her tone was there to put the young man in his place; and in truth, he didn't know that much about it. He was going to say something full of youthful confidence and bravado but hesitated just a few beats too long.

"That's what I thought. You don't know *nothin'* about pushing a record."

Dell shrugged. "How hard can it—"

"Oh, yeah! *How hard can it be?* That's smart thinkin'."

"That's what I wanted from Bearcat, wanted to find out everything I could."

"And you're not asking me?"

This was new, a note of pride in the older woman's voice. Dell heard it, waited a well-timed moment, then said, "Maybe I should ask you."

"Damn right! Who do you think was right by his side? Who do you think saw everything? Who do you think *sang on the damn thing*?"

Dell, smiling made a gesture that said, I'm all ears.

Sonesta poured herself a tall mug of coffee and heaped three teaspoons of sugar into it. Then she sat down, pulled off a swig, and faced Dell straight on.

"O.K., here's how it goes. We was younger then, of course, and maybe didn't know so much like we should've, but we *was* smart—the smartest niggers around when it came to music—and we was gonna do it ourselves. Why not? Just

'cause we colored? Just 'cause my *granddaddy was a slave?*"
Sonesta's nostrils flared.

"And we had us a good record, that *Cryin' Shame*.
We *worked* on that record, I don't know how many takes,
not like you and Miss Pretty there." Sharp look into Dell's
eyes. "Anyway, we cut ourselves master after master on
that dang-blasted machine over there—" she pointed
toward the record cutter Daisy had fixed months before
"—and then we had us a beaut! We treated that baby like
gold, not like you with that *Cadillac* thing, marching it all
over town and back, sendin' it to Nashville, don't know
where all it be."

"Sonesta, it's with Dewey Phillips," Dell interrupted, as
respectfully as he could manage, "getting us airplay. Getting
Memphis buzzing like crazy."

"Yeah, well." Sonesta rolled her eyes in that way she
was really good at, pupils actually doing full loop-de-loops in
her irises. "*Cryin' Shame*, it was one special record, and we
decided to shoot the moon, do what nobody like us ever done
before: release it ourselves. Who's gonna say no? Create our
own record company, stick the Bearcat's ol' puss right on the
label, and then distribute it ourselves. Makes sense, right?" A
loud snort.

"So how'd you do it?" Dell said, all eagerness.

Sonesta's eyes went wide and she leaned toward Dell.
She had the faint tones of a schoolteacher, but with far more
urgency.

"How would *you* do it?"

Dell thought for a moment, then said, "Well, you got it
in your hands, boxes of 'em, you just gotta get 'em into
stores." He gave a shrug. "Where people who are crazy about
it on the radio can buy it."

"And who puts 'em in the stores?"

Dell looked at her closely, then said, "You do."

"And if the stores won't talk to you? If they have what

they call *channels*? That means, they got their own pals and there ain't room for nobody new?"

"Then you get a ... distributor. Somebody got the connections. Somebody you trust—"

"Ho, ho!" Sonesta snorted. "Oh, you be's the bee's knees of record men. Somebody you trust, huh? You ever *meet* a record distributor? Makes a snake look like Mamie Eisenhower."

Dell, his head spinning, said tentatively, "So what did you do?"

"Well, like I said, we was young and thought we was smart. But we was black, too, and we couldn't go to anybody here in town even to press it up. But Bearcat, he found this little plant down in Alabam', you buy the foreman a few quarts of mash, he slip you a few boxes of discs out the back door." Sonesta settled back.

Dell nodded. "Good thinkin'."

"So we got us the record, but now we're back where we were just a second ago. How do we get it out there?"

Dell rubbed his chin, the student now, ready to learn important things. He stared straight at Sonesta till it was like he was able to read her mind. "More whiskey."

"You're learnin'." Sonesta gave Dell a big smile. "It was a *lot* more whiskey. Good thing the Bearcat had his hands in more than one pie, you know what I mean?"

Dell wasn't surprised by the big man's resourcefulness.

"Yeah, a few bottles got WHBQ to start spinning our record, and soon as people heard it, well, didn't have to bribe them: It was just like with your *Pink Cadillac* song."

"People called in, kept asking for it—" Dell started to say.

"Boy, boy, our people didn't have no telephones to call in with. But they had other ways of making themselves heard, and heard they was. This negro disc jockey they had, Mr. Carson, he gave the people what they wanted.

"Then the Bearcat, Salt and he put those boxes of *Cryin'
Shame* in the trunk of this black Chrysler we owned then, and
they took them round himself to record stores, and when a lot
of the record stores wouldn't touch the 78, they sold 'em out
of the trunk."

Dell smiled. "Smart again."

"Damn smart!" Sonesta tilted her head back. "And it
worked. We sold lots and lots of discs."

"So what went wrong?"

Sonesta, who had been leaning back, arms open, cheerfully recounting her tale so far, suddenly clenched up; she
folded her chin down into her neck, brought her arms tight
into her stomach, folded her hands in front of her wide
bosom.

"Well, success ain't so easy, always. You get to a point
where you can't do it all yourself. Bearcat, well, it was either
fold up, leave *Cryin' Shame* where it was, which nobody wanted, or get us some help. He just got the wrong help."

Dell was remembering what Salt had told him when
they were taking the empties back to town, how Bearcat had
finally sold the record up north, how it ended up going to
Tina Scott, and how the contract also bought up everything
else he'd produce. "I know Bearcat made a deal, finally, to get
money for the roadhouse—"

A long intake of breath: "Yeah."

"And then, no way he could know it, the record got to
that white—"

Sonesta gave her wide black head a quick shake, her lacquered hair even vibrating a little, which Dell understood
meant, I don't want to hear about that. So he bit off his words.

"He got too far ahead of himself," Sonesta finally said.
"Thought he knew it all. Thought that 'cuz back behind him
he had fancy, educated folks, and 'cuz he had a hit brewin', he
wasn't just another country nigger—"

Sonesta paused, and Dell waited.

Finally she looked up from a hung head and said, "Bearcat said it was stole from us, that's all he said." Sonesta rolled her eyes again. "Plumb stole from us. Like I didn't know."

"He never told you how *Cryin' Shame* got away?"

"It was *our* record, but he was the Man. Mr. Business. I was just the *arrr-tiiiste*." A snort. "No, he didn't tell me nothin'. Had to pick the whole story up on my own."

"Had to pick up what?" Dell had thought he'd had the whole story from Salt, but there was a hint of something else here in Sonesta's words. He looked intensely at the older woman. "Pick up what?"

Finally, she just shook her head. It was clear she wasn't going to say more.

Dell, trying to rescue the moment, said, "But that was all a long time ago."

That brought her back. "A long time? Maybe to a whipper-snapper like you, but it was just five years back. And we ain't done a goddamn thing since."

"Till now."

Sonesta fixed Dell with a look that could only be described as frightful. "You haven't heard *nothin'* I been saying, have you?"

"We won't deal with anybody," Dell said to the older woman, still sure of himself. "Why would we? Times've changed. I'm—"

"You're gonna make all the difference, what you know?"

"I wasn't going to say that. But together, we'll—"

"Together? You and Bearcat *together*?" She threw her gaze toward the windows, the boarded-up broken one as well as the one looking out on the parking lot. "But you ain't got a clue where he run off to?"

Dell had to shake his head.

"And you ain't been noticin' he's acting a little ... funny?" She tapped the top of her forehead.

Of course Dell had, but he remained silent and motionless.

"You ain't seen it?" Sonesta leaped up then, started throwing her still dainty hands around over her wide shoulders. "I think sometimes that man got bats flying round up his head. Little mean-faced little batty demons he don't let nobody see—but they there."

She was edging at something new here, wasn't she? "Like what?"

She looked right at him and said, "Like what he thinks about you."

Like that Dell was on guard. "What do you mean?"

"That you're runnin' a scam on him."

"He doesn't think that," Dell said, and now he was standing, too. "No way!"

"That's not what I'm hearin'. I even heard you two had words."

"He had some dumb idea, sure, but we talked it out, came to see there ain't nothing there." Dell strode back and forth agitated. What had he said to make the conversation go so quickly bad? *"Nothing!"*

"Then where that money you so proud of come from?" Sonesta lifted her hand and did a wicked mimic of the lucre finger-snap. "You know where Bearcat thinks it comes from."

"I swear it wasn't my father."

"Then where?"

"I—I can't tell."

"If I was Bearcat, I might say you was protestin' too much."

Dell turned to her, let his arms drift out, palms up.

"It's the truth. I don't care what Bearcat—*or* my father—thinks is going on, I don't have anything to do with it. All I want is to play music. Get us a hit—"

"If I was Bearcat, maybe I'd think that hit's gonna come out of my hide." The older singer stood there, her arms folded before her, her purple-rimmed eyes gazing down. "Just a word to the wise, boy. I like you, and I'm glad you enjoyed your breakfast. But remember, I got *nothing* comin' out of this *Pink Cadillac* foolishness. Ain't nothin' but trouble to me. Just keep your eyes open."

And with that Sonesta climbed back upstairs, to the private quarters, the part of the roadhouse that Dell had never been in.

He sat on the kitchen chair, thinking for the longest time, pondering the true meanings of everything he'd just heard; and what he kept coming up with was one simple notion. He had to get moving, get the record of *Pink Cadillac* out there as soon as possible. He just knew it: A hit would be their only salvation.

✳ ✳ ✳ ✳ ✳

THE THREE MALE PRINCIPALS of Dellaplane Holdings were meeting back in the leather-chaired, oak-tabled conference room. There was no great happiness in the room.

"So your son—" Jim Tucker started to say. They were seated around the table, both Tucker and Jim McNair clad in hand-tooled boots that were lifted up on the table, meaning that things weren't too tense.

"My son has been a grave disappointment."

"I'm glad you see that."

"Oh, I see it very clearly," Ransom Dellaplane said. "He hasn't done one thing for us with that nigger roadhouse situation. One thing he promised."

"And your approach, Jim?" This was Tom McNair. He casually lifted one boot heel off the table, then let it drop with a loud clunk.

"Well," the older man with the red face said. He'd started at the boot heel, and half turned now so he could look McNair in the face. "My boys been softenin' 'em up."

McNair left a long pause, then said, "*Softenin'*—I like that word." He brushed a hand back through his thick black hair. "Same word I keep hearin' from your wife 'bout you, Jim."

Tucker threw his feet off the table, spun around in his chair. His usual red face was florid.

"Boys, boys," Dellaplane said. He said it lightly, smiling. His look said: I'm glad you're diverting us from my goddamn son, but let's not let this get out of hand.

"No reason my boys can't go back out there. Just got to get a couple with a few more smarts, won't run at the first sign of a problem."

"How smart you gotta be to burn a place down?" McNair said. "Wooden place, 'specially. Some rags, some gasoline, *dead of night....*"

Tucker dropped both hands loud on the table but didn't say anything, just glowered at his coworker.

"I think what happened with your boys could've been for the best," Dellaplane said, looking from one of the blusterers to the other, noting it looked like the animosity wasn't going much further. "Indeed, they could've ended up bringing more attention down on us than we might want." There was a sparkle in Dellaplane's eyes.

"That mean you got a plan, boss?" McNair said quickly.

Dellaplane smiled. "Might."

"With your son again?" Jim Tucker asked.

Dellaplane frowned but didn't say a word.

"Oh, I see," Tom McNair said. His smile was so bright it lightened his youthful face all the way up to his shiny black hair.

"What?" Tucker said. "You see what?"

McNair spun around in his chair, looking purposefully away from Tucker. "You're going stop messing with sur'gates, right, Ransom?"

Dellaplane sat there, no discernible expression over his silver-haired, perfectly lined face.

"He's doing what you always do in bizness. He's going straight to the top, Jim." McNair spoke through a killer smile. "How come you didn't think up that?"

✳ ✳ ✳ ✳ ✳

"HEE GAW! *HEE GAW!*" Dewey Phillips leaned into the big silver microphone and let rip a whole string of his hog-calling whoop-joys. He was spinning discs, spreading the blues, beaming those thousands of watts into Memphis, goofing on his audience, squeezing his assistant's glorious ass ... he was making hits!

"Don't you just love that song, *Pink Cadillac, Pink Cadillac, oh, my Pink Cadillac*. I think we done got us what we been waitin' for, a female Elvis, a *Miss* Presley. She calls herself Miss Daisy Holliday, and she's got the rockin' and rollin', boogie woogie flu—yes, she do.

"Now some of you might remember, a few years back we played ourselves a li'l ol' song called *That's All Right*, and when we did, you lit up the phone lines with requests to hear it again, and we played it again and again and again. Then we sent one of our station assistants down to find that boy—we yanked him out of the Bijou and brought him right in here and gave 'im to you. That fine boy who loves his mother.

"Well, we got us an open invitation to Miss Daisy Holliday to come down here and talk to us. Daisy! Oh-ho, DAISY! You hear me, you pretty li'l filly, you come canterin' down here to your Uncle Dewey, *right this minute!*"

There was almost painful dead air on the radio while presumably Dewey Phillips was waiting for his filly to gallop in; though in truth he was sneaking a quick tongue jab with his secretary.

"Hee-gaw! Well, I guess we're waitin' a li'l bit longer. Still, I got me a few things I can tell you 'bout her. She's 'bout nineteen, comes this way from Kentucky, and—I swear this is truth—she met Elvis just 'fore he hied himself up to New York City, and Elvis Presley, that bad cat, he gave her one of his pink Cadillacs. Yessirreebob! That's where the song came from. Yes, yes, I know it's a lot to swallow, but it's the god-almighty truth.

" 'Cept we don't have no Daisy Holliday here, noooooo-sirreebob. And that means we got us a little mystery.

"And it also means we don't got us the record anymore. Seems the story is, without Daisy, there was just the one copy of *Pink Cadillac* your Uncle Dewey was playing, and this morning a couple gentlemen—least I hope they wuz gentle-men—came and took it away so it could be pressed up and finally make it into stores so you can all take it home and love it like I know you already do.

"So right 'bout now, when you're wishin' you could hear the original *Pink Cadillac*, well, you got to settle for li'l ol' me. That's right: a radio first. Uncle Dewey Phillips sin-gin', *'I don't care if I never come back / In my pink Cadillac, my pink Cadillac, my pink, pink, piiiiiinnnnnk Cadillac. . . .'* "

His voice was rough as barb wire, and he was close to the melody as a seven-year-old shooting bb's at a tin can, but even when he started breaking down into maniacal giggles, you couldn't really say he wasn't getting at something true in the song: A way in which it was already bedrock. Just there. Solid.

`"Well, we got us a doozy of a *real* record comin' up next, Memphis's own Mr. Howling Wolf wailing *Smokestack Lightnin'*. This is new, and comin' down to us from Chicago on the Chess Brothers label, and y'all gonna love it. *Smoke-stack Light-nin-nin-nin-nin'*. . . ."

✳ ✳ ✳ ✳ ✳

THEY WERE HEADING to New York next week! Well, two weeks ago they were heading to New York "next week," then it was a week ago and they'd sure be there by now, but this Friday night Cuth said, "O.K., the deal's a lock. I got us an audition a week from now. Well, week from Monday. I'll come up and get you next weekend and we'll hit the Big Town! What you say about that, baby?"

Daisy, wary now—how could she not be?—just said, "I'll be ready."

And she was ready. Damn ready. This cold up here in Buffalo was making her not see straight. But it was worse. Singing the pop songs she'd learned, playing for the ten or twelve people who'd show up on a freezing Tuesday or Wednesday night at the Tin Spot, knowing that by now she'd learned pretty much what she needed—stage presence, the right way to hold the microphone, smart and sassy between-song patter; all that showbiz stuff—then watching the half-drunken, probably adulterating couples groping each other in the shadows while she was pouring her heart out ... well, she had to say, this wasn't exactly what she'd dreamed of back in Bent Knee.

There was a new edge on Cuth, too—a new impatience. Something unspoken in his voice, his eyes; like he was waiting for something from her, not ready to spell it out, but not able to move ahead until whatever this was he wanted had been worked out.

Was it ... sex? That seemed the logical explanation, but if that was it, why didn't he just come out and say something? If he did, Daisy knew she'd turn him down; she, like Doris Day in the movies she loved, wasn't that kind of girl, simple as that. Not that he did much for her anyway, least now that she knew him better. That tall, mustached suave-gentleman act—well, she saw right through it. No, with this man it truly was just business.

So maybe he was picking up these impatient feelings from her, except that Cuth Starks didn't seem capable of picking up feelings from anyone. He seemed more the see-it, grab-it type. What was going on with him was a mystery, and lately it was always present when he was with her: a hesitation, a waiting, a sort of floating uncertainty. As if he wasn't getting quite what he wanted from her. That until something happened that Daisy couldn't imagine the gates to the promised land—New York City—weren't going to open.

Except they better damn fly open soon. How long could she keep singing these stupid songs? Playing for these people who just wanted a dark place to hide out?

What kept her going at all was her vision of how it would go in New York. Cuth would set up the showcase, sure, but when the spotlight fell, there'd be only one person beneath it: Daisy Holliday. And it would be the Daisy Holliday of her secret soul. There she was, a coy, smoky smile on her face as she slipped onto the stage. She was wearing some sherbet-colored thing, but it was cut tight to her hips, and she felt like a million bucks—but her own million bucks, not somebody else's.

It was like the way she'd felt in the Cadillac—her Cadillac, passed down by that boy Elvis Presley, she had convinced herself now, because of what he'd seen of her talent. On lonely nights she remembered singing with him, lifting her voice into his—the man who now had all of America in his hand.

Why couldn't Cuth Starks see who she really was? Was that what he kept waiting for: the Daisy Holliday he envisioned her as, whatever that might be? Some lounge singer? Another Rosemary Clooney? A shake of her head. Could he be that far off base? Didn't he know she was born to sing rough and ready and devil take the hindmost? Didn't he see the way she could breathe fire? How could he miss the bucking energy in her just waiting to burst out?

One night it did.

She was up on the stage, trying to keep her smile bright into the spotlight for the nine people she saw before her, to be the best performer she could, but this one time, when the band hit the usual gentle downbeat, she stopped it quick. The band leader shot her a questioning look, and she went to have a word with him. Whisper, whisper. He shook his head, but she insisted, and, well, she was the headliner, so they simply had to follow her.

A nod to the drummer, who counted the new tune off. It was a stretch for him, but there it was, finally: a real back-beat. Her hips were swaying, her eyes sparking as she stepped to the mike. A moment to make sure she caught the beat strong, and then she launched herself into that song she could really blast off with. A song to make Madame Grosgreen proud, maybe even Bearcat.

"*When you got the jump,*" she started to sing, "*and you got the quick / Ain't nothing gonna move you like your gear shift stick / Ain't nothing gonna thrill you on the midnight side / 'Cept to get in that Cadillac and ride and ride.*"

She could feel it now, the riding along, foot on the gas, wind through her hair, that lift inside her like she was shooting the moon.

> *Yeah, where we're going, nobody's gonna know*
> *Till our star burns bright all 'long Catfish Row*
> *Yeah, where we're going, ain't never lookin' back*
> *From our pink Cadillac, our pink Cadillac*

Yeah, that was it, her voice kicking, fast and rough as that New Year's Eve at the roadhouse, the words out there for all to hear, to kick them up, rouse 'em, play 'em on down....

But the drummer just couldn't hold the beat, the bassist kept missing the triplets, the guitarist lost the chords. She was half through the song when it just petered to a halt.

She blushed, faced the nine people in the audience, who didn't seem to care anyway, then picked up the bandleader's gloating downbeat and started in on *Smoke Gets in Your Eyes.*

She sang it as acridly, as heart-breakingly as she could, but all the while she kept hearing *Pink Cadillac* play on in her head. *Maybe I do care … maybe I need to get back … to my … to my … pink Cadillac.*

Damn! When were they going to New York? When was this frozen purgatory going to end?

✻ ✻ ✻ ✻ ✻

THEY WERE IN Clay's old-model Honda Civic, rust all along the bottom of the doors, the guitarist-turned-bartender throwing the gearshift (there was something off with the transmission; it grinded between second and third) and fiddling with the radio as they headed into a sparsely streetlighted part of Memphis. Booker had told Colin what he could between customers but hadn't finished the story, and finally he said, "You know, I'm getting off soon."

Colin had looked at him in a quietly eager way, and the guitar player, as if all along he'd been feeling Colin out on a silent, soul-humming level, added, "Why don't you come to my place for a nightcap?" Meaning, Colin smiled deep to himself, he'd passed a test, and was now on his way to hear the rest of the tale.

What Colin had already heard amazed him. The record had existed, it had been all over the radio, everybody who remembered it remembered it right. Daisy Holliday singing with a spark and soul nobody had ever heard from a white girl before; yet, as Clay took pains to point out, *Pink Cadillac*—not blues, but rocky-roly, he called it—was a song only a white face could do justice to.

But there was so much more. Dell Dellaplane, Sonesta Clarke, the Bearcat stomping around, the sheriff, the money from the gamblers…. These would be some liner notes—

hell, maybe a book—he'd write when, and if, they found the lost 45 and Blue Moon Records put it out.

When ... and if. Clay hadn't said anything definite yet about its current existence, and Colin knew enough not to ask. But his head was spinning. What if the record had gotten pressed up, but something had happened before it got distributed; could somewhere there be moldering boxes of ... thousands of copies of the best record nobody had heard in nearly fifty years?

Colin was getting ahead of himself. One copy would certainly do. After Clay's offer to take him home, Colin had said he'd follow the guitar player but was relieved when he'd insisted an American could easily get lost, let alone somebody from England, who drove on the "damn wrong side of the road." Colin had kept smiling through that, and Clay went right on to say it wasn't that far, and he could always run Colin back if they had trouble getting a cab. Colin of course didn't want Clay out of his sight for a second.

Over the whine of a blues guitar from the radio, Colin said, "One thing I don't understand. Are you saying here that the Bearcat had some kind of deal with the sheriff?"

"He always had a deal with the sheriff," Clay said.

"But ... sounds like you're leading up to a deal of a different—"

"It does, does it?" The bartender laughed. "C'mon now, don't go jumpin' ahead."

Colin sighed. There was so much that didn't make sense. He sat back and listened to the radio song. He recognized it as a recent recording of Junior Kimbrough, of Holly Springs, Mississippi. He was sweetly amazed to be in a place where deep blues like this could be heard over a car radio, but this was Memphis. Something about the city.... He thought for a second about Robin, how he'd always loved it that she had Memphis deep in her. That led to a soft, uncertain thought about Robin's sister, Seely. Colin heard himself inhaling his next breath: Yes, he was truly looking forward to telling her all he'd learned so far.

The Honda turned off the street, its tires crackling over loose gravel. A moment later Clay had pulled it to a stop.

They were in front of a small, what looked like a three-room house, freshly painted white, with a small concrete porch, plain but neatly kept up. Another half a dozen of the same houses stretched on in the headlight beam from where they'd parked, ending just before a copse of pines. There were camellia bushes lining a walk from the driveway, and a welcoming yellow light over the front door.

Colin remembered that Clay had suggested his wife had died, but he hadn't asked if he'd married again or was living with somebody or what?

"You said you were married, but—"

"Years ago now, cancer." Clay looked down.

"I'm sorry," Colin said.

"How about you?"

"I'm a widower, too. Memphis girl. Singer."

"Recent?"

Colin swallowed. "Nine months ago."

"Then I'm really sorry."

"Thanks." Colin heard a breath sweep out from him. "Do you live, um … is there anyone else here?"

Clay smiled. "Some nights, my friend." A slant-eyed glance at the record man. "Tonight, I don't think so, no."

Colin gave him an appreciative nod, though he was also thinking he was glad they wouldn't be interrupting anyone.

The interior of the house was sparsely furnished: a deep-burgundy couch with a plastic cover still on it; round metal table neatly set for tomorrow's breakfast; a pressed-wood entertainment center with an old turntable and a stereo receiver with a gazillion buttons. Clay offered Colin a seat in a low-slung nappy-cloth-covered chair, then returned with a Memphis State University glass already with a couple inches of Scotch in it. He flicked on the receiver, an airplane console of lights flipping on, then set it to the same channel they'd had on in the car and kept it soft in the background.

"Keepin' up with the competition," he told the record man.

"It's a great station," Colin said.

Clay smiled.

Colin was looking more closely around the room. At the foot of the entertainment center were all Clay's record albums; he could make out frayed-cardboard edges but not the titles or who was on them. From this distance, though, they looked like regular-sized albums—nothing remotely like an old 78 acetate.

"Got your CD over there," Clay said, pointing to the top of the entertainment center. "Ever sell many of 'em?"

"Some," Colin admitted. "As you no doubt know, though, Bearcat Jackson, well, he's a pretty far-away presence in the '90s." A pause, then, " 'Course, if I find *Pink Cadillac*, that could be huge news. Have to do at least a reissue of the disc. Like I said, there'd probably be TV, radio, maybe a *Pink Cadillac* tour." Colin let these promises float.

"You think?" Clay said. He was nodding to himself. It wasn't particularly revealing, just a general head bob that said, How could I have any argument with that?

"I do, yeah."

More nodding; Colin wasn't at all sure he should get any encouragement from it. Though Clay did seem slightly deeper in thought.

"So Bearcat went off that morning," Colin said, to pick up the story from where it was left off. "Who was he meeting?"

"You haven't figured that out yet?"

Colin, not wanting to speculate, really just wanting to hear the story Clay's way, simply shook his head.

"Bet you have your ideas. We all did. But all that matters, really, is that Bearcat was back that night, and up on the stage like not a thing was different." Clay was on the couch, half stretched out. He held his own MSU glass of the Scotch. "But things *was* different." He leaned down, shaking his head like he still didn't believe it. "This was like nothin' I ever saw, then or now." There was a spooky urgency in Clay's words, and Colin leaned forward. "This was the *true* blues, my friend. This was like the earth down there had cracked wide open, and all hell—*all hell*—was 'bout to break loose."

* * * * *

"WHO WANTS TO HEAR ME ROAR? *Who wants to HEAR ME ROAR?*" The Bearcat had hauled his girth up on the stage and appeared to be in the highest of moods. He stalked the stage in his ursine pad, one clumpy foot after the other, walking up to the lip and hanging over it, like he wanted to reach into the audience and personally grab 'em by the neck and shake some excitement into them. The crowd this night—the same night of the big man's mysterious morning disappearance and Sonesta and Dell's talk—was large, and some of the white kids were back, on the strength of *Pink Cadillac* on the radio and the youth grapevine letting everyone know where it came from. They also knew that Daisy Holliday wasn't there to sing it in person, but that didn't seem to matter—they wanted the beat, the jump, the whole roadhouse experience over and over. And since Dell had cleaned the place up, it didn't feel at all like a threat.

Bearcat was soaring. "We're happy to see all you folks back again, and we got us a *special* night tonight. We got Clayton Booker on his scratchin' guitar, we got Thumper Johnson on bass, Mister Sticks McGhee on the drums, and my man Dell Dellaplane on his wailin', sailin' sax. And when we come back after five, we gonna have us Miss Sonesta

Clarke doing her version of our new hit song, *Pink Cadillac*. Y'all hold tight, we'll be right back."

"So Sonesta's gonna do it?" Dell asked as soon as the musicians stepped off the stage. A loud jukebox had come on, and he had to lean over to shout into Bearcat's ear. Bearcat had come back a little before noon and had disappeared into his upstairs quarters. Dell hadn't seen him to have a word with him till they started the show.

"Gotta keep the fires burning," Bearcat said.

"But I thought—"

"Don't see no Daisy Holliday, do ya?"

"But Daisy's the singer—*she's* the hit."

"You ever hear that old one, it's not the singer, it's the song?" Bearcat said.

"That's not how I heard it," Dell said, shaking his head. "And how you know it's even gonna work with Sonesta?" He was thinking about the misguided recording session a few weeks back.

"Well, we just do us the best we can." Bearcat beckoned to Salt the bartender for a drink.

Dell pushed ahead. "I really think we oughta wait till—"

"You still think she's comin' back?"

Dell pulled his head back and stared right at the big man. "I think when the song's a true hit, when we get it pressed up and start *sellin'* it, she will, yeah."

Bearcat rolled his eyes. "Well, I ain't waitin'."

"But havin' Sonesta sing it, I don't—" Dell saw the sharp look in the big man's eyes and held his thought. "Listen, I been wanting to talk to you all day. We gotta get the record out now. I got the money—" quick thought about what Sonesta had said about Bearcat's thinking the money had come from his father, but Dell blew right past that "—and we can go press it up tomorrow."

"Tomorrow?"

"First thing. What do you say?"

"Tomorrow—tomorrow sounds just fine." Then he gave Dell a quick look and walked away.

The funny thing was, the crowd seemed to love Sonesta's *Pink Cadillac*. No, it wasn't Daisy's, and yes, it was slower and bluesier and maybe almost a different song, but when she kicked up the beat halfway into it, the boys and girls in the audience started hollering, and the cries and shrieks only grew louder as she shouted the final chorus over and over …

… and over. She was seeming downright reluctant to let the song go. Dell was totally won over. He trilled up his sax riff and blew it higher and higher. It was his song, and he had to admit, even though he'd written it for Daisy, Sonesta was making this her own.

They were still whooping out the chorus when the windows at the front of the roadhouse glowed an alarming white. It was an eerie brightness, as if a searchlight were trained on them. The light pierced the roadhouse and cast wild, spookhouse shadows over the wood walls and stage.

Slingshot at the door started bouncing on his toes and shouting something toward the band, but it was lost over the musical tumult. Dell noticed, but it all seemed lost on Bearcat.

Then the door crashed open and the roadhouse was filling with khaki-uniformed Memphis police and Tennessee state troopers.

Their batons were up, and the cops started chasing kids, who tried to squirm past them or run out the back. It was a wild melee, though nobody seemed to be actually grabbed and stopped; it was like the cops just wanted to empty the place in the quickest, most brutal way.

On the stage everyone hung there slack-jawed till finally Dell felt he had to do something. But what? Then he saw the sheriff, standing in the doorway as his men continued emptying the room.

As he made his way toward the sheriff, Dell could hear him say, "That's one of 'em." And the next thing he knew a pair of cold metal handcuffs were slapped on his wrists.

"What is this?" Dell cried. "You're ... *arresting me*?"

"We have a court order. This place is selling liquor to minors. That's a felony offense, son, and you and Mr. Jackson are the owners of record."

"But—"

"We also have an order here to close this establishment. It's been condemned by the state."

"But we paid off the taxes."

The sheriff blinked for a moment, then said, "This ain't about taxes." He wouldn't say more.

Dell struggled in the grip of two policemen, but they held him tight. Then the sheriff sidled over right next to him. Dell was sure he was about to hear something like, Boy, I know who your daddy is. You just go quiet over to the corner, when everything dies down, we'll let you out of this. Instead the sheriff simply said, "Hank, we're gonna run this boy in. You take him, I'll deal with the nigger. Start him through booking, I'll be there after a while."

Dell was going to protest, but he was sure his father was behind this somehow, and he had the gut feeling that saying anything more would be somehow giving in to him. So when the cops manhandled him out of the roadhouse and threw him into the backseat of a police car, he was all cooperation. They handcuffed him to a steel bar across the back seat, behind a wire mesh, and all the way into Memphis, as the cold steel dug into his wrists, he sat there silently, burning with rage.

In the roadhouse the chaos was beginning to settle. The sheriff's deputies had cleared the place of its patrons, kids scattered to the winds outside. Inside were still Bearcat, Sonesta, the band, and Salt and Hosea. The deputies had done their job roughly, leaving tables overturned, chairs on their sides, beer bottles clattering on the floor, grain liquor spilled sticky underfoot. One deputy was nailing another THIS PROPERTY CONDEMNED notice on the door, as the sheriff called out to Bearcat across the room, "This time it's gonna stick, Jackson. You done corrupted your last white boy out here. You played your cards too far this time."

"But what did I do?" the big man cried. "I didn't do nothin'."

The sheriff faced him directly and spoke loudly enough for everyone to hear. "Your very existence is a rilement in this town, you should know that. I don't know who you been payin' off, but ain't nobody you can pay off now."

"Sheriff, I don't care what you do, I ain't gonna leave this place. You gonna have to *shoot* me t' get me out of here. Sonesta—"

The sheriff laughed. "Jackson, you ain't gonna hide behind no woman's skirts. My friend, you got nowhere at all to hide. Bulldozers be out here in the morning before you can say Jack Sprat, roll this place down."

"We gotta get to Dell," Sonesta said sotto voce to Bearcat from where she still stood on the bandstand. She hadn't moved once and had watched with astonishment as the flood of deputies had cleared the joint. "He'll be able to get help again."

"That's why we got him on his way to the jail," the sheriff said with a wicked leer. "We ain't missin' a trick this time, lady. Right, Jackson?"

"Like I said, Sheriff, over my dead body." Bearcat puffed out his chest.

"So you swearin' you're gonna make trouble tomorrow?"

"Damn right I is."

The sheriff nodded to himself, and it was a wide, almost stagy nod.

"That case, we gotta run you in, too."

"What's your accusation?"

"Want me to go down the list again?" The sheriff leaned back and spit on the sawdust floor. "I ain't gonna bother. Sprague, you put Mr. Jackson under arrest."

A good-sized deputy started toward the Bearcat, but Bearcat was bigger, and he took a large, arm-waving step toward Deputy Sprague, and he backed off.

"*Sprague, do it.*"

Bearcat let out a roar. It, too, had a theatrical edge: The old guy leaning back and growling from deep within him. His eyes seemed light. The deputy backed off.

"This ain't a joke, Jackson. McHale, you help Sprague. Dilly, you too. Cuff the nigger and get 'im into a car."

Bearcat shook and kicked but it wasn't enough, and the three deputies got him subdued, arms behind his back, handcuffs on his wrists, one deputy in front, two behind—Deputy Sprague now kicking him with the side of his boot, moving the Bearcat toward the door.

Halfway there the deputies stopped, and Sprague said, "What's that stinky thing you got hangin' off your belt?" He jabbed at Bearcat's mojo sack with a billy club. "That some dead thang?"

"*Leave it!*" Bearcat cried, a sharp, sincere yap.

"Oh, yeah, I ain't gettin' ten feet close to that skanky thang." He jabbed at it with the stick until he'd worked it loose; caught up the bag's leather thongs and flipped it back behind the bar.

Bearcat cried out at them again, but the deputies kicked him along. At the door the Bearcat spun around and gave the sheriff a look of deep quizzicalness. There was a new surprise and pain in his eyes.

"Get him into a car, I'll be out in a sec," the sheriff said.

When Bearcat was gone, the sheriff addressed Sonesta, the other band members, and Salt and the hangers-on like Hosea still there.

"You got till tomorrow get yourselves packed up. The

roadhouse is over, no way to stop it comin' down. You hear?"

Nobody said a word.

"I'm asking you a question," the sheriff said. "*You understand?*"

Still not a sound. Everyone stood where they were, frozen.

"Well, I don't give a shit no way anyhow." And he stomped out.

At the police car the sheriff beckoned deputies Sprague, McHale, and Dilly off. He got into the driver's seat, then turned to talk to Bearcat, handcuffed to the steel bar in the backseat.

"What'm I doin' here?" the Bearcat bellowed.

"Shhhh," the sheriff went, "keep this private."

"You gonna let me go now?"

The sheriff shot a glance right, then left. Nobody was close.

"No."

"*NO?*"

"I got me orders."

"But we had a deal. You was s'posed to have the record for me. I don't see no record, all I see's me in handcuffs!"

"This is the way it's gonna play, Jackson."

"You better start talkin' now, sheriff, make some sense, or I's gonna haunt you the rest of your days."

"It's the Man, he wants to see you himself."

A sharp wariness on Bearcat. "Himself?"

"I don't ask questions, you shouldn't either."

Bearcat bared teeth. "No, what's he want?"

The sheriff sighed. "He said, drive you out to see 'im, he'd settle you up out there."

"Where?"

"Doesn't matter."

"*Where?*"

"Does not matter." Loud now. "He'll be there."

"But what's he want to see me for? I don't—"

"Jackson, sometimes you're a pain in the ass—"

"Sheriff, come on, we's friends. Talk to me."

The sheriff leaned back in the car seat and sighed again. "What he said was, 'I want to take a look at this nigger thinks he's the father to my boy.' "

* * * * *

THERE WAS A PURPLE LIGHT floating over the river, odd because it was still dark out, couldn't be later than four a.m. by Bearcat's calculation, which meant it wasn't really dawn; but there the rich purple sheen was, above the black, clumpy ripples—a post-midnight color, the hour of the true mojo if there ever was one. There'd been a brutal cloudburst not long after midnight, but now the sky was clear. Occasionally the fulsome royal purple was shot with striations of yellow or pink, and Bearcat decided they were just more signs of a false dawn. Or his old eyes playing tricks on him. All he really knew was that he and the sheriff were waiting endlessly.

After the sheriff swore for the fifth time this was the place, and refused for the sixth time to apologize for busting up the roadhouse—what would Bearcat need it for anymore, anyway?—and for the seventh time insisted they had nothing to talk about, the two men settled into an uneasy silence. The sheriff, veteran of who knows how many stakeouts, soon started snoring. The Bearcat, electricity shooting his veins, stayed awake, head pressed against the police car window, forehead cool against the glass.

It was a gamble, Bearcat knew, but he didn't see anyway else to play it. There were hands out there waiting to grab what was his the moment what was his had value—and how could he stop them? The tools given a colored man ... well, they were rusty, broken tools at best. He knew for tools, those years at his aunt and uncle's behind the plow, twelve-, fifteen-hour days, sometimes into the night. If the plow weren't sharp, you couldn't bust up nothing. If you were doin' the white-people work, that plow stayed sharp. You start plowing your *own* way, though, you see how many people line up to grind that plow for you.

Not to mention the rumors he'd been hearing lately 'bout that boy, Dell. He'd known all along 'bout the boy's father, how he was the Man downtown, one of the main players in the city's expansion; if anybody had maps up on the wall with drawings of clover leafs right there on top of where the roadhouse was, it was Ransom Dellaplane. But Bearcat had trusted the boy—had seen the true rocky-roly spirit in his eyes, in his songs, in his *saxophone*—where no way anybody could lie, least not to the Bearcat. But that was before Bearcat started hearing stories that the boy was talking with his father. Before money started showing up in that boy's pockets *out of nowhere*. Before his old broken-down roadhouse had become this high-profile showplace. Before it was the kind of joint somebody for sure was going to grab from him, the only question when—and what they'd leave him with, which of course would be what all coloreds got, one big heap of *nothing*.

But he was not going to get taken again. No! Never!

The only way Bearcat could see it, he had to grab what was his himself and run. He had it all planned out. The record of *Pink Cadillac*, with that white girl on it, could be a Northern hit as much as a Southern one and wouldn't hurt none from comin' out first up there. He just had to get the acetate to Chicago, where he had contacts from the old days, friends who'd already argumented with him long into the night. He remembered one, Sweet Home Arthur of Poker Records, who a year or so back had pulled into the dusty roadhouse parking lot in his long maroon town car, then stepped out wearing a long flowing white cashmere coat, a snow-white Borsalino on his head, a squeezy dish of apple pie clinging to his arm. Over whiskeys later Sweet Home said, "Bearcat, can't you see, the action ain't down South no more. It's up in Chitown, with Heddy Days and the Wolf and even that crazy nigger thinks he's a soda jockey, Chuck Berry. Chuck's got hits—with white kids!" Sweet Home's eyes rolled. "There's plenty for everybody. Whyn't you come?" And the Bearcat, surveying the roadhouse around him, *his* roadhouse, all he owned, true, but something he owned nonetheless, said, "Sweet, you got a point, I ain't denying, and I been givin' it some thought, who but a fool wouldn't, but I got me something right here. Might not be much, but it's all mine. Can't leave that, now, can I?"

But that was the *old* roadhouse, 'fore things started spinning away from him. Could he have done anything different? Not let the white boy in? Not record the song with that Daisy gal? He couldn't see how. He knew from the first minute that *Pink Cadillac* was his big score, his reward for sticking there, and that they was going to have a hit. Big hit. A hit with Berry's new audience, which meant Billboard pop charts, which meant … real money. That feeling you only get once or twice and it comes tingling right off your *bones*.

And it was going to be *his* hit. He was due. That boy might be ready to spring his tricks on Bearcat, take his music like all white peoples, but he had another think comin'. That was the beauty of his plan. By the time the boy got himself out of jail, Bearcat would be halfway to Chicago, *Pink Cadillac*— the *only* copy of *Pink Cadillac*—tight under his arm.

If his dangnappin' father ever showed up. This seemed pretty irregular. Bearcat had no problem dealing with the sheriff; indeed, he liked that honor, that the sheriff himself and not some flunky always came down to deal direct with the Bearcat. Not that the sheriff wan't just a flunky himself, but he was the big-cheese flunky. But this Dellaplane—he was the Cheese himself.

And there Bearcat had been, in business with the Boy

Cheese. Well, no longer. Bearcat had no illusions. The money was coming from somewhere, and Dell was his father's son. At best, he was working his own game with *Pink Cadillac*, wasn't he? And no matter what the boy cheese said, when push got to shove, how could Dell not be right there in his father's big, swallowin' pocket?

Bearcat had to laugh. Funny, how here it was Bearcat cutting the deal with Ransom Dellaplane, got the boy sitting in jail, the *Pink Cadillac* acetate 'bout to end up in the Bearcat's own hands, the Man himself wanting to—how did the sheriff put it?—"take a look at the nigger thinks he's father to my son."

But I ain't his father. And he ain't my son. And that's all there is to it.

Where is that man?

Now there was true purple in the air, a faint band in the east—real dawn at last. They'd been here must be hours now. Bearcat thought, If that man didn't have the one thing in the world I need, I would never take this disrespect, even from Ransom Dellaplane.

The sheriff stirred. Raised his thinning-haired white head and peered through the mesh separating backseat and front.

"Guess the ol' man's got him some other business," he said, yawning.

"Or don't get himself up this early."

"Oh, he'll be here, Jackson. He's a man of his word."

"Just not a man who keeps his clock running very good, huh?"

"He'll be here. What do you care? Once he comes, you're gone. Right?"

"That's our deal."

"You know, Jackson, part of me's gonna miss you. You been a good, well, guess I can't really say *friend*, but, you know ... whatever—I mean for a nigger."

"Do I say thanks?"

"You say whatever pops into your woolly head, I'm sure." The sheriff laughed. "But serious, this wire wasn't here, I'd reach over and shake your hand."

"That's downright decent of you, sheriff."

"Yeah, I mean it." And the sheriff gave the musician a wide, almost simpering grin. "Boy, you had those folks in town cra-zeee that last month, worrying they was losin' their children to that nigger music. I mean!"

The Bearcat didn't say a word.

"Yeah, things gonna be a heap quieter we get you and that nigger music out of here. Bad 'nuff they got that Presley boy singin' it now on TV. Course he's just a passin' thang. Jackson, you think that Presley boy's just a passin' thang?"

Bearcat wasn't going to answer. He was suddenly angry sick, like he'd simply had enough. He just couldn't take it any longer.

"Jackson, what you got to say 'bout that Presley boy. You's a musician, I'm asking your opin-i-on."

Bearcat was not going to say another word. Not to a white man, certainly not the sheriff. The sick was passing, but the anger was still there. O.K., he would say something more. Just one sentence. He'd tell that sheriff in words he'd obey if he cared for his life that right this second Bearcat Jackson wasn't going to take anymore, and he wanted that sheriff to drive him without no backtalk straight to Ransom Dellaplane's mansion, and then they'd see what was holdin' up their business trans—

Though it was lighter out, both men were jolted by the sweep of yellow headlights across their eyes. Then a long, black Lincoln pulled into the turnout by the river. The Lincoln pulled up from the rear, right alongside.

"Well, well, here he is now," the sheriff said, straightening himself in his seat.

Bearcat remained quiet.

The Lincoln sidled up gently, coming in head-first toward the patrol car, then the chauffeur pulled even with the sheriff in the front seat, and his window came down. The sheriff gunned his window down, too, a crisp morning breeze fluttering back and chilling Bearcat's neck. The back windows of the Lincoln were blacked out, impossible to see in at all.

"Morning, Sheriff," the chauffeur said.

"Morning, Deke."

"Got us a little somethin' for you, I guess."

"Yeah, that's why we're here." Both men's breath frosted white in the morning air.

Without another word, the chauffeur slid a small brown envelope across the distance to the sheriff's outreached hand.

"That's one of 'em. For the other, I think you might have to roll that window down some more," the chauffeur said.

"Wait," Bearcat went.

The sheriff turned to look through the wire mesh at him but paid him no mind.

"Is Dellaplane there?" Bearcat said louder. He was staring out his window at the flat black gloss of the Lincoln's rear windows.

The chauffeur was holding out a wide, flat brown package now—the size of a record. He slid it easily through the Lincoln's wide window, but it wasn't so clear it would fit the narrower window on the patrol car.

"Here," the sheriff said, riffling down his window all the way. Chill air rushed in. "See if we can work it through."

"I want to talk to Dellaplane," Bearcat said. He was trying to peer through the blacked-out glass. "Is he there?"

"I think I can grab it, Deke. 'Course I could simply get out," the sheriff said. "If I wanted to work that hard for a nigger."

Both men laughed.

"Dammit!" Bearcat cried, agitated now. His hand went

instinctively to his waist, where the mojo bag should be, but it wasn't there. "I want to see the Man."

"Looks like I got it," the sheriff said after the package had floated across the distance between the two cars. "That's it, right?"

Bearcat that second rolled down the back window of the patrol car. He still couldn't see anything in the back of the Lincoln, and it was making him crazy. He grabbed the door handle and gave it a yank, but it wouldn't turn. He pressed against it, but still nothing. This was a police car, and so it could carry prisoners, the back doors could only be opened from the outside.

"Business done," Deke said.

"No," Bearcat roared through the open window. "I want to see Ransom Dellaplane. He made me wait, now I want to see him!"

In the front seat the sheriff mimed putting fingers in his ears. "Bearcat, you got what you came for, now shut up."

But Bearcat wouldn't. Wasn't that the least they could do, let him see the man he was doing business with? Was their contempt that great? Could the man *not even have showed up*?

While the sheriff turned over his own motor, the Lincoln, in idle all along, shifted into gear and started to slide slowly forward. Bearcat leaned his head out the window hoping to see something, anything.

Then the rear window cracked open. It was just a couple inches, and so dark inside it was almost impossible to make anything out. But as the rear window of the Lincoln pulled even with Bearcat, a glint of sunlight bounced off the flank of the black-and-white cop car and shot right at the window. Though Bearcat could not swear what his eyes had actually seen, he was certain of what he perceived: a pale white, wrinkled brow, the top of a wide nose, and then, set back a little, a pair of narrow eyes under thick lashes.

What did he read in those eyes: frosty arrogance and

disdain, or a stony blankness, stippled by dots of fear and uncertainty?

Since it was almost all in his own head, there was no way to really know, though all the way back to the roadhouse, before the sheriff handed him the two envelopes and drove off, the Bearcat took what faint succor he could in believing that it was only the latter.

* * * * *

"I DEMAND TO KNOW why you're holding me!" Dell cried for what seemed the hundredth time. He'd shaken his rage when they'd tossed him in a cell; now he just wanted out. "What's the charge?"

There was a deputy at one end of the hall, sitting tilted back in a chair, feet up on a wooden desk; another was reading a magazine at the other end of the hall. Neither said anything to him.

"You do know who I am, don't you?" Dell was right up at the bars, hands grasping the cold steel tightly. He knew he had to get out of here, any way he could. He desperately needed to get back to the roadhouse.

"Question is, Dell, do you know who we are?" This was the deputy to Dell's right.

"Why should I know you?"

"High school, sport."

Dell looked down the hall as well he could, but all he saw was a white man about his age with a khaki cap tilted over his forehead and large pink ears sticking out.

"I'm sorry, I—"

"Hell, I'm not surprised. Didn't have much time for us in high school, Mr. Football Star." This was the deputy to Dell's left.

"Really, I'm—I can't recognize either of you from here."

"My name's Del, too," the deputy to the right said. "Delbert McCracken."

"And I'm Stan Blinker, Dell."

Dell racked his memory. "Did we have classes together?"

Both deputies laughed. "Warn't that many people in our class, right, Dellaplane. Figured you might remember something 'bout us."

"Like what?"

"Like you beat the tarnation out of me once in grammar school." This was McCracken.

"No shit!" Dell suddenly laughed. "I did?"

The laugh seemed to throw the deputy. He slid forward in his chair, the front two feet clapping loud on the floor, then slid his feet off the desk and stood up.

"Yeah, but it wasn't fair. You had that big friend of yours, Chick Strong, helping you."

Though Dell didn't remember, intuition told him he'd better.

"Oh, yeah, Del McCracken, I remember you now. You were one tough monkey."

"Hey?"

"Yeah," Dell went on, "what I remember was that you were whompin' shit out of me, and it was only when Chick came up that he pulled you off me. I remember it all now. Yeah, when I think of it, you're still beating the shit out of me."

"No lie?"

"Absolutely. I'm not surprised you became law enforcement, tough guy like you. You never went out for football did you? How come?"

"I—I tried. Coach—" The deputy was coming closer to Dell's cell.

"What did Coach know? I bet you woulda been a great fullback."

"Actually, I went out for end. I had speed back then."

"I remember. You ran me down during our fight, didn't you? Wasn't I running away?"

"I don't—"

"No, sure I was. Think of us meeting again like this." Dell was almost cooing now. He gave the bars a shake; they rattled a little. "Anything, Del, you can do about this?"

"We got orders, just keep you still till the sheriff gets back."

"You mean, he's not here?"

"Naw, he's got something goin'."

Dell thought quickly. "Out at the roadhouse?"

"Big doin's."

"That's where they pulled me in from. Y'all have any idea how come?"

"Naw." This was Blinker. He was up to talk to Dell, too. "They don't tell us nothin'."

"Well, the sheriff was there, threw me into a car, and they still won't say why I'm here, though I'm thinking it has something to do with my father."

"Your father?"

"Things ain't like they was when we was kids, Del."

"I'll say. Never thought I'd see you here."

"You have any knowledge of Bearcat Jackson? They bring him in, too?"

Both deputies looked at each other, then shook their heads. "Don't know any Bearcat Jackson," McCracken said. "Sounds like a nigger."

"He wasn't arrested also?"

"Not so I know," Blinker said. " 'Less they took him someplace else."

"Like where?"

McCracken took a long moment to scratch his naked chin. "Hell, even though he's a nigger, really, there ain't no place else."

"So they didn't bring him in?"

McCracken looked at Dell like he was a moron. "You see 'im?"

Dell shook off the deputy's disdain. "And no sign of the sheriff?"

"Nope, haven't seen him."

"Me neither."

"So, guys, how can I get out of here?" All brightness.

"I don't think you're goin' anywhere till tomorrow," McCracken said. He was right up at the bars now. Dell, seeing him this clearly, did faintly remember him; he remembered the fight, too, McCracken going after Dell for being rich, wearing good clothes, having a nice haircut—stuff like that. And Dell remembered beating him bloody—without the help of his friend Chick. He smiled now. "That was what we were told, anyhow," McCracken went on. "Keep Dellaplane out of commission here till tomorrow."

"Anybody ever break out of this place?"

Both deputies quickly shook their heads.

"Sorry, Dell, not much we can do."

"You mean, you're holdin' me here with no charges, not lettin' me talk to a lawyer ... and in the face of all this dubious legality, you simply got orders to keep me here all night?" The deputies nodded. "Well," Dell went on, "come, let's think this out, like old high school buds." He pointed down the hallway to a small barred window that was black as pitch. "Now look at that window over there—don't I see the dawn?"

＊ ＊ ＊ ＊ ＊

"SO," COLIN SAID, relaxed back in the chair in Clay Booker's neat living room, his ear full of the rich story, "Bearcat cut a deal with Dell's father, thinking that Dell was going to sell him out."

"That's how we saw it."

"But Dell was—"

"Dell looked on the straight up and up to me," Clay said, "but I was just the guitar player, you know." He'd replenished the Scotch in the MSU tumblers a couple times, but both men definitely had all their wits still with them.

"He got it that wrong?"

"Well, now, the Bearcat didn't get anything fun-da-men-tal wrong, I don't think. I mean, he was right to be suspicious."

"But he turned against his best ally?"

"He must've been feelin' awfully alone toward the end there, yeah."

"You said he was acting crazy, but that crazy?"

"You just had to be there," Clay said. "It was the South back then, just the way things were. But don't get me wrong, the thing you gotta understand here is that when everything started going against him, Bearcat *did* go crazy. You might've gone crazy too, anyone could've—all that pressure. I mean, Dell's father was sending the sheriff in to take out the road-house. *They were comin'!* Bearcat, all that pressure, he went plumb fuckin' *loco*."

Colin was silent a moment, then said, "Crazy enough to get himself killed?"

And Clay held fire a long moment till he answered, "He did die, yeah."

Colin leaned forward, gave a sage nod. He was getting a pretty good idea who had done it.

"Don't be too quick there," Clay said.

"But the sheriff was on his way. With deputies and guns—"

"You got a lot of story to come, my friend," Clay said, notably calm in the face of Colin's insistence. He took a sip of Scotch. "Don't be jumping—"

"But you said, I mean, what were you saying, it was just the way things were—"

Clay shook his head fast, raised his hand, palm out. "It wasn't the sheriff, and it wasn't his deputies."

Colin was teasing a remarkable idea, but he still said, "Then who?"

"You just keep listening to my story," Booker said, calm as could be. "I think you got a few surprises to come." He smiled, but there was no cheer in it at all.

* * * * *

AT THE ROADHOUSE all was a flurry of activity. It was well into the day. It had started raining again right after daybreak, though now it was just a little misty. There wasn't much light, though, it was so gray and overcast. In the roadhouse all the lamps were burning bright, including the strings of gaily colored Christmas bulbs strung along the walls. There were packing cases open on the floor, and suitcases, already packed, standing by the door. Bearcat was working away at the end of the bar. Next to him on the wood counter were the brown envelope and the large package from the night before. And his revolver.

"C'mon, y'all, we only got a couple hours till the train leaves," Bearcat called out. He was standing over his liquor supply, trying to decide how much to take with him. He put one amber bottle in an open packing case, set in some wadded newsprint, then put in another—and another.

"Bearcat, man," Sticks said, "why again we doin' this?" He was over at his drum kit, and with each move a cymbal rattled.

"Because niggers down here don't stand a chance."

"I ain't ever been to Chicago," Clay said.

"You gonna love it." Bearcat held up another unmarked bottle of 'shine hooch, eyed it with something close to devotion, then wrapped it in the newsprint and put it away. He was speaking loudly, perhaps too loud for such a mood-dampened room. "It's nigger paradise. We got us our own city round 63rd and Cottage Grove, you gotta see it to believe it. Niggers running clubs, niggers running restaurants, niggers running dry cleaning and liquor stores ... niggers running *everything you can imagine.*"

Clay shook his head. "I can't right believe that," he said, but the guitarist was very young, and there were stars in his eyes nonetheless.

"Oh, you'll see, you'll see!" Bearcat wrapped and set down another bottle, this time into his personal valise. "Now where is that Sonesta Clarke? You need her, she ain't nowhere to be found."

"She's off with her lady friends, best I know," Salt said. He was standing at the other end of the bar from Bearcat; ostensibly packing but not at all knowing what to take, he was simply sipping at a cup of coffee he kept setting down with a clatter, roughly enough to have spilled a puddle of liquid onto the wooden bar top.

"She staying out all night with Jesus now?"

"The sheriff's raid spooked her, I guess," Salt said. "Soon as you got taken away, she got on the phone, and next thing I know, she was getting picked up by somebody. You were with the po-lice, what could I do? By the way, how'd you get away from that sheriff?"

"Never you mind that," Bearcat said. He stood up, surveyed the roadhouse, the knicked and cigarette-scarred tables, the chairs askew, the walls bare except for the Christmas bulbs, the broken window still not fixed, the ramshackle stage. He looked like he was trying to decide how much else he could take with him successfully; his immediate expression, hooded eyes, pursed lips, said, Let it all go. "Y'all doin' fine now, though, you just keep packing." He looked at his pocket watch. "Damn, we don't got much longer."

"Can't we just take a later train?"

"We gotta be—" Bearcat caught his tongue. "Well,

sooner we get goin', sooner we gonna be there. Now don't that make sense?"

Everyone kept putting glasses and cooking pans into boxes, tightening down instruments cases, arranging, getting ready. Rain started falling again, beating loud on the tin roof. The light seeping into the roadhouse grew even grayer.

"Everything feels sort of, I don't know, Bearcat," Slingshot the bouncer said, "but sort of ... *mournful*."

"Hey, we's startin' a new life." Bearcat had opened one of his bottles of hooch and poured an inch into a wide glass. "That's what we's doin'. Just you keep packin'."

"Really, Bearcat, you sure we gotta leave here? This is our home—only home we know." This was Sticks, holding his last cymbal, gold light reflecting off it and glowing around his head.

"Oh, you men, you's nothin' but trouble." The old cat's voice rasped. "Who you gonna trust if not your Bearcat, huh? Who got you here? 'Sides, we're gonna have us a hit record. We gonna be the *toast of Chitown!*"

"What hit record's that?"

All heads spun. It was Sonesta, dressed in her church clothes, heavy gabardines and black wool stockings. The only thing bright on her was a charm bracelet of little crosses and tiny fishes. She came in through the back, then stopped frozen, taking in the scene of total disorder.

"My hit record!" the Bearcat barked. "And where you been?"

"Getting me a little sanctuary." Sonesta's eyes stayed round. "What's goin' on here?"

"We're goin' to Chicago," Clay said brightly.

"*Chicago?*" Sonesta briskly moved around the cases, right toward Bearcat. "What's gotten into your fool head?"

"What's gotten into yours? Don't you see we's all played out here?"

Sonesta dropped her hands onto her hips. "I see somebody runnin', that's what I see. Where's Dell? What's he say 'bout this?"

"Dell, he's out of commission. In jail."

"Jail?"

"I don't know nothin' 'bout it," Bearcat said, holding up his hands in a large shrug, "but that's what I heard when the sheriff hauled me away. Dell's in jail. Won't be there any longer than necessary, though. I'm assured about that."

"And who's assurin' you?" Sonesta was still about ten feet away from Bearcat. His leather valise was at his feet.

"Woman, none of your business." Bearcat reached down to zip up the valise, then lifted it onto a table right near the long bar. "Sling, why don't you start movin' all these filled-up cases and stuff out to the door."

"What's that?" Sonesta was pointing at the fifteen-by-fifteen-inch brown-paper envelope carefully placed at the end of the bar.

Bearcat turned back to face her. "That's none of your business, either."

"And you got your gun out, too?" Sonesta said. She started sidling through the packing cases, peeking into this one, then that. "What *is* goin' on here?"

"Listen," Bearcat said, turning to follow her. "You only got one question to ask, and that is, How long have I got to pack? And the answer is, You better skeedaddle right this second, woman, or the train be leavin' without you!" Bearcat's loud words echoed through the roadhouse.

Sonesta walked slowly around, looking at the stacks of boxes. Then to Bearcat, she said, "You think I'm goin'? Just like that?"

"You think you have a choice?"

She shook her head, mostly like she still didn't understand what was happening. Kept poking into a couple not-closed-up boxes, but all the while her gaze was slipping out toward what was on the bar. Then, wasp-swift, she was there, grabbing up the brown-paper envelope.

"It's the record," she said, holding it up, reading the hand-marked label. "That dang *Pink Cadillac* acetate, started all our trouble. How'd you get this?"

"Give it over."

"No!" Sonesta was holding up the record to the light, looking at it closely. "What you expectin' from this?"

"*Expecting?*" Another Bearcat bellow. "I'm expecting just what I deserve. A hit—a goddamn hit of my own."

"And this that one recording, the one Goldilocks sang on all that time back?"

"It's the recording that's got the hit, woman. Yeah."

"Oh, you poor man."

"What you say?"

"You take a look at this?"

"What're you saying?" Louder, worried now.

"I'm saying, how far you gonna get with a record got big deep scratches across it."

Bearcat lunged at Sonesta, and she hardly pulled back; just let him grab the black lacquer disc. He held it up to the light. The look on his face was inexpressible.

"You didn't have yourself a look at this?"

Bearcat just stared at the disc. Around him the band members and Salt and Slingshot were gathering. There were three deep gouges in the surface of the record, as if someone had taken a blunt beer-can opener to it. There was no way it could be played.

At Clay Booker's house Colin Stone felt his breathing slow. "That was the only copy, right?" he said, agitated. Clay just put a finger to his lips and went on.

"Now how'd you get this?" Sonesta said at the road-house. "What you do for it?"

"I'm gonna kill somebody," Bearcat cried. He grabbed the gun off the bar, eyeballed it to make sure it was loaded, then started waving it.

"You gonna shoot somebody *here*?" Sonesta stepped back, but she looked unalarmed. "We didn't do this to you. Now you tell me who did."

"It's that boy."

"What boy?"

"Dellaplane!"

"How's it that boy?"

"He sold me out. Damn!" Bearcat started moving around, stamping his feet loudly on the wood floor, head tilted back, raging. "I knew it, knew he had lyin' eyes. Knew he was in cahoots with his father. Just thought I was faster—"

"What's his father got to do with it?"

Bearcat whirled on Sonesta. "You don't get it? His father's the man who wants this property. He sicced the sheriff on us, gonna come and bulldoze the place down—"

"But you said they put Dell in jail." Sonesta was shaking her head in lack of comprehension. "Why'd the boy's father do that?"

Bearcat looked like he was thinking fast. "Must be some kind of trick." Bearcat held up the lacquered disc again, squinted at it. "I knew it, I knew it. He wanted to keep that song to hisself, that boy. That's why it's all scratched up. Damn!"

"That boy loves you," Sonesta said. Another baffled shake of her head. "He wouldn't do nothin' to hurt you. And he certainly wouldn't do nothin' to hurt his *record*."

"Woman, don't you got eyes?"

The woman singer took another step forward. "How'd you get the disc?"

"What're you sayin'?" Bearcat immediately flew back at her, quick defense.

"How ... did ... you ... get ... this ... record?" Sonesta was bearing right in on the Bearcat. At the same time she moved back over to the bar, eyes glancing at the other envelope lying there. "Last I heard, that record was with that white disc jockey Dewey Phillips. Last I heard, Dell Dellaplane was waiting around to talk to you about going to get it back. Talking to you to see 'bout taking money he got and going and pressing it up. We was talkin' 'bout that together. Waiting for you. He wanted to get it right out to be pressed. I was the one telling him—"

"What were *you* tellin' him?" Bearcat had a wild light in his eyes now.

"Just that the whole thing was foolishness, you know. *Nothing new.*"

"Then why's the record like this?" Bearcat held up the gouged black lacquer disc. He looked fiercely in pain. "I mean, it ain't gonna be a hit now—ain't gonna be nothing. Thing is dead!" And with a furious thrust Bearcat took the black disc and broke it over his knee. The lacquer shattered into large triangular shards that Bearcat let fall to the floor.

Colin felt his heart drop, his head start spinning. He grasped the side of the chair as if afraid to let go.

From the sofa across from him Clay gave him a stern look. "Don't go giving up now," *he said.* "I told you, we got us surprises. Story ain't over by half."

Bearcat looked around the roadhouse, eyes lit with fury. Then a glance at his watch; under his breath he muttered, "Shit, what'm I gonna do now?"

"You're gonna tell me what this is?" Sonesta was just where she was when she pulled out the ruined record.

"Now what, woman?"

"This thing here." Sonesta held open the smaller envelope on the bar, looked inside. "I smell money—a stack of money."

Bearcat gave the room one more helpless glance, then out went his chest, puffed up with awkward pride. "You don't think I'm givin' anything up for nothin', do you?"

"Giving what up?"

"Bearcat sold the roadhouse," Sticks the drummer

stepped forward and said. "That's why we're all goin' to Chicago." There was a clear tone in his voice that said, Sonesta, can *you* talk some sense into him?

"You sold this place out from under us?" Sonesta's eyes suddenly broke open with a terrible understanding. "That's what all these boxes are about?"

"I did—did what I had to do," Bearcat said. He was standing tall now, chest out, voice as deep and powerful as he could make it. "They was gonna take it anyway, even you said that. I was just gettin' top dollar!"

"Top dollar?" Sonesta was sliding the bills out of the envelope. "You didn't even take yourself a look at *this*?"

Bearcat leaned forward, then muttered, "It was dark."

"Dark! Look at this." Sonesta held out the inch-high stack of bills. "You fool! *You damn, damn fool!*"

Bearcat took the stack, which Sonesta passed to him already fanned open. There was nobody in the room who didn't see a few true $100 bills on either side of the pile, the rest plain pale green paper cut to size.

"Look at your sorry ass," Sonesta bore in, carping. "You don't trust nobody, you can't even bring yourself to trust a white boy who loves you, yet you go all stupid with his daddy. *Look at you!*"

Bearcat grabbed his heart, dropping the bills at the same time; they fluttered to the floor around the broken pieces of the disc. He staggered backward as if he'd been clubbed in the chest. The Christmas lights on the walls were flashing around him. Then he saw the gun on the bar counter and lunged at it. He clutched the black pistol tight before him.

"Where you goin', brother?" Sticks said. He was eyeing Bearcat close.

The big man had the gun in his hand, but it wasn't clear that he was in total control of it—or himself. He kept staggering around, moving toward the front door. Part of the time he was swinging the gun out freely, a dull light curling along its barrel, but then the Bearcat would pull it back to his chest. Slingshot and Salt were behind him, shadowing him, but the Bearcat was wily. He waved the gun just crazily enough to keep them off guard.

"Bearcat, come on," Salt said.

Bearcat flashed the gun out at the bartender, who jumped back. Then the big man pointed the pistol right at his own right temple. He pressed the round barrel against his flesh. Everyone sucked in their breaths. The Bearcat's eyes were huge, unreadable. A second later when Bearcat pulled the gun away, it left an odd pink ring on his dark skin.

"Bearcat, man, come on, give me that," Slingshot said. He tried to use his own size to move the Bearcat, but the big man paid him no mind. Slingshot reached out. "Come on, easy, man."

Bearcat kept reeling around the room, still heading toward the door, the gun leaving his head only to be brandished at his shadowers, then as if on an elastic cord snapping back at his temple. The two men kept by him, but gingerly. Each time a certain dark light went off in the older man's eyes, Slingshot moved closer and Salt circled, ready to make a last-ditch grab for Bearcat's raised hand; but then out swept the the pistol's barrel, aimed right at them, and they scurried back. Fortunately, the whole dance looked like a stalemate.

All through this Sonesta stood there, one foot stretched out, shaking with fury. Her religious charm bracelet kept clinking ominously.

"What you want, woman?" Bearcat looked right at Sonesta. *"You want me to do it?"*

Sonesta was so full of anger she could only glare back. Bearcat's gaze locked on hers, and it was clear some deep-running battle was reengaged. Salt and Slingshot held back, seeing that Bearcat was distracted from himself. Indeed, a moment later, Bearcat lowered the gun to his side.

Sonesta bore in. Bearcat held her furious gaze as long as

possible, then lowered his eyes. A moment later he called out, "Where's my mojo bag?"

"Your mojo bag?" Slingshot repeated. Then loud, to everyone: "Where's Bearcat's mojo bag?"

All the musicians in the room started scurrying. Looks cast everywhere. Finally, Clay found it hanging behind the bar and grabbed it. "Here it is!"

"Gimme it! Gimme my mojo bag." The gun hung by the big man's side, almost like it was forgotten. "I gotta have my mojo bag!"

Clay tossed it to Thumper, who caught it with his quick hands.

"Lissen, Bearcat, how 'bout we make us a trade? Gun for the sack."

Bearcat gave the bass player an indignant stare. "Give ... me ... my ... bag!"

But Thumper held it back. "You just ease that pistol over to 'Shot, I'll give you the bag. Come on, that's a fair trade—"

"You traitor!"

Now Sonesta took a few steps toward the big man. The contest between her and her former lover looked put aside. When she spoke, there was even a kind of wary tenderness in her deep voice.

"Bearcat," she said, "listen to the man. Get that damn gun out of your hand 'fore you hurt somebody."

Bearcat whipped his head around at her. His eyes were flaring like fireworks. Then he gave everyone a huge, mollifying smile. "O.K.," he said in a trumped-up tone, "hand me the bag—I *need* the bag—and I'll give you the gun, yes, I will."

Nobody moved.

"Here." The Bearcat held out the gun but kept the barrel pointed out, and it was no different from aiming it.

All the musicians and hangers-on stayed frozen.

"Hey, come on. I'll make your deal. *Just give me the goddamn bag.*"

Thumper took a deep, loud breath, then walked toward the Bearcat. There was a moment when Bearcat blinked and his hand jolted, and it looked like the gun was about to go off right in Thumper's face, but it didn't get fired; and Thumper kept the mojo bag in front of him, until with a lightning lunge the Bearcat grabbed the rank sack with his left hand, then pulled back the gun and effectively buried it in his heavy right paw.

"*Heh, hey!*" he called, shaking the bag furiously in their faces, then he ran fast toward the front door and disappeared outside.

As soon as Bearcat was gone, Thumper said, "We gotta do something! The old man's gonna hurt himself!"

"Oh, you think?" Sonesta said, moving now to pick up the true bills and phony green paper scattered over the floor. She let the broken lacquer pieces lie.

"I've never seen him like this," Salt said.

"I don't think so." Sonesta shook her head, but her attention was on counting the money. The top bills were two deep; there were two more on the bottom of the stack. Four hundred dollars. She looked up at all the musicians. "Bearcat Jackson, he ain't got hurtin' himself in him." A snort. "It's all an act. Question is, though, what he's done to *us*. He's got us set up to get thrown out of here, right?"

"He was taking us to Chicago," Slingshot the bouncer said. "Never told us why."

"This roadhouse ain't long for the world now," Sticks lamented.

"Can we stop it?" Thumper said.

Sonesta was quiet a moment. "I don't know how. The white men, I'm sure they got court orders, and now they probably got some paper with Bearcat's signature on it giving 'em all the rights. You think even the best colored lawyer could get out here with a cease and desist when the bulldozers are rollin'? Even if we could afford him?"

"Where we gonna go?" Sticks said in deep lamentation.

"Oh," Sonesta went, and it was a long sigh. She was over by a box of dishes, looking at the way they'd been stacked inside. She shook her head, glanced upward as if to say, That silly man probably packed this ol' box, then said, firm as she could, "Oh, we'll make out somehow. Always have. This ain't the first—"

"It worked! It worked!" rang through the room. Everyone's head spun toward the door where Bearcat stood, filling the opening. The big man was shouting over and over, "It worked. *It worked!*"

Puzzled faces. The Bearcat was rattling his mojo bag, the weird bones and rocks clattering inside. His pistol was tucked conspicuously into his waistband.

"What in hell is it?" Sonesta finally called out.

"Look who it is! She's back!" Bearcat moved aside, and there in the doorway was framed Daisy Holliday.

She looked different, *weathered* was the word that came to Sonesta, and not just from the wetness she stood in the doorway shaking off her blonde hair. The girl had lost her color, was pasty-white in fact, and seemed thinner, as if she'd worried off a few pounds. She also didn't seem to have that bubbly thing she'd shown up with the couple months or so before. And yet, in ways this Daisy Holliday seemed more substantial, solid. Sonesta was seeing traces of something deeper running through her, just shadings on the surface really, a wrinkle here, a lift to her blue eyes there; but if Sonesta had to come up with another word for the girl, it'd be *the blues*: Like she could understand 'em now, might even be able *to truly sing 'em.*

"Howdy," Daisy said. She was still standing there, hesitant to step inside the well-lit room. She scanned it closely, though, her gaze not settling on—or finding?—just what she was looking for.

"Hello, sugar," Sonesta said. Yeah, it was the blues; the

girl done got herself a serious case of the true-blue blues wherever she been with that carny man. Sonesta felt a twinge of pity; *she* knew the blues. And what *had* that man done to her?

"So, this is it," Bearcat said, lifting his hands in a shoo-ing motion as he swept into the room. "Sticks, Thumper, Clay, you get yourselves set up."

"What you sayin'?" Sonesta said.

"THIS IS IT!" the Bearcat shouted. He was moving toward the bandstand, still waving his arms. At first the other musicians just stood where they were, but Bearcat went over and grabbed Sticks and pushed him toward his drum set. Then he took Clay by the elbow, almost lifted him up on the stage. Thumper went on his own and picked up his bass.

"Don't you see?" Bearcat said, rushing ahead. "We gonna make ourselves the record again. We're gonna do *Pink Cadillac*—do it right!" He pulled an old harmonica out of his pocket.

Sonesta's jaw dropped in disbelief. "Are you crazy?"

Even Daisy looked astonished. "But—but where's Dell?" she finally said.

"He's not here. Come on, time's wasting."

"Not here?"

"Dell's in jail," Sonesta said.

Daisy's voice flew up. "He's what? What's he doing in jail?"

"Why don't you ask the harmonica man."

Daisy crossed over to the stage. Her stride was firm, purposeful; indeed, she looked much more certain and together than she had the few moments before when she came in. "Bearcat, what's she saying?"

Bearcat didn't say a word. Stood there watching the two women.

"Oh, you missed a lot down here," Sonesta went on. The quiet fury was back in her voice. "You missed this great man here making a deal with the white devil to sell out his own true son."

"I don't—" Daisy started to say, turning to the Bearcat. "You—"

And the harmonica man lost it. With animal quickness he leaped at Sonesta and popped her right on the back of her head. It was an open-palmed blow, but hard.

The older woman reeled away, grabbing the back of her head.

"You stupid—"

Like that Bearcat was standing above her, raising his fist. That was all it took. Sonesta dropped to her knees, tucked in her head, pulled her elbows into her side, and lifted a crooked right arm above her. But she could hardly control the lower part of her body. Her heavy skirt rose up her thick hips; her black-wool-stockinged legs splayed out awkwardly.

The scene might have stayed frozen there, the big man standing above the cowering woman, arm raised, Sonesta with her arm protecting her head below him, and Daisy looking on appalled, but for a loud noise in the parking lot. It was the grinding of gears and axles on large-sounding trucks. Everyone heard it. Salt ran to the window.

"Bearcat, it's—"

Two workmen in khaki work clothes and bandannas appeared in the open doorway. One of them held up a piece of paper.

"This place is supposed to be empty. What're y'all doin' here?"

"We own this place," Bearcat told them.

"You a Mr. Jackson?"

"That's me." Bearcat left Sonesta, put a big smile on his face, and went over to the workmen. They sized the big man up. Noticed the rank sack hanging from his belt. Must have seen the gun butt stuck out of his pants.

"Well, what we got here is a vacate and demolish order."

"There must be some mistake." Bearcat moved up on the two men, and the one holding the paper turned it for Bearcat to see.

"Well, I don't have my glasses, but I know this is all a mistake."

"Well, sir—" a glance down at Bearcat's gun "—this is from the city. Property been condemned. We got a road coming through here, clover leaf we gotta build."

"Not this place."

The lead workman cocked an eye at Bearcat. "We don't want any trouble, but we have a job to do."

"You tear down the wrong building on the wrong day, then everybody got trouble."

"Look, it says Jackson, this address, and here it is, March 9, 1956. Where's it say anything wrong?"

"It says the place be empty."

"Looks like it's almost empty," the workman said, glaring around at the bags and packing cases on the floor. "Looks like you people just a little *slow*."

Bearcat pulled out his gun. "No, no, looks like *you* a little slow. Little slow to see we're not goin' anywhere. Now skeedaddle."

The two workmen recoiled visibly at the gun being pulled on them. They looked one to the other, then the one who'd done all the talking said, "Well, Mr. Jackson, I think we're going to go confirm this."

"Confirm my ass!"

"Bearcat, man, hey—" Thumper started to say.

"I mean," the man said, with his partner backing up now toward the door. "Maybe we are mistaken. We're just gonna go now and—"

Bearcat fired a shot. It wasn't at all at the two men, way over their heads, pinging into the lintel above the door, but that was all it took: One couldn't beat the other fast enough out the door.

"Bearcat, have you—" Sonesta went.

"We don't got time to waste on you, you foolish old woman. Daisy, get up there. *Get up there and sing!*"

They all heard the door start opening again; all turned toward it.

Bearcat raised his pistol. "I told you—"

But it was Dell who walked in.

"Those two men running out of here, what were they. . . ?" Dell stopped. Focused on Daisy, astonished. "You're back?"

"You're out of jail?" This was Bearcat.

But Dell was looking right past him. "I can't believe it. You look—" He was peering at the young singer, her hair still wet and limp; and though what he saw looked more like a wet, dazed animal than the bright woman who'd kissed him all night that time by the levee, what he said was, "You look great." And he meant it.

"Oh, no, no," Daisy said, cheeks reddening. "I look—well, it was hard."

Sudden concern in Dell's eyes. "Daisy, what'd he do to you?"

"He didn't—" Dell was next to Daisy, looking right into her face. "He really didn't do. . . ."

It was his silent pleading that caught her up.

She looked straight into Dell's eyes and said emphatically, "He did not do anything like . . . that. No, it was something else."

"What do you mean?" Barely less concern from Dell.

"It was—" Daisy gritted her teeth, looked like she was using everything she had to get the explanation right. "I started . . . started forgetting who I was." She shook her head, as if it was strange hearing her own voice talking about this; as if she hadn't explained it at all to anyone before, not really even herself. "He had me up in Buffalo—Buffalo, New York. Snow everywhere. Cold, cold, cold." She gave an involuntary shiver. "I was all alone, he left me alone most of the week, and I had all kinds of funny—funny things in my head." A shake of her blonde hair. "I'd only see Cuth on weekends, he'd come up and start telling me how to dress, how to do my face, laugh, what to sing. It was like all week I was ... and then—"

"He didn't have you doin' anything with that *Pink Cadillac*, did he?" Bearcat said.

Daisy turned to him, shook her head from side to side. She paused a second, but when she spoke, it was like she'd quickly gathered strength to herself, as if she was realizing finally that she was really back.

"It's funny with that song, 'cause that was the final straw." She looked at Dell, a faint smile now on her pink face. "You shoulda been there. Cuth, he promised to take me to New York, but he had me singing this Patti Page stuff. And I was doin' it. But one night—last night I was there—I finally got the band to learn it good, and I got up there and I sang it all the way through. Sang our song—"

"*Pink Cadillac.*"

"Yeah, I really ripped it, too." A loud, snorting laugh popped out of Daisy, just like that. Surprised her as much as anybody. "It was something."

"And then?" Dell said.

"Then." A wince. "Well, Cuth was there that night. He—he came backstage, and he ... he hit me." She flinched further as she said it, but there was a furious look in her eyes. "No man's *ever again* gonna get away with hittin' me."

There was silence—even, one could say, an embarrassed silence. Certainly nobody looked in Sonesta's direction. The older woman was looking at the younger one with an unreadable face.

"I left right then. Got on a train, didn't know where I was gonna end up. But it just—well, here I am."

Daisy showed the brightest smile she could.

"And you're here to stay?" This was Dell.

Daisy swung her gaze around the room, seeming to notice all the packed-up boxes for the first time. She looked like she was just then understanding that things weren't as she'd left them; that the whole safe world of the roadhouse might have changed. The look in her eyes quickly went from What's going on? to Is some of this *my* fault?

What she actually said, after a long moment was, "If you'll—you'll forgive me."

The silence lengthened. Daisy looked toward Dell, who didn't seem able to answer right away. He looked down, then back up at her, but before any words left his lips, Sonesta spoke up.

"Sugar, of course we will." The older woman spoke with an empathy that surprised everyone. She stepped toward Daisy to hug her in welcome, but Bearcat swiftly interposed himself.

"Oh, yeah, we've been dyin' for you to come back. Baby, this is your *home*. Home of the *Pink Cadillac*!" Bearcat took Daisy by the arm. "An' now you and Dell be back here, you're gonna sing." He turned, spoke quick to the band, then said, "Sling, you go bolt that door, don't let nobody in. Dell, snap to it, son, get your sax. Boys, you start playing—"

Everybody stood there dumbfounded.

"Come on, *git*!" Bearcat flapped his arms again, herding the musicians to the stage. Sticks, Thumper, and Clay moved slowly to their instruments.

"Come on!" Bearcat cried. "The devil's standin' right outside our door. *Play!*"

The musicians started a half-hearted intro to *Pink Cadillac*, went up to where the verse started; but since no one else was with them, they paused, then played the intro again.

But Dell wasn't going anywhere. He kept looking around at the packed boxes and suitcases, trying to under-stand what was going on.

"Dammit, boy, why aren't you movin'?" the Bearcat said. "Song don't really work without your sax-o-phone."

"Why are you so fired up about doin' this now?"

Bearcat whirled, pistol outstretched. "We gotta make that record."

"But I can just go get the disc back from Dewey Phillips. Why all this—"

Sonesta snorted. Bearcat raised his hand at her again. And though she looked determined to stand tough, she couldn't; involuntarily, like a long-whipped dog, she cowered back again.

Daisy at first flinched, then moved protectively toward the older woman.

"Yeah, well, it's not really goin' down that way," Bearcat said.

"What happened to the acetate?"

Cognizant of the pistol in Bearcat's hand, nobody said anything, but enough gazes fell to the floor where the broken pieces lay for Dell to follow them and see the remains.

"It was you—you who put me in jail," Dell suddenly cried. "I was sure it was my father, but this—this was all *your* doin'—"

"You don't know the half of it," Sonesta said.

Bearcat, the pistol still in his hand, waved it at her.

"Bearcat, how could you—"

"How could *you*?"

"Me what?"

"Gettin' that money from your father. Cuttin' God knows what kinda deal with him. Handing our record over to that white man, couldn't get it back—"

"Bearcat, I didn't cut any deal with my father. Didn't do a thing. Didn't take a cent from him—"

"Oh, yeah, then where'd it all come from?"

Dell looked around the room. Diamondback had been there all along, but in a corner with the country boy, Hosea.

Dell caught the old gambler's eye, got a short nod. "I went down to Beale Street, ol' compadre of yours. Hocked my whole future to a man called Beauregard T. Washington—"

"Snake Eyes?"

Dell nodded. "Like the guy slid everywhere on his belly, yeah. But he had the scratch, Bearcat. Got us the roadhouse rebuilt, was gonna get us the damn record distributed." Dell looked again down at the floor at the broken pieces.

"The money came from *Snake Eyes*?" Bearcat looked shaken, confused.

"It was all I could think of. I never knew it would—"

The Bearcat stood there for a long moment, looking like his whole world was spinning vertiginously around inside him; his balance looked precarious. But then a visible wave went through him, visibly rippling, as it would through ursine fur; and when it passed, he was quickly focused back on the stage. In a surprisingly firm voice he said, "What's done is done. Come on, we don't got any time."

But the enormity of what had happened just slammed into Dell. "Bearcat, you did all this—"

"Damn you all," the Bearcat cried. "Start playin'!"

There was a loud rapping at the door. Everyone froze. Slingshot the bouncer put his shoulder to the door. Then came a louder banging, the sound of something like a bat pounding against the wood.

"Bearcat, it's those workmen come back," Salt called out from the good window. "They got a machine, got a ram on it."

"Damn!" Bearcat cried. "I said we don't got a second to waste. Gotta make our record here, now! Gotta get that *sound* again."

The loud rap against the door had silenced everyone. Finally, Dell looked at Daisy. "Are you up for this?"

"I—I'm still a little in—"

Another loud pounding at the door. It shook on its hinges.

"Gotta move right this minute!" Bearcat cried.

Dell was looking at the door, and Daisy followed his gaze, and then something silent but powerful passed between them—and that was all it took. Like that, Daisy gave a quick nod O.K., then ran to the record-cutting machine. Just as she had five months before, she got it hooked up in a flash. Bearcat was plugging in microphones and cables; pops and static startled the room till he got the plugs settled right. The band kept playing the intro, just marking time, but tightening down each time through. Dell, who'd had his sax taken from him when he was arrested, hunted around for it and finally found it, tucked into its case, safe behind a cast-aside group of chairs. Finally, Daisy went to the lead microphone.

"Except for two times in Buffalo, I haven't sung *Pink Cadillac* in—"

Dell, his sax around his neck, went to her, leaned in. "You don't lose it, babe. Not you. Just open your mouth and let it—"

An even louder pounding at the door. This time the whole flimsy roadhouse shook, but the door held.

Slingshot mouthed words to Bearcat, who cried, "Don't bother me with that now."

Dell trilled a run up the sax. Moved his mouth as if it had just brought chills to him.

The band kicked into a higher gear.

Sonesta went toward the door and peered through the window. "Jackson, you listen to me. It ain't just a couple workmen now. It's the sheriff. And a whole lotta men."

Bearcat shook her words off. Everything was moving too fast. "That cutting machine going?"

"Someone's just got to flip the final switch," Daisy said into the main mike.

"Hosea, get your sorry ass over there, turn that machine on when I tell you."

"Boss, I don't know machines," the overalled man said.

"Just do it!" Bearcat started listening to the band, see-ing if they needed anything. "Sticks? Thumper? We on, right? Sounds good." Then Bearcat was right next to Daisy, in front of the microphone. He tucked the gun back in his belt, then adjusted it. "Testing, one, two, buckle my shoe. Three, four, keep the devil from our door. Good. O.K., boys, you ready?" Bearcat leaned his ear into the band, cooking a little. "Yeah, that's good, you got the true jump now. O.K., *let it rip!*"

Wham! The rhythm section churned again through the intro to *Pink Cadillac.*

"Good, good. Daisy girl, you ready? O.K., Hosea, hit it!" Bearcat mimed flipping the switch, and the country boy actually did it right, setting the lathe-cutting platter spinning.

Daisy put her hands together almost as if in prayer, then stepped into the microphone just as Dell trilled the last thrilling note of the intro solo.

She started right in on the first verse, *"When you got the jump and you got the quick / Ain't nothing gonna move you like your gear shift stick / Ain't nothing gonna thrill you like the mid-night side / When you get in that Cadillac and ride ride ride. . . ."*

Clay Booker said to Colin, "You should've heard it. We were all stunned by her voice." He told the record man that it had the same giddyap charge of the first take those months before, that kick your spurs and go, but this time it wasn't just a carefree afternoon run down the road; though you could still feel the wind blow through her hair and soar on the sheer power of the Caddie's engine, now the ride was truly darker.

In the roadhouse Dell thought, She'd never nailed that line about the "midnight side," but she had it now. He felt a tingle rip his spine: This take was all black night and furtive thrills.

Not for the first time he said to himself, This is one woman you'd go anywhere with.

When Daisy launched into the chorus, *"Yeah, where*

*we're going, nobody's gonna know / Till our star burns bright all
'long Catfish Row / Yeah, where we're going, ain't never gonna look
back / From our pink Cadillac, our pink Cadillac,"* they were all
riding together. And it wasn't just midnight now ... there was
light ahead.

*"That's what we all thought, and the way Sticks was digging
into his toms, yeah, we were playing it, too, driving us toward that
light opening up past all the bullshit and all the shame."*

That's what Dell was thinking, Yeah, Daisy just *had it*,
we're roaring now, and no matter what is happening to the
roadhouse, no matter what Bearcat's done, no matter how
fucked up everything looks, we ... are ... truly....

Then a huge, room-shaking whomp hit the front door
again, much harder than before, as if they workmen had gotten the battering ram aligned perfectly.

*"That noise, it was curious: It fell right on the downbeat
before the bridge; stopped Sticks and Thumper cold, but only for half
a second, and though it felt like the whole world had just plumb
halted, right there we kicked back in, and we were wilder than
ever."*

"Running, we're running," Daisy sang, improvising.
*"Ain't gonna catch us, ain't gonna match us, just gonna let us run
free."*

When the sheriff and his men slammed their ram into
the door again, the band was ready for them, and they didn't
miss a beat.

Sonesta was still at the window. "They gonna break the
place down," she cried.

Bearcat, by the disc cutting machine now, waved his
hand at her, mimed for her to be quiet. The band was making
such a noise he was pretty sure her voice hadn't gotten picked
up. And there were only two more verses and choruses to go.

"Jackson, you listen to me, they got guns out there!"
Hysteria skirled up her voice.

"I got me a gun, too," Bearcat said, pulling the pistol

from his belt. He'd taken a few steps toward her to say it, still far away from the microphone on the stage feeding the cutting machine.

"Oh, you fool!"

"Damn you, shut up!" Bearcat was hissing, trying to stay under the sound from the band.

Another huge whomp at the door. The whole roadhouse again shook. Dell had half an eye on it. He could see the hinges bow. He also saw Sonesta standing there, with Bearcat moving on her.

He too thought, Only two more verses to go. He looked back at Sticks, jabbing with his head to get across the idea they'd better jump that tempo. Then at Sonesta, who was turning her head wildly from Bearcat to the window outside.

Daisy was into the second-to-last verse: *"When you're riding, don't know what's up the road ahead / You got your dreams, got your schemes, got your flirtin' with the dead / You got your sunshine and, baby, you got your rain / Ride this Caddie hard enough, gonna ride right past your pain."*

Yeah, Dell thought, that's how we wrote it. *Ride right past your pain.* From the corner of his eye he saw both Daisy belting her soul into the microphone and the way the Bearcat was almost on Sonesta. Nervous ripples up his spine: He was remembering too many scenes from the days he was half living there.

The pounding on the door this time knocked the bottom hinge off, then cracked away the bottom of the wood door. A triangle of gray light swept across the floor. Dell could see heavy, wet leather boots out there, but the door's two other hinges were still holding, and there was no way anybody could get in the way it was now. Faster, he thought, *faster.* One verse to go.

"Yeah, better run this Caddie like it might be your last / 'Cuz what is is what is, and what's not is what's past," Daisy sang, and each word rang surprisingly clear.

If we can just get to the end, Dell though, this has gotta be one monster hit.

"Jackson, they got their guns out," Sonesta cried, and this time she had to be loud enough to make it onto the recording. "If they burst in here, *they're gonna kill us*!"

She was at the door now, and fumbling with the lock.

"Don't!" Bearcat cried, not even worrying now if he could be heard. "Stop it!"

And like that Bearcat was on her. He pulled her back from the door, took his hand and hit her hard across the cheek. Sonesta fell to the floor. He leaned down and hit her again, then stood over her, his right fist raised, the gun loose in his left.

And now, though Daisy should be crying off the final half of the last verse, she instead shouted, "Stop it!"

Bearcat looked up in alarm.

"Don't hurt her anymore!"

"Dammit, sing, girl. *Sing!*"

But Daisy wasn't going to. Sonesta stayed on the floor, and it was the way the older woman was pulling her legs up to her chest and wrapping her arms around them, as tight and protective a ball as she could make, and yet, Dell understood, not safe at all ... well, he knew everything was going wrong, and no matter what, Bearcat had to be stopped.

Dell blew one last desperate honk on the sax, as if that could stop the big man, then laid it down. Left the bandstand and moved up on the Bearcat.

If I can just get the—

Another crash at the door, and it shuddered back, half off the second set of hinges.

Bearcat left Sonesta and went to the front door. He put his shoulder to it.

"Come on," he shouted at Dell, who was close now. "Help me!"

But Dell had come over to Sonesta's thinking: Got to

get the gun away from him, he'll just get himself—maybe us—killed.

Bearcat seemed to be holding back the door by himself now. The gun dangled from his left hand. "Come help me!" he cried.

Dell took a grab at it. He couldn't get ahold of the handle, but he did knock it from the Bearcat's grip. The black pistol skittered across the floor.

"What the fuck are you—" Bearcat turned, shouting at Dell.

Dell went for the gun, but the Bearcat was faster. He elbowed Dell away, sending him flying, then dove at the gun.

Dell leaped on Bearcat's back just as he was bending down for the gun, and though he couldn't actually knock the big man over, he threw him off his course. Bearcat bellowed, spun around, and backed hard into a wall, crashing Dell into it.

The wind flew out of Dell. But he stayed solid. Bearcat was going back toward the gun, but Dell took a leap at him again, trying to hit him low, just like opposing football players used to hit him. He knew it was all physics, use your body like a fulcrum. But he came at the Bearcat too high. The big man took his lunge, then pushed Dell down. He fell face-first on the dirty floor.

"We couldn't see the gun," Clay said. He was looking away from Colin as he said this. "It had to be down there on the ground, but we couldn't see it."

Dell was sprawled on the floor. He was starting to push himself up when Bearcat moved right above him.

"You gonna pay, boy. You and your goddamn father." Bearcat, all fury, kicked at Dell. *"You gonna pay now."*

"Stop it!" Sonesta cried.

Bearcat looked up at her with enraged eyes.

"What are you...?" Bearcat cried.

Dell started to get up again. Bearcat sensed him move and turned to kick him again, this time his foot going right at

Dell's face, but Dell scrambled aside. Sonesta was moving about next to the Bearcat, shouting at him, but Bearcat was kicking at Dell. Dell was facing up, and when Bearcat's boot was inches from his nose, a shot went off.

"We didn't know what had happened," Clay told Colin. "We'd been playing all the while, even though Daisy had gone frantic to try to stop the fight. But when the gun went off we stopped.

"We just stood there. It was horrible. Nobody moved, then finally the Bearcat slumped to the ground. God, there was blood all over his chest, pouring out. He let out a long cry, and . . . then it was just silence."

"Oh, my God!" Daisy brought her hand to her mouth. The band left the stage and formed a circle around Bearcat.

"Dell got himself up and went to Bearcat, too. He took his wrist, feeling for a pulse. We all watched him, then he raised his head and silently shook it."

"Dell had the gun, right?" Colin said.

Clay didn't answer right away. He looked at his young interlocutor, then said, "No, that was the weirdest thing. It must've been ditched, because Sonesta, she had it. Must've found the gun on the ground after it went off, because next thing I know, she's holding it."

There was another pounding at the door, and this time it nearly busted loose.

"Sonesta looked like she was in utter shock. That black pistol just dangled from her hand, pointing straight down. Then I saw Daisy go over to her, put her arm around her."

Like that the sheriff's deputies burst in, There were five of them, and they all had their guns drawn. The sheriff followed.

"What happened here?"

Nobody spoke. Dell, Daisy, Sonesta, and the hangers-on were grouped around Bearcat.

"I said, 'What in tarnation happened here?' "

"I—I shot him."

"That was Dell, right?"

"Of course."

"And he had the gun, now, didn't he?"

Clay raised an eyebrow that said, You're paying very good attention, aren't you?

The sheriff turned to Dell.

"You what?"

Dell stepped forward, the pistol held out before him, letting it dangle unthreateningly.

"He was gonna—he was gonna shoot you when you came through the door, but I got him first," Dell said. He kept the pistol out before him, though he was holding it somewhat tentatively.

"He was gonna—" the sheriff started to say in disbelief.

"He was lying in wait," Daisy said, stepping forward. "Dell—Dell saved your life. He's a hero."

The sheriff's eyes narrowed. "That's the story, eh?"

"Yeah, that's just the way it happened." Dell spoke now with absolute conviction.

The sheriff looked around the room, as if he was trying to see something else than what was just before his eyes. He saw the musicians standing about, and the roadhouse's hangers-on, and the sobbing black woman comforted now by the lovely blonde. Then he glanced down on the motionless mass of flesh at his feet.

"Tha's how it happened?" he asked Sticks, pointing a finger at him.

Sticks blinked. "Yassuh," he said.

"And you agree?" To Slingshot.

"Yassuh, that's it exactly. The white boy here shot 'im so he couldn't shoot *you*."

"And you?" He was pointing at me." Clay lifted his glass of *Scotch. "And I just nodded, too."*

The sheriff kept an eyebrow lifted, but his eyes themselves brightened.

"Then I guess I got to thank you, son," he said to Dell as he took the pistol from him. He didn't even bother to hold it carefully, just wrapped his whole hand around it. "Looks like this pretty li'l lady's right—you gotta be *some* kind of hero."

The Pink Cadillac

S O LET ME GET IT STRAIGHT," Colin said, a strange
excitement fizzing away in him. "There were *two*
recordings, the original one that Dell's father got from
Dewey Phillips, then scratched all to hell, and that Bearcat
broke."

Clay nodded.

"But then there was the recut."

Another nod. "That's it."

"And the recut—"

"Yeah, it kept running—"

"That great performance?"

"Daisy Holliday, yeah. Like nobody ever heard before."

"All of it?"

Clay nodded. "My friend, *all* of it. It heard it all."

"Bearcat? *Dell?*"

"Everything."

Colin swallowed hard.

"Which would make *that* not only the sole recording of
Pink Cadillac, but also ... evidence. Of what Dell had done."

"That's how we saw it, yeah."

"But Dell beat the rap, right? Didn't it go down as just
self-defense?"

Clay was silent for a second, then said, "That's true."

"But the record was still sitting there."

"Yeah."

"On the cutting machine." Colin was so far into his
imagination he could see the disc. "Freshly-grooved black
lacquer."

"So what happened to it?"

"Well," Clay said, drawing out the word. Colin had the sense that the guitar player was thinking over every one of his words. "Here, let me take you back to the roadhouse. Let's see it all from another angle.

"The shot's gone off, we's all laid down our instruments. I remember clearly taking my Fender, carefully turning the white knob to zero so it wouldn't feed back, then leaning it against my amp. I went over to where Bearcat was lying on the ground. Blood was flowing from his chest; his hands were up there, but he couldn't stop nothing. His eyes ... never forget those eyes, they was clearly halfway to heaven—or halfway to hell—already. Yeah, he was already gazing on the other side. And I don't got me much doubt which one it was.

"Then I looked over at the record machine. Don't know why nobody else thought of it but me, but there it is. Sheriff, he's about to arrest Dell, but I'm thinking fast: Don't want to give him too much to work with, know what I mean? So I reached down and switched that record machine off, then swung the arm away, and lifted up that lacquer disc—"

Colin grabbed a breath, then said, "*You* took it?"

There was the longest pause, then Clay made a slight headshake gesture. Colin leaned forward, and Clay softly said, "Sorry. I never had it."

"Then who did?"

That long pause again. "Um, it was Sonesta, she took it."

"Sonesta? What would *she* be doing with it?"

"It was worked out with Daisy, I don't really know. Guess they thought it'd be safest with her. Who'd look in her direction?" Clay shrugged, as if that made the only kind of sense. " 'Sides, that record didn't do anyone no good, you know. I mean, that record just got a man killed. I was *glad* I didn't get it."

Colin was impatient now, spoke right over Clay. "But Sonesta had it?"

Clay shrugged. "That's my recollection."

"And she's dead, right?" Colin said this in a voice that made it clear that he was seeing the end of his quest. "Anything she had probably just thrown—"

"Dead?" Clay said quick, lifting an eyebrow.

"Yeah." Colin shrugged. He was thinking of how Seely had said she and Robin had seen the old singer, but that was still years ago. "I tried to find her when I did the Bearcat CD but couldn't. I just assumed—" he flew toward Clay "—you mean, *she's not?*"

Clay shook his head. "'Less she had herself a heart attack in the last month I didn't hear about."

"You know where she is?"

"Well, that's not so easy. 'Less you try the Peabody Hotel."

"*Peabody*—"

"Hotel. Last I heard, she's still runnin' the laundry there. Workin' nights." Clay laughed. "She's so old, nobody can get rid of her." Then a pleasant smile. "She sings some, too, though hasn't in a few years I know about."

Colin was still leaning forward, though it was taking him a while to process all this. Finally, he said, "And she ... might have ... the record?"

Again that hesitation. "Oh, I wouldn't know 'bout that. You'd have to ask her." Clay smiled. "Doubt if it's come up in, what, forty-some years."

Colin just shook his head.

Clay stood up. "That's about it," he said, then looked out the window, where a faint yellow-pink light was scratching at the windows. "Looks like we stayed up all night."

Colin yawned at that. His head was a murky jumble of all this information, shot through by the lightning flash that there might actually be an extant recording. He couldn't quite believe it; felt it was too much to hope for. Still, if Sonesta was still O.K....

"Guess it's 'bout time I run you back to town," Clay said. "Have a feeling you're gonna want some sleep before you go headin' down to the Peabody." He harrumphed.

"That'd be great." Colin was truly lightheaded. "If it's not any trouble."

"Not at all, my friend."

Clay got up then, swayed a second, took a halting step till he had his balance, then walked on rubbery legs over to the door. He muttered something like, "Ain't used to goin' all night anymore."

"I really appreciate this," Colin said, following him.

Outside the morning sky was all lemons and oranges spread across a cool night blue. Colin checked his watch: 7:15.

The drive back to town went quickly. Both men were yawning something crazy and didn't say much. Clay pulled up outside the bar, where Colin's car was sitting alone in the parking lot.

"Looks like it's safe," Clay said, peering through the windshield. "You're lucky. This ain't the best part of town."

When the Honda came to a stop, Colin told Clay thanks again, then said, "I—this has been more than I could've expected. I'll be in touch."

Again that hesitation. "Um, that's O.K." Clay made a wry face. "I think I already know more than I need to 'bout that *Pink Cadillac* record." He leaned across from his seat and shook Colin's hand. "Hope your luck stays good, my friend."

They shook hands again, and Colin was left alone.

As he got behind the wheel of his rented car, he noticed he was breathing a little too fast; he also kept gesturing with his hands, not signifying anything, just bouncing them before him in some insistent way. It was nerves, through and through, he decided. A deep breath.

As he drove back to town he came up with a plan. Clay was right, he should sleep; especially since it would be hard to find Sonesta during the day, since he'd combed the phone books four years back when he was looking for her. He also had another thought, and when he pulled into the parking lot for the Skyway Motel, the first thing he did was call the Longworths and ask Robin's mother if he could talk to Seely. She gave Colin her work number, and he got through immediately.

He quickly sketched what he'd found out, then told her he'd like her to go with him tonight to look for Sonesta. Seely asked why.

"I think you'd be a big plus. You've seen her perform, and you're, well, a woman."

"You think that'll matter?"

"I—I don't really know." Colin let out a huge yawn he hoped Seely didn't hear. "But I know I'd like you there."

A slight pause, then Robin's sister said, "No problem. Come by the house about six-thirty, we can go out for some dinner."

"I might be too excited."

Colin could feel her laugh. "Been a while since anybody was too excited to have dinner with me. But, hey, whatever. I'll see you then."

When Colin hung up he wasn't at all sure if he'd made some kind of subtle mistake or not. But he was ... so tired. Luckily, he fell asleep as soon as his head touched the pillow.

✳ ✳ ✳ ✳ ✳

AS HOT AS IT was this July night in Memphis, the air where they were now was so nearly scalding and steamy that it struck Colin as a veritable Hades. They'd pulled into the parking lot of the Peabody Hotel, descended down a narrow set of stairs, went through turns and twists of concrete and pipe cata-combs, till they came to the laundry room. They had to dodge huge metal baskets heaped with wet sheets and pillowcases, press their fingers to their ears to keep out the incessant buzzing from the wall-high washers and driers. Everyone here wore weird white pajama-like pants and shirts, as well as brilliantly white 'do rags to keep back their hair, and so the other image that leaped into both their minds was Heaven: A place so clean, white, and pure in a world burning hot.

The old woman had her own office, and when she shut the door behind her, it was suddenly almost perfectly quiet—and cool.

She looked like she knew how surprised they were.

"When they promoted me, and it wasn't easy getting promoted, black woman like me, in a place like this, but when I did, I said I wouldn't last more'n a week or two I had to hear all that any longer, so I made 'em soundproof it. Some kind of space-travel material they use." She gave them a spry wink. "Not bad, huh, for a seventy-eight-year-old."

There was only one extra chair in the room, and Sonesta put Seely in it; Colin stood against an institution-green wall, next to a bulletin board with sundry announcements. He was looking closely at the old woman's face. She looked pretty good, could pass for ten years younger. She was stocky but not corpulent, as if the heat of the laundry had rendered off any possible fat, and not very tall; indeed, she had some of that shrunken old lady look, her spine curved forward slightly. Her hair, coifed in large rolls, was full around her face. Her nose was full, her chin doubled, yet her brown eyes were bright. She was wearing a pants suit with a faded bird print on it and solid white nurse shoes.

Sonesta leaned back in her wood swivel chair, then said, "So, why do you want to see me?"

Seely looked back to Colin, who said, "I don't know if you know of me, but I'm the man who owns Blue Moon Records. We put out a CD with your song *Cryin' Shame* on it a few years back—"

"And now you're here to pay me for using it?" Sonesta raised an eyebrow.

"Of course," Colin said quickly. "And I want to apologize, I didn't—didn't think—"

"You thought I was dead. I know." Sonesta leaned back, planted her folded hands behind the nape of her neck, just like some plutocrat behind his yards-long desk. "Once Elvis Presley died, it was, Well, everybody from the old days must be dead. Right? 'Course he was just forty-some years old, and he had himself a little *abuse problem* by then."

"I'm sorry, I just couldn't find you."

"Well, where you think I was?" A sprightly glance around her nondescript office. "Where was I but right here?"

Seely gave out a pleasant, involuntary chuckle, and Sonesta's eyes twinkled. She leaned forward and patted Colin's companion on the knee and said, "See, the pretty girl here understands. Don't you, dear?"

A glance up at Colin. "I think Mr. Stone should be lucky you don't sue his pants off."

A loud cackle from Sonesta Clarke. "Say it, sister!"

Seely turned her head and winked at Colin. All right, he was thinking, if she has to make a little fun of me to win the old woman over, so be it. But his ears burned nonetheless.

"But there's another reason we're here," Seely said, just a second before Colin was going to use the same words. All right again, maybe it was better that she lead. "Mr. Stone here has been doing some more research into your music back in the '50s. In particular he's looking for a record of a song called—" a pause, as if Seely wanted to prepare the older woman "—*Pink Cadillac*."

Sonesta didn't react at first, unless you counted the fast flicker that shot between her limpid eyes. Indeed, she sat stone still in her wooden chair. Finally, she simply repeated, *"Pink Cadillac?"*

"A song recorded by Bearcat Jackson, along with Dell Dellaplane. Feisty young woman singer—" there was that word, but it seemed to Colin all the women he'd been coming across, Sonesta, Daisy Holliday, his wife, of course, and even Seely were just that: *feisty* "—named Daisy Holliday."

Sonesta nodded silently to herself. There was a hint of white-yellow tooth above her lower lip. Her eyes seemed larger, amped a little, but she was still not giving anything away.

"And you think I ... know something about this?"

"My friend Colin here," Seely started to say, "has been investigating it. He's talked to a lot of people. We know that you were there."

"Where?"

"Bearcat's roadhouse," Colin said.

"You say that like you actually been there, Mister," Sonesta said, pulling back just a whit. "You say it like some part of you thinks you own it."

Colin blanched. Was he that obvious? But he thought back to just the night before, when Clay Booker had told him the long story. He *had* been there, hadn't he? He had as good as heard them make the record—it still played huge in his mind.

"That was the trouble," Sonesta went on. "White boys *always* thought they owned it. Only one man truly owned that place, and that was Thomas Jackson, and when he passed—God rest his soul—there wasn't no roadhouse anymore. Wasn't no *Pink Cadillac*. Wasn't *nothing*!"

"That's what Colin—that's what we've both heard," Seely said softly. "But we also hear there was ... a record—"

Flashes like sparks in Sonesta's eyes. "Damn right there was a record. Little pretty singing that rocky-roly, sure. *Pink Cadillac*. But that record, it got busted up." She threw her hands up in the air as if she were scattering leaves. "Broken into a thousand pieces. By Thomas himself."

Sonesta's eyes almost bulged out; she sat there, her arms now folded across her bosom, a glower on her face. There was a long silence after this while Colin figured what to say next.

"That's the story I've heard, Miss Clarke. But—"

"It's Mrs. Horner. Wife of J. Howard Horner, may God rest his soul, too—"

Quickly Colin thought, So that's why I couldn't find her. An encouraging glance to Seely, who had leaned over and gently patted the older woman's shoulder.

"Mrs. Horner," he went on. "But I've heard there was a second recording."

Sonesta was shaking her head.

"A second recording, done on the same day that Bear—um, Mr. Jackson—died. Same day the roadhouse got torn down."

Sonesta was still shaking her head, but more slowly now. She still didn't speak.

"That Daisy was there, and Dell on the saxophone, and Bearcat on the harmonica. And you were there, too."

Sonesta had stopped moving her head; instead, she'd brought both her hands to her face, cupping them like a church steeple and placing them over her mouth. She was listening closely.

"And what I've heard, Mrs. Horner, was that the . . . second recording . . . went home with you."

A long silence, then Sonesta said, "Who be tellin' you stories like that?"

Colin didn't answer, instead said, "It's true, isn't it?"

A shake of her head again, but wanly. "It was a long time ago—"

"It's all right," Seely said, patting the older woman's shoulder again. "Colin told me all about it. It was a horrible day, wasn't it?"

A deep sigh from Sonesta that rose over the sound of the air-conditioning. Then it was as if she were a transformed woman: sad, dismayed, deeply shaken.

"Honey, it was the worst day of my life."

"I can imagine." Somehow Seely had gotten Sonesta to

peel away her hands from her face; now she held one of them, light in her own hands. "You lost your—"

"My lover." A tear came to Sonesta's eye. With the hand Seely wasn't holding, she daubed at it. "My love."

"Bearcat was a great man," Colin said. "That's why I put out the album on him. So *everybody* could know that."

"But they've forgotten Jackson, haven't they?" Sonesta said after a moment. There was still a dampness in her eyes. "I know what you did, but they still've forgotten him."

"The record," Colin said from his perch by the wall. "*Pink Cadillac.* It couldn't have been done without Bearcat. And because of—because it was a white girl singing it, back then, when nobody else could, and with black musicians, a record like that is going to get—" he took a step forward "—a lot of attention."

Sonesta suddenly looked even more upset, almost stricken. Seely shuffled in her chair so she could be more comforting to her.

"Everyone would hear it—"

"Yes," Colin said. "Yes, yes, yes."

"Hear ... all ... of ... it?"

Colin paused a moment to decide how best to put what would come next. He glanced at Seely, who gave him a quick, encouraging flicker of her eyes.

"I know what you're worried about," Colin said. "That the whole ... whole killing of Mr. Jackson ... the whole thing will come out. I know it's on the surviving disc. But that was all taken care of over forty years ago. I don't—"

But there was fear in Sonesta's eyes. Colin saw it clear as the sun. It momentarily halted him.

"Colin's told me that up to now the story of Mr. Jackson's death," Seely started saying, "is, well, pretty murky. He also says there're ways of editing the recording, new ways—with computers, they can do magic. But it's also nothing to do with you, right? You were just standing by—"

As soon as Seely said this, Colin knew. Those gaps in the way Clay had told him the story, the intuitive questions he himself had simply been suppressing in his excitement to hear that the record of *Pink Cadillac* actually existed ... he read it in the older woman's eyes.

The way Seely paused, as if she'd come to some similar understanding, or maybe there'd been an electric flinch in Sonesta's hand—well, Seely stopped speaking. The silence in the room was immense.

"The story I heard," Colin started to say, softly and quietly, "was that there was a fight. Bearcat had a gun, but he was wrestling with Dell Dellaplane, and the gun got away from him. Then Dell was on the ground. *Nobody* had the gun. Bearcat was kicking Dell. He maybe looked like he was going to kill him. Then the gun went off. Somebody shot him. *Somebody*—"

"Why—why have you come here?" Sonesta cried. Her mouth was contorted, her eyes looking everywhere.

"I'm sorry," Seely said, patting her hand.

Colin said, clearly and forcefully, "Tell us about it."

Sonesta flinched.

"It's all right." Seely gave Colin a startled look, but kept her hand on the older woman's loose-fleshed one.

Colin kept looking at Sonesta, but after Seely's glance, didn't say anything further, just took a long breath.

"We're here as friends," Seely said. "I think you'll feel better if—"

"I'd like—"

"If you tell us what happened," the young woman went on. "We'll understand."

Sonesta lifted her head and looked right into Seely's eyes. She was looking for something, and after a few silent, heavy beats, she finally said softly, through gentle whimpers, "Anybody would have ... done it."

"Done what?" Colin took another step forward, then

admonished himself. This was no interrogation, this was an old woman being dragged into something horrible from her deep, lost past. He was beginning to feel truly terrible.

"Done what had to be done." There was determination in Sonesta's voice now.

"I'm sure you're—" Seely started to say. But Sonesta leaped ahead.

"He—he was gonna, gonna *kill* that boy." Sobs now, but also a steely focus. "Kicking 'im in the head. Him down on the ground. What could he do to protect himself? What could *I* do?"

This wasn't a real question, and nobody in the room said a word.

"It was just ... lying there. That horrible black thing. I always hated that Thomas had himself a gun, though I under-stood—*I understood*. But he wasn't...." Her chest was heaving. "He wasn't supposed to turn it on those ... who loved him."

Colin didn't move except to nod in encouragement. A part of him didn't want to hear this. This was *not* what he'd been looking for when he'd heard there was a lost 45 that could change the world. *Not at all.*

"But it was just lying there, and somebody had to do something. He was gonna—" A shudder. The older woman was thumping her chest crazily with her free hand. To the other Seely hung on with firm compassion. Then a wild shake of Sonesta's head. "I just took it up, didn't really know what I was doing, but somebody ... had ... to do ... something."

"It was self-defense," Colin said. "What else could it be?"

Sonesta looked as if she was surprised to hear a voice like this. Gave her head one curious nod.

"That boy, *he* was the hero! Way he stood up for me. Negro lady didn't give him anything but grief. And ... Daisy. She stood up, too. She was a hero, too."

"They arrested Dell, right?"

"Oh, yeah, they arrested him. Took him down to the

jail. Kept him there all of about six hours. Let him go. They called it self-defense with him, too. Trouble was, they also called him a hero ... for killing that uppity nigger who was corruptin' Memphis's precious youth." A fierce scowl replaced Sonesta's stricken expression. "That was the real crime, you ask me. Way that Memphis was *overjoyed* that Thomas Jackson was dead."

Seely was shaking her head in a kind of anger and grief. Sonesta noticed and flipped her hand over, so that now she was comforting the young woman.

"I—I haven't spoken of this in...." Sonesta shook her head. "I don't think I *ever* told anyone. Lordy, Lordy!"

"But ... like you said ... somebody had to do something. You did only what—"

Sonesta fixed Colin with a withering look. "Don't you patronize me, young man. I killed him. I did it! I killed the only man I ever loved. I killed my lover! Me. With a gun in my hand, God protect me. *Me!*"

No one spoke. It was as if they were all holding their breath, far beyond what was possible. Everything stayed still and frozen except for the subtle hiss of the air-conditioning.

Finally, Colin spoke. "I'd like—we'd like—" But he couldn't go on. Somehow the *Pink Cadillac* record seemed wholly unimportant at that moment.

After the silence stretched beyond imagining, Sonesta gave a long sigh, then said, "You saw some of them? You said—"

"All of them I could," Colin told her. "Clay, the guitarist. Dell Dellaplane. Even Daisy Holliday."

Sonesta was shaking her head in a kind of disbelief. "Really, they're all still with us? They're all all right?"

Colin held his thought, then said, "They seemed O.K. More or less."

"God, that was so long ago. And yet, I just close my eyes, and it was like ... it was ... yesterday."

"You weren't that wrong, Mrs. Horner," Colin said, "when you said earlier it was as if I'd been there. I feel like I *have* been there."

"There wasn't any place I've ever been quite like it," Sonesta said. She seemed better, almost recovered. "No place at all like that roadhouse—the music in that place, the power." That fiery flare again. "That's why they had to destroy it."

And now Colin felt he could speak. "That's why I want to get the record out. *Pink Cadillac*. Let everyone hear for themselves."

Everything had changed. Sonesta was listening to him now. And not fighting him or pulling away.

"I could see that," she said softly.

"Believe me, this would be big news. And it would … bring the roadhouse back. Bring Bearcat back. I know it."

Sonesta nodded to herself. "You might be right."

Seely looked nervous, not quite sure this turn to a kind of business talk was right. She glanced at Colin, who understood what she was thinking but who also knew he was O.K. with Sonesta now and had to move ahead. He hoped Seely would see that and be with him.

"And you still have it?" This was Seely. Colin let a silent sigh of relief out.

"I—I haven't thought about it, haven't looked for it, in all those years. But, yes, I think I know where that damn recording is."

"And you'd—"

"It's all right, Honey. You're being very kind to me, but it's all right. It's actually—" Sonesta halted, looked like she was turning that word *actually* around in her head "—you were right, it actually *is* a relief." She gave out a wan smile. "You think you know yourself. Think you just have to get through a few more years. Then—"

"Could we have it?" Colin said. "The record?"

That was the question. Sonesta looked from Colin to Seely, then back again. Everybody was stone still. Then she nodded.

"Yes," she told them both. "Actually, that might—well, I want you to hear it. Not sure you're gonna want to do anything with it, though. That record, it ain't done anybody no good, you know."

Colin nodded encouragingly. He saw that Seely was giving him a look that said, Don't forget this woman here. Don't forget what she's been through. Don't forget what might happen to her. He nodded back at his wife's sister that, yes, there would be no problem.

"I'll give you my address," Sonesta said, "you come by tomorrow, O.K.? I get off here about two, then I gotta sleep. Make it around two tomorrow?"

"We'll be there," Colin said quickly before Seely could interject. Not that he thought she might. But he couldn't take any chances.

"Well, all right then." A glance at the big round clock behind Colin. "And I guess I better get back to my damn job. Who knows what mischief those children out there'll get into I'm not watching them every minute."

And like that the older woman was back to work. A little officious but understanding, too.

In the parking lot of the Peabody, Seely turned to Colin and said, "I'm not feeling one hundred percent about all this."

"I know."

"You do?" Surprise in her voice.

"Of course. I was picking up everything in there."

"Then you know what I'm thinking?"

Colin nodded. "You have qualms about what we just put Sonesta Clarke through, but you're telling yourself that that's done. What you're really worried about is what could happen to her if the record comes out."

Seely's eyes brightened as she nodded.

"So what are we going to do?"

"We're going to her place tomorrow and get the record. We're going to listen to it—I have to hear it. And then we'll decide."

"*We* will decide?"

"We'll talk it over, yes. Hear what the lacquer sounds like. Think it all through."

"*We* will."

"Yes, both of us." These words surprised him, but he realized immediately that he meant them.

"All right, then. I just don't want to—"

"I know. I can see the problems. And not just with Sonesta, with Dell, too. With Daisy."

"Still, it might be a great record," Seely said, an upturned smile coming to her face and a clear light seeming to pass behind her eyes.

"It better be," Colin said as he ushered her into the passenger seat of his rented car. "That's the whole damn point of all of this, isn't it?"

* * * * *

THEY WEREN'T TALKING much on the drive to Sonesta's. She lived south of town in a neighborhood of small houses and tinier yards, old-model cars lining the streets, and vacant lots sprawling at times for half a block at a time. Seely was driving, which Colin acceded to when she said that his hotel was more on the way than her parents' house was, and that she knew Memphis better than he did.

"I think I'm getting to know it pretty well," he'd told her on the phone.

"Yeah, but this is my *home*."

There was something in her tone, a kind quiet, tense meaningfulness, and the worst of it all was that it was exactly the tone—the manner—that Robin had got when she was mad at Colin. Tight lips, tighter brow, silence ... until she blew up at him anywhere from hours to a day later, and it all came out, whatever it was, and then everything was all right again. But Robin was his wife, and Colin had learned how to nurse along her silent fury, how to massage it until it puckered up and like a boil burst. He didn't know Seely well at all, though at the times like this when she had such a familiar Longworth trait, he felt that in a way he'd known her all his life.

In any event she was driving, a late-model Lexus, picked up in the separation from her husband, she let him know; and she did know Memphis, as well as Colin could tell, not making a wrong turn as they headed into a part of town far from the suburb the Longworths lived in.

But she was silent. And it *was* getting on Colin's nerves.

"You're not excited?" he said, then realized it was probably the wrong thing. That had been true with Robin also: When she'd gotten uptight like this, it had thrown him off his stride; he'd say something just to get something out of her, but he'd feel his voice cajoling, even supplicating, and often it just made her quieter, madder.

"I am what I am," she said.

Whoo, a doozy. Colin thought back to the night before with Sonesta Clarke. What had he done? He'd just gone after the record, and the singer had offered it. Had he been too hard? Seely had objected to something, but right now as they got closer to Sonesta's house, he couldn't remember exactly what it was. Damn! And then he realized how much he wanted her with him on this. Finding the lost 45 wouldn't be half as good without her there.

Should he tell her that? A look at her, her pretty head straight, eyes forward, her dark hair pulled back over her ears just the way Robin had tucked hers away when she was going out to talk business, her lips cut tight. No, better just let her be.

Sonesta's house, not unlike Clay Booker's, was one of the neatest ones on her block, though in her case the whole block smacked of clean, well-tended small houses. Seely was able to pull her Lexus right up in front. Colin noticed it was far from the only fine car on the block.

Sonesta had left the front door ajar, and after Colin hit the buzzer, he heard her call out from inside, "Y'all come on in."

Colin followed Seely. Saw her walk, to his relief, not exactly as his wife had, though not all that different—.

"I've been waiting for you," the older woman said. She had on a midnight-blue dress with maroon piping that hung loose on her, thick black shoes, and sported a gold bird, wings lifted in flight, pinned on her chest. "Don't get visitors too often, I think I'm a little rusty. Can I get y'all some ice tea?"

"That sounds good," Colin said.

"Honey?"

Seely shrugged, then shook her head. Colin was following her gaze around the room, taking in the blocky, old-fashioned heavy wood furniture, the framed pictures on the wall—on closer inspection, Colin later saw, they were drawings of negro league ballplayers: Must be J. Howard Horner's legacy, though you never knew.

"Oh, come on," Sonesta said, ushering them to chairs at a thick oak dining table in an alcove off the main sitting room, "it's not polite to not take anything. 'Specially when I need the practice." Sonesta smiled, eyes lit quick, and that seemed to take Seely off guard. She started to lower herself into one of the proffered chairs, then stood back up.

"May I have some coffee, then?"

Sonesta made a face. "Haven't had a coffee drinker in this house since, well, since I gave up the bridge 'bout seven years ago. I might still have some instant though, want me to look?"

It must've been something in the idea of seven-year-old instant coffee that got Seely to crinkle up her nose, then give their host a smile. "I'm sorry," she said. "It's that I don't want to be any trouble to you." She stood behind her chair at a kind of stiff attention. "I just think we're going to be nothing but trouble."

Sonesta cocked her head back. For a moment it looked like she wasn't sure what all Seely was saying, then she gave out a slow nod.

"Honey, I don't know what you're worried about, but I'm enjoying this. Yes I am. It's nice to have young visitors. Now sit."

Seely gave every indication that she didn't want to sit. That that wasn't what she was saying.

Colin stepped in. "Mrs. Horner, what Seely is saying is that she's sorry we're stirring up everything from your past like this." He gave the brown-haired woman a quick look: Am I speaking out of turn? But Seely looked at him with a muffled kind of relief. "And I think she—well, I am, too—we're both worried about this record, what it might do to you."

Sonesta was shaking her head. "You didn't hear me at all last night, did you?"

"Hear you how?" Colin racked his brain, but again all he could remember was that she actually had the lost 45 and promised it to him.

"Like I said last night—least, like I think I said—I want you to have the record. I—"

"Are you sure?" Seely interrupted. "I just think—well, we barged in there and all—"

"I've been thinking about it," Sonesta continued. She also sat down on her side of the table, dropping into her chair with a swift movement that said, If you're too stupid to take a load off your feet, I'm not! "Thinking it all night. I couldn't—well, that doesn't matter."

Now Seely pulled back her chair and lowered herself into it; when she was seated, Colin did the same.

"But what I was thinking was, the whole business been with me more than I thought. I figured it was—was so long ago. But I saw it clear, that maybe it was always down there, eating at me. Like I never got away from it. 'Spose I never will—"

Seely made gestures as if she were going to speak, but Sonesta held up a small, steely hand.

"And I don't know if it's having that record here in the house with me or not. I mean it when I said I didn't much think about it, but last night I realized I always knew it was there." The older woman lifted her head as if listening to her words to see if they were the right ones. "I mean, part of me, some part of me, knew I had it in that drawer." She turned her head, threw a glance at an intimidating maple hutch against one wall. "In there in the bottom drawer, with the fancy linens and tablecloths, where it'd be safe from being jostled or scratched, but way in the back, so's I had to have people over 'nuff for maybe three whole affairs before I'd ever have to dig *that* far.

"And I never had to. That was what I realized. Remembered once when I was celebrating our daughter's wedding—did I tell you 'bout my daughter with J. Howard?—well, I went out borrowing linens and such rather than go that far back in the drawer.

"You see, that's 'cause I always was aware. *Always.* Maybe always waiting in the back of my old head for this. 'Cept maybe I thought it wasn't going to be a sweet couple like you two but maybe the police or the sheriff."

Seely shook her head swiftly, then said, "If you don't want us to disturb you, just say—"

"Honey, you don't understand. This is such a ... relief. Such ... a ... relief!" The older woman's eyes brightened. "I can't tell you. It's like this thing, whatever it is, it's been down in this ... cave ... so long. Gotten all moldery and spooky and strange. Now you two come 'long, gonna drag it into the light. Light is good, darlin'. I learned one thing in my long life, Light Is Good."

"Is it still there?" Colin said. "In the drawer?"

Sonesta suddenly looked a little meek, gave a tight, pained smile to him.

"You couldn't even look at it, could you," he said. "It's all right. I'll get it for you. I can, can't I?"

He was looking at Seely as much as he was at Sonesta, keeping both women in his line of sight. And he wasn't sure which one nodded first, because nobody moved right away, but finally they both did. He could tell the sigh that flew from his chest was loud enough for them all to hear.

"I'll get that iced tea for you now," Sonesta said, "and, Honey, how 'bout some juice. I got some nice V-8 juice in there. Cold. All them vitamins—"

"V-8 would be fine."

When Sonesta left the room, Colin threw one last glance at Robin's sister, who gave him the faintest of nods, and then he bent down and pulled open the bottom drawer in the hutch. It was hard to open, filled to the top with neatly folded and starched cotton cloth. He had to stick his hand into the drawer and press down, then work the drawer slowly back and forth till he got it most of the way out. He reached in farther. Felt around for something hard. Found ... a china serving plate. Found ... a large silver spoon. Found behind it something thinner, made of plastic, and then he felt the grooves....

When he held it up, it looked pristine. Muted black lacquer, no label, grooves running almost all the way to the spindle hole. The way he held it before him, his own reflection showed up in a flat, pewterlike way. Was it distortion, or were his eyes really that large?

"Oh, my God," Seely said softly.

Colin turned to her. Looked past the lost record. Was curiously moved: Her eyes were as large as his.

Colin had a quick intuition: Put the record out of sight before Sonesta came back in. He heard the refrigerator door shut. Heard liquid splash into a glass. Heard the sputter of coffee spurt out of a coffee maker.

"Can I have your keys?" he said. Seely seemed to understand right away what he meant, pulled them out. It made him nervous to have the record out of his sight now, but as he slipped it into her car, carefully positioning it beneath the passenger's seat, he knew it was a risk worth taking to make sure Sonesta herself didn't actually have to see it.

"I have your coffee," she said when he was back inside her house. As she leaned across him to pour it, Colin believed he saw tension fled from her shoulders.

"Thanks."

"And your V-8. I just love that V-8," Sonesta said, as she sat back down. "Always have."

She's not going to even ask about the record, he thought. Then he said, "Can I ask you a few questions more?"

She moved her head just enough to make it a yes.

"So, Dell Dellaplane was in jail only that afternoon, right?" A nod. "Did you ever see him again?"

"He came to the funeral, yeah. That was three days later. Took all of Dell's father's money, then some, to pay for it."

"And Daisy?"

"She was there, too."

"But anything else?"

"You mean, do I know what happened to them?"

"Yeah, anything."

"Well, I don't know." For a moment there Sonesta looked much older, and more confused. "You better ask specifics."

"Well, Dell Dellaplane. Was there ever even a trial?"

Sonesta shook her head. "No trial. Far as I know it was all worked out that one afternoon. 'Course, he was a Dellaplane, didn't hurt. But like I said, even the judges back then, they would've built him a statue down on Front Street for what he done before they woulda put him in jail."

"I saw him in California, I guess he went out there not long after all this." Colin leaned forward a few inches. "What about Daisy?"

"She was just gone. I don't have any idea what happened to her."

"And as far as you know, she never sang *Pink Cadillac* again?"

Sonesta grimaced slightly, then shook her head. "All I remember, there was something—something in her eyes." She took a napkin from the table and daubed her forehead. "Something dead and haunted. I don't think anybody could've got her to sing that cursed song again for *nothing*."

"She and Dell?" This was Seely. Both Colin and Sonesta turned to her.

"I don't have any information there, Honey. You'd have to talk to them to find that out. Whatever, didn't seem to stick, though, did it?"

Seely made an I-can't-know gesture.

Colin looked from Seely back to Sonesta. "And the roadhouse?"

"What do you think happened?"

Colin looked pained, as if he were about to hear someone beloved had died.

"They tore it down?"

"Of course." Sonesta pushed herself up, a flash of indignation on her face. "Of course. Right away. Thomas's body was still warm! We didn't own it anymore. Dell's father did. That deal Bearcat struck, you think it wasn't a gonna-stand-up deal?"

Colin was seeing it, this place he'd been imagining for weeks—years, if you counted work on the Bearcat CD—a place he'd come to know so well he could just close his eyes and breathe in the air of it.

"Yessir, right in front of us, too. They didn't but load Bearcat in the back of this station wagon they thought was good enough of an ambulance for us coloreds, then all those construction men, they did what they'd come for." Sonesta closed her eyes then, and there was wetness in the corners. She shook her head. "That was the end of it. After that place.... You know, I had my problems with it, with what Jackson was doing there toward the end, but that place ... it was ... my home."

"Where'd you go?" Seely asked.

"Oh, I was lucky. I was able to get my job back at the Peabody. And I just stayed there. Married Mr. J. Horner. Got us this house here. Had me a child even, old as I was. God, even that was a long, long time ago."

"One more question," Colin said, glad to see there was still clear, attentive light in Sonesta's eyes. Now that he had the record, there was still one thing he had to know. "That car. The pink Cadillac—"

"You mean that damn Elvis Presley car that started it all?" Her eyebrows flew up. "Pardon me."

"It was still at the roadhouse that day, right?"

Sonesta pursed her brow. "I guess. I don't really remember." A deeper wrinkling. "I'm pretty sure it was still sitting there."

"But you don't remember it after that?"

Sonesta shook her head. It was clear to them she was trying to be helpful, that she didn't know.

"Could the sheriff have taken it?"

The older woman nodded. "Maybe. He took darn near everything else."

"But you didn't see it?" Colin was leaning forward.

"I just don't know *what* happened to it."

Colin nodded silently. He'd never really thought he'd find the car; that would be too much. It was enough that they had the record. He thought of it now, with a quick sear of desire to hear it.

He thanked Sonesta, then got up and said, "Anything

that happens to the record, Blue Moon Records won't forget you."

"I'm doing fine."

"I know. But I just want you to know that."

The older woman smiled, looked from Colin to Seely, then said, "Maybe it'll bring the both of you better luck than it did any of us."

Seely smiled. "I hope so," she said softly.

Back in Seely's car Colin pulled out the lacquer disc he'd hidden beneath the seat. He was sure he was imagining it, but it actually felt hot in his hands. He still couldn't believe he actually had it. And what would they soon hear off it?

Seely was obviously thinking the same thing. "Do you remember seeing that old-fashioned record console in our den?" she said. "It was handed down from our grandparents. I'm pretty sure it has a 78 setting."

Colin could faintly remember something large, wooden, and hulking in the den. He said, "That'd be great." A pause. "And you're ready to hear it?" There was more in those words than only those words.

Seely didn't answer right then, just drove along for a while, then came up on a tricky left into traffic, and when they were safely headed back north into Memphis, said softly, "I'm sorry for earlier."

The way she said it caught at Colin's heart. He was so focused on the disc in his hands that her conciliatory tone seemed to come out of nowhere—out of a dream. But it was exactly the way Robin would apologize. Softly. Carefully. Only once.

"No problem," Colin said. "You were just thinking about Sonesta, I understand."

"A man who understands!" Seely cried, bright and laughing. "No wonder Robin married you."

Colin didn't even try to call back the gasp that flew from his lips.

✳ ✳ ✳ ✳ ✳

THE FIRST TIME SHE HEARD IT (and she was to hear it many, many more times in the next few months), it sneaked up on her as if out of nowhere, and though she couldn't believe her ears, she was able to convince herself that it had to be some kind of trick she was playing on herself. She'd been driving in her gray Mercedes to the club, a 3:30 tennis date with Samantha Randall, and was spinning through the radio dial, stopping for a moment on the Phoenix oldies station, when she heard a gripping young woman shouting down a chorus that sounded a lot like that song she'd sung over forty years before, *Pink Cadillac.* Her hands immediately tightened on the steering wheel, her attention flew off the traffic to the radio, but there was only a line or two, then the song ended, somewhat abruptly, and was followed by a commercial for a *Cops* show that night on Fox.

She was so startled though that she pulled over to the side of the road and just sat there. *Could it be?* But finally she decided it was only a turn of her imagination, brought on no doubt by that visit a month back by that young Englishman.

Still, the wisp of what she thought she might've heard preyed on her, and when she got home, feeling young and flush from the tennis match, she lingered for a minute in the circular driveway, then went to the door of the huge garage her husband had put in when he built the house.

She couldn't remember the last time she'd gone to look at it. Even the last couple years, when Jerry Crenshaw from the Texaco had come out for his biannual start-it-up and servicing, she'd been out or busy in her office or ... something.

But today she wanted to see the car whole. The door was locked by a combination lock she didn't know the numbers to, but once you were in the garage, it was easy enough to go from one bay to another.

Leaving the bright sun she couldn't make out anything for a while; moved carefully, even though her husband, Harold, kept the place immaculate. Her eyes were adjusting when she got to the final room. She looked up first, for the string that turned on the overhead light, then pulled it, and....

It sucked away her breath. Just like that. The flared fenders, the sweet curves, that stunning pink enamel paint just as perfect today as it was forty years ago.

She hadn't driven the pink Cadillac in at least twenty years; Harold hadn't either, even though in her secret heart she half credited the car with making him notice her and falling in love with her when she'd first moved to Arizona.

First, though, she'd gone to Hollywood in the car, though once she was there she kept it secret in a garage. Why? She'd fallen back in with Dell Dellaplane, who was in Elvis Presley's Memphis Mafia, and she didn't want to stir up the past. She and Dell were even getting close again when one night Elvis beckoned to her, and she didn't resist. She and Presley didn't last long, but Dell was nothing but curt after that. She fell out of Elvis's circle, didn't see Dell again, and years later drove the pink Caddie to Arizona.

In the desert her car and her Hollywood tales promised endless youth and adventure to the up-and-coming Phoenix builder. By that point Daisy was ready to settle down, and she let the car's magic do its job. Though it hadn't been long before Harold seemed in a way jealous of the car, and the man who had given it to her—and the life it suggested. Harold himself parked it in the farthest-away bay and then stopped driving it, even mentioning it. By then it was simply easier for Daisy to let it go, too.

But it was so beautiful. She'd forgotten. A host of memories flew up, and before she knew it, she'd found the keys, sprung the combo lock, pulled the large door open, and started it up.

Vrrrooooom! Vrrrrrrrooooooooooooom!

It *ripped*. That was the word. The question quickly came

to her: Had there been anything in her life quite as thrilling as running this car down the road?

> *Where we're going, ain't never lookin' back*
> *From our pink Cadillac, our pink Cadillac*

Like that the words were with her. As she backed up the car, she was humming the tune.

> *Sitting round the house, can't wait to bust the door*
> *Grab a deep breath, slam that peddle to the floor*

Good thing Jerry kept the car tuned up. The way the V-8 engine growled—had anyone heard a car roar like this since they first made these?—that growl ran right through her, unsettling her deeply, exactly a *physical* unburdening. There was something about having all that power at her touch that teased her with the sensation that her life might not be as stuck as it usually felt.

> *Yeah, gotta run this Caddie like it might be your last*
> *'Cuz what is is what is, and what's not is what's past*
> *Not that you ever thought you'd have more than one shot*
> *Pink Caddie's your best chance of never getting caught*

Well, she had gotten caught; they'd all gotten caught. Still ... thrum! thrum! *thrum!*

She spun the Cadillac's wheels along Hayden Road, past the municipal airport, then with a wide-open straightaway before her, she blasted off into the desert, the top down, the wind flashing through her still thick blonde hair. When she got the car up to ninety, she slowed down just long enough to tie the fluttering strands back in a ponytail.

It only seemed right.

Acknowledgments:
Pink Cadillac couldn't have
been done without the help of
David Jiranek, Schuyler Bishop,
Nancy Ramsey, Anna Manikowska,
Peter Guralnick, Judy Peiser,
Bruce Diones, Carol Robinson,
Joni Blackburn (copyeditor extraordinaire),
and, always, Patricia Woodbridge